Dave Edlund (signature)

RELENTLESS
SAVAGE

a Peter Savage novel

DAVE EDLUND

 Light Messages

Relentless Savage (Peter Savage, #2)
Dave Edlund
www.petersavagenovels.com
dedlund@lightmessages.com

Published 2015, by Light Messages
www.lightmessages.com
Durham, NC 27713
Printed in the United States of America
Paperback ISBN: 978-1-61153-129-9
Ebook ISBN: 978-1-61153-130-5

This is a work of fiction. All characters, organizations, and events portrayed in this novel are either products of the author's imagination or are used fictitiously.

In loving memory of Mom and Dad... may you forever share the peace and love that was so elusive in life.

***

To our service men and women, wherever they may be, thank you for your patriotism, your sacrifice, and your dedication.

ACKNOWLEDGEMENTS

WRITING A BOOK REQUIRES the contributions from many, and *Relentless Savage* is no different. So, as I am acknowledging those contributions, I have to begin with my best buddy, Gary.

Thank you, Gary.

Although language is the primary means of expressing emotion, in this case it is inadequate. Even before those words escape my lips, it is clear how insufficient they are. Gary, your extensive comments, edits, feedback, and suggestions made this story so much better. You were instrumental in pointing out plot deficiencies and incongruities, and you found many mistakes that I am embarrassed to have let slip.

Many thanks are also due to my very good friend Gordon, also a writer and a gentleman, who freely gives with no expectation of return. Not only have you given me motivation, but your insight and critical review are highly valued. There is no doubt your feedback has shaped this novel for the better.

No novel may be considered complete without the help of an editor. There's editing for grammar, punctuation, spelling—and there is editing for content. Both are difficult tasks—and the later borders on mystical in my opinion. So I am once again indebted to my editor, Elizabeth, for her significant contributions, encouragement, nudges, and suggestions that have refined this story and helped me find my voice.

Finding and correcting all the typos, misspellings, etc. that an author places in a manuscript is an exceedingly challenging task, and any errors that remain are solely my responsibility because I put them there.

This novel, and its predecessor *Crossing Savage*, have strong elements of real science and engineering woven throughout the adventure. I have to acknowledge my parents, Barbara and Melvin, for their willingness to not only encourage my studies, but to nurture that interest, which evolved into a lifelong passion. Mom and Dad died in 2011, but they are never far from my thoughts.

Last, but far from least, I wish to acknowledge my wife for her never-ending support and optimism. From the time we met, she has been the light in my life, my cornerstone. I cannot imagine what she ever saw in me, but her influence has made me a better man.

Finally, I want to offer my deepest appreciation to you, the fans of Peter Savage, James Nicolaou, and the rest of the crew, for your support. I write these novels for your enjoyment and it would be great to hear from you on my web site www.PeterSavageNovels.com.

AUTHOR'S NOTE

DNA. DEOXYRIBONUCLEIC ACID. The double helix. We have come to know this essential biological material as the unique identifier of every man, woman, and child. It has become the most damning of all possible evidence in criminal cases; yet equally powerful in freeing those wrongly convicted and imprisoned for crimes they did not commit.

Although I'd argue that science has not unequivocally proven that no two persons can possess the same genetic code, there is no doubt that DNA defines the characteristics of not only people, but all plants and animals. Every physical feature—the color of your eyes and hair, your height, the tone of your voice, how strong you are, even the freckle on your left shoulder—is defined by the sequence of only four nucleobases in your DNA.

Over the past six decades, beginning with the discovery of the double-helix structure of DNA by Watson and Crick in 1953 (based on pioneering X-ray images taken by Rosalind Franklin a year earlier), genetic research has produced phenomenal results, ultimately yielding a map of the human genome.

As breakthroughs laid the foundation for further and more

rapid achievements, we now understand that our DNA not only dictates our physical characteristics but also plays a pivotal role in mankind's susceptibility to disease. A prime example is the so-called 'delta-factor'. There is compelling evidence that this genetic mutation, traced back to survivors of the Black Plague, lends extraordinary resistance to HIV infection.

Of course, DNA is also the key ingredient of cloning—the insertion of foreign DNA from a host into a recipient. The cells of the recipient accept and incorporate the foreign DNA, and gradually the recipient becomes biologically defined by this new genetic material. Although the ethics of cloning will be debated for generations, the scientific capability to clone plant and animal species has been firmly established.

Will genetic engineering ever be applied to humans? Never say never.

For example, cancer cells are very much like normal cells, except that cancer cells don't know when to stop replicating. That part of their genetic code that would normally stop cell division does not function properly. The result is massive tumors and the disease, as we know it. Conventional treatment attempts to target the cancerous cells and selectively destroy them. Of course, the problem is that cancer cells and normal cells are very much alike—so killing cancer cells without killing the normal cells is a delicate task.

Enter genetic modification. Imagine being able to insert new DNA into cancer cells. The new DNA would have the correct base sequence—literally, the genetic code—that causes runaway cell replication to cease.

No more cancer.

Impossible? Outrageous? We've mapped the human genome. We know that many diseases such as sickle cell anemia, cystic fibrosis, hemophilia, Parkinson's disease, and breast and colon cancer—I could go on—are caused by mutations to normal human DNA. Now apply cloning—insertion of correct DNA into the cancerous tumor—and it is easy to imagine where this is going.

But science has no morals. That is why people must exercise their conscience. Science is knowledge. And knowledge can be used for good or bad. It is our choice.

This is the moral of *Relentless Savage*. I hope you find hours of enjoyment on these pages...

DE

PROLOGUE

LIGHTNING FLASHED AGAIN, lighting the cave entrance. A moment later the thunderclap resounded like canon fire. The adult females and children had retreated deeper into the cave, fearful of the passing storm. It was early morning and the approaching sunrise painted the eastern horizon a deep crimson purple. The two younger males who would be part of the morning hunting party warmed themselves by the fire, preparing for the hunt.

Multiple lightning bolts split the dark sky silhouetting the lone figure at the mouth of the cave. Tok was the undisputed leader of this clan. He was large for a Neanderthal, standing a full hand taller than the other mature males; he was also much stronger and heavier, weighing a third again as much.

Tok had ruled this clan for the past six winters; ever since his father had been killed hunting the wild boar. Like most of the large mammals of this period, the wild boar was much larger and more aggressive than any modern porcine. A large

1

boar could weigh upwards of 1,300 pounds—four to five times Tok's weight. Combined with outwardly projecting tusks measuring over ten inches long and four inches around at the base, this animal could eviscerate even the largest predators, including the short face bear and saber tooth cat.

Tok did not fear the heavenly pyrotechnic display. He stood at the mouth of the cave, gazing at the dark sky, wearing a warm bearskin cape and holding his short spear. The shaft was made from a young, sturdy hickory tree he had selected for its diameter and straight growth. To the end of the spear shaft Tok mounted a massive obsidian thrusting point, eight inches long and five inches wide at the base, securing it in place with bison sinew.

The massive thrusting spear weighed close to 20 pounds, but to Tok it was a natural extension of his arm. He wielded it with fluid grace and tremendous power. When thrust or swung like a sword, the razor-sharp point could effortlessly penetrate and slash the toughest hide and muscle.

Soon it would be light, and Tok would lead his party of three hunters, not returning to the cave—to the clan—until they had killed their quarry. Without turning his gaze from the plains and patches of brush mixed with deciduous trees, Tok lifted his thrusting spear and tapped it firmly on the ground once, then twice. The two other males rose and gathered their spears to join Tok.

The group walked down the slope away from the cave, following a familiar path toward the expansive plain, rich in flora and fauna. Flashes of lightning periodically illuminated the well-worn path. They walked quietly in single file, Tok in the lead. Their senses grew keenly aware of the surroundings. As sunrise drew nearer, the sky lightened to a dark shade of gray. There was little sound save for the occasional rodent scurrying to the safety of a nearby bush.

The hunting party continued to walk forward in silence—watching, listening, scenting the gentle air currents. Like all beings in the wild, each relied on finely developed senses, brute strength, and cunning to survive.

Tok was now moving very deliberately, although still walking at a reasonable pace. He swung his head slowly from side to side, eyes penetrating deep into the bushes and clusters of trees. Flaring his nostrils, he drew in a deep breath.

Suddenly, Tok froze; the two hunters behind him followed suit immediately. There was a faint odor, a familiar and distinct musky scent. It was the smell of the beast that had killed his father many seasons before. Although Tok had no fear of this creature, he did respect its strength and agility. This would be a worthy prize.

The air swirled gently, almost imperceptibly, but it was enough for Tok to get a crude bearing on the direction the scent was coming from. He turned slowly to his right while giving a discrete hand signal to the other two males to hold their positions. He concentrated on the scent, listening for any sound of movement, eyes searching for any indication that the boar had detected the presence of the hunters. They had arrived downwind from the boar and had approached without a sound.

Twenty or so strides to his front, Tok saw a dark tangle of scrub trees and thorn berries. This is where the boar would be lying. Shifting his gaze to the soft dirt, Tok could see the tracks left by the boar. He motioned for the younger hunters to move carefully around the dense brush lair. They would approach from the opposite side and drive the boar out to Tok.

The hunters split and each circled around the brush from opposite sides, giving it a wide berth so as not to be scented by the boar. The air was very light this morning, so the odor of the Neanderthals would take time to diffuse to the boar's den. The hunters intended to be moving toward the den before the boar realized it was surrounded.

Tok waited patiently, spear low at his side, ready to thrust the black obsidian point into the chest of the boar. The hunters did well, demonstrating countless generations of instinct and training. Upon circling to the far side of the dense cluster of brush and trees, the hunters slowly approached the boar's den.

The party spread apart and advanced on the thicket with sufficient stealth that it was their scent, more than sound, that eventually raised the awareness of the slowly awakening boar. The animal rose to its feet, alert. It looked in the direction of the two approaching hunters. Seeing them, the huge boar became agitated. Although the boar was easily eight times larger than either of the smaller male Neanderthals, the animal instinctively avoided these predators whenever possible. If they could not be avoided, the boar would fight to the death with a primeval ferocity that had earned the animal great respect from Tok and his hunters.

Not sensing any other threat, and with a clear path of egress out the opposite side of the brush, the boar stealthily snuck out and trotted away. The creature did not immediately see or smell Tok, as he was crouched close to the ground, looking much like a rock or stump in the gray predawn light. When the boar was almost upon Tok it scented him and startled, turning to run.

Tok jumped to his feet and lunged, driving his spear into the chest of the approaching boar. The heavy obsidian point penetrated deep into the animal's chest just behind the front shoulder, piercing the beast's heart. Blood gushed from the wound, saturating the spear shaft in crimson. Tok forced the point deeper. The beast howled and cried in surprise and pain. It quickly retreated, pulling free of the spear and causing the obsidian point to slice further through both lungs and severing the aorta. The boar twirled in confusion and then collapsed to the ground—dead.

Tok approached his fallen prey, spear pointed at the beast, ready to deliver a final blow if necessary. It was not.

The other two hunters trotted up to Tok and the dead boar. They nodded and grunted in their primitive language. There would be plenty of food for the clan. Nothing would go to waste. The meat would be consumed before it spoiled. Bone and sinew and hide would be used for clothing, rudimentary tools, and strong binding cord.

The youngest hunter, observing his place in the clan hierarchy, laid down his spear and removed a flint hand-blade from a pouch at his side. He began the laborious process of gutting and quartering the boar. The other hunter exchanged words with Tok then left for the cave; the hunters would need help to quickly bring this magnificent prize back to the safety of the cave. Soon, the scent of blood and entrails would draw in other predators that would fight for this carcass.

Tok stood watch, spear at his side, his head constantly scanning the brush and trees for movement. It was easier to see now as the clouds began to part, the thunder now distant.

The youngest hunter worked steadily and swiftly. As he scooped out the intestines, he glanced at Tok. He could see by the way he stood, ready and able, that there was no fear—only confidence. The young hunter had only recently reached the age when he was recognized as an adult. He still had much to prove, and much to overcome, especially his fear. He took comfort in knowing Tok was standing guard. Surely, Tok could defeat any creature—even the most terrifying this world had to offer.

The young hunter returned his attention to the work at hand. He began to split open the breastbone, especially hard work on such a large animal. His flint and obsidian blades were razor sharp and unyielding. He pried open the chest and braced it with a stick, and then he removed the remainder of the internal organs—the heart and lungs. The hunter was bloodied up to his shoulders, and he smelled musky of boar sweat and urine.

The sky was much lighter now. Tok listened to the familiar morning sounds as the animals inhabiting the plain became active. Birds chirped and flitted about; squirrels began scampering in search of food. In the distance, Tok saw a deer bounding away, tail raised in alarm. He wondered what had frightened the deer.

No sooner had this thought entered his mind when the familiar morning sounds grew quiet. Tok was immediately on edge, unconsciously tightening his grip on the spear shaft. What had caused such widespread fear in the animals? Then, he heard the low growl.

The sound came from behind him, and he spun around searching for the source. Tok tensed, his legs in a crouch, ready to move swiftly in any direction. He still could not pinpoint the sound, but he knew what had made it—a saber tooth cat.

With the spear gripped firmly in both hands, point facing forward, legs braced, Tok finally spotted the cat. It was crouched low, in an expanse of brush no more than waist tall. The large male cat was undoubtedly drawn to the smell of the butchered boar, and now it saw an easy meal for the taking. Tok was almost directly between the saber tooth cat and the young hunter now quartering the dead boar; so intent on his work that he had not yet registered the low guttural growls.

The cat's eyes darted between Tok and the butchered carcass, sensing that Tok was an impediment that the cat would have to deal with. After a long pause, the cat charged and then sprang—flying through the air and striking Tok's head. The leap was so swift and powerful that Tok had little time to react. He had just managed to raise the point of his spear, slashing a rear leg of the large cat, before the blow to his head knocked him to the ground.

The animal landed and with a second, shorter bound, was on the boar carcass brushing the young Neanderthal hunter aside.

Terrified, the young hunter lashed out with his flint knife. The knife sunk deep into the rear quarter of the cat, but the blade was a short working tool and it failed to reach anything vital.

The saber tooth cat roared and swiveled, stretching a mighty clawed paw in an enormous swipe at the Neanderthal. The blow struck the young hunter in the chest, four sharp claws tearing his flesh, crushing ribs, penetrating deep into the hunter's lungs and heart. The young hunter crashed to the ground, never even murmuring a sound, his lifeless eyes staring blankly at the sky.

The cat roared in victory, the sound echoing off the mountains, and then returned its attention to the carcass. Biting deep into a 300-pound rear quarter, the carnivore raised its head, effortlessly picking up the huge chunk of meat.

But Tok was not going to surrender his prize. He had killed the boar and claimed it for his clan. He slowly stood, shaking his head from the blow. He gripped his spear and charged the cat.

With the thrusting spear low at his side and powerful legs pumping, Tok rushed forward toward the cat. He released a blood-curdling scream and threw himself at the beast just as it turned to face its attacker.

With a mighty collision, Tok slammed into the cat and pushed the spear deep into the animal's side. The two predators crumbled to the ground in a tangled ball. Tok was stunned by the collision and had difficulty catching his breath. The saber tooth cat recovered first, despite its wounds. It untangled itself from the Neanderthal hunter, spear still hanging from its side.

With a defiant roar, the cat stumbled away from Tok and twisted, biting at the spear and the source of its pain. Tok rose—first to one knee, and then slowly standing on wobbly legs. He searched the ground for his spear, only to realize it was still stuck firmly in the cat. The cat now caught his gaze, and roared again.

Tok lowered his hand to his waist and retrieved a long and stout hunting knife. Like his thrusting spear-point, Tok had painstakingly shaped the long knife from a superb specimen of obsidian, and he fashioned the handle from a large fang of a saber tooth cat his father had killed when Tok was a young child. The fang, filled with hardened tree resin for additional strength, was as long as the blade, with the point of the fang opposite the point of the blade.

The saber tooth cat lowered its head and started to move toward Tok. Standing firm, the Neanderthal did not give ground. The cat was not accustomed to these creatures behaving defiantly—normally they fled in the face of a charge. But this one, this hunter, behaved very differently.

Sensing something abnormal, the cat stopped and roared again, trying to intimidate Tok. But rather than run, Tok let loose his own war cry and then lunged at the large cat. They collided head on with Tok wrapping his massive arm around the cat's neck. He stabbed his knife into the shoulder of the cat, attempting to strike a vital organ or artery, but the blade was not long enough to cause mortal wounds from this angle.

The cat shook free of the hunter and lashed out with a powerful swipe with its paw. The cat's claws easily shredded the bear-hide cape Tok was wearing, but were deflected by an undergarment of body armor fashioned from the shoulder cartilage of a boar. The blow knocked Tok aside, snapping the leather straps holding the cartilage plate over his chest, but he quickly recovered and regained his balance. Pushing the useless hide garments off, he stood naked, knife at the ready, facing the saber tooth cat.

The cat charged.

Tok parried bringing the blade down across the side of the cat's neck in a vicious slash. The serrated obsidian blade cut deep through the thick muscles.

The animal's momentum carried it beyond Tok. It roared in pain and turned to face its nemesis. Again the cat charged—and again Tok deflected the blow by pivoting to the side. This time he swung outward at the passing cat with the heal of the knife. The saber-tooth-fang handle connected with the shoulder of the beast, sinking deeply into the muscle. The beast stumbled, weakened from its wounds and loss of blood.

The cat staggered, nearly falling. Tok knew it was near death. But the beast, with adrenaline still coursing through its veins, would not quit the fight. Again the cat charged, slower this time. Tok stood his ground. With a closed fist, he delivered a mighty blow to the cat's head while at the same time sinking the hunting knife into its neck, severing the carotid artery.

The cat stumbled and toppled to its knees. Slowly, the beast rolled over onto its side; breathing shallowly—its eyes not focusing. Tok took a deep breath, and looked down at his foe, knowing the cat was mortally wounded and would soon die. Tok retrieved his spear and raised his arms, bellowing in triumph.

By the time three adult males from Tok's clan arrived, the boar was cut into quarters and placed on the creature's hide, separated from its body in one large piece, hairy side against the dirt. Tok had just laid the young hunter in a shallow depression he scrapped in the earth. His arms were folded across his chest, the short flint knife clasped in one hand. All three males helped Tok gather stones to layer over the corpse. Eventually, they knew, scavengers would pull away the rocks and scatter the bones.

This basic ritual completed, each Neanderthal lifted a quarter of the boar and began the hike back to their cave. Tok kneeled and wrapped the boar hide around the last rear quarter, then he hefted the load to his shoulder, gripping the thrusting spear in his right hand. He watched for a few moments as the other three Neanderthals walked away single file, each loaded with meat for the clan. One by one they fell from sight as they crossed a slight rise and descended down the far side.

Tok stood motionless. He flared his nostrils, drawing in the air, sifting out the hundreds of unique scents. He pinched his eyebrows and slowly turned his head, searching for movement. Again, Tok inhaled deeply. There it was, a foreign odor—almost, but not quite, masked by the musky smell of blood and urine and viscera.

Slowly Tok turned to face into the slight breeze, his eyes searching, piercing the flora for signs of movement, of danger. Several moments passed as Tok remained absolutely motionless, scanning left to right and back again.

And then he saw them, three of them. They had arms and legs, like Tok, but they looked different—not Neanderthal at all. These creatures were slightly taller than most of the males in Tok's clan, and they were thinner.

They approached Tok, initially attempting to conceal their movement, but once Tok spotted them the closest one stood, and then the other two did as well. Their skin was dark, and they carried spears and clubs.

This was the first time Tok had encountered Homo sapiens. Like Tok, the Homo sapiens were also confused by this new discovery that looked something like themselves, but yet not the same. But they certainly recognized the meat Tok held on his shoulder—and they were determined to take it.

The closest of the strangers was noticeably taller than the other two, and a full hand taller than Tok. Staring directly into

Tok's eyes, he spoke in a commanding voice. Tok understood the attempt to communicate, but it was an unfamiliar tongue. Then the tall stranger nodded to his companions, and they began to separate while also moving toward Tok, spears gripped firmly with both hands, points lowered.

Recognizing that they intended to surround him and attack, Tok dropped the boar quarter and planted his feet, legs slightly spread and knees bent. When the two shorter Homo sapiens were about opposite each other, they charged Tok. As they closed, Tok quickly took three steps to his left and thrust his spear into the stranger. Yanking the hickory shaft, Tok swung the obsidian point like a broad sword just as the second Homo sapiens approached within reach. He swung his own spear down to block the blow, only to have the shaft snap in two on contact with Tok's massive thrusting point.

Tok allowed the point to continue its arc, and brought up the butt of the hickory shaft, connecting with the stranger's cheek. Bone shattered and blood and saliva sprayed outward from the impact, forming a mist that wafted over Tok. The stranger fell to the ground, dead.

Seeing his two companions defeated, the leader gripped his spear in one hand and a club in the other. His arms outstretched, he bellowed a fierce cry—his eyes showing a rage that burned inside. He ran at Tok, slowing just enough to throw his spear when he had closed the distance a dozen paces. The spear sped at Tok, who fell to the side to dodge the deadly projectile.

With Tok off his feet, the Homo sapiens pressed his advantage, closing the gap and rearing his club. Tok had only risen to one knee when the club swung downward at his head. He ducked to the side and raised his arm, the heavy club striking squarely on Tok's upper arm. The blow would have crushed the skull of another Homo sapiens, but the Neanderthal's thick muscles and heavy bone resisted the impact.

Tok had to regain his footing. He pushed upward, knocking back the tall stranger, who still had a tight grip on his club. Now Tok had the advantage with the longer reach of his spear. The two warriors circled each other, each watching for the other to make a move.

It came with blinding speed as Tok swung the butt of his spear downward. As expected, the stranger blocked the blow with his club, but in doing so opened up his other side to attack. Tok instantly reversed his swing and brought the obsidian point slashing down across the stranger's neck and chest.

The club slipped from the stranger's hand. He collapsed to his knees and briefly looked up at Tok, his face devoid of expression. And then he fell to his side, blood still draining from his wounds even though his heart no longer beat.

The leader of the Neanderthal clan did not live through the coming winter, succumbing to a disease that had mysteriously infected his clan following Tok's encounter with the strange beings. Tok, the mightiest hunter and chief of his clan, was buried in a nook at the far depths of the cave, his spirit believed to offer protection over the clan much as he had done in life. Primitive paintings applied to the cave walls commemorated his hunts, which had allowed his family to thrive.

In the cool and dry depths of the cave, Tok's body very slowly desiccated, preserving his tissues for many centuries. Eventually, over the millennia, only his bones remained—as they were left in reverence by his clan.

Tok's spirit could offer no protection to his extended family. Within three years the last of Tok's clan had succumbed to disease.

CHAPTER 1

THE GUARDS NEVER GOT USED TO the frequent grunting and howling. It was a primitive form of speech, one which they did not yet understand. The linguists were studying these sounds and patterns, but since their subjects seemed to have lost most of their ability to communicate in their native language, progress was slow. The creatures' appearance was no less unnerving than their speech: exaggerated eyebrows, heavy cheekbones, jutting jaw, and thickly muscled neck. Hideous abominations, the guards thought.

The brute strength of these creatures was also intimidating, and the guards always worked in pairs when socializing and training them. Armed with cattle prods, pistols, and clubs, the guards still felt uneasy. They relied heavily on the cattle prods to instill rudimentary obedience before the more sophisticated military training could commence.

It was like breaking a wild horse, one guard said. But once accomplished the results were impressive—an obedient soldier that possessed enormous strength and keen senses. Even more significantly, these soldiers did not fear battle, and they never questioned orders.

The compound housing the creatures had been built mostly in secret and had been completed only six months earlier. The Chinese government exercised complete authority over the camp and the 360-degree perimeter around the compound extending two kilometers beyond the outer fence. Roving patrols of heavily armed foot soldiers and mounted units ensured that no one accidentally, or intentionally, strayed too close.

It was no secret that China and Sudan had forged very close relations, but exactly how close was still a carefully guarded secret. The relationship was symbiotic—China needed oil, provided by Sudan. In return, Sudan needed—craved is really a better term—more money and military weaponry.

But President Hassan al-Bariqi was not about to spend his newfound wealth on his impoverished citizens. Rather, his money was spent on palaces, yachts, lavish aircraft, weapons, and other expensive toys of war and status.

The price for this one desert compound and associated real estate was the equivalent of 500 million U.S. dollars, paid to al-Bariqi's government, and the People's Republic of China didn't hesitate to consummate the deal.

"Colonel Ming. Seven new subjects have been prepared for the treatment. Do you wish to examine them first?"

Ming was conducting his customary morning inspection of the holding cells, accompanied by two junior medical officers.

"Were the subjects recently captured? Where are they from?" Ming inquired.

"They are from the Masalit tribe. They were turned over yesterday by the Janjaweed militia under the command of Korlos. All are male, between the age of 16 and 30, and all are in satisfactory health. None were shot; they suffered only the usual beatings."

"Very well. Instruct Dr. Hsu to continue using procedural modification 33vK. He can use a different test group for his experiments with the new viral infection procedure 26rh8.

"And make certain Dr. Hsu knows that I want a detailed report on the subjects' initial physiological responses by 2200 hours today. Is that understood?"

Ming did not wait for a reply before walking away at his usual brisk pace.

CHAPTER 2

"SO, WE WOULD TAKE THE SUMMER TERM off from the academic curriculum, but get credit for the volunteer work? Sort of like a short stint with the Peace Corps?" Ethan asked the speaker.

He was dressed in gym shorts and a yellow polo shirt, gym bag over his shoulder. Standing next to him, arms folded across his chest, was another young man, similarly dressed. Joe was Ethan's best friend. They had just completed a session of racket ball and were on their way back to their dorm.

Of Scandinavian and Irish decent, Ethan had blue eyes, light brown hair, a moderately pale complexion and average build—very common by any measure. His personality, however, made him stand out from a crowd, or draw the attention of one. He was outgoing, engaging, both witty and humorous—at times overt and at other times very subtle. He was intelligent and focused; two attributes his professors especially valued. But he had yet to declare a major and he was halfway through his second year at the University of Oregon, his father's Alma Mater.

Ethan's grandfather was a Professor Emeritus at Oregon State University, and the rivalry between the two universities was as intense as any. Despite the fact that both schools were highly ranked and had good athletic programs, the family arguments were known to get somewhat heated during the Civil War basketball and football games, although always in good nature.

"Yes," the speaker replied. "That's basically the way the program works. We recognize that a multiyear commitment is difficult for many people, especially students. It's understandable that recent graduates would want to start their career path right away, and they may be uncertain if serving with the Peace Corps is the right step to take. This program was designed to provide a hands-on introduction while earning college credits, so you can determine first-hand if volunteer work helping impoverished people is right for you."

Ethan Savage nodded understanding. He had often thought that helping poor and under-educated children would make the world a better place for everyone. *But how much difference can one person make? Or even a bunch of people? The problem is so enormous, and the gap between the wealthy and poor growing ever larger*, he thought. Ethan found appalling the fact that nearly one-third of the world's population—about two billion people—had no access to electricity.

Even as a young boy, Ethan remembered his father, Peter, talking about these issues. His father had explained that education was the key to improving, albeit slowly, global standards of living and improving ethnic and religious tolerance. Ethan believed this and wanted to do something meaningful, but he felt like he never could find the right opportunity.

Maybe it's because opting out is easier than getting involved?

Ethan shook his head; he wasn't ready to truthfully answer that question.

Now he had an opportunity to travel with a student group—the Peace Corps Reserve—and spend three months working at an impoverished village in Darfur—literally meaning Land of the Fur—or maybe at an aid camp for refugees, victims of on-going persecution by the government of Sudan. He had read a bit about the political unrest and violence in the western region of Sudan. Although there appeared to be some abatement after the Republic of South Sudan seceded as a new nation, the region was still rife with ethnic violence on both sides of the new border. Still, that was half a world away, and it all felt so abstract and remote to Ethan.

It would be so easy to come up with an endless list of reasons why he couldn't do this, but who was he kidding? Ethan was running the debate in his mind. *I can keep telling myself I want to do something, but words are cheap. Action is what really counts.*

Ethan leaned toward Joe and whispered so as not to disturb the surrounding students listening to the speaker. "What do you think?"

"I don't know—sounds like it's hard work and the living conditions look pretty rough. Did she really say that they sleep in tents? On canvas cots in sleeping bags?"

"Yeah, so what? It would be like camping. Besides, what if we could help put in a well, or a solar panel and some batteries at a village so they at least have some electricity."

Joe was skeptical. "So what? What can they do with one PV panel and a car battery?" he scoffed.

Joe's dismissiveness irritated Ethan. "Lots, that's what. How about powering a PC and a radio, maybe a small refrigerator to store vaccines and other medicines."

At that moment, Ethan made up his mind. He was young,

healthy, smart, and strong. Would there ever be a better time than now? He would help... he wanted to help.

"I'm in," he said aloud still looking at Joe. The speaker, hearing him, smiled enthusiastically. "Fantastic! You're doing a good thing."

Joe frowned. If Ethan was going he had to also, or he'd never hear the end of it. "All right... me too." Although the words were there, the enthusiasm was plainly lacking from his voice.

Leaning toward his buddy, Joe mumbled, "Remind me again why you're my friend?"

There was a growing murmur amongst the student audience as more and more spoke up. "I'll go, too. I'm in."

The line to sign the registration sheet was long. Twenty-three young men and women had followed Ethan's lead and signed up to travel to North Africa.

Exactly what they would do was presently unknown, but that didn't matter. Somehow, they'd be able to make a difference. At this moment they were all united in their belief that soon they would each trade a few months of their lives for the betterment of people they didn't know and most likely would never see again after this short tour of duty.

CHAPTER 3

"YOU DID WHAT!" Peter shouted into the phone.

"Calm down, Dad. This is what you always said people should do—what I should do. I'm going to Africa to help refugees in Darfur. It's only for three months, and I get academic credit for the quarter I'm not at the university."

"I understand, son. And this is a very good thing you're planning to do. It really and truly is. But Darfur? Why couldn't you go someplace else—someplace where there isn't so much violence?"

"Yeah, someplace where they don't need our help? Is that what you really think, Dad? By U.N. estimates there are between one and two million refugees along the border with Chad—and every one of them needs help. Did you know that the so-called developed countries can't even agree that genocide is happening in Darfur?"

"Look… I understand your feelings. But that's a dangerous place. Do you understand what's happening there?"

"Duh… Of course I do. I've spent some time researching the conflict. I know that more than 300,000 civilians have been killed as a result of the fighting since it officially began in 2003. I also know that there's been tension between the ethnic African farmers and the nomadic Arabs going back at least several decades, probably longer. The American media has over-simplified this as an ethnic struggle between black Africans and lighter-skinned Arabs. But that's not what's at the heart of the struggle."

"Really?" Peter was surprised by the veracity and depth of his son's explanation.

"Yes, really. It's about resources—food, water, minerals, oil. That's exactly why those people need my help—our help. They've been abandoned by everyone else." Ethan paused for a moment before continuing.

"Dad, surely you realize this."

Peter was silent. He had always been too busy to help others at the magnitude of commitment that his son had just made. The list of reasons—excuses really—was long and, at the time, compelling. First there was college and completing his degree while working full time. Then he was fully occupied starting his career and a family. Later, it was the time needed to get his business established. Sure, Peter had always preached to his children the need to help others, and he had always donated generously to many charities. But deep inside he knew that it was far easier to give money and material than it was to give time, sweat, and knowledge.

In the innocence and naïveté of youth, Ethan had taken his preaching to heart, which had genuinely surprised and moved Peter. As a child growing up, Ethan was never very serious. He was always having fun goofing off and doing only a little better than average in school. He made friends very easily but didn't show much interest in organized sports or, for that matter, any organized activity.

With this one phone call Peter's image of his son abruptly changed. The carefree boy had a serious and deeply caring side that had been previously masked, hidden from view even for those closest to him. And now Peter's only son was about to travel halfway around the world to a very dangerous place to provide assistance to people who sorely needed it.

"Okay, okay. You win. It's just that I'm worried about your safety. You know I always have been… you and your sister. If anything happened to either of you, I don't know what I would do."

"I'll be fine, Dad. We're part of a large group sponsored by Uncle Sam. And I've checked out the situation there. For the last couple years the violence has been way down, and the French military has helped to stabilize the borders Sudan shares with Chad and C.A.R."

"C.A.R.?"

"The Central African Republic. There are lots of international aid groups on the ground and no one seems to be having any problems."

"I hear you, son." There was another pause as Peter choked back his emotion. His son had become a fine young man, and Peter was proud. "Your mother would be very proud of you; you know that."

"Yeah, I know. Look, this is what you and Mom always said people should do. I want to do this; I'll be fine."

"I know you will. Now, tell me all about this expedition you're about to embark upon."

Although the sound of dread had vanished from Peter's voice, he could not vanquish his anxiety. He had simply pushed his fears to a far corner of his consciousness. They would arise later, mostly in the dead of night, to haunt him. He knew that; he had experienced it when Maggie was in the hospital following the car accident.

For days the doctors had been brutally honest—his loving wife, the mother of their children, had suffered irreparable damage to her brain. There was no hope to be offered by modern medicine. Without sustaining life-support machines, her body would cease to function.

For five whole days, Peter refused to accept the truth. Every time he felt himself sliding into a restless sleep, he was haunted by Maggie's image—laughing and running through the mountain meadows with Ethan and their daughter, Joanna. Peter hardly slept for those five days. He would will himself to put aside the fear that she was gone, to believe that there was hope she would recover. But each time he closed his eyes the logical portion of his mind told him that she was gone and that he needed to let go. After days of holding onto false hope, Peter had finally agreed to execute Maggie's advance directive and instructed her physicians to terminate life support. Maggie perished that night, and with her so went part of Peter's soul.

"Well, I don't have all the details yet. I just signed up two days ago. But we'll fly out a day or two after finals week. I think we're flying from Portland to New York, and then on to Paris, then to… I'm not sure. But the final leg is by truck—that I do remember. We can bring one duffle bag and a backpack with personal gear, that's all."

"And I suspect that you will have far more in that one duffle bag than any of the refugees you'll be helping."

"You're probably right. I'm going to load up with candy and chewing gum for the children. The aid groups are providing everything we need other than our personal gear."

"Do you know what projects you and the others in the group will be taking on?"

"We talked a little bit about that during the orientation meeting yesterday. The group leader—her name is Samantha

Ward, but she goes by Sam—said that we would do a lot of teaching, maybe help to install a water treatment system on at least one community well, and assist with medical checkups." Ethan sounded very excited. There was no trace of fear or apprehension in his voice.

"I didn't know you had any medical training," Peter quipped, trying to inject some humor into the conversation.

"Oh, I know a little first aid. But we would only be assisting trained doctors. You know, Doctors Without Borders? I think our job will be to comfort the patients and try to teach them about preventive care. Sam said we would have to go through training on the local diseases and common injuries. Oh, and I'll need to get a bunch of vaccinations before I go, for illnesses I've never heard of!"

"And make sure you do!" Peter replied in as stern a voice as he could muster.

"Trust me, Dad. I don't want to get a rare illness and become the subject of a research article in some medical journal. I'll get every vaccination they recommend."

"And you'll take your cell phone so we can talk periodically, right?" As soon as Peter asked the question he realized he was treating Ethan like a child rather than the man he had become.

"Of course I will! When have you ever known me to be without my phone? But, Sam says that electricity is scarce and you can't count on having a socket to plug into. I think we'll be out in the country somewhere near the border with Chad."

"Well, that makes sense if you're in a refugee camp. I would guess those camps are rather primitive, and they probably don't all have diesel generators for electric power. I'd guess it's like a primitive RV park."

"That's what it looked like in the slide show they showed us. We'll wash our clothes by hand in a communal water trough. And sleep on cots in tents with kerosene lanterns for light. I'm planning to bring several paperbacks to pass the time when we aren't working."

"If you're out in the country away from cities, will you even get cell coverage?" asked Peter.

"Sam says we will. I guess even the most distant locations in western Sudan are being connected. Anyway, I'll bring spare batteries and a solar charger, and my camera too."

"Why not just use your phone for pictures?"

"Not enough memory. I plan to take loads of photos to share with everyone when I come back home."

"It sounds like you're well on your way to getting it all figured out."

Ethan laughed. He knew this was hard for his father.

Peter continued, "Promise me that you will come over to Bend for a family dinner before you leave. I'll check with your sister; I'm sure she'll want to see you off as well."

"Only if you promise to barbeque steaks!

"Tell Sis I said hello."

"I'll let her know. You take care now, okay? And do well on your finals—I want to see solid grades."

"Sure, Dad. I'll talk to you soon. Bye." As Peter hung up the phone he could not dismiss the growing feeling of dread in the pit of his stomach.

CHAPTER 4

LAND OF THE FUR
JUNE 5

THE SUCCESSION OF PLANE FLIGHTS separated by endless waiting in airport terminals had taken a toll on the young Peace Corps Reserve volunteers. Ethan and his new friends were exhausted despite the excitement.

Riding in the back of a UN-blue, covered cargo truck, sitting on metal bench seats with their duffle bags at their feet, no one could see the surrounding country as the truck bounced along on the final leg of their journey. The two-hour ride was uncomfortable, and Ethan's buttocks and lower back ached. Soon, they were told, the truck would arrive at the refugee camp and they could rest for the remainder of the day. It was late morning, and the volunteers would have their mid-day meal upon arriving at the camp.

The truck's brakes squealed a greeting as the vehicle slowed and came to a stop. A cloud of reddish-tan dust engulfed the truck as the driver walked to the back and dropped the tailgate. Then he placed a stool on the ground at the back of the truck so that the student volunteers could more easily exit the bed onto the dusty ground.

The volunteers exited single file; Ethan was the last to step out into the bright sunlight. Looking around, he took in the refugee camp. There were a few large tents nearby with the sides rolled up to allow what little breeze there was to flow through the walls of insect netting. The tents were old and battered, and several cloth patches were evident on the netting and the canvas roofs. It was already hot, and there didn't appear to be much shade other than what the tents offered.

Stretched out in wavy rows were hundreds of smaller walled tents, each about the size of a four-man tent that Ethan was familiar with. They were all faded on top to a bleached gray-green color while closer to the ground the canvas was stained reddish-tan from the dirt. None of these tents had insect netting or walls that could be opened to allow cooling ventilation. As he surveyed the camp, he saw a woman and six children leave one of the nearest tents. Then a man followed them out.

"How many people are living in each tent?" Ethan asked of no one in particular.

From behind him a voice answered, "Initially we assigned one tent per family. That meant there were about four to eight persons in each tent." Ethan turned around. It was Sam who had answered him. She must have arrived earlier.

"About two weeks ago a new group of refugees started to wander in, and we don't have enough shelter for all of them. Many of the young men have chosen to sleep outside. Since it's so dry there are no worries about getting rained on. But the insects can be a problem. We've issued mosquito netting and that helps, but there isn't enough to go around. We had to begin doubling up in the tents that were sheltering smaller families."

"How do so many fit in those small tents?"

Sam shrugged. "The refugees are still streaming in every

day. The population in the camp has risen 30 percent to about 2,000. I'm glad you've all arrived—there's a lot that needs to be done beginning with basic sanitation and food preparation."

Samantha Ward looked over the group of volunteers. It had been almost three months since she had spoken to the students at the University of Oregon, and she remembered not only the faces but also the names of those who signed up. She scanned the motley bunch of men and women standing before her.

Slowly she went from face to face, naming each person. "Trent... Wendy... Susan... Brad... Ethan... Joe... Matthew... James. Welcome. I know you're tired and have lots of questions. But first, please follow Bob." She pointed to their native driver. "He'll show you to your tent. I'm sorry but you will all have to share one tent since space is in short supply. Just drop your bags off and then meet me at the mess tent, which is over there." Sam pointed to the nearest of the large tents with an assortment of bench tables.

Ethan picked up his duffle bag and walked with Joe. "It's hard to imagine how these people survive," he said.

Joe nodded and looked at a group of small children playing in the dust. "I suspect we're going to learn firsthand." They completed the walk to their tent in silence. Whether it was fatigue or the grim reality of the refugee camp beginning to sink in, everyone was solemn.

The tent was set up with eight cots—four to a side with a narrow isle between them. Duffle bags had to be stored beneath each cot; there was no other space. A flap opening was at each opposite end of the tent; the flaps were presently tied back, and the two other canvas walls were rolled up. Still it must have been 20 degrees hotter inside the tent than it was outside. Ethan could feel the heat radiating down from the fabric roof like an oven. Each person selected a cot and placed their bag on it before walking out the opposite opening and sauntering over to the mess tent.

Sam was waiting for the new arrivals. After everyone seated themselves on the benches running along either side of the table, she began with a brief orientation. While she was speaking, two middle-aged women—refugees recruited to help prepare meals—brought bottled water, a broth soup, and bowls of rice to the table.

"This is a typical mid-day meal," explained Sam. "The staff and volunteers eat the same food as the refugees. We don't always have bottled water; it depends what supplies are delivered. The well-water is safe—it just doesn't taste as good; kind of a soapy taste from the dissolved minerals."

Ethan pulled a bowl of rice toward him and began to eat. It was very bland. He guessed salt and pepper were also in short supply and he thought how wonderful it would be to add a few dashes of his favorite hot sauce to the rice. He took a sip of the hot, thin soup. It had an unusual flavor but reminded him of beef broth. He decided not to ask what it was made from.

"The evening meal is served at dusk... about 6:00 p.m. Don't expect it to cool much at night. The temperature only falls 15, maybe 20, degrees. The breeze helps, and after a while you get acclimated."

Wendy spoke softly, but still loud enough to be heard. "A shower sure would feel good." Ethan glanced her way and smiled.

"Sorry, Wendy... no showers. The well is already taxed to provide enough water for drinking and cooking. A new well is being dug about 300 yards west of the main well, but it will be another three or four weeks before it's finished."

"Four weeks without showering? I can't do that!" said Wendy very seriously.

Sam smiled. "Sure you can. Look around you and you'll see 2,000 people who haven't had a shower in the last six weeks, maybe longer for many. Use your washcloth and take a sponge bath. Occasionally we also get baby wipes with the humanitarian aid."

"Isn't there a stream or river that can be used for bathing?" asked Trent.

"Yes, but the water is very low now and it's so muddy you'd come out worse off than when you went in... I don't recommend it. If we get some rain and the water rises and clears, then bathing in the river is an option. But please, relax everyone. You're making a bigger deal out of this than you should be. I told you it would be primitive."

Ethan didn't want the conversation to dissolve into whining and grumbling, so he decided to change the subject. "What's our first project? Will we be working on the new well?"

Sam smiled. She appreciated his positive attitude. "This afternoon I want all of you to rest. Following dinner I'll brief you along with the other team that is arriving later today."

Matthew asked, "How many new volunteers are in our group?"

"There are nine volunteers from Oregon State University arriving today, soon I think. I'll be working with this team and the OSU team, and I'm hoping to see some friendly competition. We'll refer to you as Team Duck and Team Beaver following your school mascots." Matthew and Joe both smiled at the thought of some hometown rivalry.

"I'll cover all the ground rules this evening prior to the project briefing. You know where the latrine is located. It's reserved for the volunteer staff—a small token of our gratitude—and I'm sure you will highly value it before you leave here." The students chuckled in response.

"Any other questions?" prompted Sam.

"Yes, I have one," replied Joe. "What's the reason for the influx of refugees?"

Sam paused before answering. "There have been renewed attacks on villages to the northeast, about 20 or so miles from here. As you all know, the international press has not been allowed free access across Darfur. So what little we have been able to piece together is based on what the refugees are telling us."

Sam instantly recognized the concerned expressions. Perhaps she should have shared this information earlier. She pressed on. "We think the attacks were isolated events, and we have no reason to believe that the peace that was brokered in Qatar is unraveling. Still, we can't be certain just yet."

Ethan asked the obvious question, "What does this mean for us? For our safety?"

"There is nothing to worry about. At the first sign of danger, we will all be evacuated along with the refugees. The villages that were attacked are a long way from here, so I don't think there's any imminent danger at all. Once journalists and aid groups are allowed into the area and can make independent assessments, we'll know more."

"It's the Janjaweed, isn't it," Trent said.

Sam nodded. "Yes, that's what the refugees are saying. They rode in without warning and burned the villages and crops. Most of the young men were taken away. The women were raped and beaten. And then a war plane dropped napalm canisters on the villagers. Many were killed; even more were burned. The injured are at a United Nations field hospital north of here. But there wasn't enough room at that camp, so those who are able are now walking here.

"We can't handle many more, but there's no sign yet that the numbers are diminishing. Some of the elders that arrived yesterday explained that several villages were attacked—they didn't know how many, only that it was more than just their own village."

"How will you care for everyone?" asked Wendy.

"Our quota of rice and water was increased earlier this week, so we can cope for the moment, but unless we get more shelter and more food and medicine, we won't be able to keep taking them in. I pray that the exodus is nearing an end."

The students were quickly realizing they really weren't prepared for this current situation. What they had been prepped for was far less intense than this heightened element of danger and the refugees' overwhelming struggle to survive. They were in as strange a world as any they could imagine. But none of the volunteers had any regrets; they were eager to begin helping.

CHAPTER 5

DARFUR
JUNE 5

DR. HSU WAS ACCOMPANIED by two staff researchers, each carrying a tablet computer for recording notes. They all wore surgical masks containing activated charcoal embedded with silver nanoparticles. The masks were designed to trap and sanitize air-born microbes.

The doctor was conducting his morning rounds. He stopped at the foot of a simple metal-frame bed with a clipboard hanging from the footboard. Fastened to the clipboard were the subject's medical charts. The male subject lying in the bed was asleep.

As Dr. Hsu scanned the notes on the charts, he pinched his eyebrows. "This subject was injected two days ago?"

"Yes, doctor," replied one of the researchers after consulting the computerized records.

"I see the subject is showing the normal early signs of infection. Good… as expected." Dr. Hsu put the clipboard down and moved to the next bed.

This subject was awake as he approached and lunged for the doctor. It was a weak effort, easily restrained by the nylon straps binding his arms and legs to the bed frame. The man shouted in his native language, no doubt some curse aimed at the doctor and his staff. No sooner had the words come out when he retched in convulsions, his body going into spasms, trying to double over. As his muscles contracted, his arms and legs yanked against the straps and further chaffed—the skin already rubbed off in many places.

"This subject was injected with the virus three days ago," commented the other researcher.

Dr. Hsu nodded and studied the medical chart. "Severe cramps, nausea… vomiting began earlier this morning. Make sure the subject stays on a saline drip; I don't want him to dehydrate. Begin administering Halotestin, 60 milligrams per day, IV drip. And take a bone sample; I want to monitor the rate of progress of the cellular reconstruction."

Both researchers bowed, indicating their obedience.

Although there were other beds and other subjects in the room, the trio left with Dr. Hsu in the lead. He entered the hallway and walked only a short distance before entering another room, this one rather small and equipped with numerous air intakes that allowed the room to be maintained at a slightly negative pressure of filtered and sterilized air. The door shut behind them automatically.

Hanging on the wall were white, sterile, hooded jumpsuits. Hsu slipped into one and zipped it up all the way to his chin, pulling the hood snuggly over his head and neck; the two researchers did likewise. Next, they each donned a pair of nitrile gloves and then a full facemask. The mask fit tightly, sealing the hood against the chin, cheeks and forehead.

Attached to the facemask was a device that looked very similar to a diver's rebreather. It consisted of an aluminum tube mounted horizontally. The tube contained sodium peroxide, a chemical that liberates pure oxygen when it reacts with the moisture and carbon dioxide exhaled by the user. A mesh pad impregnated with silver nanoparticles filtered the oxygen to provide an added measure of safety by destroying bacteria and viruses.

After checking to make sure that his mask was properly fitted and sealed, Dr. Hsu opened a second door and entered a large room with twelve beds arranged in two rows of six; four of the beds were empty. Along the wall behind each bed ran a green pipe containing oxygen with a gas regulator located at each bed. Attached to the regulator was a length of clear plastic tubing connected to a simple facemask that could be placed over the subject's nose and mouth. LCD monitors above each bed displayed the subject's blood pressure and pulse in real time. A portable defibrillator was pushed off to the side of the room.

All of the subjects exhibited signs of bleeding—extreme in some cases. The evidence was all over the bed sheets. The room was quiet, except for an occasional groan.

"These subjects—" that's how Hsu thought of them, as subjects rather than patients, "—were all infected with the most recent variation at the same time?"

"Yes. Formula 26rh8. They were infected almost nine days ago," one of the researchers replied.

Dr. Hsu knew that this formula was based on a derivative of the Ebola-Sudan virus, a variation of the Filoviridae virus that causes hemorrhagic fever.

The other researcher added, "Four of the subjects died during the night."

"The cause?" demanded Hsu.

"It was a combination of blood loss, liver damage, and systemic shock."

Dr. Hsu smiled. "Excellent! Keep me informed as the symptoms progress in the remaining subjects. Once the control experiment is complete we can test the new viral carrier for the foreign DNA."

The two researchers exchanged a confused glance; then one dared to ask the question that was suddenly burning in both minds. "I don't understand, sir. Did you say this is a control experiment?"

Hsu spun on his heels, he did not care to be questioned. "Of course! How else would we know if the viral insertion is inducing any new side effects? Besides, the mutated viral strain we are using—with similarities to both the Sudan strain and the Zaire strain—has not been studied in depth."

"I'm sorry, sir. I just don't understand why the Filoviridae virus is considered a candidate host to insert the foreign DNA into the subjects. The virus induces such severe systemic damage to the subject's body... the mortality rate is as high as 90 percent."

"Yes, and our control experiment will certainly verify that result."

"But with such a high mortality rate, how can the procedure be effective?"

"Effective can have many different meanings. With procedure 33vK the subjects are likely to survive the transformation, and we have seen the results, which are quite impressive. But the Ad14 virus is weak; it can be treated and killed with new drugs. In contrast, the Ebola virus is far more robust." The gleam in Dr. Hsu's eyes shone through his clear plastic face shield.

"There are few effective treatments for hemorrhagic fever. What treatments there are remain expensive and in short supply, partly due to the ease with which the virus naturally mutates into a distinctly new strain, still deadly but resistant to prior medications. It is the perfect carrier for the foreign DNA!"

The researchers stared back at Dr. Hsu, admiring his twisted brilliance but also not fully comprehending his ultimate objectives in these experiments.

"It is evident you don't understand."

The two researchers had blank expressions.

"It should be obvious." Hsu was imagining himself lecturing to a room full of students. "The Ad14 virus infects hundreds of millions of people each year. Even though it is relatively harmless, it is a nuisance. Drug companies and medical labs will eventually find an effective vaccine, and when they do... well then, procedure 33vK will be far less *effective*.

"But, the Ebola virus—aside from the occasional regional outbreaks—infects on average only a few *hundred* people each year and therefore, even though it is quite lethal, it usually does not merit much attention. There simply is not enough profit to be made by developing an effective treatment, let alone an effective vaccine."

"But if the mortality rate remains high," one of the researchers interjected, "then most of the subjects will die before the transformation is complete. I don't see how this moves us toward the Committee's goal of engineering a superior soldier?"

Dr. Hsu smiled behind the surgical mask, his eyes reflecting excitement. "You seem to confuse effectiveness with yield. If the mortality rate of 26rh8 is high, it simply means we need a larger population to infect. This is not a difficult problem."

Both researchers stared blankly back at Dr. Hsu.

"These issues do not concern either of you." Hsu moved on to the next bed and then the next. After completing his inspection, and satisfied with the data, he turned back to the two researchers who were following three steps behind.

"When this control experiment is finished, we will move into the next phase. This work is very important. Procedure

33vK has proved sufficient for making a super soldier, and that work showed us possibilities never before imagined. You see, once we perfect the 26rh8 formula and procedure, we will have an invincible biological weapon. One for which there is no vaccine and no cure."

CHAPTER 6

WHEN THE PEOPLE'S LIBERATION ARMY first agreed to fund Colonel Xao Ming's genetic engineering experiments, none of the generals really believed the work would successfully lead to a vastly superior soldier, as Ming had boasted. Yet, he had strong ties to powerful political allies and the generals felt it was in their best interest to appease the colonel—at least for the moment. That was seven years ago, and Ming's work had achieved even greater success than was promised.

When the research reached a critical point where human subjects were needed, it became too dangerous to continue the work on Chinese soil. Serendipity played a key role when the turmoil and violence in North Africa reached new levels in western Sudan. The People's Liberation Army saw a unique opportunity to build a secluded and secret military research facility that was well isolated from prying eyes. And the government in Khartoum was all too willing to cooperate with China's military leaders, including asking no questions.

Colonel Ming presided over the conference call from the seat situated at the center of the table. Dr. Hsu sat to his immediate right, and several other top scientists and doctors occupied the remaining seats. He was about to address General Cai of the People's Liberation Army over a video and voice link. On the wall facing Ming hung two large flat screens, one for the video link and one for displaying the slides that would also be transmitted to the General and his staff.

"Colonel Ming," greeted General Cai, his hands folded on the table as he looked straight into the camera. "I expect you have substantially more promising results to report on this... gene therapy... than you did during your last briefing. You may begin."

"Thank you General." Ming bowed his head slightly. "Using adenovirus 14, or Ad14, we have shown that the foreign DNA is successfully inserted in human DNA."

"Excuse me, Colonel." The interruption came from one of the General's aides. "I was under the impression that you have been using the Ad14 carrier for close to two years. Certainly you have some new results to share with this committee?"

Ming forced a smile. "If the General will indulge me for just a moment and refer to the first slide, I will explain our transformation procedure 33vK." As Ming explained the details of the viral infection procedure he noticed the bored expressions on the faces of General Cai and his staff, their faces displayed in detail on the flat-screen monitor.

The idiots can't grasp the significance of my work, thought Ming. Still, he pressed forward. "The symptoms are very reproducible. Within 48 hours of exposure, an otherwise healthy subject develops coughing and sneezing, similar to a bad cold. The symptoms quickly escalate and within 60 hours the subject exhibits fever and signs of nausea as well as muscle ache and cramps, which are severe in most cases."

Ming was flashing through slides with photographs documenting the various stages of infection as he was describing the effects. "As the infection spreads, the pain becomes so intense it is common for the subjects to scream continuously for days. Physical exhaustion is typical as the subject is unable to rest or sleep."

No longer bored, General Cai and his staff appeared perversely fascinated by the pictures. Ming clicked the mouse activating an embedded video. It was only fifteen seconds long but recorded a young man doubled over while lying on a concrete floor, his arms wrapped around his stomach. His body was thrashing back and forth and his face contorted in agony, his loud screams recorded on the audio track.

"These symptoms continue for up to three weeks. If the subject is in poor health, especially with a weak heart or circulatory deficiency, death usually results. If the subject survives the transformation, all symptoms of the infection vanish after 30 days."

"Please explain the cause of death." This question was asked by the General's aide, the same who had interrupted Ming earlier.

Without prompting, Dr. Hsu replied. "Autopsies on 63 subjects indicates that death is the result of heart failure or stroke, brought on by severe physiological stress."

"For this reason," added Colonel Ming, "we only use male subjects between 17 and 35 years of age, who are in good health."

"That seems rather selective," observed General Cai. "Are you able to gather sufficient subjects?"

Ming flashed a disingenuous smile again. "Fortunately, that has not been a problem. The Janjaweed militia are very efficient, and they are suitably motivated by a token payment for each subject they deliver in good condition. They find the hard currency very useful for black-market transactions."

"I see," General Cai answered. "Please continue. You have not explained yet why you have proclaimed your work an unqualified success."

"Adenovirus 14 is an extremely virulent strain that is closely related to viruses responsible for pink eye, the common cold, and several upper respiratory illnesses. Because Ad14 is so easily transmitted from one human host to another, it is an ideal carrier for inserting foreign DNA into human cells. However, as you know, we succeeded in merging Neanderthal DNA with modern human, or Homo sapiens, DNA two years ago. But that alone was not sufficient.

"We sought a procedure that implanted the Neanderthal DNA in such a way that it fused with modern human DNA synergistically, allowing cellular reproduction. General, I am pleased to report that procedure 33vK achieves this goal."

Ming clicked the mouse and advanced to the next slide. It was a photographic collage showing a half dozen creatures, the result of the new gene therapy procedure. A collective gasp was transmitted over the voice link as the General and his staff saw the photographs of grotesque beings.

"General, you are looking at photographic evidence of the first hominid species created by mankind. A true hybrid between Homo sapiens and Homo neanderthalensis. My staff calls these beings Homothals. Although not scientifically correct, there is a certain ring to the name, don't you think?"

General Cai turned from the images back to the video camera. His eyes were wide and his mouth slightly agape.

Ming sat back and folded his hands, enjoying the moment. Dr. Hsu continued with some of the more technical aspects of the briefing. "Samples of bone, muscle tissue, skin, liver, and kidney were taken from living subjects at various stages of the transformation to document the progress of the mutation. Autopsies on subjects failing to survive the process, or who were intentionally sacrificed, confirmed that the transformation quickly infected all parts of the host—organs as well as the muscles and skeleton. What results is rapid cellular reproduction, altering every aspect of the host."

"A bonus is that, when wounded, the Homothals heal in roughly half the time required for a healthy human." Ming added, his eyes gleaming brightly.

The General's staff continued to talk amongst themselves, creating a murmur that seemed to be distracting to General Cai. He held up both hands, silencing his staff.

"Continue," General Cai said, more as a request rather than an order.

"Following recovery from the initial infection, subjects are given high doses of anabolic-androgen steroids. This greatly accelerates the rate of muscle and bone growth. Secondary effects include hair growth and increased aggression, but we've learned how to control that and use it to our benefit."

"Your scientists do not object to experimentation on human subjects?" This question came from another of the General's aides.

"By human, I presume you mean people?" Ming asked, but did not wait for a reply. "As I have already explained, once the genetic transformation has taken place, the subjects are no longer human, as you say."

"I do not wish to quibble over terminology, Colonel," Cai said, his voice carrying an edge of irritation.

Ming bowed his head ever so slightly. "My staff is very loyal and obedient. They see these Homothals for what they are, test subjects. However, as a precaution, science and medical staff are forbidden from having any contact with the native captives brought to the compound in order to avoid any feelings of empathy for the test subjects. The prisoners are received at the compound by my soldiers under the direct command of Lieutenant Li and are kept in cells holding up to six persons. Only when a specific prisoner is designated for procedure 33vK or another experiment, is the medical staff allowed to have contact with him—and then only as necessary."

"How did you achieve success after so many failures?" said General Cai. "Your gene therapy procedure is essentially unchanged from what you reported six months ago, except that now you only infect the strongest subjects."

"Very good General! Yes, you are correct. I am pleased that you are beginning to grasp the more important details of my work."

Cai frowned and glanced to the aide on his right. The aide wrote something on his notepad, a reminder to continue this discussion later with the General.

"In the early phases of my research, combinations of infection procedures and viral strains failed for many different reasons—but most commonly because the fused Homo sapiens and Neanderthal DNA did not result in viable, reproductive cells. In hundreds of cases the subject's autoimmune response was triggered by the foreign DNA, the T-cells eventually destroying their organs from within resulting in extensive hemorrhaging, not unlike the symptoms of hemorrhagic fevers such as Ebola.

"However, that changed with the introduction of a new strain of Neanderthal DNA, recovered from the marrow of bones well preserved in an ancient burial site deep in a cave in southern Spain, near Gibraltar. The DNA was much more robust than earlier strains and, unlike earlier samples, this Neanderthal DNA has a short but unique nucleotide sequence—only 253 base pairs—found only in modern human DNA."

"What is the significance of this discovery?" asked one of

the aides.

"Other than the obvious?" Ming didn't wait for a reply. "This suggests that somehow genetic material from Homo sapiens had become mixed with the Neanderthal DNA in the donating specimen. Whether by interbreeding or disease, I cannot say. It could also be the result of a natural mutation, although unlikely. Whatever the reason, the results are unambiguous. When attached to the Ad14 virus, more than 83 percent of human hosts are infected without triggering the autoimmune response, as well as, for the first time, reproduction of infected cells.

"My staff has examined all known samples of Neanderthal DNA, and only this one donor gives rise to the results I have shared with you. But that does not present any barriers. My staff can replicate the DNA and prepare an unlimited supply of genetic material."

"I care little about your scientific accomplishments, Colonel Ming, however important they may be," General Cai said. "Give me your assessment of the fighting capabilities of these creatures you call Homothals."

"Their physical strength, suggested by their obvious appearance, is easily equal to three or four men. Anatomically, they have thick bones, tendons, and ligaments. They exhibit exceptional endurance and agility, easily exceeding the best of my soldiers. Their senses—sight, hearing, smell—far exceed that of modern humans and is on par with wild animals. In addition, my soldiers swear the Homothals have an ability to sense when they are being tracked or stalked."

"Do they follow orders without question? All the rest is meaningless if they are not good soldiers." General Cai's staff was nodding in agreement with their boss.

"The transformation erases much of the human will to question or defy authority. At the same time, it has also eliminated nearly all linguistic capability, leaving a rudimentary—at best—function of speech. Autopsies of the Homothal larynx fails to reveal any functional deficiency. We are still studying this. However, we have already developed simple and effective training programs."

"Are you telling me that these Homothals cannot speak? Even in their native tongue?" the General asked.

"Yes, that is mostly correct," Hsu answered. "They communicate verbally through a collection of grunts that at first seems to have little variation. After further study, my linguists were able to identify a small vocabulary. The phonological sounds, morphological structure of words, and syntactical construction of sentences are all much more simplistic. The semantics and the way the sounds and meanings relate to each other in their simple language, and even more importantly, their lexicon or mental dictionary, suggests that the Homothals have regressed mentally. I believe the foreign DNA has changed the brain function as well as other physiological functions already noted. The Homothal is a very simple creature, without modern language abilities, and they show no signs of attachment to any prior aspect of their lives."

Hsu continued, believing further explanation would help the General's staff fully comprehend the importance of this result. "Other than basic aggression, often triggered by the desire to mate with a female, there are no emotional expressions from the subjects. They function like animals—satisfying the basic needs of food, water, and shelter appear to be their only concerns. They are given a basic nutritional supplement in their daily rations, but the normal human desire for variety of food, friendship, family, material possessions—all observations indicate these emotions are completely absent."

"Without this baggage, the Homothal enters battle without fear. It has no concept of mercy. As you can see, through my genius *I have created* the perfect fighting organism," Ming proclaimed as he held his head high.

General Cai pinched his eyes and looked directly at Ming. "It would do you well, *Colonel*, to remember that your work is allowed to proceed specifically for the benefit of the PLA and the Party."

Colonel Ming dipped his head slightly, although it was not quite a bow. *Ignorant fools. Soon enough, you will answer to my orders.*

"I expect your full report, Colonel, along with the complete data package. It seems your boasts are substantiated, and I will discuss the next steps with the Chairman and the Committee."

The video ended and the conference call was terminated.

"Should I organize the data for transmission?" Dr. Hsu asked.

"No, those fools do not understand what I have achieved. I have other plans, and when the time is right, General Cai and his staff will be shown the power that I wield at *my* discretion."

CHAPTER 7

AT THE END OF THE CORRIDOR, Colonel Ming slid his security badge through an electronic lock and exited through two doors into a large fenced courtyard. The fencing was electrified and separated a central region, where Ming presently stood, from a large parade ground. This parade ground was further bounded by the compound's perimeter fence stretching twelve feet in height and topped by concertina razor wire. It, too, was electrified with 10,000 volts. A red flashing light on a tall conspicuous pole indicated when the wire was energized.

The test subjects were about to be released from their solitary holding cells, and Ming wanted to observe their behavior as they mingled. Socialization had proven to be challenging—perhaps a side effect of the anabolic steroids, or maybe some aspect of Neanderthal behavior surfacing. A satisfactory degree of social acceptance and tolerance had finally been managed, however, through a regimen of strict discipline and training. But not before several of the weaker subjects had been brutally beaten by the others.

Daily exercise was forced upon the Homothals—partly to build their strength and endurance, and partly as a release for aggression. The regular dosage of halotestin was reduced to a moderate level of 40 milligrams as a further measure to control belligerent and violent behavior.

Ming did not have to wait long before the steel doors at the rear of each holding cell opened. Slowly the Homothals emerged into the daylight. The creatures were distinctly humanoid in appearance, yet clearly different from modern humans. Their bone and muscle structure were obviously massive, as evidenced by exposed arms and legs and their huge barrel chest. The aptly proportioned head appeared quite large in comparison to a modern human, with the pronounced extension of the jaw, large lips, and squashed nose of the Neanderthal. And their eyes, unlike any human eyes, possessed a cat-like quality except that the retinas were universally yellow-orange.

The Homothal's movement and mannerisms were suggestive of a wild beast. It was clear why the guards feared them. Whenever a Homothal sensed it was being observed, its reaction was to freeze and lock eyes with the observer, remaining perfectly still with unblinking yellow eyes that bore into the human observer until, invariably, the human broke contact and moved on.

All of the subjects were naked except for loose-fitting shorts. They intermingled with suspicious restraint, not showing any tendency to interact with the other Homothals, but not avoiding them either. All the specimens were male; Ming had learned that introducing females into the population catalyzed aggression as the more dominant males fought viciously—usually to the death—for possession of the females.

Two minutes passed before a siren sounded and the Homothals—47 in all—assembled into three rows in front of

Colonel Ming. The creatures had been well trained and showed discipline. This was remarkable since none of the subjects had ever received military training prior to their transformation.

As the Homothals stood at attention, Lieutenant Li strode to Colonel Ming's side, stopped, saluted his superior officer and stood at attention. At first, the colonel didn't acknowledge the presence of the lieutenant, but after two minutes passed in silence, Ming spoke to Li without ever taking his eyes off the Homothals.

"What is your assessment of the fighting skills of the subjects?"

"Sir, the Homothals have exhibited above-average tactical skills, exceptional strength and endurance, and excellent discipline. They are all proficient with small arms, RPGs, and grenades," replied Li. He had taken six of the best trained Homothals on prior raids to see how they performed outside the structure of training exercises.

"Yes, yes. This I know. I have read all your reports on the raids on the villages south of Hajar Banda. What I want to know, Lieutenant, is do you have complete confidence in the subjects as soldiers? Will they follow their orders to the death?"

Lieutenant Li faltered at this line of questioning. He had been extremely thorough, including all details, no matter how small, in his reports. His mind raced, trying to understand where the colonel was leading with these questions.

"Lieutenant?" prompted Ming.

"Yes, Sir. I trust the Homothals completely. They are excellent soldiers, and I would not hesitate to lead them into battle."

Colonel Ming nodded approval. "Excellent, because tomorrow you *will* lead them into battle against the refugee camp eleven kilometers west of Bendesi."

Li didn't understand. "Sir?"

"Are my orders not clear, Lieutenant Li? I want you and Sergeant Wong to lead the Homothals on an assault against the refugee camp. It seems that your training exercises—the raids against villages along the border with Chad and the Central African Republic—have been less than complete. Large numbers of natives have fled to the refugee camp you are now going to destroy."

"Sir, I don't understand. It is just a camp full of old women and children. Our raids have not allowed any men to escape. They were all killed or taken prisoner for further experimentation here."

Ming was not accustomed to being questioned, and he abruptly faced his lieutenant. "I do not need to explain my orders," he hissed. "You will follow them, is that clear?"

Suitably rebuked, Li stiffened and barked, "Yes, Sir!"

Ming studied his first lieutenant. The man had served under his command for more than ten years and had always been unquestionably loyal. "However, since you have asked… it seems that the Homothals have drawn some attention during the raids. There is talk of half-man creatures with yellow eyes. No one believes it, of course, but I don't want the international press to hear these stories and start an investigation."

Li was silent, but he nodded ever so slightly.

"Make sure the attack is thorough—there are to be no survivors. Make certain to leave evidence so the blame is laid squarely on the Janjaweed militia. Understood?"

Before the lieutenant could answer, Colonel Ming spun on his heels and left the courtyard for the air-conditioned comfort inside the compound, leaving Li alone to contemplate his orders.

Li summoned Sergeant Wong and the commander of the local Janjaweed militia, a brutal man by the name of Korlos.

Korlos usually stayed at the compound—he considered it a privilege since the accommodations were far more plush and comfortable than the tents his militia used. Yet the real reason Colonel Ming hosted Korlos was to keep a close watch over him. Ming considered the Janjaweed militia merely as pawns in his game and it would not be good if Korlos developed too much independence. Better to treat him as an honored guest and inflate his ego; that would make him much more agreeable to Ming's orders and subtle suggestions.

With Korlos and Sergeant Wong assembled in the communications room, Li began his briefing. Standing before a large regional map pinned to a corkboard on the wall, Li illustrated the plan of attack. There would be two teams: Korlos would lead his militia cavalry while Li, with Wong under his command, would lead a force of sixteen Homothals. The two teams would approach the refugee camp from opposite directions in a coordinated assault.

The mounted Janjaweed would attack from the south and encircle the camp. Simultaneously, the Homothals, transported by truck, would attack from the north. The Arab militia was to use the speed and intimidation of the mounted raiders to prevent anyone from escaping the camp while the Homothals would enter on foot to conclude the attack.

"And what are we supposed to do with these refugees?" demanded Korlos.

Li fixed his gaze on Korlos. "Colonel Ming has made his orders very clear. Everyone is to be killed."

Korlos smiled ever so slightly. "As you wish," he bowed modestly.

"My men will be pleased," Korlos added. "They grow impatient and yearn for the excitement of battle!"

Korlos disgusted Lieutenant Li. "Shooting unarmed women and children is hardly battle."

Korlos was not about to be drawn into a debate. He was simply pleased that he was being given free rein to resume his murderous attacks on the people he hated. "Nevertheless, we will fully carry out Colonel Ming's orders."

"Of course," was all Li could manage in reply. Li deeply despised him, and Korlos knew it.

"When is the assault to commence?" inquired Sergeant Wong.

The question brought Li back to the subject at hand. "Tomorrow morning, 0600 hours. The camp will just be waking, this will add to the surprise and shock."

Korlos and Wong nodded, but remained silent.

"If there are no further questions, you are dismissed. Brief your men and make necessary preparations."

The two men turned to leave, but Li called to Wong before he stepped out of the room. "Sergeant Wong. There is one other matter I need to discuss with you."

After Korlos had left the room, Li approached Wong and spoke in a hushed voice. "There is one more point I want to make you aware of. This is not to be shared with Korlos or his blood-thirsty band of raiders."

Wong looked slightly confused.

"The Homothals will be issued older type 81 assault rifles. You are to make certain some weapons are left behind."

This rifle was widely distributed and would not attract any more attention than would an AK-47, especially in this part of the world where second-hand weapons were the norm. Colonel Ming had made sure that the Janjaweed militias, fighting on behalf of the Sudanese government, were supplied with sufficient quantities of the type 81 rifle. Any foreign observers coming across the weapon would naturally assume it was from a fallen Arab militiaman.

"Of course. The Homothals have trained with the type 81

and are quite proficient with it. They will be ordered to drop their weapons within the encampment once the attack is concluded."

Li hesitated for a moment. He took a deep breath and exhaled before speaking. "Sergeant Wong, we have served together for many years. You are a good soldier, and a friend, and I trust you with my life."

Wong replied, "As I do you. What troubles you?"

"We cannot fail. This is different from the training missions before. This time we are tasking the Homothals to work in a coordinated strike with the Janjaweed militia. The Janjaweed are poorly trained and unpredictable. They do not know discipline. Should any of the Homothals fall, we cannot allow them to be left behind."

"Understood."

"I am not sure you do, my friend," replied Li. "What I am saying is that we cannot trust the Janjaweed. Korlos is a psychopath, and he would prostitute his own mother to advance his agenda. For all we know, he could be negotiating with Khartoum or a neighboring government for the promise of a modest payoff. But whatever motivates Korlos, rest assured it is not in the best interest of China and the PLA.

"If Korlos turns his soldiers against the Homothals, or if he abandons the attack, Colonel Ming has ordered me to call in all necessary force to eliminate the Janjaweed along with the camp. If that becomes necessary, I will radio for an airstrike… they will drop thermobaric warheads over the entire area and obliterate the camp and everyone within a thousand meters."

"Including Korlos and his men?"

"They and the Homothals will all be incinerated. If it becomes necessary to call in the strike, you must evacuate immediately, do you understand?"

"If you issue the order, we will evacuate together."

CHAPTER 8

THE MILKY WAY THAT NIGHT glowed bright from its ancient starlight, as if painted by the hand of God to both amuse and befuddle mankind. Ethan had chosen to sleep outside the tent, taking full advantage of the cool evening air. He had seen similarly beautiful night skies when camping as a boy in the Cascade Mountains back home. He always found the sight mesmerizing. He could spend hours lying on his back watching for meteors and satellites to streak across the sky. The practice brought him peace, and his mind often wandered, as it did earlier on this night. He needed to be alone with his thoughts.

Ethan found himself thinking about the refugees surrounding him. During the evening meal he had sat across from a widowed mother named Bebe. There were so many in the camp that he knew he would never meet everyone, but he had introduced himself to her and struck up a conversation. Ethan was mildly surprised to discover that she spoke English with a strong British accent.

Bebe explained that she was fortunate to have been born in a village that had a school, and she attended for several years until she was old enough to work all day to help support her family. It was at school that she met Allison, a young volunteer from Dover in the U.K. She taught Bebe how to read and speak English and shared her modest collection of fiction novels with Bebe. A fast learner, Bebe enjoyed the compilations of Jules Verne and H.G. Wells.

"I would say you are fond of science fiction," observed Allison one afternoon when Bebe reported she had finished reading *The Mysterious Island*.

"What is science fiction?" inquired Bebe.

Allison smiled. "It is a type of story. You see, there are stories that are set in the present time and based on what we know to be true, or science fact. But science fiction stories are not based on science fact. The writer can make up things, like the creatures found on the Mysterious Island."

Bebe laughed. "Yes, I like science fiction."

Allison also entertained Bebe for hours at a time with stories of Dover, the English country, and London. Bebe found it hard to imagine what a big city was like—all the lights and people with restaurants and stores open until late in the evening. But what Bebe enjoyed most were Allison's stories about the theater.

"Actors dress in costume and play a role—they pretend to be a character from the story on a stage in front of a large audience. They usually have very ornate decorations on the stage to help you imagine you are part of the story. A long time ago an English poet named Shakespeare wrote many plays that are still very popular," explained Allison.

During dinner and then after, Bebe and Ethan talked for hours about her family. Ethan learned that in Bebe's tribe a family unit included all the grandparents, aunts, uncles, nieces and nephews. A family could easily total more than 30 people.

When Ethan asked what had caused her to come to the refugee camp, Bebe explained that her village was raided by the Janjaweed about a month ago. The raiders rode in on charging horses, shooting their rifles. The villagers were defenseless and terrified. It was very chaotic during the attack, and she was quickly separated from her husband and brothers.

Her four sons—all under the age of thirteen—were killed, and she was raped by three men, then left to die. She could not protect her daughters from being beaten and raped by other Janjaweed men. Her youngest daughter didn't survive the brutal attack—she was only ten years old.

Bebe had told her story so straight forward and honestly, sparing no details, as the tears slowly inched down Ethan's cheeks. But Bebe did not cry—she said she had cried for days after the attack and could cry no more.

Later, after the raiders left, her husband and brothers were nowhere to be found. Bebe left her razed village with her two surviving daughters. They wandered on foot for three days, walking west toward the border with Chad. Finally they stumbled upon a Peace Corps team conducting a survey for new water wells.

When Bebe and her daughters reached the camp they were exhausted and dehydrated. Slowly, word of the refugee camp spread, resulting in first a trickle and then a flood of survivors, mostly older women and young children—almost all girls, since nearly all the boys had been killed. But none of the adolescent and adult men from her village had made it to the camp, leading the refugees to believe that they were all either killed or captured.

"I'm very sorry, Bebe." Ethan didn't know what else to say.

"Such is the way of the Janjaweed and their allies," she said. To Ethan, she sounded rather philosophical about the brutality, and this made it even harder for him to understand. How could

Bebe so readily accept the violence that had been wrought upon her family and village? Throughout her retelling of the devastation she had suffered, not once did Bebe complain. She simply reported the facts without displaying emotion and outrage. Ethan couldn't understand her detachment.

"You said the Janjaweed have allies?" Ethan asked.

"Oh yes. The Janjaweed have powerful allies. The army of Sudan helps them. The government says no, but we saw the airplanes bomb our village. The Janjaweed have no airplanes."

"Why do they kill your husbands and children and drive you from your homes?" Ethan asked.

"We do not know. They just do." Bebe spoke as if her reply was at once both obvious and without need of explanation, as if she had been asked why the lion attacks the antelope.

Bebe could see the shock and sorrow in Ethan's eyes. She was used to disbelief from foreigners who had not witnessed the atrocities. Yet, Ethan also communicated a sincerity and innocence that she had not seen in the visiting journalists. As if to test his willingness to learn, she continued. "Some say that it is not only the Arab Janjaweed that attack my people. Some say that a half-man creature also preys on us."

This statement surprised Ethan. He had read much about the conflict, and at no time had he read of such superstitious claims. He carefully studied Bebe's face. Until now, she had seemed very rational. But this... this suggested either Bebe was unbalanced or the shock of it all had caused her to retreat somewhat into native superstitions.

Perhaps that is how she is able to deal with this horror; to somehow rationalize it as actions of evil spirits.

"A half-man creature. What do you mean?" Ethan asked.

"I have not witnessed it myself. But they say the creature walks on two legs as a man but has yellow eyes and is strong like a wild animal. It is said to speak a language that is not human—

it grunts, barks, and howls. Like a dog, but not the same."

"It would seem to me that the behavior of the Janjaweed is more like wild animals than civilized men. Are you sure that this creature isn't just a wild militiaman?"

"I am only saying what others have spoken to me."

"Do these half-man creatures appear often?"

Bebe shrugged. "No, not so often. And always at night. Do you think it is a superstition, a made-up story?"

Ethan didn't want to confess his true opinion to Bebe. "I believe what you are telling me, that villagers think they have seen a strange man-like creature. What you and the other refugees have survived is horrible. But what happened was done by men... nothing more and nothing less."

As Ethan recalled Bebe's words he considered the circumstances of her life. Although she was not very old— Ethan estimated her age to be about 30—she had already given birth to seven children. From Ethan's perspective, Bebe's world was filled with impossible struggles and hardships; it was so foreign to him that he doubted he could ever truly understand it. He wondered what Bebe would be like if she had been born in another place where survival was not so hard.

Life is so fragile, he thought. He had experienced personal tragedy when his mother died, but even that paled in comparison with what people like Bebe were enduring daily. Then, as now, he thought about how quickly everything that a person takes for granted could change due to a freak stroke of bad luck.

Eventually, Ethan fell asleep. It was a fitful rest at best, and when the sun began to rise in the morning he awoke easily. Although still tired from the exhausting trip to Darfur, he was stimulated as the morning sun struck his face. This was a new day, a new beginning, and the symbolism wasn't lost on him.

There were few signs of activity yet—most people in the

camp were still asleep. The pungent odor of smoldering wood and animal dung, probably a cooking fire, hung in the still air, and he heard the faint sound of a small child crying in the distance.

Still wearing the same clothes he had on yesterday, he walked to the mess tent hoping that at least one of the staff was also up. He parted the mosquito netting, happy to smell the aroma of strong coffee.

As Ethan sat down to savor his mug of coffee he noticed a few people beginning to move around outside the tents now. Soon that would change, he surmised, as the sun gained elevation and began to turn the tents into oversized solar ovens.

Two more staff members, both women from the Masalit tribe, entered the mess tent and continued with preparations for breakfast. Sitting in silence, sipping the black coffee, Ethan noticed a cloud of dust growing in size to the north of the camp. At first he thought it was a dust devil or some other type of atmospheric disturbance. It continued to grow as it approached the camp. After a few minutes he could see that the dust was emanating from a cluster of vehicles driving fast across the dirt and sand.

The two Masalit women preparing the morning breakfast looked up and began to speak in excited voices. Ethan couldn't understand what they were saying, but it attracted his attention and he looked in the other direction where the women were pointing to see another dust cloud. This one was rising above a hundred or more horses. Then he heard a word he did understand… "Janjaweed!"

Within seconds, panic erupted across the entire camp. People poured out of their tents—women carrying babies, young children running and crying, older women simply sitting and weeping, physically unable to enter the mass exodus.

Ethan stood transfixed by the rapidly unfolding drama in

front of him, having no idea what to do. The two dust clouds approached relentlessly from opposite sides of the camp. Within the camp itself, the scene was complete and total chaos. Refugees ran away from the Janjaweed only to see another force approaching from the opposite direction.

Out of nowhere, Sam appeared and shouted to Ethan. "You must leave! If they find you they will take you prisoner, or kill you!"

Ethan stood looking at Sam, dumbfounded. Had he heard her correctly? *What the hell is going on?* Only 24 hours ago he arrived at this refugee camp with assurances that everyone was safe.

"Didn't you hear me? Go! Run! You have to hide until they're gone!"

Ethan remained rooted, staring at Sam.

Seeing that she wasn't getting through, she shoved Ethan. "Go! Get out of here—now!"

Slowly at first, Ethan turned as his eyes searched for any sanctuary. He spotted a small grove of trees about 200 yards away and he ran for them, hoping to get there before he was seen by the approaching militia. He ran hard, thinking of nothing more than reaching the trees, never looking back over his shoulder. He could only hope that his friends were doing the same.

The thunderous roar of approaching horses and vehicles was almost deafening, but the screams of women and children pierced through the din, amplifying Ethan's fear. He stumbled into the trees and tripped over a log, crashing to the ground. He pulled himself up behind the fallen tree trunk. As he rose to peer over the log he was almost kicked in the head by his friend Joe who had been right behind him.

Joe cleared the log easily and slid to a stop, crawling back to where Ethan lay. From this position they were sheltered from view but could still see the mess tent and a large portion of the camp.

"Did the others get away?" asked Ethan.

"I think so. I'd just gotten to the mess tent when I heard Sam yelling for you to run. So I did, too. I think Brad and the rest of our group ran out that direction," Joe pointed to their right where the small grove of trees continued.

By this time Ethan and Joe could see the mounted militiamen circling the camp, firing their rifles into the refugees while running down and trampling the elderly and young. The noise was horrendous—gunfire, screaming, shouting voices, children crying. The unarmed and helpless refugees were falling quickly before the onslaught. And still the mounted Janjaweed circled the camp firing their rifles at point-blank range into the panicked crowd. Ethan was sickened by the sight, but couldn't force himself to turn away. He couldn't believe that this was real.

Then Joe spotted Brad and Wendy as they ran into the grove of trees. A couple dozen yards behind them were three more people, but Joe couldn't be sure who they were in the dust and confusion. They were also running for the trees, aiming to enter where Brad and Wendy had just entered moments before.

A Janjaweed soldier also saw them and aimed his rifle. Firing without hesitation, the solider brought the three to the ground. Joe yelled, "No!" and started to rise. Ethan grabbed his arm and yanked him back down.

"If they see you, they'll shoot you, too!"

Joe realized the truth in Ethan's statement. Neither Joe nor Ethan could escape the horror and brutality of what they were witnessing. The refugees were being slaughtered and the Janjaweed showed no sign of letting up.

"Come on, we need to move back and find better cover," Ethan told Joe. "Stay low and follow me."

The two crawled deeper into the grove, being more

concerned with staying low and moving quickly than they were with making excessive noise. It would be impossible for anyone to hear them above the roar of the massacre.

Ethan spotted a leafy thorn bush of some sort to their left. Next to the bush was a large boulder, and it looked like small animals had worked out a bedding area next to the boulder and under the sheltered protection of the dense foliage. He changed his direction and crawled faster for the bush.

Ethan told Joe to squeeze in first, and then he followed, scratching his face and arms on the inch-long, hardened thorns. It was tight, but they were fairly well camouflaged. It would have to do, but if they had been seen it would not be long before the militiamen would find their hiding place. Ethan and Joe could only hope and pray that they were safe.

Looking through the thorn bush Ethan saw a narrow sliver of the butchering occurring just outside the shelter of the grove. It was well over 200 yards away, but he still saw the terror in the faces of the women and children as the Janjaweed prevented their escape from the refugee-turned-death camp. Joe was pushed against the boulder behind Ethan, and he couldn't see anything of the carnage.

And then Ethan glimpsed something unbelievable. Trotting into the mess tent was some creature that looked to be half man and half animal. As if it sensed Ethan spying it, the creature froze and turned its head, looking directly at Ethan with intense yellow eyes. The creature was holding a rifle, just like the ones the Janjaweed had.

Ethan blinked his eyes and wiped the sweat from his face. Looking again, it was gone. It happened so fast Ethan wasn't sure if what he had seen was real or just his imagination playing tricks.

"What are we going to do?" whispered Joe, causing Ethan to pull back his focus to their more immediate concerns.

"I don't know. What can we do? If we go out there we'll be killed. We don't have any guns. Hiding here may seem chicken-shit but without weapons we'll just be slaughtering ourselves."

Ethan's mind was racing.

"Wait… maybe we can do something."

"Like what," Joe scoffed weakly. "Call in the marines?"

"Not quite, but close," and Ethan retrieved his cell phone from his pants pocket. He dialed a long string of numbers. "Please be in range," he said silently to himself.

The number connected and he heard a ring tone. Finally, the other party picked up. "Hello…"

"Dad, it's me! You have to…"

"You've reached Peter Savage. I can't take your call, so please leave a short message and I'll get back to you. Cheers." Then there was the requisite beep signaling to leave a message.

"Look, Dad, I can't talk long. The refugee camp is under attack by Janjaweed raiders. They're shooting everyone! You have to get help!"

As Ethan spoke softly into his phone he saw a pair of dusty sandaled feet appear not more than ten feet in front of the bush. He reached back and firmly squeezed Joe's arm sending a nonverbal message to be silent and still. Ethan held his breath, daring not to even breathe for fear of being heard.

Only seconds passed, but it seemed like an eternity to Ethan. Then the body attached to the sandaled feet bent down and pointed a large rifle into the bush. The face appeared next. It was deeply tanned with the typical features associated with Arabian nomads of North Africa and the Middle East—black hair and short beard, sharp nose, prominent cheek bones. The face grinned, exposing two gold teeth. His head and body were wrapped in dirty white linens. He motioned to come out, saying the same thing in Arabic.

"Okay, okay!" said Ethan. His phone was still open and

he hoped the connection to his father's voicemail had not terminated. "Don't shoot! We're coming out!"

Ethan and Joe slowly and painfully crawled out from their hiding spot, earning more scratches from the sharp thorns. They were terrified and expected to be killed right there. The man kept saying something that they couldn't understand. From the way he was dressed, the two concluded he was a Janjaweed militiaman.

The militiaman motioned with his rifle. Then two other Janjaweed soldiers arrived. They, too, held their rifles pointed at Ethan and Joe, just in case one rifle was simply an insufficient threat against the two unarmed volunteers. One of the men stepped forward and spoke in broken English.

"You are aid workers, yes?"

Ethan nodded. "We're volunteers with the Peace Corps Reserve."

"What is that in your hand?" he asked, looking at Ethan.

"My phone."

"Give it to me!"

Ethan extended the phone and the man grabbed it. Looking at the phone, he could see that a call had been made and maybe the line was still open. He dropped the phone onto the sandy ground and stomped it with his foot, breaking the phone into pieces.

"Hey!" shouted Ethan and he lunged forward. But Joe wisely caught his arm and pulled him back.

"Who were you calling?" he demanded.

Ethan just stared at him, refusing to answer

"Who were you calling?" he shouted, inching toward Ethan.

Joe answered to deflect the obviously growing irritation of the Janjaweed soldier. "He was on the phone with the U.S. Marines, that's who. And when they get here, they're going to kick your ass! You can count on it."

Ethan wished Joe hadn't said that. Antagonizing the Janjaweed was only likely to get them killed sooner.

The man studied Joe and then said, "No one will ever know what has happened here. Even if they do, do you really think they would care? America doesn't want to become involved in African affairs."

Joe's arrogant attitude did not reflect his true feelings. He and Ethan both knew that help would be slow to arrive, if it ever did. Clearly, the Janjaweed militias had been allowed virtual free reign for so long that they were confident there would not be any military intervention from the rest of the world.

One of the militiamen stepped forward and jabbed the barrel of his gun into Joe's belly. "Raise your hands and move."

Joe and Ethan did as they were told. The Janjaweed led them out of the grove of trees, but not back to the camp.

"Where are you taking us?" asked Ethan.

The only reply was a sharp poke in his back with a rifle barrel.

The small party exited the trees on the far side from the refugee camp. There were another dozen Janjaweed soldiers as well as Brad, Wendy, and Sam. They were all assembled at the rear of a military truck with a canvas tarp over the back, but it was clear that most of the militiamen were traveling by horse.

"Get in," the man motioned to the truck.

Without any other choice, the five aid workers climbed into the back of the truck sliding onto bench seats on either side of the truck bed. Underneath the dark-green canvas tarp the heat was stifling. Two guards climbed in after them; one sitting on each side at the rear of the truck. The two men had their rifles lazily aimed at the students, not that any of them entertained ideas of trying to overcome the guards and escape.

"Where are you taking us?" asked Sam. The only reply was the falling canvas flap covering the opening. It was dark inside and even hotter now that the only source of air had been closed off.

Sam looked at Joe and Ethan. "Did any of the others get away?" she asked.

Joe shook his head. Ethan looked at Sam and then at the floor of the truck. "We saw three people running for the trees right behind Brad and Wendy," Ethan paused. He seemed to have trouble finding the words. His faced wrinkled as if it was painful to speak. Then he swallowed and regained his composure.

"They didn't make it to the grove. A Janjaweed raider shot them in the back."

Sam stared at the floor of the truck bed as tears slowly ran down her cheeks. Wendy and Brad remained silent as they reflected on what had happened to their friends.

"What's going to happen to us?" Wendy finally asked, breaking the silence among the volunteers.

"I don't know," Sam replied tearfully. "I don't know."

CHAPTER 9

BEND, OREGON
JUNE 7

PETER SAVAGE HAD BEEN ON THE PHONE for most of the morning trying to get answers from anyone in the Federal Government who might even remotely be in a position to help. Finally, he called his high-school buddy, James Nicolaou. The number he dialed rang to Jim's phone at The Office—the headquarters for SGIT, the Strategic Global Intervention Team. Peter had played the voice recording over the audio connection so that Jim could hear Ethan's entire message.

"Is that all there is to it?" asked Jim.

"I'm afraid so. I was at a restaurant when he called and I had the phone off. I didn't get the message until early this morning."

"All right... try to stay calm. I know that's hard to do, but try. Let me make a few calls. Other aid workers may have also had a chance to get word out. Chances are good that someone in intelligence is aware of the attack and can shed some light on the matter."

"Thank you, Jim. You'll check on this ASAP, right? In the

meantime, I'll be getting ready."

"Ready for what?" Jim was almost afraid to ask, knowing Peter's penchant for action that more than once had him running off half-cocked. He had hoped Peter would give him some time to come up with answers before reacting.

"Surely you don't expect me to sit here and wait for Ethan to be freed, do you?"

"Now slow down. We don't know anything about the situation. We don't even know where Ethan is being held." Jim couldn't bring himself to add the obvious—or if he is even alive.

"I know enough. I know he was at an aid camp in western Sudan. Someone with the Peace Corps can give me the location—I have a call in to them and expect an answer soon. I figure it will take close to two days to get there. While I'm traveling, you'll be getting answers. You can keep me posted while I'm en route."

Jim took in a deep breath. "Look, Peter. You know that I love Ethan as if he were my own family. But I can't interrupt everything I'm doing to work this problem right now; I have superiors to answer to, and I can't feed everything to you that I learn. Nearly all of my intelligence work is highly classified."

Jim paused and tried a different approach. "And what do you think you're going to do even if we can find him?"

"Everything I can to get him back from the bastards that kidnapped him."

"Listen to me... this isn't the Wild West! You're talking about going into a foreign country; you have to follow their laws!"

Silence hung across the airwaves. Finally Peter answered, his voice steady and calm, like a machine. "I will do whatever is necessary to get my son—*whatever is necessary.*" Peter emphasized the words so there could be no misunderstanding. "I would think you'd understand that," he added softly.

Jim knew the conversation was over. "I do understand." He sighed heavily before continuing. "As much as I hate to admit it, I'd do the same. Just give me one hour, can you do that? Just one hour. Let me see what I can learn, and I promise to call you within the hour. Can you give me that?"

"One hour," and Peter hung up the phone.

Rather than waiting to hear back from Jim, Peter immediately dialed another number.

"Gary, it's Peter."

"Hi Peter," replied Gary Porter. "Haven't heard from you in a while. How's everything going?"

Gary was a year older than Peter. They grew up in the same neighborhood in Sacramento and became fast friends at an early age. As teenagers they went camping and hunting together, and both men shared a love for nature and the outdoors. Gary remained in central California and ran a very successful computer-security consulting firm with Nancy, his wife of 25 years. It wasn't uncommon for Gary and Peter to go twelve to eighteen months without uttering a word to one another, but they were as close as any two brothers would be.

"It's bad, Gary, that's why I'm calling. Ethan was in Sudan doing volunteer work at an aid camp. Last night—early morning in Sudan—the camp was attacked and Ethan was kidnapped. He was barely able to leave a voice message on my cell phone before he was cut off."

"Oh man, I'm so sorry. Okay, let's stay calm."

"You're the second person to tell me that and I'm tired of hearing it."

Gary understood his friend's frustration and fear. "Do you know where he's being held?"

"No, but I have connections working on that as we speak."

"There's nothing going on here that can't wait for a while, and Nancy can keep an eye on the business. What do you need me to do?"

Peter smiled. "I knew you'd say that; you've always been there when things get rough."

"That's what friends do."

"I have a bad feeling about this, Gary. It could get very ugly in a hurry."

"And your point is?"

"My point is this. I'm going to Sudan to get Ethan back. I don't know how I'm going to do it, but I will bring him back with me. I don't know where he is, but by the time I get there I trust I will know. I expect this to get bloody... very bloody."

"Nancy and I did a consulting gig in Egypt last year. The best way to get to Sudan is through Chad, via Paris. I'll start packing. If I remember correctly we can book a night flight from San Francisco."

"Thank you. I expected as much from you, but I wanted you to know the score before you committed."

"Sounds like I should bring some firepower?"

"Bring your hunting rifle and your Colt revolver. I think the airlines limit each passenger to eleven pounds of ammo. You should double check the regs and max out. As far as the airlines and customs agents are concerned, we're on safari."

"Got it. I always wanted to hunt in Africa."

"I hope that isn't a wish you later regret. We'll meet you at the airport in San Francisco this evening. If we can't get a commercial flight from Bend to San Francisco, I'll book a charter plane."

"Who is 'we'?" Gary asked.

"Another buddy—a guy I work with—Todd Steed." Then Peter added, almost as an afterthought, "Todd has also been itching to go on safari in Africa."

CHAPTER 10

JIM NICOLAOU SLAMMED THE PHONE down after Peter abruptly ended the conversation. "Damn it, why does this always happen to me?" No one was in the room to answer him. His dark brown eyes blazed with frustration and anger. Jim's Greek heritage brought along a sharp temper, and right now he needed to rein in his emotions.

He pushed a button on his desk phone. "Lieutenant, we have a problem and need to talk… now!"

Fifteen seconds later, there was a soft knock on his office door. Lieutenant Ellen Lacey entered, closing the door behind her. She knew there was no expectation to follow official military protocol in this office, so she sat down in a leather chair opposite Jim's desk.

In contrast to her boss' muscular stature, black hair, and dark complexion, Ellen was tall and thin. Her pale skin went well with her soft, shoulder-length red hair. She was a bright woman with advanced degrees in both political science and general science, and Nicolaou relied on her analytical capabilities.

"What do we know about a raid on a remote aid camp yesterday in western Sudan?" Jim asked, foregoing any greetings or courtesy.

Lacey had long ago learned not to take it personally. "Not much. There have been two or three brief references that came across my desk—reports from the DIA to all of the principle U.S. intelligence agencies. I didn't pay it much attention."

"Well, better go back and see what you can dig up. This has suddenly become very relevant."

"Sir, may I ask what this is about?" she asked cautiously.

"Ten minutes ago Peter Savage called. Do you remember him?"

"Yes. We met following the attempted terrorist mission in the Gulf of Alaska. As I recall, Peter played a key role in foiling the terrorist's plot and saving the lives of several hostages."

"And one of those hostages was his father."

"Didn't that all end with the death of Ricky Ramirez?"

"Yes, and with the death of his brother Vasquez Ramirez," replied Jim, seemingly lost in thought. "But that's not what Peter called about. That raid on the aid camp?"

"Yes," replied Ellen, waiting for the punch.

"Well, his son, Ethan, was there. He was taken hostage, presumably by the Janjaweed militia. Peter called asking for help locating his son."

"But we couldn't give him that information even if we knew—and honestly, we don't know. We don't even know he's alive."

"Hell, Ellen, you don't have to tell me that!"

"Sorry sir," said Ellen, suitably rebuked.

"But I can't just sit back and do nothing. There has to be something we can do within the prerogative of my command.

I know Peter well enough… he'll be on a plane to North Africa within 24 hours and he'll go gunning for anyone he thinks is even remotely responsible for kidnapping his son." Jim paused, reflecting on his choice of words before continuing.

"Are you that certain?" asked Ellen.

Jim swiveled in his chair and opened a file drawer in a cabinet behind his desk. It only took a minute to find what he was looking for. He laid the file on his desk. "Look for yourself."

Ellen picked up the file. It only held two pages. "This is a psychological profile of Peter Savage," she said without lifting her eyes from the documents.

"That's right. The department psychologist constructed it from the video and audio recordings of Peter's debriefing after the incident on Chernabura Island."

Ellen read the first page quickly, then flipped the paper and continued to the second page.

"The psychological profile is consistent with my observations as well," said Jim.

"So the conclusion is that Peter is suffering long-term emotional trauma triggered by the death of his wife. That's not so unusual," said Ellen. She continued by reading the concluding remarks. "In times of severe emotional stress, the patient is predisposed to view his environment in terms of absolutes; good and evil, black and white. This clinical perspective is likely to be accompanied by unwillingness to compromise as well as an intense drive to take any action perceived necessary to rectify injustice, real or imagined."

Ellen let out a soft whistle. "Well, if I was in trouble he's the friend I'd want helping me. But I get your point."

Jim looked directly at her, his face seemingly aged twenty years. "He lost his wife. He's not going to lose his son."

The level of personal involvement suddenly became clear to Lieutenant Lacey. She nodded, not knowing what this would ultimately mean to her, but she was committed to supporting her boss... and friend.

Jim continued to think out loud. "I have no doubt that Peter will be killed in the process if I can't help him. He'll be going in unprepared, out gunned, and without backup."

"Yes, sir. Let me see what I can learn. I'll be ready to brief you in 30 minutes. We can pull in Beth and Mark and work up a plan."

Jim shook his head. "Just you, okay? Keep this under wraps for now."

"Sure thing, Boss Man," replied Ellen. She never used his call sign, *Boss Man*, informally, so Jim knew she was in the game and playing for keeps.

The loyalty and dedication of his team were two reasons why Nicolaou had consistently refused promotions. He enjoyed his work, knowing he was truly making a difference even if the rest of the world would never know. But he was also smart enough to know that it was his team—his people—that really achieved the necessary outcomes, consistently resulting in successful missions. No other group of people could accomplish what his team could, and each member would do whatever was required to help the team succeed.

Twenty-seven minutes later Ellen knocked on Jim's office door. "It was definitely a refugee camp that was hit. Reports indicate that a large group of young adults—college students— enlisted with the Peace Corps Reserve had just arrived at that camp the previous day. The camp is located in western Sudan, close to the border with Chad, eleven kilometers west of a small town named Bendesi. There have been numerous raids in that area from rebel factions originating in both Sudan and Chad, and more recently from central Sudan."

"Who's responsible in this case?"

"Can't say for sure, but intelligence suggests it was the

Janjaweed militia. There were very few eyewitness reports, but it seems the raiders came in on horses firing indiscriminately into the camp. Typical MO for the Janjaweed. Casualties are very high. Near as we can tell the camp housed only women and children—refugees from previous raids. I don't know how many survived, but initial estimates place the number at less than ten."

Jim rubbed a hand across his chin, disgusted by the senseless violence and waste of life.

Ellen continued. "The DIA is recommending U.S. military intervention. The Janjaweed and Sudanese government may have gone too far with this attack. It seems that one of the students is the daughter of a Congresswoman from California— Lois Bennett. She serves on the Defense Appropriations Subcommittee. She's a rising star in the Republican Party and some of the talking heads are suggesting she could be a good candidate for presidency... if not the next election then the following one."

Jim perked up and leaned forward, reaching across his desk for the file Ellen was reading from. He quickly read the first page while Ellen continued, reciting from memory.

"Congresswoman Bennett's constituency is in San Diego County. She has served in Congress for fourteen years. She was recently re-elected by a large margin, in part due to sizable campaign donations from some of the largest defense contractors. General Atomics, Lockheed Martin, Spawar Systems Center Pacific, General Dynamics, L3 Communication—"

Jim held up his hand, palm facing Ellen. "I get it," not taking his eyes from the report. He read further.

"Her daughter is Wendy Bennett. Says she's also a student at the University of Oregon."

"Is there significance to that?"

Jim nodded. "That's where Ethan is attending, so they're likely in the same aid group. If we can locate Ms. Bennett, I bet we'll find Ethan as well."

Ellen nodded. "Makes sense."

Jim handed back the file. "It's time to clean house."

"Congresswoman Bennett is stirring the pot. She's authoring a House Resolution condemning the attack. It's expected to be up for a vote later today or tomorrow and to pass with little or no opposition. That will put some pressure on the administration to act."

"Do you think the President will authorize a strike based on the outrage of a few members of Congress?" Jim understood the practical side of politics better than most.

Ellen shrugged. "The Pentagon hasn't made any recommendations yet, but it's still early. My guess is that the President will first seek the support of a U.N. Resolution calling for a no-fly zone, maybe bolstered with limited military strikes."

"The wheels turn slowly. But God help anyone who's caught in the path." Jim wanted to start planning the mission now, but he knew it could be weeks before the order came down… if it ever did.

"All right. Here's what I want you to do. Send a memo up the chain, all the way to the top, and copy everyone between me and the Joint Chiefs. Diplomatically suggest that this is a mission tailor-made for the Strategic Global Intervention Team. Explain that SGIT can infiltrate discretely, we carry plausible deniability in the extremely unlikely event of capture or causalities, and we have an unequaled record of success. Remind them of the Aleutian Islands mission where we averted a terrorist strike on U.S. soil and assisted with the capture of a Russian Spetsnaz sniper team as well as their stealth submarine launch vehicle. I *want* this mission— understand?"

Lacey nodded.

"I'll phone Colonel Pierson directly after the memo goes out, see if I can get his support, too."

"Yes, sir."

"That should do it. I sure hope it does. We need to be there to set things right."

"Yes, sir. I'll let you know the instant we have a response." Ellen folded her notepad and stood to leave.

Jim stopped her. "Just one more thing."

"Yes, sir?"

"Does the name Abdul Wahid el-Nur mean anything to you?"

"Yes. He's the leader of a splinter group of the SLM—the Sudanese Liberation Movement—in self-imposed exile in Paris."

"That's right." Jim opened a bottom drawer in his desk and retrieved a cell phone. He threw it to Lacey, who caught it one handed. "Here. I want you to contact him. Tell him I asked you to call. He'll remember me. We've done business before and I've saved his ass more than once. Tell el-Nur I want him to meet a mutual friend. If he says no, remind him that he owes me, and I aim to collect. And be sure to use the electronic voice alteration system when you call."

"What do you want me to do after I speak to him?"

"Call Peter and give him Wahid el-Nur's name and phone number in Paris."

Ellen looked at the phone and then a wily smile crossed her face. "A throw-away phone? Plausible deniability?"

"I wouldn't have it any other way. Would you, Lieutenant?"

"No, sir!" Ellen turned smartly and left Jim's office.

CHAPTER 11

UNDER DIFFERENT CIRCUMSTANCES, the trio would have enjoyed the business-class seating on the Air France flight to Paris. But their thoughts were heavy and dark, wondering how they would first find Ethan and then bring him home safely. All three men tried to rest—sleep was impossible—knowing they would need to remain vigilant and sharp when entering Chad and Sudan.

After landing at Charles de Gaulle airport and clearing customs, Gary and Todd found a comfortable spot near the airline counters. They would keep a tight eye on the gun cases and luggage while Peter hailed a taxi to take him into Paris. Just before boarding the plane in San Francisco, during a tense call to the phone number he had been given anonymously, Peter hastily arranged to meet with Abdul Wahid el-Nur.

At first, el-Nur had been skeptical. He had many enemies, and why should he risk harm by meeting with a total stranger on short notice? It sounded too much like a set up. But there was something in the man's voice that was genuine. The concern and fear for Ethan's life came through clearly, and equally clear was the speaker's attempt to hide this most-human vulnerability.

Besides, el-Nur had been told by an unidentified caller that this meeting would be payback to Commander Nicolaou... it would clean the slate, and they would be even. Abdul el-Nur wished he had time to verify that claim, but he didn't.

Against his better judgment, el-Nur agreed to meet with Peter at a public location in Paris—the Shakespeare & Company bookstore on the east bank of the Seine River. The quaint old store was packed with books and frequented by casual as well as serious collectors. The shop and the rooms were small, such that it would be difficult for anyone to approach without first being noticed, and this gave Abdul el-Nur a slight sense of security.

Educated in the U.K., the revolutionary leader had chosen to flee to Paris to avoid persecution from the Sudanese government. A large man, but not tall, Abdul el-Nur wore a beige suit over a charcoal collarless shirt. His dark complexion and cleanly-shaven face and head contributed to his sophisticated appearance.

Upon meeting Peter, he quickly realized that his instincts were true; this man was no personal threat. He took Peter by the arm. "Come, let's wander through the stacks, shall we?"

They strolled aimlessly, and Abdul's eyes were flicking about, scanning every face as the patrons moved about. He didn't see anything to cause him to be alarmed; mostly young people leisurely browsing through books pulled down from the miles of shelves. No one even paid the slightest notice to Peter and el-Nur.

As they continued to shuffle through the narrow halls and rooms stuffed floor to ceiling with books, many old and worn, Peter explained how his son, a volunteer in the Peace Corps

Reserve, had been captured during a raid on the refugee camp.

"How may I be of assistance?" asked the leader of the SLM.

"I know where the refugee camp was, but I don't know where my son may have been taken. I'm hoping you can help me answer that question."

"Assuming I can answer your question... then what?"

"That's my business. I'll take care of the rest."

As his finger moved across a collection of leather-bound French poetry, Abdul el-Nur pondered this man standing next to him. *Typical American. Thinks he can do anything, anywhere.*

"You make it sound so simple. I tell you where to look for your son and you... you... do what? You are but a single man and the Janjaweed are many."

Peter looked directly at el-Nur and clenched his jaw, but didn't say a word.

"Do you think I will lend you my rebel army?" he scoffed.

"No. You tell me where my son is... that's all I ask. The rest is up to me. I will get him; you can be assured of that."

"What do I get in return for this information you seek?" Abdul el-Nur was amused, and he decided to play along. In the end he would provide whatever information he could regarding the location of the man's son. That would repay his debt to James Nicolaou.

Peter spoke slowly, choosing his words precisely. "Your enemy is my enemy. To free my son I expect I will kill some— maybe many—of them. That should be sufficient payment for your information."

Peter Savage surprised el-Nur. At first he appeared to be barely in control of his emotions, stricken with grief. But now... now he was as cold and hard as stone. There was little doubt that he would indeed kill anyone preventing the rescue of his son, or die trying. The latter was more likely, the SLM leader thought.

Peter Savage was not to be treated lightly, he decided. Maybe he could be of assistance. Perhaps, just perhaps, this American could help strike a significant blow against the Janjaweed.

Breaking the silence, Abdul el-Nur said, "Perhaps I wish to up the ante."

Now it was Peter's turn to be surprised and confused. "What do you mean?"

"I have no interest in the welfare of your son. My people have suffered far beyond your imagination."

A young woman approached the pair and eyed a set of blue-bound screenplays by Lillian Hellman. She stopped and removed one of the books from the shelf and gently turned the pages. Abdul el-Nur nudged Peter along into the next room, which was empty except for the aged, musty-smelling tomes.

He continued, his voice firm. "Where were you and your countrymen when my people's villages were being burned? The Janjaweed have murdered the men, raped the women, burned our villages and crops, and yet no one came to our side."

"I am an American, but I don't run my country. I don't have control over policy, and I don't have the power to send armies to help others. There is little I can do to influence the future... and I'm damned sure I can't change the past," Peter replied. "It was wrong, but I can't change it. I am truly sorry. And yes, now I need your help. Just one answer; that's all I'm asking. Please. Where is my son?"

"I cannot tell you with certainty where your son is being held. But I may know."

"Go on, please. What do you want in return? Name your price."

Abdul Wahid el-Nur thought for a moment before answering. Peter Savage was an odd mix of compassion and hardness. He had an edge barely tempered by his devotion to everything that he believed was good. He studied Peter further, not saying a word. He saw, buried beneath the veneer of civility and kindness, a capability of violence that may be boundless.

Abdul el-Nur had read of Peter's resourcefulness in the redacted file that the unidentified caller had uploaded into a secure, virtual drop box for him to retrieve. The caller had only reluctantly agreed to provide the file so that el-Nur would have some knowledge of the stranger he would meet. Peter's exploits on Chernabura Island against a well-trained and armed band of mercenaries were remarkable to say the least. Just then an idea came to el-Nur.

"I do not ask for money."

"Then what? Tell me."

"An enemy of my enemy is my friend. Yes?"

Peter answered, "I'm familiar with the proverb. Yes."

"Then I want you to lead my soldiers against your enemy—against *our* enemy. That is my price for the information you seek."

"I'm not a military man. What makes you think I can do this?"

"I know something of your past. You are a resourceful man when faced with adversity."

Peter didn't answer.

"I see a rare mixture of compassion and violence in your eyes. You are a man who knows the difference between good and evil and who does not shirk from fighting evil in the most forceful ways imaginable—without hesitation or mercy." Abdul el-Nur paused, watching for a response from Peter. There was none. Peter remained completely passive, peering into the eyes of the exiled revolutionary.

Abdul el-Nur nodded. "I see my analysis is accurate."

Suddenly Peter turned to leave, his face flushed with frustration. He took two steps and stopped, looking back over his shoulder at the man he hoped would provide critical information. "I came to you with a simple question. I am truly sorry for the suffering your people have experienced, but I can't change history, nor am I responsible for it. As a father, I appealed to your sense of humanity and goodness. How different are you from the devils who attacked the refugee camp and took my son?"

Immediately Abdul Wahid el-Nur was in Peter's face. "I am very different from the Janjaweed, I assure you. Otherwise I would have cut your throat within the first minute of our conversation."

"Look, I'm sorry. It's just that I need your help. Where do I look for my son? That's all I am asking. Can't you understand that?"

"Yes, I do understand," he answered in an even, low voice. "And I also understand that you are a man to be trusted. You are a man who will do what is right, no matter the cost. That is why I need *your* help."

Peter was stunned. He had grossly miss-read his contact and now regretted his outburst.

"Okay," Peter said, "let's assume I agree. What do you want me to do? As I said, I am not a soldier, and I've never served in the military."

"No. But I see in you a natural leader. And, you are motivated. I want you to lead my men against those who butchered the women and children in the refugee camp and then kidnapped your son. I want you to inspire them, to lead them against what is likely to be a superior force. When you fight..." el-Nur leaned close for emphasis, "...I want you to give no quarter. That is the saying, yes?"

"I understand the meaning," replied Peter. Although it was one thing to say this, he knew that when it came to killing another man, that decision did not come lightly. Having gone down that path before, he knew it weighed heavily on his conscience. Even now, long after the shootout on Chernabura Island, Peter would still occasionally awake in the dead of night, drenched in a cold sweat, reliving that nightmare and the actions he was forced to take.

Despite his self-doubt, Peter knew he had no choice but to accept the terms. "The raiders who attacked the camp will receive no mercy from me if they bear arms. They can surrender or die."

Abdul Wahid el-Nur had a smug look and folded his arms across his chest. "I'd strongly prefer the latter."

CHAPTER 12

North Africa
June 10

FOLLOWING THE MEETING with el-Nur, the trio of Americans boarded a flight that would take them to N'Djamena, the capital city of Chad. Getting all of their firearms checked in at Charles de Gaulle International Airport proved to be more challenging than they had thought. The French authorities were thorough and made it abundantly clear that they preferred not to have civilians checking baggage containing guns—it didn't matter that it was for sporting purposes.

"I fail to see the threat," mumbled Gary. "The guns are in locked cases in the baggage compartment beneath the passenger cabin of the airplane. Do they really think we're going to somehow find our way down there and dig through piles of luggage just to hijack this flying crate?"

Gary Porter had a cheerful appearance; his blue eyes and wavy blond hair caused most people to think of him more as a surfer dude than an accomplished software engineer. He had always been rather direct, but his quick wit and humor could get him out of most confrontations.

The Air France agent looked at Gary sternly. Before she could comment Peter stepped forward, smiled politely and asked if everything was in order. At the same time he raised his left foot and discretely kicked Gary in the shin.

"Oww!" Gary yelped, but he got the message and shut up. Todd Steed, standing several steps away from the check-in counter, smiled inwardly at the exchange—he was quickly taking a liking to Gary.

In contrast to the Paris airport, the security at N'Djamena International Airport was nearly nonexistent. Fortunately, Peter, Gary, and Todd had deplaned quickly and were waiting at the baggage claim when their duffle bags and gun cases arrived. All three men feared that if they had not immediately claimed the gun cases someone else would have.

"Feels like I've been stuffed in a box and shipped all this way," Peter complained. Although he was not one to follow a regular exercise routine, he disliked long periods of inactivity—it caused his whole body to ache.

Gary stretched, alternating between arching his arms back and then bending over to touch his toes. "I'm with you. I'd really like to run at least a mile right now. My butt is killing me."

"Sorry, that's not happening. Best I can offer is a 500-yard walk to the private air terminal. Our charter flight should be waiting for us."

Gary and Todd scooped up their bags and followed Peter out the door. Their destination was the neighboring building that handled the logistics for the private aircraft that shared the runway with the commercial flights. Although Peter and Gary were breathing hard from the physical strain of carrying their bags and gun cases, Todd wasn't showing any sign of fatigue. Being a practicing machinist, he constantly handled heavy metal with an ease and endurance that most men would find impossible to match. The result was impressive upper body strength and a bone-crushing handgrip.

Peter introduced himself to the young lady behind the counter. "We have a reserved charter flight; I believe it is scheduled to leave about now."

The lady looked at a list of names, destinations, and times on a sheet of paper held to an old-fashioned clip board. "Ah, yes. The pilot has already fueled and is waiting for you. Just go through those doors," she pointed over her shoulder. "It's the red and white airplane; you can't miss it."

"Thank you," Peter said.

With Peter in the lead, Todd turned toward Gary and spoke softly so as not to be overheard. "Security was a breeze. I could get used to flying private planes."

"I don't know," Gary answered. "I kinda like the pat downs by TSA."

For the final leg of their journey they boarded a 1974 Piper Seneca I, a workhorse for ferrying people and supplies to the remote areas of North Africa. Peter had specifically requested the twin-engine plane. He knew they would need both the payload capacity and the space for their baggage. In addition to a large duffle bag for each man, they brought along a formidable arsenal. Gary and Todd had each packed scoped .30-06 bolt-action hunting rifles. Peter had brought two rifles: his favorite .340 caliber Weatherby and .30-06 Winchester. By bringing three rifles in the same caliber they could share the ammunition they brought—the maximum amount allowed by commercial airlines—which they had distributed throughout the three duffle bags. In a separate locked case they had also packed three large-caliber handguns.

Peter and his friends stuffed their bodies into the confined space of the Piper cabin. They were not small men, each standing six feet tall, give or take an inch or two.

The charter plane took nearly three hours to cover the 520 miles to their terminus—the border town of Foro Burunga. Mercifully, the time passed quickly as the rhythmic sound and vibration from the engines lulled all three men into a light sleep.

It was late in the day, almost dark, when the Piper landed on the dirt airstrip. As Abdul Wahid el-Nur had promised, they were met by a man who introduced himself as Hamaad. Dressed in camouflage fatigues and wearing a black ball cap, he said he was a scout in the Sudanese Liberation Movement, and he was directed to meet Peter and his companions and to take them to his camp along the Little Deriba wadi where they could rest. Tomorrow, he said, there was much work to do to plan the attack on the Janjaweed. Abdul el-Nur had refused to tell Peter where the militia was expected to be camped, only that his information was good.

After brief introductions, Peter asked Hamaad, "Do you know if my son is being held at the camp?" Peter needed hope that he was still alive if he was to have the strength to continue.

Hamaad nodded. "Yes. Three nights ago I went with two of my men. The Janjaweed sometimes camp at this special location because it has shade trees and a well close by. It is on an old trail sometimes used by goat herders. We thought they might go there after the raid on the refugee camp. It was late at night and we were able to get close. Sound travels far on a quiet night, and we could hear some of the militiamen talking about a blond woman. They mentioned another woman also."

"But what about my son?" Peter persisted. "Did they say anything about the men that they kidnapped?"

Hamaad nodded again. "They also spoke about some American men, but they were much more interested in the women."

"But is my son there? Did they mention any names? His name is Ethan."

"No. No names."

"Are they alright? Are any of them hurt?"

"We were on a ridge overlooking their camp and it was dark. We could not see them. There was one tent that was guarded. The Americans are most likely in that tent."

"Where is the Janjaweed camp?" Peter pressed.

Hamaad smiled, his yellow-stained teeth looked white next to his dark skin. "I cannot answer your question. Please forgive me." Hamaad bowed deeply. He had been strictly ordered not to reveal the location of the encampment to reduce the risk that the Americans would move out on their own.

With this meager knowledge, Peter felt more hopeful than he had since the ordeal began over 60 hours ago. Now he knew that there were several hostages, and he had to believe that Ethan was one of them.

"Please, let me help put your bags in the truck," offered Hamaad. "It is maybe one hour to our camp. We should go."

They carried their bags and gun cases to a Toyota extended cab pickup truck that had certainly seen better days. The body was dented everywhere, and the left front quarter panel was missing entirely. The bed was rusted through in several areas, and the tailgate was absent.

Hamaad opened the door and retrieved three small, worn cardboard boxes from the front seat. Turning, he gave them to Peter.

"We have been carrying these boxes of ammunition in our stores for many months. It is left over from the American soldiers who fought here in World War II."

Peter read the label on one of the boxes, "Rifle, Ball Ammunition." He handed it off to Todd and Gary.

"If I'm not mistaken, our friend just gave us three more boxes of .30-06 ammunition. It's old, but should still shoot."

With the bags piled on the truckbed and Todd and Gary

wedged into the back seat, Peter rode shotgun, his medium-length brown hair flapping in the breeze. The air conditioner had long since quit working, but it wouldn't have mattered since the windows were all broken out. With an air temperature of 96 degrees, they were sweating despite the air flowing through the cab.

"How long have you been with the SLM?" Peter asked.

Hamaad spoke English reasonably well. "Almost three years. I was a teacher. The Janjaweed attacked my village and burned my tukuls... my huts."

"Do you have any children?" asked Todd

"I did," answered Hamaad. "When the Janjaweed attacked, they shot the men. Those who weren't killed were tied together with a large rope. Then the Janjaweed clubbed the children and raped the women. When they were done, they shot them all." Hamaad was speaking softly now. The pain, even after three years, was still evident in his voice.

"I'm sorry," said Todd. "I didn't mean to..."

"It is okay," answered Hamaad, "you didn't know."

"How did you get away?" asked Peter.

"The Janjaweed let a few of us go. They said we were to warn other villagers what would happen if they didn't leave."

"Leave and go where?"

"Anywhere! It does not matter. Chad, the Central African Republic. The Janjaweed and the government in Khartoum want to clear western and southern Sudan of the tribal people. They want to repopulate the land with political allies."

"You mean Arabs?"

"Yes, and Arab sympathizers. It was the British Empire that forced the tribal people of the Fur to become part of Sudan. It was a foolish act born of arrogance and ignorance."

"Yes, it was," Peter added. "And if I remember correctly, it was the distinguished British military officer, T.E. Lawrence, also known as Lawrence of Arabia, who advised against it."

"That is true. He understood the tribal politics and knew that such a forced union would never last. The same is true here and elsewhere in Africa where the Colonial Powers invoked make-believe and foolish boundaries."

"How many people have left their villages?" Gary inquired.

"It is hard to say," replied Hamaad. "Many fled to Chad; many just moved further south. But the Janjaweed militias continue to raid; burning villages and crops, raping the women, killing—always killing."

"I read somewhere that U.N. estimates place the number of refugees in the range of a couple million," Todd commented. "And they also estimate that more than 300,000 civilians have been killed directly by the conflict. But President Hassan al-Bariqi wants everyone to think that the number killed is only around 10,000."

"Yeah. Like 10,000 murdered civilians is okay," interjected Gary. "What was it Stalin said? 'One death is a tragedy, one million deaths is a statistic.'"

"There's something else I don't understand," Peter said.

Hamaad glanced at Peter and waited for him to continue.

"I thought the Janjaweed mostly killed the men and children. When did they start taking hostages?"

"Only recently. Maybe a little more than two years ago they started. It was not very many at first—only men. They do not take old men and never women or children. They never asked for ransom, not that the villagers could afford to pay anything. The men simply vanish." Hamaad's eyes scanned the desert around them. "The tribes call them the 'un-dead' because the family does not have a body to bury and the men are never seen nor heard from again."

"So when did the Janjaweed begin kidnapping Western aid workers?"

Hamaad glanced at Peter, and then continued looking at the rough dirt road stretching out toward the horizon.

"They have never taken foreigners hostage."

Peter, too, stared off in the distance, not knowing what to think. "So, Hamaad, do you think they want ransom?"

"Perhaps for the men. The women will be sold into slavery. That's what they were saying. They believe the blond woman will bring a very high price."

"Sick bastards," Todd declared. "I'm thinking I can arrange a meeting with Allah for all of them Janjaweed."

Hamaad continued. "I have heard that some groups within the Janjaweed grow tired of waiting for the next raid. They are a nomadic people, warriors, and do not adjust well to staying in one place, just waiting for something to happen. I have heard rumors that some have spoken of rebellion against their commander."

"Who is their commander?"

"An Arab named Korlos Ismail."

"How do we get to him?" asked Peter.

"You cannot. He does not stay with other militiamen."

"And this group of Janjaweed that are holding my son and the other American hostages... are they loyal to Korlos?"

"They talk of rebellion. I think that is why they kidnapped the aid workers. They need money to buy food, weapons, and ammunition."

"How many are there?" asked Todd.

"Hostages?" answered Hamaad, sounding confused by the question. "We don't know. As I told you, they were in the tent; we did not see them."

"How many militiamen are guarding the hostages?" Peter clarified, growing impatient. The fatigue of travel and the stress was taking its toll.

"Forty, maybe 50," said Hamaad.

"And how many soldiers are in your camp?"

"We have lost ten men to illness. I am not sure of your word for it, but they keep going to the toilet."

"Dysentery," Gary mumbled, staring at the passing scrub brush and endless stretches of rock and dry, dusty dirt.

"How many able men do you have, Hamaad?" Peter repeated his question, this time a little louder.

Hamaad seemed to squirm in his seat. He glanced slightly to Peter, before looking straight ahead again, still not answering.

"Hamaad, please answer my question." Peter's blue eyes bore into Hamaad, while his right hand was clutched tightly on the 'Jesus' bar attached to the upper doorframe for added stability over rough roads.

"Including me?" he answered.

"How many!" Peter shouted.

"We have—I think—18 able soldiers."

"Twenty-one against 50. Sounds like fair odds," commented Gary.

Peter let out a deep breath and sank in his seat, his head flopping against the headrest. "Great."

CHAPTER 13

PETER SAVAGE WAS STILL WEARING the same clothes he had been in for the last three days—a khaki shirt and khaki long pants, boots, and a light-tan canvas brimmed hat with ventilated crown. Due to the heat, the long sleeves of his shirt had been rolled up ever since landing in Chad. The underarms as well as front and back of his shirt were stained dark by sweat.

He stood, back to the rising sun, hands cradling a cup of strong camp coffee. He was staring toward the northwest, his mind lost in a tangle of intersecting thoughts mostly centering on his son. "Just how in hell am I going to get you out of here?" He spoke softly to himself.

"We'll get him," came an unexpected reply from behind him. It was Todd.

Peter turned, "You startled me. I thought I was alone."

"You were; I just walked over."

Todd's eyes were focused on some unseen object far off, rather than the man he was talking to, and his mouth—framed by a chocolate-brown goatee and mustache—was tight and almost down-turned, eyebrows pinched together. He had his arms folded across his chest and appeared to be deep in thought.

"You need to be confident, Peter. You always find a way to solve tough problems. I've been working for you long enough to know that if anyone can figure out a solution to a problem, it's you. Whether you're solving a technical design challenge or handling government bureaucrats or tracking a monster bull elk you're huntin' across an alpine meadow—you always come up with a plan. No matter how stretched it seems, you always achieve your goal."

Peter studied Todd for a moment before answering, trying to read his thoughts. Todd was not one to speak volumes, but when he had something to say it was usually important.

"This is different Todd, you know that."

"It is, and it isn't." Todd turned to face Peter. They had known each other for more than ten years, and had worked together closely, each possessing a deep and genuine respect for the other's skills and accomplishments.

"You know what I mean," continued Todd. "It's a problem, right? Work the problem, and never give up. Identify it, break it down into manageable pieces, and make it happen. As long as we're breathing—the three of us—there's still a chance, another option. There's always another option. You taught me that."

Peter turned, affected by the veracity and wisdom of Todd's words. Never had Peter heard Todd speak so plainly and powerfully.

Peter was stunned to realize that subconsciously he had begun to give up—doubt of success was creeping into his mind. What was it that Henry Ford had said, Peter asked himself. *Whether you think you can, or you think you can't—you're right.*

Peter turned again, facing Todd. "You're right. We'll get

Ethan back—and the rest of the hostages too."

"There we go. So, what's the plan?" Todd inquired, a rare and faint smile crossing his face.

"I have an idea building. Let's go back to camp and round up Gary and Hamaad."

Neither man uttered a word during the short walk back to the campsite. The camp itself was little more than a collection of tents and three beat-up Toyota pickup trucks. One was the familiar vehicle that they had ridden in with Hamaad at the wheel.

"Hamaad, you said that the Janjaweed are camped about 20 kilometers north of here, correct?" asked Peter.

"Yes," replied Hamaad. "Here, I'll show you." He used a stick to draw a crude map in the dirt at their feet. Even though they were standing in the shade under a canvas tarp, the heat was already building and Gary had a trickle of perspiration running down his forehead.

"We are here," Hamaad pointed with the stick to a spot in the dirt map. "There is a low ridge just north of our camp. If you go over that ridge and then follow the wadi, or old river bed, to the east, it soon turns north. Continue following it and you will come to the Janjaweed camp. It is in a few trees and there is a well with good water; that is why they camp there."

"Makes sense," nodded Gary. The camp they were currently in was a dry camp and all the water had to be transported in 55-gallon steel drums. It was warm and tasted foul, but it was better than no water. From the taste, Gary suspected they alternated using the drums for both water and kerosene.

"What is the terrain like surrounding the camp?" Peter inquired.

"It is a wadi," Hamaad shrugged and looked around at the Americans.

"Yes, I understand. But are the banks steep or shallow at the sides of the wadi, especially to the east of the camp?"

"Ah." Hamaad now understood the question. "The banks of the wadi are not too steep, but not shallow. A man can climb them. They rise maybe 30 meters above the camp on the east side."

Peter nodded and looked at Gary and then Todd. As if they could read each other's minds, the three men reflected an understanding that Hamaad missed.

Hamaad's eyes flicked back and forth across the faces before him. "What is it? What are you thinking?"

"Hamaad," began Peter. "The Janjaweed have us outnumbered almost two to one. They have the hostages to use as shields. We don't have much of a chance if we attack directly."

Hamaad nodded understanding. "And they will certainly hear all of us coming up the wadi long before we can get there," he added.

"So we are going to change the rules of engagement. May I have the stick?"

Peter focused on the map scratched in the earth. Using the stick, he drew an oval representing the ridge to the east of the militia camp. "We are going to use surprise and stealth to our advantage. Hamaad, how close can you get us to the camp in your trucks?"

Hamaad shrugged. "We can approach to within two kilometers—the Janjaweed won't hear our engines."

"Good." Pointing at the map, Peter continued. "Late tonight, after midnight, when most of the militiamen are asleep, we…" he motioned with his left hand to indicate himself, Gary, and Todd, "are going to position ourselves on top of this ridge looking down on the camp. At the same time, I want you and your men to position yourselves on the western ridge." Peter pointed to a spot on the dirt map to emphasize the point.

"It is imperative that you and your men are not detected, do you understand?"

Hamaad looked confused, and shook his head. "No. What is the meaning of im-per-a-tive?" He said the word slowly, carefully repeating each syllable.

Gary answered. "It means you have to do this, you can't fail. If the Janjaweed know you guys are moving into positions on the western ridge, we're all dead." As usual, Gary wasted no time getting to the point.

Hamaad had been looking seriously at Gary. "Yes, now I understand. We will not fail," he proclaimed proudly. "My men are well trained." Hamaad paused, thinking, before adding, "imperative... this is a good word."

The three Americans smiled. "Okay," Peter continued. "I want everyone in place and ready by 4:00 a.m. We need that time to watch the activity in the camp before it gets light. Hamaad, do you have any NVGs, I mean night vision goggles or scopes?"

"Yes, night-vision goggles, from your American army. But only two sets and we don't have any batteries so we cannot use them."

"Not to worry, we can provide batteries. Todd, you have some extra double-As?"

"Sure thing," Todd responded. "After we're done here Hamaad, I'll get you set up."

Peter pressed on. "Hamaad, you and your second in command take the NVGs. We're going to be scoping out the camp from the east ridge. We don't have any military gear, but our commercial night-vision scopes will be fine provided we can stay within 300 yards or so. We can use your portable radios to communicate and coordinate the assault."

"What's the general idea?" asked Todd.

"I'm thinking we watch these goons as the camp begins to come alive in the morning. Hamaad can tell us what tent the hostages are being held in… we should also see one or two guards at that tent. That will confirm we have it right. I want to use the element of surprise—rising sun at our back, long-range precision shots—to take out the guards and any other armed men in the immediate vicinity of the hostages. That should cause confusion and chaos. At that moment, Hamaad, I want your men to come in fast. Round up all the hostages and move quickly, double-time, to our position. We will continue providing cover fire."

Peter looked around at each face, locking eyes, searching for any indication of concern or disagreement. He didn't see any, only solidarity.

To be sure, he added, "That's the best I can come up with. If anyone has other ideas, let's hear them now. Once we get out there, it's too late to have second thoughts."

"Sounds good to me boss," replied Todd.

"My men will be ready," said Hamaad.

Peter looked at Gary. He just stood there, hands on his hips. He almost looked bored.

"Gary?" prompted Peter.

"Let's get the rifles sighted in. I say we check the zero at 250 yards, cold barrel and hot. I don't know what distance we'll be shooting at, but a 250 zero will give us an on-target hit out to 350, maybe 400 yards."

Peter smiled. "Agreed; but let's be miserly with the ammunition when sighting in, okay?"

The meeting ended and Hamaad went to brief his men while Gary, Todd, and Peter picked up their rifle cases and walked a couple hundred yards away from the camp. Gary paced off 250 yards and placed an empty wooden crate on the dirt and then on top he stood an empty cardboard box, originally used to package cans of fruit. Inside his rifle case were four paper targets. He always kept some there for trips to the range at home. With two pieces of duct tape he fastened one target to the cardboard box.

Looking back to Peter he yelled, "Okay, what do you read?"

"Two-hundred-sixty-three yards! Bring it in a little!" Peter yelled. He was using his rangefinder binoculars to measure the exact distance to the target.

Gary moved the target closer, estimating the distance. "How about now?"

"Two-hundred-fifty-two yards! Good enough!"

Gary jogged back to join Peter and Todd on the firing line. They would sight in their rifles from a prone position as this was the position they expected to be in on the eastern ridge overlooking the Janjaweed camp. Actually, the process was more correctly checking the zero on the weapons, as they had already been sighted in. The main concern was whether the scopes had been knocked out of adjustment during transport. Each man fired two shots. The first shot would heat the barrel and possibly change the point of bullet impact, so the second shot proved how true the sight alignment was.

Luck, combined with good quality equipment, was paying off. The scopes were fine and no adjustments were needed. This meant that their precious supply of ammunition was not wasted on adjusting the sights.

"I know you both know this, but I'll say it anyway. Just run a dry patch down the barrel—no oil." Peter didn't want to take any chances of oil fouling the first bullet in the morning; and with all the dust and dirt they were exposed to he didn't want excess lubricant to hold grit in the action of each weapon. This was much more than their usual hunting trip; lives were at stake.

As they gathered up their gear, Peter remembered how he felt on Chernabura Island when he was looking through the scope on his Weatherby rifle—the very same rifle he had with him now—at the terrorist threatening to shoot a U.S. marshal.

"You know," he began, and then paused, rethinking his words. "Tomorrow morning, you'll be sighting in on men, not animals. This isn't like hunting big game."

Gary clasped Peter's shoulder. "We knew the stakes when we agreed to come along, and Todd and me... we're big boys. Besides, I disagree with your assertion."

"What do you mean?"

"Well, it's pretty simple," replied Gary. "As I see it, these Janjaweed militia have terrorized, murdered, raped, and kidnapped innocent men, women, and children. They're holding your son and some of his friends against their will, and they're talking of selling the women into slavery. All things considered, that makes them much lower than any animal in my book."

Peter tried once more. "You do understand they'll also be shooting back at us."

Todd looked at Gary, and then turned to face Peter. Nodding, all he said was "Yep."

CHAPTER 14

DARFUR
JUNE 12

"WE HAVE TO GET OUT OF HERE!" exclaimed Joe. He and Sam were whispering to Ethan, trying desperately to avoid being overheard by the guard in front of the tent. Brad was snoring, which offered some cover noise. They were lying on reed mats laid out on the dirt. The tent didn't have the luxury of a canvas floor.

"So, what's your plan?" asked Ethan skeptically.

"We sneak out underneath the back wall of the tent. The stakes there can be pulled up easily. I already tested it. Then, we quietly make for the edge of camp. If any guards get in our way we just have to overpower them." Joe made it sound like child's play.

"Sure, we just overpower guards with automatic weapons. Get real," Ethan replied in a whisper.

"Well, what's your idea then if you don't like Joe's plan?" asked Sam.

"I'm not the one who started this, remember?" Ethan said.

"Shush, keep it down," Joe admonished.

"Well, I'm telling you that either we find a way to escape or we're as good as dead. That's what I heard them saying this afternoon." Sam understood Arabic fairly well, though she only spoke a little bit. "They said that after the ransom was paid, you, Joe and Brad would be turned over to Colonel Ming. Wendy and I will be sold into slavery. I'd rather be shot than sold into slavery. Do you know what happens to women who are bought as slaves?"

Ethan didn't want to think about that.

"Who's this Colonel Ming, and what would he want with any of us?" Ethan asked, mostly to change the subject.

"I don't know. But everyone laughed when they said you would be given to Ming, so it can't be good."

"So, what do you want to do?" Joe asked, counting on Ethan to come up with a better plan.

After a brief pause, Ethan said, "Okay. You're right. The only way out of the tent is under the back flap just like you said." Joe smiled briefly at the recognition. "But we go one at a time. If we all go together we are more likely to be seen or heard. Then we need to make it to the trees along the wadi where there's cover."

Joe nodded agreement. "What about Wendy and Brad?" They were both asleep… or at least pretending to be asleep.

"You heard them last night," whispered Sam. "They don't want to go. They think they'll stand a better chance staying put and don't want to risk getting captured and beaten. If even one of us can escape from camp, we'll have to find a way to get help and rescue the others." The concern in Sam's voice was evident.

"All the more reason for us to go one at a time—it increases the chances that at least one of us gets away to call for help," Ethan acknowledged. "Just remember, if any of us gets caught the guards will surely beat the hell out of all of us, right?"

"Yeah," replied Joe somberly. "So don't get caught."

Ethan nodded. "Sure thing."

"Sam, do you have any idea where we are?" Ethan asked.

She shook her head. Ethan thought they had ridden in the truck for about two hours. The dirt road had been very rough and he estimated that they averaged about ten, maybe fifteen, miles per hour. But since the truck was covered, it was hard to tell what direction they had traveled.

"Okay. Then we need to go in different directions because we don't really know which direction will bring us to help. Right?"

Joe and Sam nodded agreement.

"That will also lessen the chance that we all get caught once the guards figure out we're missing," Joe added.

"Sure," Sam agreed, "they'll probably assume we'd stay together for safety."

"Okay. Unless one of you has a better idea, I'd say that Sam goes west, toward Chad. Joe, you go east—I remember looking at a map in the mess tent and there should be several villages to the east assuming we haven't traveled more than 30 miles from the refugee camp. I'll go south. North would only bring me further into Darfur where several villages have already been raided; south is likely to land me in the Central African Republic. Agreed?"

Sam and Joe nodded again.

"I know how to find west when the sun is up, but what about at night?" Sam tried to hide her concern, but it crept into her voice nonetheless.

"It's easy," Joe replied confidently. "Just use Polaris to locate true north."

Sam hesitated. "I don't think I know how to find the North Star."

"Do you know how to find the Little Dipper or the Big Dipper?" Joe asked.

Sam nodded. "Yes, I think so."

"Okay. It's the last star in the handle of the Little Dipper. Or you can follow the two stars on the edge of the ladle of the Big Dipper. Just imagine a line through those two stars and follow it past the opening of the ladle; they connect to the North Star."

"Can you do this, Sam?" Ethan asked.

She nodded again. "Yes, I've looked at the Little Dipper a hundred times, never knowing that I was also looking at the North Star."

"What if one of us gets caught?" asked Joe.

Ethan was grim. "Don't let it happen. Best case is they move us to a different location. They'll beat all of us for sure. Worst case is they kill us. I just hope that at least one of us makes it out. But if one of us does get out and calls for help, and yet they've already moved the rest of us to a new camp…" Ethan didn't need to finish, Joe and Sam understood.

"But if what Sam is saying is true," Joe whispered, "then we really don't have any choice, do we? We're as good as dead if we stay here."

Ethan knew that Sam and Joe were staring at him in the darkness, but he couldn't make out their facial expressions.

"Sam, what time do you think it is?" Ethan asked.

The Janjaweed militia had stolen all their watches, cell phones, and jewelry when they were captured. Apparently, the militiamen believed they could be both good Muslims and good thieves at the same time.

"I can't be sure; maybe 3:00 a.m.," she answered.

"Yeah, that'd be my guess, too," Joe agreed.

"All right then. Let's rest for another couple hours. The guards will be getting tired so they may fall asleep, or at least not be paying as much attention. The relief guards won't take over until after dawn. It shouldn't take more than five minutes, ten at the most, to get away from camp. So we should stagger our breakouts by about five minutes. That will give the first person time to disappear into the darkness. We'll have to estimate time, that's all we can do. Who wants to go first?"

"It's your idea, you should go first," said Joe.

"My idea? You brought up…" Ethan couldn't see Joe's smile, but knowing he'd been played, Ethan agreed. "Fine. I'll go first. Sam, you go second—and Joe, you go third. Now, let's try to get some rest."

CHAPTER 15

PETER, TODD AND GARY were stretched out on the eastern ridge overlooking the Janjaweed camp below. They were spaced about 25 yards apart and each had a generous supply of rifle ammunition. Arriving right on schedule at 4:00 a.m., they had snuggled into the earth, making themselves comfortable so they each could spy on the camp and, when the time came, place carefully and accurately aimed rifle fire on the militiamen. It would take Hamaad's men another hour to circle around the north end of the camp to the opposite ridgeline, allowing plenty of distance so as not to be heard.

The moon had nearly set, and the sky was as clear as crystal, the stars shining surprisingly bright—enough so that the commercial light-amplification night-vision spotting scopes revealed the detailed layout of the Janjaweed encampment. The three men on the east ridge of the wadi were using their see-in-the-dark capability to methodically survey the location of the tents, the number of guards, and the features of the terrain.

The tents were pitched randomly on the level ground. A grove of trees to the right of the camp would offer some shelter from the relentless mid-day heat later in the day. Peter assumed the well, or spring, was located somewhere in the clump of trees. To the left of the scattered tents, seemingly marking the southern boundary of the camp, was a fallen tree lying across the dry earth. He thought the large log formed a convenient natural barrier to stop vehicles that might otherwise drive up the wadi unimpeded.

Having settled in, there was nothing to do but watch and wait for the SLM rebels to arrive at the opposite side of the encampment. As Peter lay in the earth, he wondered if he could kill again. Then he thought of Ethan and the other hostages. At this moment what he wanted most was to be home, safe with his son.

Before the emotion could well up inside him, Peter pushed away those thoughts, returning his focus to the camp below his position. It was not only Ethan and the other hostages who were relying on Peter, but also his friends who had followed him halfway around the world on a foolhardy mission.

Yes, if I need to kill to bring my son and friends home, so be it.

Todd was the first to spot the fleeting motion across the wadi on the opposite ridge; Hamaad and his men were just coming to position. Although they were over 500 yards away, Peter could barely make out their movements as they deployed across the ridge. Hamaad had only sixteen men, including himself. He had lost two more men yesterday to dysentery. Still, they were well armed with AK-47 rifles and each man had two or three full magazines. If they fought as well as Hamaad had claimed, then this just might work. *It has to work*, thought Peter.

When Peter determined that Hamaad and his men should be in position, he called to check on their status.

"Hamaad, are you in place and ready?" he whispered into the radio.

"Yes," was the brief reply.

It was pre-dawn and Peter could easily see two guards slowly roaming around the campgrounds. *Why can't these guys just be atheists and drink themselves into a stupor before passing out?* he thought.

Gary called him on the radio. Whispering, Peter could barely hear his friend. They were using a single frequency so Hamaad would also hear. There were no secrets to keep, and coordination was of paramount importance.

"There's a solitary guard stationed next to one of the tents—the third tent from the left. None of the other tents appear to have a posted guard."

"Yes, I see what you mean," Peter replied. "That must be where they're keeping Ethan and the other hostages."

"Yeah, that's what I was thinking." Gary put down the radio and raised his rifle, taking careful aim through the scope. The star light was sufficient to make out targets if there was a contrasting background. In this case, the guard appeared as a light-gray silhouette against the darker color of the tent and the earth.

"I can take him out when you give the word."

"Not yet, Gary. Hold on. Let's watch a little longer and see what happens—make sure we're not missing something. Besides, we're better off using the rising sun to screen our position. If you shoot now, the muzzle flash will give away our position."

They continued to watch and wait. Soon the horizon would be turning pale and then the sun would rise quickly. When the sun was just peaking over the horizon, the three civilian snipers would have their best advantage. But they would have to move fast because it would only take minutes for the sun to rise above the horizon, illuminating their position. They would be exposed on the open dirt.

As the minutes ticked by, the eastern horizon was becoming grey, no longer pitch black, signaling the coming of dawn.

Suddenly, there was movement from the tent where the guard was posted. From the eastern ridge Peter, Gary and Todd all saw it—a person crawling out from under the canvas on the far side from the guard. Peter tensed. He didn't expect this. Someone—could it be Ethan?—was trying to escape. What should they do? If they fired on the guards below, their positions would be quickly revealed in the dim early-morning light since the muzzle flash from each rifle would be like a flash bulb going off in the approaching twilight.

They watched as the escaping figure paused just outside the tent, a solitary dark figure crouching low to the ground. Then it scurried away from the tent, rushing toward the wadi, heading south to escape the camp.

The figure stopped again, at the fallen and weathered tree, next to the aged mass of roots that had once held the tree firmly to the ground. Crouching, apparently sensing that a roaming guard was approaching, the figure was all but lost against the dark undefined clutter of roots and tree trunk. Using another tent for screening from the guard, the figure hid, waiting to move on.

"Peter, what do you want to do?" prompted Gary.

Peter paused, waiting and watching. "Wait, not yet," he answered.

The eastern sky was getting brighter as the earth rotated toward the sun at a thousand miles per hour. Soon, the bright yellow sphere would peak above the horizon. Initially just a sliver of light, growing quickly in size and blinding brightness. *Come on!* the words screamed in Peter's head. Even though the air was relatively cool, he was perspiring heavily—rivulets of sweat running down his forehead. He wiped away the salty liquid before it got into his eyes. His heart pounded in his chest, hoping beyond all hope that the shadowy figure that had just escaped from the tent was Ethan.

The specter squatting next to the fallen tree began to move again. Everyone watched, willing it to move when the coast was clear and to freeze when it wasn't. But the escapee had no idea there was anyone on the ridge watching. The figure could not communicate with them to know when it was safe to move and when it wasn't. Peter knew that the odds were not good for whoever was trying to escape, and yet he still prayed it was Ethan—for that would mean Ethan was alive and within reach.

The camp was relatively open; the tents were placed a good distance apart and there were no bushes or rocks or trees to shield movement throughout the camp. This allowed the two roaming guards and the one stationary guard to be rather effective. They were armed with automatic rifles and Peter had to assume that whoever was trying to escape was not armed at all.

Come on, sun. Come on! Peter kept thinking to himself. It was close now, maybe another two minutes and the first slice of intense light would appear at the horizon, just above the snipers' heads.

The figure rose up and began to run, first circling around the large root ball of the fallen tree and then running full out, trying to put the encampment as far behind as possible, for the coming light would not be at all helpful. The fleeing person covered 30 yards, making for the small bushes in the wadi, when the first guard spotted him. The guard never sounded the alarm, he simply raised his rifle and fired a short burst at the running figure. The bullets all impacted the dirt, forward and to the right of the runner, kicking up small puffs of dust where each bullet cratered into the ground.

The figure immediately darted to the left, away from the bullet impacts. The sound of gunfire drew the other guards' attention, and soon they also spotted the escaping prisoner. One of the guards recklessly fired from the hip, the bullets completely missing their mark.

"What do you say, boss?" Todd broke his silence.

"Shit!" exclaimed Peter.

"Care to be more explicit?" Gary asked. "They'll cut him down if we don't do something."

Peter looked over his shoulder. It was almost time. He could just make out the beginning of the sunrise. Within a minute at most they would have the cover they needed. Only they didn't have a minute.

"Todd, you take the guard on the far right. Gary, you take the one on the far left. I got the middle guy." There was a momentary pause before Peter finished the order, each man using the time wisely to draw his rifle in tight and settle the cross-hairs on his respective target. "Okay, on my mark... now!"

The rifle shots were simultaneous, and an instant later the three guards fell to the ground. Peter immediately chambered another round and was searching for new targets. The gunfire had awakened the remaining Janjaweed and they were beginning to pour out of the tents, startled and confused. They were carrying automatic rifles and firing blindly in all directions. The runner continued down the wadi away from the camp.

One shot at a time, the militiamen were falling to the sniper fire coming from the eastern ridge. The sun cast a brilliant yellow-white light at exactly the level of the eastern horizon, masking the muzzle flash of the weapons; the echo bouncing off the opposite bank of the wadi further served to confuse the Janjaweed. Shot after shot, the Americans continued to pick off the militiamen running about. The rifle fire continued from the eastern ridge, and more Janjaweed went down one by one.

But Peter knew they would not remain invisible forever. As the sun rose higher, someone finally spotted the flash from one of the rifles and all of a sudden a dozen assault rifles began firing at the three men. The shots were not well aimed, and they all missed, but it served to keep Gary, Todd, and Peter down as miniature fountains of sand and dirt erupted all around them.

"Hamaad, now!" Peter shouted into the radio.

The trio could only occasionally rise to take a quick shot, and their hit rate had gone way down. But then Hamaad's men charged down the western ridge and started to shoot their weapons into the Janjaweed, who were mostly facing away from this new attack.

The SLM rebels came in fast and hard with weapons rapidly firing a deadly spray of bullets. All of these men had lost family members to the Janjaweed and seen their villages burned to the ground. Their hatred fueled their fury.

The Janjaweed broke off from the eastern ridge assault to face this new threat. Gary, Todd and Peter didn't waste any time getting back into action. The Janjaweed number had been reduced to half of the initial estimate, and yet they still outnumbered the SLM soldiers.

Hamaad's rebels were yelling and firing as they rushed toward the militiamen. But the Janjaweed were experienced fighters and were not easily intimidated. They quickly regrouped to face the charge. The handful of SLM rebels had no cover to hide behind as they ran down the western ridge toward the encampment. They would have been annihilated had it not been for their three guardian angels firing once again from the east.

One by one, the trio of snipers took careful aim and felled more militiamen. Then Peter noticed the motion of a lone guard at the tent where the hostages were believed to be held.

Peter aimed and squeezed the trigger on his Weatherby rifle. Less than a second later the large bullet blasted through the guard's chest.

Quickly two other Janjaweed soldiers ran for the tent. Peter reasoned that they wanted to use the hostages as shields and to barter for surrender. They had to be stopped. He aimed at the closest and fired. *BOOM!* The report was deafening and the guard fell. Peter cycled the action of his rifle, ejecting the spent cartridge and slamming the bolt forward to load another.

Then he shifted and took aim on the remaining guard. He was closing on the tent and was carrying his rifle low and pointed forward, at the ready.

Peter steadied himself...

Tracking the running guard...

Gently squeezing the trigger...

Click! It was the worst sound he could imagine. The chamber of his rifle was empty, and he had no time to reload.

Peter's heart sank as he frantically yanked the bolt back, a litany of curses unconsciously rolled off his tongue. He inserted another round into the chamber, now taking precious seconds to reload the rifle magazine. And yet he knew he would be too late. He rammed the bolt home and looked through the scope at the guard who was now only feet away from the tent.

Suddenly... *BOOM!*... and the guard fell. Peter glanced to his left. Gary had also been tracking the guard as he ran toward the tent; in the second it took Peter to reload, Gary had taken him down. Peter momentarily lowered his head in relief, but only for a moment—Hamaad and his men still needed help.

By now the SLM rebels were within the camp, and the fighting was reduced to very close quarters shooting and hand-to-hand combat. Still outnumbered, the SLM fought violently and ruthlessly, and with the advantage of precision fire from the high ground to the east. Every time a rebel was about to fall to a militiaman an unexpected bullet altered the outcome. The fighting continued until only four Janjaweed warriors remained. Realizing they could not prevail, they dropped their weapons and raised their hands, preferring to surrender than to die.

Peter, Todd, and Gary stopped firing and surveyed the scene before rising and beginning a slow trot down the ridge to the camp.

The remaining militiamen were rounded-up into a group surrounded by the SLM rebels. Having just achieved victory against overwhelming odds, the rebels relaxed somewhat. That was the only mistake they would make.

One of the Janjaweed dropped his hands and slipped a grenade from underneath his robes. He had just pulled the pin when an SLM soldier saw what was about to happen and pulled the trigger on his rifle, killing the militiaman instantly. The grenade dropped to the ground, the pin still clutched in the fingers of the dead man.

Shrapnel from the exploding grenade sliced through the remaining Janjaweed militiamen, killing them and three of Hamaad's men instantly, and wounding six more.

Peter and the others ducked at the sound of the explosion, bringing their rifles to the ready. As the dust settled, they could clearly hear the screams of the wounded. Peter saw the ripped and bleeding bodies. Picking up the pace, he ran down the slope to the camp, followed closely by Todd and Gary.

Hamaad was spared injury and ordered his remaining men to treat the wounded. Peter and his friends ran to the hostage tent. They pulled the flap to the side and looked in. Huddled together, terrified, were four Americans. Peter scanned their faces, but Ethan was not there. His heart sank.

"I'm looking for my son. His name is Ethan Savage. Do you know him?"

Joe nodded, "Yes, he escaped this morning just before the shooting began."

Peter dropped the flap and turned to Todd and Gary. "Let's go," and he started jogging south toward the wadi, in the direction they had seen the runner depart just before the fighting began.

They traveled down the wadi approximately a mile when they stopped to catch their breath and have a drink of water. "He couldn't have gone too far," Todd said encouragingly between drinks of water.

"We have to keep going; we've got to find him," Peter said, already starting forward again.

And then Peter heard the sweetest sound he could imagine. "Dad! Is that really you?" It was Ethan. He came out from behind a tight knot of bushes a few yards away in the wadi.

"Ethan!" Peter rushed to greet his son. "Are you hurt?" Their embrace brought rare tears to Peter's eyes.

Peter held Ethan by the shoulders and stood back, at arm's length, looking over his son for signs of injury. "Are you alright?" he asked again.

Ethan nodded, "Yeah, Dad. I'm fine." He didn't look fine. His right cheek and eye were bruised pretty badly, and there was a long cut on his forehead right at the hairline.

"How did you know where to find us?" Ethan asked, still not fully believing his father had rescued him.

"I got your message and had some help. The Janjaweed have made lots of enemies, and one of those enemies was quite willing to help us."

Peter handed Ethan his canteen and he took a long drink. Then Ethan noticed Todd and Gary and recognized his Dad's friends. "Hello Mr. Porter; Mr. Steed."

"Man, are we glad to see you!" greeted Gary.

Ethan nodded. "Thank you... thank you so much." He

almost choked on the words, trying to hold back tears that were welling up in his tired blue eyes. "We were being held for ransom, but they were planning to turn Joe, Brad and me over to someone named Colonel Ming… and Wendy and Sam were to be sold into slavery. We owe you our lives."

"Your friends are alright. Can't say the same about those damned Janjaweed, though." Todd looked over his shoulder in the direction of the camp.

"Come on, son. Let's meet your friends and I'll introduce you to Hamaad." Peter placed his arm around Ethan's shoulder as they walked back to the camp.

CHAPTER 16

DARFUR
JUNE 12

"DAD, THIS IS WENDY… Brad… Joe… and Sam. Samantha Ward is our manager; she also recruited us at the U of O," Ethan explained as he introduced his friends. They were huddled together under the shade of a large acacia tree.

"This is my Dad and his friends, Mr. Steed and Mr. Porter."

"Please, call me Peter," he said as they shook hands.

They all looked very tired, faces uniformly smudged with dirt and dried sweat stains. Both Wendy and Sam had shoulder-length hair that was matted and stringy. Bruises were evident on everyone's face, especially Wendy and Brad. Brad seemed to fair the worst—he sported a swollen right cheek as well.

"How can we ever thank you? You saved our lives. I overheard the Janjaweed discussing our fate yesterday," Sam said, her voice drifted softer, the thought clearly very disturbing.

Gary broke in. "You don't need to go into it—Ethan explained. It's all over; you're safe now. We can go home."

Those few words energized Sam and the others. The effect

was almost instantaneous as they realized they were no longer captives. Each looked up with relief and new-found hope.

Wendy, a brunette who reminded Peter of his daughter, was nodding her head, smiling and crying at the same time. "Thank you... thank you." With the back of her hand she wiped away the tears before continuing. "Does my mother know that you're here?"

Peter was confused. "No. Who is your mother?"

"She's a Congresswoman from California—San Diego. I thought maybe she helped you organize this rescue team."

"No, these men are my friends. They came because I asked for their help."

Wendy nodded understanding, but Peter wasn't convinced and suspected she was in shock. "Look, Wendy, I've never met your mother. But I'm sure she will be relieved and very happy to know you're safe. As soon as we get back to Hamaad's camp we can use the radio—I'm sure we can get word to your mother."

Then Joe stepped forward, extending his hand again to Gary, Todd, and Peter. "If you hadn't come along when you did... well, I don't know what would have happened. We—Sam, Ethan, and me—we were trying to escape. We had a plan, and—"

"They almost shot me," Ethan interrupted. "It didn't work. We all would have been killed."

Joe averted his eyes to the ground, rubbing his shoe in the dirt. He knew Ethan was right.

"Come with me," said Peter. "I want to introduce all of you to a friend of mine, and a friend of yours."

Peter led the group the short distance to Hamaad. He was talking to his second-in-command when they walked up. Feeling Peter's presence, he completed his conversation and turned.

Hamaad was surprisingly cheerful. Seeing that Peter was

accompanied by his compatriots and the American hostages, he said, "I just ordered my second-in-command to drive the trucks up to the acacia grove."

Peter nodded in response.

"I see you have found our lost children!" Hamaad smiled broadly.

"Hamaad, I'd like you to meet my son, Ethan." They shook hands.

"And this is Wendy... Joe... Sam... and Brad."

Ethan didn't hesitate; he knew he owed much to Hamaad. Looking the SLM commander squarely in the eyes, he said, "It's an honor to meet you, sir. I can never thank you enough for what you and your men have done to free me... and my friends."

Hamaad's face lost its shine as Ethan finished. He glanced over his shoulder at the bodies of his comrades lying on the dusty, parched earth.

"We hate the Janjaweed. It was the right thing to do. No thanks are necessary."

Ethan, Joe, and Sam all looked beyond Hamaad toward the dead and wounded SLM soldiers. The deceased had been laid side by side. A few of the bodies were covered in dirty linens; others had a shirt or jacket draped over their faces. The wounded soldiers were sitting quietly in the shade.

"Hamaad, I can never repay the debt I owe you," said Peter.

"But you already have. We have defeated these Janjaweed. That is payment enough." Hamaad spoke very philosophically. His family gone, the only reason the former teacher had to live was to fight and to kill his enemy. This singular need filled the void in his life. It wasn't much, but it was sufficient.

"Your father is a good leader, Ethan. You and your friends should be very proud of him; never forget this day."

That pushed Ethan over the emotional edge and as he

nodded in agreement, tears streamed from his eyes. Even Joe's macho veneer cracked as his eyes moistened and he wiped away a tear.

"We're very sorry at the loss of your men," replied Peter.

Hamaad shrugged his shoulders ever so slightly. "We are used to suffering and dying. It is what Allah wants us to do—it is our destiny. We do not know why… but we do it well."

Peter remained silent. Yes, Hamaad's people had been subjected to a life that was intensely cruel and harsh. But what could he do—what could anyone do?

He brought his mind back to the present. The wounded still needed care, and he desperately wanted to get Ethan away from the camp, to get him started on the journey back home.

"Hamaad, are there any other Janjaweed patrols nearby?" Peter asked.

"You are worried of a counter attack?"

"Yes, I am. The sound of the battle will have carried far. We need to get out of here and retreat back to your camp. I don't feel secure here, and we need to get your wounded evacuated."

"This was a rogue group. They were not functioning within the structure of the main battalion commanded by the demon Korlos. But you're right; we should be moving on."

Peter scanned the southern horizon, searching for any sign of danger, but no threat was visible. He couldn't explain it, but a feeling of foreboding had suddenly come over him.

"I'll feel better the sooner we get out of here." Peter agreed. "We can load your dead and wounded in the trucks. We leave the rest, unless you want to bury them."

Hamaad spat on the ground. "Those animals are not Muslim and they are not Christian. They are pigs and do not deserve burial. Let their bodies rot in the sun." Hamaad turned and swiftly walked away to issue new orders to his men.

"Well. He was certainly clear on that topic," Gary said.

"Yes, I guess he was," said Todd with a smile on his face. "Can't say I cared much for those Janjaweed fellas either."

Todd had no sooner finished his quip when the first RPG round exploded against a tree just to their left. Instinctively, everyone ducked and looked in different directions, not knowing where the round had come from. Almost immediately, the sound of automatic rifle fire filled the air and bullets kicked up clouds of dirt and sand, but luckily no one was hit. Another RPG round exploded close to the first one.

The counter attack that Peter had feared had just begun.

CHAPTER 17

DARFUR
JUNE 12

"GET YOUR MEN INSIDE THE TREE LINE, and take the students with you!" Peter shouted to Hamaad as he stripped the two rifles off his back and shoved the Winchester .30-06 into Ethan's hands, keeping his prized Weatherby.

Ethan didn't need any instructions, and he recognized the rifle as much by the familiar feel as by sight. He had shot and hunted often, usually with his father but sometimes solo. As he took the rifle, his mind flashed to the pine-forested mountains he knew well and loved. The beauty and serenity of the wilderness, the quiet and peaceful surroundings—at this moment it all seemed impossibly far away and out of reach.

Ethan opened the bolt just a fraction, checking that a round had been chambered. He locked the bolt and put the safety in the fire position, keeping the barrel elevated and looking to his father.

Waving with his left hand, Peter wasted no time. "Get behind the log! They're coming up the wadi from the south, just as we did!"

Gary, Todd, and Ethan all jumped into action, running past the scattered tents and sliding into the earth behind the fallen tree. The trunk was long; maybe 25 feet or more between the large root ball and the first thick, barren branches projecting randomly in many directions. With a diameter of about two feet, the tree would offer protection from small arms fire. Peter could only hope the RPG accuracy would not improve.

Hamaad and his remaining SLM soldiers took up defensive positions within the grove of acacia trees, spreading out and guarding against a possible attack from the north. Wendy, Brad, Joe, and Sam were huddled in the center of the grove.

From his position kneeling next to the ragged root ball, Peter scanned the wadi. Scattered bushes and occasional boulders dotted an otherwise desolate dry creek bed. The RPGs had been fired from somewhere in that bleak landscape.

After the initial barrage, it had suddenly become eerily quiet. All eyes were probing the wadi in front of their position. Sweat dripped profusely down Peter's forehead, his chest and back were drenched, and his senses were on high alert. Ethan was next to his side, and further off to his right Gary and Todd were peering over the top of the tree trunk, calmly sweeping their rifles back and forth, looking through their riflescopes, trying to locate the enemy.

Peter glanced over his shoulder to the acacia grove and Hamaad's men behind him. Quickly he did the math: the SLM number had been reduced to nine men plus six wounded. Peter didn't know if the wounded were capable of fighting. He assumed they were not. That left only thirteen able men, counting himself and now Ethan—an unlucky number.

If the attackers didn't number too many, given their defensive position, they might stand a good chance of prevailing. But he knew that his rifle ammunition was getting low, and he had to assume the same was true for the rest of his men.

"Don't shoot unless you have a clear target," he said. "We can't afford to waste ammo."

They didn't have to wait long. Ethan spotted the Janjaweed militiaman first. Moving quickly up the wadi in a low crouch, sprinting between positions of cover, the man was dressed in flowing robes that had probably been white at one time but were now multiple shades of tan from the dirt and dust. He carried a Chinese-made type 81 assault rifle with a bandolier of ammunition pouches strapped across his shoulder and chest.

"Ahead, maybe 300 yards," he whispered just loud enough for his father to hear. Then another militiaman appeared, following the first. Then another, and another. Where moments before there was only dirt and scattered bushes and rocks, there was now a swarm of more than a dozen Janjaweed approaching the horizontal log.

"Here they come," said Gary, making no attempt to keep his voice down.

"Hold your fire… hold… hold… now!"

The skirmish line at the fallen tree opened up with random, well-aimed shots. The Janjaweed were unaccustomed to the long-range accuracy of the scoped sporting rifles—weapons designed and crafted for the singular purpose of placing their deadly bullets in a two-inch group at 200 yards, or further. And the skillful owners of these rifles were very capable of hitting their targets out to 400 yards and beyond.

In contrast, the obsolete surplus military rifles used by the Janjaweed were equipped with open sights and had been badly abused for at least the last three decades. In addition, the Janjaweed militiamen were neither trained, nor practiced, in marksmanship. This combination of factors meant that they could place accurate shots to a distance of perhaps 100 yards—a far shorter distance than the Americans they were squaring off against. The militiamen simply pointed their weapons in the general direction of the Americans and pulled the trigger, expecting the volume of automatic fire to yield a lucky hit.

Under the circumstances, the militiamen were outgunned and outclassed. Still, they kept coming—and dying before they could approach to an effective range.

WHOOSH… BOOM! Another RPG struck just short of the root ball. Dirt rained down on Peter and Ethan. Peter shouted down the line, "We have to keep those RPGs out there. If they get close enough to aim effectively, we're done!"

The bolt-action rifles kept firing; militiamen falling with each shot. Peter had lost count of the number they had killed or wounded, but thought it must be 30, maybe 35.

As effective as the sporting rifles were, they did have a serious drawback: their magazines only held four rounds. Peter's .340 Weatherby was even worse, holding only three rounds due to the large caliber of the cartridge. As much as possible, three men would continue aiming and shooting while one reloaded.

Peter checked his ammunition supply. He was down to his last box and he laid it open on the ground within easy reach. He glanced to Gary, "How's your ammo?"

"Getting low. If they keep coming, we're going to have to fall back to Hamaad and let his soldiers share the fun."

"Yeah? I just hope the Janjaweed haven't split their force trying to do an end run."

"If they do, if they try to flank us, they'll run squarely into Hamaad. I sure wouldn't want to… those SLM soldiers are pretty pissed right now."

So far, the attacking force remained focused on the southern line and none of the militiamen had gotten close enough for the SLM rebels to engage them. So Hamaad held his men in position in the grove of trees, ready should the tide of battle change. For now, they were perfectly happy that the odd Americans were picking off the enemy.

Then, just as suddenly as it started, the rifle fire ceased as the militiamen stopped advancing up the wadi. Just as suddenly as they had appeared, they seemingly melted into the parched earth, no longer visible, no longer targets.

The skirmish line was silent, but no one dropped their guard, expecting a new threat to emerge at any moment.

"Stay sharp!" Peter shouted.

One minute passed, then two. It remained quiet. Peter was wary. A bead of perspiration threatened to roll into his eye, and he wiped the back of his arm across his forehead. His eyes were darting back and forth, probing for any sign of the enemy within the wadi or on the slopes at the side. No movement. He released a deep breath, finally allowing himself to relax.

Peter had been kneeling, and now he felt his legs cramping. He fell into a sitting position, his back against the fallen tree, and looked down the line at Gary, Todd, and Ethan—rifles leaning against the horizontal tree trunk. Gary rolled onto his side and faced Peter.

"Well, that was interesting. What was the point?"

Peter shook his head. "I don't know. I thought a counter attacking force would number many more. How many did you count?"

"I got twelve; two were wounded and crawled away."

"I got eleven," said Todd and, reflecting a morbid sense of humor and one-upmanship, he added, "none were crawling away though."

"Add six or seven for me, I think," Ethan added, his voice soft and lacking the bravado exhibited by Todd and Gary.

Peter added it up in his head, accounting for the number of Janjaweed militia he had taken down. The attacking force numbered only 44 or so, less than the size of the group that had been holding the American hostages for ransom.

Peter finally gave up trying to figure it out and decided he should be thankful that the force was small. He turned to face the grove of trees.

"Hamaad, anyone hurt?"

Hamaad stepped out from behind a tree. Slowly the other eight men did as well. He looked over his ragged group and then answered, "No casualties." The six men wounded earlier by the fragmentation grenade were being attended by a man who had been designated as their medic. He actually had little medical training, but more than his colleagues.

Wendy, Joe, Brad, and Sam were also huddled next to the wounded. They remained deep in the grove where they had the most protection.

Peter stretched his legs, trying to get the circulation flowing again. Ethan didn't make any move to get up and join his friends in the acacia grove. As the intensity of the fight waned, Peter witnessed the emotional shock beginning to set into his son.

"Are you okay?" he asked.

Ethan looked at his father, eyes glazed, face devoid of emotion. To Peter, he looked more like a mannequin rather than a man. He didn't know what to make of his son's reaction. He had expected Ethan to be frightened, terrified maybe, even revolted by the immediate need to kill or be killed. Instead, he didn't see any emotion at all, and that truly worried Peter.

"I'm sorry that you had to go through that. I wish none of this had happened to you."

Ethan didn't say anything, he just looked at his father.

"I've always told you and your sister that the world is not fair. It can be—and often is—a very cruel and violent place. Most people back home only see the violence in news reports. They'll never have to experience what happened here."

Ethan nodded, barely perceptible at first, and then more so. He looked down at his hands, examining them as if he had never seen them before, thinking of what he had done. They were trembling. He spoke very softly without looking up. "I never imagined that I would have to kill another person."

Peter reached out, grasping his son's shoulder. "Listen to me. You did what had to be done. Without your help, we couldn't have held the line… we may have all been killed."

Ethan looked up at his father. Tears were running down his cheeks, making brown wavy lines where they mingled with the dust caked on his face. Peter pulled his son close as Ethan wept.

CHAPTER 18

"HEY CHIEF!" Todd shouted. "This doesn't look good!" Both Todd and Gary had remained alert, watching for any new threat from the remote reach of the wadi.

No sooner had Todd called out when Peter heard the faint mechanical rumble. He could see a distant dust cloud far down the wadi, and it was growing closer with every passing minute.

"Hamaad! I thought they just had horses and small arms!" Hamaad dashed up to Peter's position to look at the approaching threat.

"That is mostly true. But sometimes they have trucks and tanks from the Sudanese army."

"Oh, that's just great," Gary said. "And I was beginning to think we might live to see tomorrow."

Todd and Gary had pulled in close to huddle with Peter and Hamaad. "That must've been just an advance recon team we fought," suggested Todd.

"I hate it when I'm right," Peter said with a scowl on his

face. "Their force was too small." They were all exhausted and running out of ideas as well as ammunition.

"Hamaad, is there anything around the camp we can use to take out those vehicles? RPGs… maybe a mortar?"

"We haven't had time to search the camp yet; we'll look now." Hamaad called two of his men to help and set off to quickly search the tents and equipment stores.

Peter continued issuing orders without wasting a second. "Ethan, tell your friends to help load the wounded into the three trucks as quickly as possible. Hopefully they can slip away before the Janjaweed get close enough to waste this camp. Hurry!"

As Ethan jogged off, Peter continued, "Okay, this isn't looking good. At least General Custer had the advantage of high ground… we don't even have that."

"Hey! We didn't come all this way to rescue Ethan and save those kids, just to have our butts kicked by a bunch of third world hoodlums!" Gary exclaimed. Peter wasn't sure if the cocky attitude was real or an attempt to mask the fear they all must be feeling.

"I'm open to any suggestions guys," Peter stared hard at his two friends.

Todd held Peter's stare while he shoved cartridges into his rifle's magazine. Then, to punctuate his answer, Todd pushed the bolt closed and locked. Peter nodded, understanding completely.

He took a deep breath and exhaled. "All right," he said softly. "We make a stand here. Take out as many of the bastards as we can before our ammo runs out. Watch each other's back."

"Like we always do," Gary replied and he smoothly drew the Colt Python .357 magnum revolver from his belt and inspected the cylinder, ensuring that each chamber was loaded. Todd and Peter also checked their handguns one last time.

Hamaad rushed to Peter with a big smile. "We found a mortar and five shells!" he proclaimed proudly.

"Fantastic! Get it set up by the fallen tree, over there where it begins to branch out. Maybe we can slow them down a little."

Two of the SLM rebels ran forward—one carrying the base plate and the other the mortar tube—and did as directed, aiming the mortar directly down the wadi toward the center of the oncoming force. Two other soldiers hustled forward with three wood crates housing the high explosive shells. The enemy was too far out to estimate the size of the force, or the precise assets—trucks, tanks, horses—and they were still coming fast.

Peter looked to the left of the acacia grove and saw that the six wounded rebels had been helped into the Toyotas; two per truck, lying lengthwise in the bed. It would be a rough trip but it was the best they could do.

Sam, Brad, and Joe agreed to drive the wounded soldiers further up the wadi to the north, away from the fighting. While he watched, Wendy slid into the passenger seat beside Sam. Ethan was standing at the driver's window talking with Joe.

"Get those trucks out'a here!" Peter yelled, hoping they could get far enough away to avoid the forthcoming onslaught and carnage.

Returning his gaze to the oncoming Janjaweed force and then checking again on the mortar team, Peter prayed that they knew how to aim and fire the weapon, because he didn't.

"General Santa Anna approaches..." Peter mumbled.

"Promise me one thing," Gary muttered without breaking his concentration on the approaching dust cloud, "if we live through this you'll stop with the negative metaphors! First it was Custer, now the Alamo... next you'll be comparing us to the Spartan's final stand against the entire Persian army!"

Peter glanced sideways at Gary, somewhat amused by his ranting. "Actually, I was just waiting for them to get a whole lot closer before using that one." Both men smiled grimly.

Back to business, Peter raised his binoculars and strained to make out any details in the approaching column. He could just discern the distinctive outline of numerous mounted soldiers, and in the center of the mass he thought he counted two... no, make that three... drab-green heavy trucks. There looked to be something mounted on the trucks, perhaps machine guns, but he couldn't be sure. At least he wasn't seeing any tanks or other armored vehicles.

"Looks like the cavalry is coming. Too bad they're not on our side."

Todd had also been spying through his binoculars. "They're still out there a ways, maybe 2,000 yards. Two far for rifle fire with these guns." Peter confirmed that the leading edge of the column was beyond the 1,300-yard limit of his rangefinder binoculars.

"But not too far for mortars. Hamaad! Have your men target the leading edge of that column. Distance 2,000 yards. Fire only one round for distance."

Hamaad gave the order and his mortar team adjusted the aim and azimuth of the mortar tube and then dropped one round down the muzzle, immediately leaning away as the round launched from the tube. A few seconds later, the high explosive round impacted the earth right at the forward edge of the attacking formation. The explosion sprayed shrapnel with devastating effect and Peter, watching through his binoculars, could see a score of men and horses go down.

"That's it!" Peter yelled. "Pull your distance back 30 yards and fire all remaining shells—now!"

The mortar team didn't wait for Hamaad to relay the order, and within ten seconds the last of the mortar rounds was flying down range in a high ballistic arc. The explosions tore through the Janjaweed cavalry. Men and horses scattered in all directions as the formation crumbled.

Still scanning, Peter could now recognize an even more deadly threat. The trucks, all three of them, showed no sign of slowing and had taken over to lead the charge forward. Now, without the cavalry kicking up dust, Peter and Todd both saw that the trucks each bore quad-anti-aircraft guns.

"Hamaad, pull your men back!"

No sooner had Peter given the order when the anti-aircraft guns opened up, raining lead into the fallen tree and acacia grove. The two-man mortar team was slow in moving back and was cut down as they ran for cover. The tree trunk serving as the front line for the defenders only moments ago was chopped to kindling by the large caliber bullets tearing into it.

At the sight of the quad AA guns Peter, Todd, and Gary had taken cover to the left of the root ball in a slight depression that looked like the weathered hole left when the tree fell years earlier. Bullets were chewing up the acacia trees behind them, and bark and leaves were flying in every direction. Given the distance of the trucks, the men could actually hear the sound of hundreds of bullets impacting the trees and earth, something normally masked by the accompanying deafening report of gunfire.

After a very long minute, the shooting halted and Peter carefully raised his head. He saw the two dead SLM rebels who had failed to retreat from the mortar position. The mortar itself was a jumbled mess of scrap iron, not that it would be of any further use without additional shells.

Peter crawled forward to get into a prone shooting position. He was determined to fight, even if he stood little chance. But his resolve nearly evaporated in an instant when Ethan slid to the ground next to him, holding the Winchester rifle he had been shooting only minutes earlier.

"What are you doing here? You were supposed to leave with

your friends!"

"I couldn't, Dad. You need all the help you can get."

"Ethan, you've got to leave now, while you still have a chance! You can't stay here." Peter's left hand was clutching his Weatherby and with his right he clasped Ethan's shoulder.

"Dad, I'm not leaving you. You risked everything to find me and bring me home. I'm not leaving you! We'll go home together."

"Look... there is nothing we can do to stop those trucks, do you understand? Those AA guns will tear up this grove! We're only trying to slow them down to give you guys a chance to get away!"

Ethan looked squarely into his father's eyes with a determination he had not shown before. He was no longer Peter's little boy, no longer the terrorized youth that Peter had consoled just a short while ago. He had changed. Under the extreme conditions, Ethan was emerging from the cocoon of youth as a man, and Peter knew he had to accept that Ethan would—and should—make his own decisions.

But there was even more to it than that. As Peter looked into Ethan's eyes he swore he caught a glimpse of his son's soul. What he saw made Peter avert his eyes. But as he looked back at Ethan, it was still there... a hint of ruthlessness and determination that Peter had thought only resided in himself, brought to the surface following his wife's death. In this moment, he recognized it in Ethan, too.

Todd called out, breaking the silence.

"What are we going to do, boss?"

Peter glanced at Todd and then turned back to Ethan.

"Son, this is very bad, do you hear me? We are not likely to make it out of this one."

"All the more reason that I'm not abandoning you." There was no waver or hesitation in Ethan's voice. "I sent the trucks on; they're gone."

Peter nodded silently and then hung his head down, eyes clenched tight. With a moment's pause, he resigned himself to accept his son's decision.

"All right then," Peter continued. "Spread out on the lip of this depression. Aim for the drivers and pray to God they don't have armored glass. If the bullets fall low maybe we can puncture the radiators and kill the engines."

The trucks had approached to within 600 yards. A long shot for sure, but still within the effective range of the rifle cartridges they were shooting. Hamaad's remaining men spread out within the acacia grove, kneeling beside the largest trees. The grove was not huge by any measure, barely a half acre in size, so they could not expect to hold out long. It was only a matter of time before the Americans and SLM rebels alike ran out of ammunition. The Janjaweed had time and resources on their side. They could simply sit out there and slowly cut the men down with the AA guns.

Peter looked at Ethan off to his right. He was busily laying out the few remaining .30-06 cartridges for the Winchester.

"I'm so sorry I couldn't protect you from this."

"Dad, you didn't make this choice… it just happened. Like you said, life isn't always fair. But if there is one thing I learned from you, it's to make the best of whatever situation you find yourself in. It's what we have to do."

Peter nodded. "Son, I'm very proud of you. And in case we don't make it out of here, I want you to know how much I love you."

Ethan paused in his preparations. "I know you do, Dad. And I love you, too."

Just then a group of mounted Janjaweed militiamen came riding over the ridge to the west, charging into the acacia grove, firing their weapons into the flank of the defenders. The SLM rebels were ready, and turned quickly, returning fire at their loathsome enemy.

Using acacia trees for cover, the rebels were surprisingly effective even though the mounted militiamen were moving swiftly, never offering a stationary target. The rebels laid down a spray of fire, easily shooting as many horses as militiamen. Their choice of target didn't matter, because when a horse was shot it went down, dropping the rider and making him an easier target to pick off.

After a brief but intensely violent skirmish, only four Janjaweed were left to ride off in retreat. Fortunately, none of Hamaad's men were seriously wounded.

Peter surmised that the AA guns had ceased fire to allow the mounted attack. Now that it had been repelled, he didn't have to wait long for the guns to open up again, only now they were much closer at 500 yards.

The aim was high and the acacia trees took the full impact of the assault—bark, leaves, and tree limbs rained down to the ground. Without waiting any longer, the Americans took careful aim at the truck drivers and began to return fire. One by one the three trucks stopped advancing.

The stricken drivers were not replaced and the trucks remained stalled, allowing the Janjaweed to keep their distance while continuing the barrage of automatic fire. The ground in front of Todd and Gary erupted in dust, sand, and dirt as a barrage of bullets slammed into the earth, and the gunners manning the AAs adjusted their range.

The roar of the large guns was much louder now that the trucks were closer. "Aim for the gunners," Peter yelled above the noise. The Americans altered their aim accordingly.

One militiaman fell, and immediately his body was unceremoniously dragged off the truck. Another man took his place and the gun chattered again.

Groups of Janjaweed clustered around the base of the trucks, shooting at their stubborn foe with their limited-range automatic rifles. The American riflemen maintained concentration on the real threat... those damned AA guns.

"Yeah! I got one!" Gary shouted to no one in particular.

"Only one? That's number three for me," Todd replied calmly as he rammed another round into the chamber and took careful aim.

Suddenly a stream of heavy-caliber bullets cut from left to right across the grove, striking three of Hamaad's rebels.

"Down to my last five rounds," Ethan calmly announced.

Peter only had four shots left. They were just about out of time. Once they ran out of ammunition, there would be nothing to keep the antiaircraft trucks at bay.

Maybe they'll also run out soon, Peter thought. The AA guns were chewing up ammo at an extreme rate. Fortunately, the militiamen appeared to have little skill in using the weapons; otherwise they would have been shot to ribbons by now.

Then Peter saw an opportunity. One of the guns had jammed, maybe it was overheated. As the gunner was desperately trying to clear the jam, he exposed himself. Peter didn't wait. Holding the cross-hairs about two feet above the target's upper chest, Peter slowly squeezed the trigger. Everything seemed to move in very slow motion as Peter watched the rifle bullet strike the man in the abdomen. There was a bright splotch of red as the soft-point hunting bullet passed through him and he immediately doubled over as if struck forcefully by a baseball bat.

But a moment later he was pushed aside, landing on the ground in a jumbled heap. Another man climbed up and worked to clear the jammed gun. Peter took aim again, but before he could shoot the AA gun was back in action. Peter fired anyway and saw the round impact the ammunition can hanging off the side of the AA gun, hopelessly jamming the ammunition feed and unexpectedly taking the gun out of action.

Peter's concentration was interrupted by a sudden cry from his left. "Ahhh... Damn it!" He glanced over and saw Gary cycling the action of his rifle with his right hand while using his chin and shoulder to hold the rifle steady; his left arm remained limp, extended on the dirt in front of him. And then Peter saw the bloody and torn cloth on Gary's left shoulder. Gary ignored Peter's gaze, taking careful aim and firing.

"How bad is it?" demanded Peter.

"I'd be lying if I said I'll live. But I came into this fight knowing that." He kept clumsily cycling the rifle bolt and firing.

Despite the deafening sounds of battle, to his right Peter clearly heard the 'click' as Ethan pulled the trigger on an empty chamber. His son didn't say anything when he looked down at the now useless rifle before him.

Then Todd announced he, too, had run out of ammunition.

Peter's head spun as he scrambled to consider what they could do. What could he do? There had to be an answer. He analyzed the problem from every conceivable angle. There had to be a solution, right? His mind was running in circles. There was always another option, another possibility. He had believed this to be a universal truth. Only now it seemed to be a cruel lie—a deception born from the vanity of his belief that knowledge, technology, and determination could solve any challenge.

Now, with the lives of his son and his best friends on the line, he was at a loss for any scenario that offered even a slim chance of survival. He needed a miracle, but his faith had not been strong in a long time. *How do I ask God for a miracle? How do I ask God to help me kill these bastards?*

BOOM! The ground shook and the sudden new sound of explosions drew Peter back to reality. He looked around expecting to see his friend's shredded bodies from a mortar or RPG attack. Finding no such carnage, he looked up the wadi and saw two of the AA trucks on fire. As he slowly tried to comprehend what had happened, the third truck exploded in a ball of fire.

"What the...?" Peter mumbled, still staring in disbelief at the burning wreckage.

"Nice shooting," Todd chuckled, believing either Gary or Peter had landed a lucky shot.

"It wasn't me," Gary admitted.

The AA guns were silent, and yet there were still several dozen Janjaweed militiamen pressing the attack, sensing that their enemy was out of ammunition since their rifles had silenced.

As the Janjaweed advanced on foot toward the acacia grove, Peter regained focus and fired his remaining two shots, killing the two lead militiamen. His rifle now useless, Peter withdrew a Colt 1911A1 .45 pistol from the tactical holster on his right thigh. He saw that Todd had also armed himself with his sidearm, a Berretta 9mm.

Gary fired the last shot from his rifle and lowered his head, clearly suffering from pain and exhaustion. He tried to pull the revolver from his hip holster but rolled too far to his left and winced in pain.

"Let me help you," Peter said as he reached over and pulled the large revolver from its holster, placing it in Gary's right hand.

As Gary took the Python, he looked at Peter. "What did you do to knock out those trucks? Did you hit the gas tank?"

Peter shook his head, not understanding what had happened either. "I didn't do anything. They just exploded."

The Janjaweed continued to advance, faster now that the accurate rifle fire was no longer coming. Hamaad still had four of his men, but they were also out of ammunition. With no means of defending themselves, they all stayed hidden behind the trees. Occasional rifle rounds impacted the trees and dirt.

As the Janjaweed approached to within about a hundred yards, Gary raised the Colt Python and cocked the hammer. Looking toward Peter with a grim smile he said, "Is this where Butch and Sundance make their last stand?"

Peter chuckled, but he wasn't sure why. They were facing death.

"I promised I wouldn't utter any more morbid allusions, remember?"

"You're off the hook. That deal was only if we live through this. Right now, that doesn't look likely."

They were both silent as they watched the enemy advance. Peter had no hope of hitting anything smaller than an elephant at 100 yards with his pistol, so he just watched and waited.

"You know, Gary, you've been like a brother to me."

"I know. And you're the brother I never had."

Todd cut in. "Okay Butch and Sundance. Don't go all sentimental on me. It ain't over yet. The fat lady may be warming up, but she still ain't singin'."

Peter turned to Ethan, his face a mixture of regret and the love of a father for his son, a love without limits or qualifications. Never in his worst dreams had Peter imagined it would all end this way... in the dry desert of North Africa, thousands of miles from home and family. He wondered if his daughter, Joanna, would ever come to know what happened here... to understand why her father and brother never came home.

Battle sounds pulled Peter's focus back to the advancing enemy. A barrage began to pepper the line of approaching Janjaweed warriors. The sound of explosions was quickly followed by a high-pitched buzz, the distinctive sound made by a minigun.

Like toy soldiers being swept over by a child's hand, the Janjaweed fell to the onslaught. It happened quickly, and within a minute, they were all dead.

CHAPTER 19

DARFUR
JUNE 12

AN OVERWHELMING RINGING assaulted Peter's ears from the gunfire and explosions. Otherwise the surroundings had grown strangely quiet and still—Peter thought it to be the calm before yet another storm. Taking advantage of the unexpected reprieve, Peter crawled over to Gary's position, followed by Ethan, while Todd kept watch, alert for yet another attack.

Between exhaustion and blood loss from the wound to his left shoulder, Gary didn't look good. His eyelids partially covered his eyes as if he was about to blackout, and his complexion was extremely pale; his skin felt cold and clammy. His body was going into shock.

"We're going to get you out of this, buddy," Peter offered, but the conviction was lacking from his voice.

"Yeah, sure we are Sundance," Gary replied weakly.

Peter reached over Gary's back and probed gently at the ragged slash across the upper portion of his left arm and shoulder. It looked to be deep and long. Fortunately the bullet appeared to have missed bone; an inch lower and the round would have entered the upper part of his torso and exited through his pelvis, immediately killing him.

"Hamaad! Do you have any more bandages?" Peter called. Hamaad had been hunkered down in the acacia grove with his few remaining rebels.

Hamaad scrambled to Peter and slid to a crouch next to him, handing him a sterile, sealed bandage and a packet of powdered antiseptic; both appeared to be surplus military and decades old. Peter dressed the wound as best he could, tearing off Gary's shirt sleeve and slicing it to strips so he could secure the bandage to the shoulder and arm.

"How come I can't have a pretty nurse?" asked Gary weakly.

"Shut up and be grateful I don't have to give you mouth-to-mouth." Peter offered Gary some water from his canteen—he sipped eagerly. His blond hair was wild and wavy as ever, but his blue eyes were dull, and his face was smudged with grime and sweat; he looked to have aged ten years in the past seven hours.

"Look sharp... we got more company!" Todd announced firmly, but keeping his voice down.

As Peter looked up, Todd added, "To the west, beyond the ridge of the wadi."

"Hell, why can't we seem to get a break," muttered Peter as he fumbled to check the safety on his Colt and moved closer to Todd. Ethan was already there, gazing forward and still clutching the empty rifle whose only use now was as a club.

"Where are they?" demanded Peter, not yet seeing the new threat.

Todd pointed without lowering his binoculars.

Peter squinted to make out any movement without the aid of optics; he had left his binoculars by Gary.

Todd lowered the glasses and offered them to Peter. Then

he removed the Berretta from his holster and checked the magazine yet again. "Bring it on! I'm not out of fight yet!"

Peter adjusted the focus. There were now several armed men visible about 400 yards away and slowly walking along the west ridge; the same ridge that the Janjaweed cavalry charge had come over during the earlier assault, and from which Hamaad's men had launched their dawn attack. The armed force was spread some distance apart and seemed to be in no particular hurry to reach the ragged group of Americans and SLM rebel survivors in the acacia grove.

As Peter continued to watch the approaching soldiers, Todd spoke again. "I say we find some cover in that grove and ambush them when they get within pistol range."

Peter carefully studied the figures.

"What do you say, boss? We can't take them on out here in the open. We're down to only pistols now."

Peter lowered the binoculars, but he was still looking at the approaching force, which numbered eleven men. There was an odd vehicle moving along slowly behind them, but it didn't appear to have a driver. Peter wondered if it was a remote-controlled cargo hauler of some type.

Peter again pressed the binoculars to his eyes. "I think our luck has just changed," he said, as if talking to himself.

"Are you saying those are good guys?" Todd asked in disbelief.

Peter nodded his head. "Certain of it. Those are the good guys. In fact, unless I'm mistaken, my friend Commander James Nicolaou is the point man."

"Jim Nicolaou? Didn't I meet him at the shop close to a year ago?" Todd recalled, his voice betraying a hint of disbelief.

"One in the same. See that man on point? The one with the cowboy hat?" Peter handed the glasses back to Todd so he could have a better look.

"Yep," Todd answered.

"That's Jim."

"No shit… how did he find us out here? Not that I'm complaining."

"Maybe he listened to me after all."

"Sorry?" Todd wasn't following Peter's random comment.

"Right after I got the voice message from Ethan that he'd been kidnapped, I contacted Jim. He said he couldn't help, and I'm afraid I had no patience with him. But I'm certain he was the anonymous organizer behind our meeting with Abdul Wahid el-Nur in Paris, and it looks like he arranged for more than just that meeting."

Dressed in digital desert camouflage in muted shades of tan, the soldiers moved with a well-trained combat readiness while their eyes scanned for threats in all directions. They carried an assortment of rifles and machine guns at the ready. The team rapidly closed the final distance to Peter and his friends.

Jim walked up to Peter as casually as if they were meeting in a city park. He extended his hand. "Good to see you Peter!"

Jim shouldered his H&K 416 rifle and removed his Stetson hat, cradling it under his left arm. His thick black hair was plastered to his head. There were droplets of sweat all over his face, and his fatigues were wet from perspiration.

The desert camouflage fatigues seemed to accent Jim's Greek heritage. The dark olive skin tone, thick black mustache, and dark eyes typified his Mediterranean ancestry.

Peter had yet to shake his mild state of shock. He had just survived three intense battles, and it wasn't even 5:00 p.m. yet. Now, contrary to all logic and reason, not only had the cavalry arrived, but it was led by his good friend. *It doesn't get any stranger than this.*

"Man, are we glad to see you!" exclaimed Peter, and before Jim could utter a word, Peter continued. "How in hell did you know where to find us? And what brought you here in the first place? You said this wasn't something you could get involved in."

Jim nodded agreement. "All true at the time. But events escalated quickly once word got out of the Janjaweed attack on the refugee camp. Since this type of localized emergency is exactly what we do best, it didn't take long to get the Joint Chiefs and then the President to authorize SGIT to strike back. Our objective was to rescue the American hostages. Normally, the kidnapping of a few Americans wouldn't attract so much high-level attention. But this case is different."

"Wendy, the Congresswoman's daughter?" Peter asked.

"That's right. How did you know?"

"Met her earlier today," Peter explained.

"Her mother has a number of connections in the Defense Department, and she didn't hesitate to call in a whole lot of favors." Even as Jim was explaining these events, his head was swiveling from side to side, scanning everyone in sight.

Not seeing any women or other Caucasians, Jim asked "Where are the other Americans? I have specific orders to find and return Wendy Bennett."

"We rescued her, along with my son and three other volunteers, early this morning. With the exception of Ethan, they all drove north in Hamaad's three Toyotas. There's six wounded SLM rebels with them."

"We'll pick them up. Are any of the Americans hurt?"

"Nothing serious as far as I can tell," Peter replied. "Wendy and Brad were roughed up a bit, mostly bruises."

"Sulu, T-Bone, Rambo," Jim summoned three of his men.

"Conduct a quick search of those trucks we blew up. Bring back any papers, cell phones, anything that may have intelligence value. Same thing for any satchels or backpacks you come across."

"Yes, sir." The three soldiers moved out at a brisk pace.

"So how did you know where to find us?" Peter repeated his question.

"I'll explain in a minute. Let me finish the immediate business first."

Jim turned to his left, surveying the acacia grove. He couldn't miss the wounded SLM rebels sitting in the shade. They were being treated by one of Jim's medics.

"Homer, Ghost," Jim said.

Two men came running. "Set up a defensive perimeter. I want to know if anyone approaches within a thousand yards of our position. We're going to be here for a while, so do it right. And get the mule over here. I want everyone fully provisioned."

"Coyote!" Jim called.

Pointing toward a beat-up ancient flatbed truck with several rusted barrels clustered on the bed, he continued his order. "See that truck over there? See if it's operational. We need some wheels to catch up with the students. Shouldn't be too hard to track them in this dry soil. And we can use the drones to help."

"Will do, sir," replied Coyote.

With his men busy, Jim turned to Peter. "We have a mutual friend—Abdul Wahid el-Nur. Quite a network that man has."

"Let me see if I have this right," Peter said. "You sent me to el-Nur knowing that he would pass me along to some local faction of the SLM. Then you tracked me through his contacts."

"Not exactly, but close enough. In my position I could never provide you with information to contact el-Nur... still, I'm glad someone did. It was lucky for us—and you—that he was willing to meet with you and could offer assistance."

Peter smiled at Jim's cagey reply... he knew the truth and understood fully that Jim had stepped beyond his official authority in providing that help. But he still didn't understand how Jim could have found their current location so quickly.

"But I still don't get it… we didn't know that Ethan and the other hostages were being held here when we met with el-Nur in Paris. In fact, it was Hamaad and his spies who discovered the location only three days before we arrived at the SLM base camp southwest of here."

"That's right. Based on intel from el-Nur we flew directly to the SLM camp. From that point we employed three drones to scout the surrounding desert until, late this morning, we confirmed your location. Those drones can home in on the sound of gunshots and explosions. Ours are also armed with air-to-surface rockets; they took out those truck-mounted AA guns."

Peter nodded briefly, but otherwise was silent, thinking through the events leading to this miraculous rescue.

Jim faced the young man standing next to Peter. "This must be your son, I assume?"

"Uh, yes… Ethan."

Jim extended his hand in greeting. "Pleased to meet you. Even more pleased to know you are alive and well. Your father was really pissed at me when I couldn't help right away."

Jim turned his attention from Ethan back to Peter. "I knew you'd go flying off and do something impetuous like this."

"You'd do the same if it was your son." Peter offered no apologies.

"Yeah. I suppose you're right."

Todd stepped forward and offered his hand to Commander Nicolaou. "Jim… I'm Todd Steed. We met at EJ Enterprises about a year ago. Remember?"

"Of course I remember. Your handshake is just as strong now as it was then. Peter is fortunate to have a friend like you."

"I'm not dead yet!" Gary mumbled.

"Oh, sorry," Peter grinned. "This is Gary Porter. He's another close friend."

Once introduced, Jim immediately noticed the bloody bandage around Gary's shoulder. "Medic!"

Somewhat embarrassed for ignoring Gary's wound, Peter admitted, "I put a field dressing on it, but I'm sure your corpsman can do a better job."

The squad corpsman, call-sign Bull, quickly ran over to Gary, his medical kit flopping at his waist. Bull eased the dressing back and thoroughly examined the gash. He applied more antiseptic powder and a fresh bandage. Then he gave Gary a shot of a potent antibiotic combined with a pain killer—a morphine derivative without the addictive characteristics—followed by more water with added sucrose and electrolytes.

"Once we're secure, Boss Man, I need to put a couple dozen stitches in that tear to keep it together. Looks like he took a grazing hit from a large caliber round. Lucky it wasn't any lower."

Boss Man was the call sign for Jim Nicolaou. All his team used *noms de guerre* when on a mission to keep their true identities private. It was rumored that each man carried a foreign bounty on his head of 100,000 dollars.

The Strategic Global Intervention Team, a highly classified intelligence and strike force unit, operated under authority from the Defense Intelligence Agency, or DIA. As the name suggested, SGIT was tasked with intervening covertly in matters of strategic importance to the United States. Their unique combination of brain and brawn was often the best tool for solving thorny international issues in an increasingly hostile and complicated world.

They brought the analytical expertise of the DIA and melded it with the surgical strike capabilities of a Navy SEAL team. The unit was made up of former Special Forces soldiers and intelligence officers and led by Commander James Nicolaou, a former Navy SEAL himself.

"Jim, I also want to introduce you to Hamaad," Peter said as the rebel leader approached.

The two men shook hands. "One of my medics is treating your wounded, Hamaad. They will get the best care possible."

"Thank you," Hamaad replied, bowing deeply as he said the words.

Jim shifted his attention to Ethan. "I realize this has been a very difficult day. But I need to ask a few questions of you, okay?"

Ethan shrugged. "Sure."

"Do you know why the Janjaweed kidnapped you and your friends?"

"I guess so. At first they said they wanted ransom from the government. But later they were talking about selling Wendy and Sam into slavery."

Jim shook his head. "It doesn't really add up. They'd be taking a big risk just to sell two women on the black market. The Janjaweed have never taken Western hostages before and demanded ransom. Why would they start now?" Jim didn't expect an answer.

"Is there anything else, maybe something that you saw or overheard?"

Ethan thought for a moment before replying. "Well, it isn't much, but Sam—uh, Samantha Ward—understands some Arabic, and she overheard the guards talking. She said they mentioned that Brad, Joe, and I were going to be turned over to someone named Colonel Ming."

Instantly Jim's expression changed from one of contemplation to deep concern. "Are you sure that was the name—Colonel Ming?"

Ethan nodded.

Jim looked at Hamaad and asked, "Do you know of a Colonel Ming operating in this area?"

Hamaad shook his head. "No, that isn't a name I have heard before."

Jim looked worried. He was rubbing his chin and staring at the ground.

"Is that name significant?" asked Peter.

"It could be…" Jim responded.

CHAPTER 20

DARFUR
JUNE 12

JIM REMAINED DEEP IN THOUGHT, running through unspoken scenarios—in each case weighing the odds of success and possible casualties.

"What's this about?" Peter inquired, trying to understand it all.

"There are rumors… I don't have a lot of details. But it doesn't matter. You and Ethan and your friends are going home."

Peter smiled and looked at his son, grateful that he was alive and well.

Jim spoke into his throat mic. "Coyote, what's the verdict on that flatbed?"

The answer came back immediately as he heard the engine cough a few times, and then rumble to life. The extensive coating of rust and the scouring of wind-driven sand had long ago erased the paint from the truck.

"She's running." Coyote's voice sounded clearly in Jim's ear bud. "Can't guarantee how long though. It's a Dodge. My guess is it dates back to the early forties, probably surplus U.S. Army. There are still a few patches of olive drab inside the cab and under the hood."

"Hamaad, we'll take your wounded along with Peter, his son, and friends, to Chad. I'll make sure your men get proper medical help."

"How will we get home?" Ethan asked.

"Two of my men, New York and Chico, will go with you. We have a military transport on standby. It's not first class, but it's faster and easier than flying commercial. You'll be debriefed during the flight."

Gary and Todd shared a high-five. Ethan simply closed his eyes and smiled ever so slightly, overjoyed at the prospect of being safe at home again.

"But isn't your entire team going?" Peter asked. "Once we catch up to Wendy and the others, your mission is over, isn't it?"

Before Jim could answer, a loud explosion split the air. Rock and debris rained down on the area where the Janjaweed trucks had been stopped. A cloud of dust obscured any sign of the vehicles.

Immediately Jim was speaking into his mic. "T-Bone... Rambo... Sulu..." He was answered by persistent static.

"Homer! Ghost!" Jim practically yelled, even though he knew his mic was perfectly capable of picking up the softest whisper. "Do you have contact with any hostiles?"

"Negative, sir."

"What happened?" Hamaad asked.

"They must have booby-trapped the trucks. Bull, Magnum. Check it out, and be careful!"

"What can we do to help?" Peter asked.

"Right now, nothing. Just sit tight. My men may be torn up pretty bad. Until we have the situation under control, I won't risk any more lives."

They all watched as Bull and Magnum ran toward the settling dust, fearful of what they would find.

When they reached the site of the explosion Bull and Magnum were gulping down air, trying to slow their breathing. Dust was still hanging in the air. They quickly took in the scene, before reporting to their commander.

"We've got Rambo and Sulu, sir... and what's left of T-Bone."

Jim closed his eyes as he felt the full weight of the news.

"Rambo and Sulu are alive, but hurt. Blast must have stripped their com gear."

"How bad is it?" Jim asked. The seconds dragged by while Bull completed his preliminary examination.

Thirty seconds later, Bull reported. "Rambo can walk, but he can hardly hear, maybe ruptured eardrums and probable broken wrist. Sulu took shrapnel... arms and legs. Their body armor saved them for sure. We've got to get these guys medevaced."

"Stabilize them as best you can. We'll get them on the flatbed and heading toward Chad."

"Affirmative, sir."

"What the hell happened?" Jim knew it had to be an IED, but he wanted to know more.

"Sulu says that one of the Janjaweed appeared to be alive. They approached with T-Bone in the lead, and when they got close the guy dropped a grenade into a satchel. The explosion was too large for a single grenade, and Sulu thinks there were more explosives in the satchel. Maybe grenades, too, we passed several scattered around as we approached. T-Bone didn't stand a chance..."

"Damn it!" Jim shouted.

"Sir, the truck is gonna be a slow and rough ride. I'd rather call in a Blackhawk."

"That's not an option," Jim retorted. "We came in on foot for a reason—no air support."

"Understood, sir. I can patch them up, stop the bleeding… they should make it."

Jim didn't pause before issuing his next order. "Chico, New York. Get Hamaad's wounded on that flatbed. Then get our wounded loaded… and do what you can to gather up T-Bone's remains."

"Yes sir. We'll put his remains in a body bag," Chico replied. When the SGIT team was operating covertly in a foreign and potentially hostile country, they always brought along a few body bags. Should a team member be killed, it was not acceptable to leave his body behind. Officially, the risk of political fallout was considered too great. However, the standing order was hardly required. All of the team members lived by an unspoken code of honor that would not allow any man to be left behind. Alive or dead, every soldier under Jim's command would return home.

"I want you to head north," Jim continued. "Follow the tracks from the Toyotas that drove away with the hostages. New York, you pilot the drones from the back of the truck; scout ahead and try to locate them.

"As soon as you get the students and other wounded, you get to the border as fast as you can. Once you cross into Chad, radio in your location. I'll have the medevac cleared and on standby before you get there."

"What happened?" Peter asked.

"An IED… triggered when they walked up. T-Bone is dead. If it had been mortar or artillery shells, all three of my men would have been vaporized."

"How was it triggered?"

"Manually, by a Janjaweed militiaman. Simple enough to rig the charge using a grenade as the detonator when my men were close enough."

"So we didn't get them all," Todd observed.

"It only takes one," answered Jim.

"I'm sorry, sir." Ethan spoke in a soft voice. He had seen too much killing.

Rambo hobbled back, aided by Magnum, while Bull carried Sulu slung over his shoulders.

By the time Magnum and Bull arrived, Jim was already on the satellite radio.

CHAPTER 21

DARFUR
JUNE 12

WITH THE LOSS OF HIS SCIENCE EXPERTS plus the number of wounded, Jim knew the prudent decision was to abort the mission. It took about a minute to get through to Colonel Pierson, and Jim quickly briefed his boss.

"Under the circumstances, I am recommending that we abort the second part of the mission, sir. We can medevac from Chad with the civilians."

Colonel Pierson was characteristically direct. "Negative."

"Say again, sir?" Jim knew what he heard, but he wanted confirmation.

"I say negative, Commander. We have new intel—intercepted radio transmissions. Seems your field exercise was noticed. Radio traffic from the approximate location of the complex has been unusually high during the previous two hours. NSA is warning that they could remove key evidence and obscure the true function of the compound. We can't afford to abort and come back in a month or two."

"Colonel, I am down to six men and my specialists are out of play."

"Improvise, Commander. That's what you get paid to do."

Jim didn't agree with the decision, but it wasn't his call. "Understood, sir. Will proceed with the mission. Civilians and wounded will medevac from Chad."

Jim terminated the transmission and turned, facing Peter, his thick mustache unable to hide the newly-formed frown.

"You've been ordered to continue the mission even though you lost almost half your team," Peter said. He could see Jim didn't like the message he'd received over the radio.

"That's *my* concern. My men will adapt. You and Ethan and your friends need to get on that truck. The bus is leaving."

"Wait a minute Jim. I owe you. Let me help."

Jim closed the gap to Peter until he was less than an arm's length away. He clenched his jaw and focused on his friends face, trying to read his mind, weigh his commitment, measure his skills. The silence served to amplify the tension, and then he made his decision. "T-Bone and Sulu were my science specialists. I could use your help."

"If Peter is stayin', so am I," Todd announced.

"Me too," added Gary, his strength slowly returning with hydration and pain medication circulating through his body.

Jim wondered what Colonel Pierson would say, but then quickly dismissed the thought. *He ordered me to improvise.* "Under the circumstances, I'm not going to argue. Ethan can load up and head out with the wounded."

"No way. I'm not leaving without my Dad."

"Son, please listen to Commander Nicolaou. You should go home."

"No way, Dad. I told you before; I'm not leaving unless we leave together."

Peter looked at Jim, his eyes pleading for an answer that Jim would not give.

"Look," Jim said. "I don't like this, and Colonel Pierson will probably relieve me of my command and bust me two grades for doing it. But I'm down five men, including my two geeks. I won't order any of you to stay, and if you choose to leave you need to get on that truck now." Jim paused looking for a reaction from the civilians—no one spoke or moved for the truck.

"Okay. As of this moment you are all volunteers and under my command. This is a military mission of highest priority."

"What, exactly, is this mission?" Peter asked

Jim took a deep breath and exhaled before continuing.

"It's about Colonel Ming. NSA has a hunch that he's here, but there's no actionable intel. We weren't even certain he was alive… until Ethan mentioned his name."

"So who is Colonel Ming, and what does he have to do with this?" Peter asked.

Jim took a second to organize his thoughts before answering. "Colonel Ming is a very elusive character. He is reported to be a brilliant scientist. Trained in medicine and genetic engineering, specializing in viral diseases. He completed two post docs in the U.S.—Harvard and UC San Francisco Medical Center—by age 30. Then he left the U.S. and reappeared a few years later in Beijing. Over the last two decades he worked mostly for the North Koreans and the PLA—People's Liberation Army—researching and developing bioweapons.

"About eighteen months ago the CIA started to receive unconfirmed reports that Ming was in Sudan, but without agents on the ground we were never able to develop actionable intel. A lot of the information we have on Ming was obtained through the Mossad. They refer to him as a modern-day Dr. Mengele, Angel of Death—but the locals here have another name for him."

"And what would that be?" Peter asked.

"They call him the Devil of Darfur."

Peter was repulsed by these references to Colonel Ming. He knew a little about the atrocities committed by Nazi doctors in the 1940s, and his imagination conjured up horrific images of sadistic human experiments. In a brief moment, his face revealed the horror he was feeling. Jim saw it, too.

"You have good reason to fear Ming. Based on our intel, he is pure evil."

"What do you mean?"

He is rumored to have proposed a radical project, years ago, related to inserting foreign DNA into humans. Supposedly, even the Chinese government was too disgusted and frightened to support it... we're not sure about the North Koreans. But nothing was ever proven, and his location remains a mystery."

"If nothing was proven, why so much interest in him?"

"Because we've heard other rumors as well. According to some sources, Ming actually conducted experiments on human subjects—mostly violent criminals and homeless men—learning how to successfully insert abnormal DNA into the DNA of living people."

A chill ran down Peter's back.

"My team was sent here to accomplish two objectives. The first priority was to rescue Wendy Bennett and any other American hostages. I hoped that would include your son. You and your friends helped us to achieve that goal."

"What is the second objective?" prompted Peter.

Jim took in a deep breath and folded his arms across his chest. He looked squarely at Peter before continuing.

"We have some intelligence from reliable sources—don't even ask where it came from—that suggests a large number of the tribal people in western Darfur have been disappearing. Eyewitnesses report convoys of trucks carrying men only—never women, children, or the elderly—into the desert, to a remote complex of buildings. The sources say that no one ever leaves."

"What?" Peter couldn't believe he had heard correctly, or understood the true implication of what he was being told.

"Satellite photos picked up a newly constructed compound about 20 clicks from here. The analysts think it may be a death camp."

Peter's mouth hung agape, his head moving subtly side to side.

"Once we have secured the hostages, my orders are to investigate the compound, discretely of course, and report what we find. If Ming has been directing research there, the analysts will find evidence of that. Any recourse will come through other channels."

"That's it?" asked Peter.

Nodding, Jim replied simply, "That's it."

"You think Ming is here, don't you?"

Jim nodded. "And if he is, I think he's experimenting again with human subjects."

CHAPTER 22

DARFUR
JUNE 12

WITH DUSK RAPIDLY APPROACHING, the promise of cooling temperatures seemed to improve the mood of almost everyone, except Peter. Despite his exhaustion, or maybe because of it, his mind seemed to be caught in an endless loop as he kept trying to process what Jim had told him about the mysterious Colonel Ming. A thousand questions raced through his mind. Some instinctive warning kept crawling to the front of his thoughts; Ming was near, and he was definitely evil.

In sharp contrast, Todd was sitting with his back against a tree trunk, sipping water from his canteen. His eyes were closed as he spoke. "I can almost imagine that I'm on the beach in Cabo, enjoying an ice-cold Corona with lime."

"Hey, man. I'm with ya," replied Gary. "You know, I think I can taste it… oh yeah."

Gary's vitality and spirits had definitely improved since receiving Bull's treatment. He was hydrated and the color had returned to his complexion; the pain medication contributed enormously to regenerating his usual optimistic and witty character.

Ethan just shook his head and laughed. His Dad definitely had some odd friends.

"You guys can't be serious! This is warm, stale water."

Todd opened his eyes and looked incredulously at Ethan. "Of course! It's the illusion... you don't get it, do you?"

"No, Mr. Steed. I suppose I don't," he laughed.

Commander Nicolaou walked over and joined the group. Peter remained quiet, almost brooding.

"I gather you men fancy yourselves as riflemen?" Jim asked. It came across as a genuine question, not a challenge to their egos.

"Yep," answered Todd, not one to waste words.

Gary added, "My philosophy is, why get close enough that the bad guys can shoot back?"

"Doesn't appear that your strategy worked so well," Jim chuckled as he eyed Gary's bandaged shoulder.

Gary shrugged, and then immediately winced from the brief stab of pain. "Reality and theory don't always follow one another."

"We packed along a lot of supplies including spare ammo, but I'm afraid I don't have ammunition for your rifles. The venerable .30-06 cartridge hasn't been standard government-issue for a long time. As for Peter's preferred long arm..." Jim glanced over to Peter who had been watching the banter and was grinning ever so slightly. "...Uncle Sam has never knowingly issued any weapon chambering the .340 Weatherby cartridge."

"A simple oversight, I'm sure. In fact, I have an appointment with the Secretary of Defense next week to review the superb ballistics and advantages of the Weatherby Mark V rifle and .340 cartridge for long-range precision shooting." Peter commented, and then flashed a grin.

"Be that as it may, what I can offer you is the M107 Barrett .50 caliber rifle."

"You brought extra rifles?" asked Ethan.

"Sort of, I guess. All my men are trained to be experts with a very broad range of weapons, including the M107. It's standard practice for my team to deploy with a primary and a secondary weapon assignment.

"The team I detached to escort the Peace Corps hostages back to the Chad border is traveling light, they were ordered to take only their primary weapons and sidearms. That leaves me with four extra 107s."

"So you're saying that you have four Barrett .50 caliber sniper rifles... is that right?" asked Todd, just to be sure he heard correctly.

Jim nodded. "I want you all armed and proficient with your weapon, although I'll do my best to keep you shielded from immediate danger. Magnum!"

A camouflage-clad soldier quickly reported to his commanding officer. Magnum—his call sign, although he liked to use it on informal occasions as well—stood a hand taller than Boss Man at six feet one inch. Like all of the team members, he was fit and muscular, with short cropped hair and looked maybe three to four years younger than his true age of 30.

Magnum—whose given name was Percival Dexter— had been a professional soldier all of his adult life. At the age of eighteen he joined the navy to see the world, which he believed would be far more attractive and interesting than his neighborhood in South Central LA. He loved the challenge and reward, and the seemingly endless opportunity to advance. It was not long before Percival, Percy as his friends called him, won a position with the elite navy commando SEALs.

With a distinguished combat record in both Iraq and

Afghanistan, it wasn't long before he was recruited by Commander Nicolaou to join SGIT. Percy never hesitated to accept any challenge, and he viewed this offer no differently.

"Sir." Magnum reported his presence.

"Magnum, I think we have just recruited four new snipers to the team. Please issue each man the M107 and see that they receive proper instruction as to its operation and maintenance."

"Yes, sir!"

"Oh, and let's see if we have enough daylight left this evening to give these men a few minutes of trigger time—best way to get familiar with the sighting system. They seem to know their way around a rifle. Now I want you to make certain they can handle the Barrett in the excitement of a firefight."

"Yes, sir." Magnum motioned to the new recruits.

"Please come with me, gentlemen. There's not much daylight left but if we stay on task I can get you outfitted and you will still have enough time to squeeze off a few rounds."

Magnum led the group a short distance to the mule; a remotely piloted hybrid vehicle that essentially was a cargo carrier. It had a large, flat bed the width of a small truck and was just over eight feet long. With a small diesel genset that charged on-board lithium-polymer batteries, combined with an electric motor, the mule could be stealthy when needed and still traverse long distances.

"Gentlemen, this is the mule. We call her Bessy. Since Bessy carries most of the load, we can cover large distances and still be fit and ready to fight."

"I see that Bessy also packs a punch," Peter said, noting the electric Gatling gun mounted onto the mule's deck.

"The platform is flexible. For this mission Boss Man opted to have the Dillon Aero M134DT mounted on Bessy's deck. This is the light-weight titanium version. It came in real handy in taking out that mass of Janjaweed terrorists charging your position earlier.

"The Dillon fires the standard NATO 7.62mm cartridge at 3,000 rounds per minute. It is devastating against an infantry charge or other soft targets. There's nothing equal to it on the battlefield."

"Since we were down to pistols by that point in the battle, I'm truly grateful that you showed up with Bessy and her minigun," Peter commented.

Magnum reached onto the deck and pulled over a large black water-proof gun case. There were five more like it. He opened the case to reveal the M107 snuggled deep within egg-crate foam.

"Gentlemen. The model 107, Barrett, caliber .50." Magnum picked up the rifle with one hand, not even registering the 30-pound weight of the weapon. He held it at port arms as he lectured.

"Ten round box magazine..." he pointed to the magazine extending below the rifle's receiver, never breaking eye contact with his students.

"Twenty-nine inch barrel. Chrome chamber. Folding bipod..." and he extended down two metal legs near the front of the rifle.

"But the most deadly feature of this rifle is here... the optical sighting system."

Peter was staring intently at the scope as it had already caught his attention. Rather than a traditional riflescope—essentially a tube that is flared or belled at each end to contain ground-glass optics—what he saw on the rifle before him was a conventional scope with a small box attached to the top of the tube on the end closest to the shooter.

"Working with Mr. Ronnie Barrett and his team of engineers, we have enhanced their BORS integrated electronic ballistic computer to include range measurement via an internal laser range finder, and automatic windage adjustment. These rifles are equipped with the Leupold 8.5-25x50mm scope."

"I'm rather fond of Leupold scopes myself," Todd commented.

"Glad to hear that, sir."

"Magnum, what exactly does this modified BORS do for us?" Peter asked.

"Quite simply, it takes the guesswork out of long range shooting. The built-in laser range detection system accurately measures distance-to-target out to 2,000 yards. The internal meteorology suite continually measures ambient temperature, humidity, barometric pressure, angle of inclination, wind speed, and wind direction. A GPS receiver nails the elevation. There's even a sensor that detects and compensates for rifle tilt... left or right. Basically everything you would input to calculate a ballistic solution is measured. The microchip then computes the ballistic arc and translates that to the small LED display overlaid on the image in the scope. You'll see key data, like distance to target, wind direction, and speed.

"But the most important feature is the red dot. That is the calculated point of impact—where the BORS computer says the bullet will strike home. All you have to do is adjust the elevation and windage knobs until the red dot merges with the cross hairs."

Ethan was completely absorbed with Magnum's instruction while Todd had a blank stare on his face, not quite taking everything in at the speed Magnum was dishing it out. Like Ethan, Gary seemed to be processing the information just fine. "So let me see if I follow. The cross hairs in the scope shows the apparent point of impact and the red dot shows the true ballistic point of impact based on measured environmental data. So, adjusting the elevation and windage knobs alters the sighting point to match the true point of impact. Do I have that right?"

"Yes sir, Mr. Porter. That is correct. I see you have a knack for technology."

Gary grinned at both Todd and Peter.

"Oh, give me a break," grumbled Todd.

"Hey, this is my thing. I do computer security and stuff, I dig this, man, okay?"

Even Peter rolled his eyes now.

Magnum continued. "It takes about two seconds for the data to be measured and fed to the BORS microprocessor, so it's not always practical to calculate prior to each shot. That's why Mr. Barrett didn't completely eliminate the traditional cross hairs in the scope. Pressing this button here at the front of the trigger guard engages the BORS computer. The red dot will be positioned based on the ballistic calculations and it will remain there until the BORS completes the next calculation."

Pointing toward the muzzle, Magnum said, "The rifle has a muzzle break to compensate for recoil generated by the exhaust gases. But she still kicks! You'll need to practice good shooting form and hold the stock tight into your shoulder."

Magnum pulled forward three more cases and distributed the rifles plus ten rounds of ammunition. "This is our special load, manufactured by Nosler. With a 750 grain bullet and muzzle velocity of 2,900 feet-per-second, these are hot loads. We also have a few mags loaded with the Raufoss Mk211 armor piercing rounds for vehicles and hardened targets. Any questions?"

No one spoke up.

"All right. Let's see what you can do."

The mule was parked at the edge of the grove of acacia trees, and Magnum led them about 30 yards away. Removing a small range finder from a pocket in his trousers, he sighted a boulder about the size of a man and 678 yards distant. The boulder happened to lie between two small bushes, so it was easy to identify.

"Gentlemen. I want each of you to take a prone position here, give yourselves some space as the muzzle blast is fearsome. Then, I want you each to sight on that boulder between the two small bushes. It is about 680 yards from here. Let me know when you are ready. And mind you, we are going to lose daylight soon."

Ethan, Todd, Gary, and Peter all took up firing positions as instructed, allowing eight to ten feet between them. Gary gently eased into a prone position, favoring his wounded shoulder but still showing adequate dexterity.

"Ready, Gentlemen?" Magnum asked. He received a unanimous yes.

"Fire at will."

Slowly, and one by one, the rifles belched their deadly loads. The report with each shot was truly deafening, but at Magnum's suggestion everyone had stuffed a small wad of tissue in their ears.

Amazingly, each shot was a hit; not just close hits, but right-on hits.

After each man had fired his ten rounds, the make-shift range became silent. Ethan rolled to his side and looked at Magnum. "The kick isn't near as bad as I thought it would be."

"That's the muzzle break and spring recoil dampeners. They work wonders, I can tell you."

"That is totally awesome!" exclaimed Gary. Todd also had a huge grin on his face, testimony enough to the impression the weapon system had made on them.

Peter looked to Todd. "Remind me when we're back in Bend that we need to adapt one of these BORS to our impulse guns. Should be able to extend the accuracy out at least to 1,000 yards, don't you think?"

Characteristically Todd's answer was short and direct. "Yep."

Gary and Todd helped Magnum clean and repack the rifles in their hard cases. The chatter was light, mostly about the BORS optic system. Peter placed a hand on Ethan's shoulder, and they walked away several yards.

"How are you doing?" Peter asked.

Ethan shrugged. "What can I say. I'm here and we have to do this."

"You shouldn't have stayed. You should have evacuated with your friends. This is no place for a—" Peter stopped himself.

"No place for what? A child? I'm not a child anymore Dad."

Peter forced a smile, but his eyes glistened with anguish. "You'll always be my son. I know you're grown up now, but seems like it hasn't been that many years since you were just a little tyke." Peter turned his head, forcing back the sadness that felt all consuming. "I'm sorry. I didn't mean to offend you."

"Dad, look at me."

Peter slowly faced his son. He bit his lip, sniffled, and composed himself. He had to be strong, and right now that seemed impossible. "You should have gone home," he said again, this time his voice tender.

"No, I couldn't. After all you and your friends and Commander Nicolaou and his team have risked to save me…" Ethan squared his shoulders, choosing the right words before going on. "No, I have to be here. I can't run away from this; I can't."

Peter threw his arms around Ethan, resigning himself to the fact that he had no power to change the situation. Just as when Maggie died.

Jim had been standing well behind the firing line and was impressed by the shooting skills of these men. Although he was not close enough to overhear the private conversation between

Peter and Ethan, there was no mistaking the raw emotions. Jim knew this could present problems later on, and he would have to pay close attention to father and son.

Stepping forward his order was clear and concise. "Pack'em up. We're moving out in two hours. I want to be at the coordinates for this mysterious compound before sunrise. We'll rest during the day, and tomorrow evening we will see if Colonel Ming has set up a new shop of horrors."

CHAPTER 23

COMMANDER NICOLAOU'S TEAM was bolstered in number by the new recruits—Peter, Ethan, Gary, Todd, and Hamaad. Whether they could fight or not was another question. Having sent the surviving SLM soldiers out with his own wounded, Jim asked Hamaad to stay with his team. He believed Hamaad could prove useful as an interpreter if they encountered any local residents.

They made good time considering how exhausted some of the men were. An hour before sunrise, they arrived at the coordinates where the satellite photos had indicated the compound was located. The night started out very dark, but a nearly full moon had risen early in the evening and was still hanging low above the horizon at dawn. The air was blessedly cool for the long march, but everyone knew that once the sun rose it would quickly become unbearably hot.

Right now, the first priority was to establish shelter from the merciless sun while remaining out of sight of anyone who might inhabit the compound.

Jim deployed his men on the reverse side of a rocky ridge overlooking the collection of buildings, which lay on a desolate plain below them. The remnants of a dry riverbed wound between the base of the ridge and the structures. A smattering of bushes dotted the riverbed suggesting that water was still to be found beneath the swirled sand and gravel.

The ridge ran roughly from the southeast to the northwest, with the compound about 2,000 yards to the west of the ridge where Jim had chosen to make camp. A collection of shallow caves—really not much more than overhanging rock—provided shelter on the eastern slope of the rocky ridge near the top.

Of course, there would be no campfires and no lights of any type other than as absolutely necessary. It was vitally important to the mission that their location not be detected. By climbing 30 yards to the ridge crest, the SGIT soldiers would observe the target buildings using light amplification scopes at night and standard spotting scopes during daylight.

"All right men, listen up," Jim said.

"I want everyone to get something to eat and plenty of water. I want you hydrated. The civilians need to get some sleep... you are all on the ragged edge of exhaustion."

"You're telling me. I'd swear I was sleep walking the last three miles," Gary complained.

"Ghost and I will take first watch. We're Team Alpha. Two hours on, four hours off. I want that compound under constant surveillance. Magnum and Bull, you are Team Bravo; you will relieve Team Alpha. Coyote and Homer, you are Team Charlie; you will relieve Team Bravo. Questions?"

Jim knew his team exceptionally well. Although he always asked if there were questions, he knew there would rarely be any. His men were sharp, motivated, dedicated, and knew the drill.

"Okay then. Remove your communication gear and stow it. Any time you are within ten yards of that ridge..." Jim pointed to the top of the rock ridge from which they would observe the compound, "...no one says a word. Standard hand signals only."

Each member of the team was equipped with an ear bud and throat microphone connected to a secure, encrypted net that allowed every member of the team to communicate during missions. The head set was voice activated and did not require a free hand to operate. Even though the system was engineered for short-range communication, it did operate on standard but randomly changing radio frequencies. This made it difficult, but not impossible, to detect.

Colonel Ming had escaped surveillance for the better part of two decades, so he was crafty and smart, and although Commander Nicolaou could not be absolutely certain Ming was at this remote base, he wasn't going to take any chances.

Next, Jim addressed the civilians, who were completely new to military operations. "I know you men like to hunt, and you want to exercise many of the same practices here. If you smoke... don't. If you need to relieve yourself... do it quietly. Don't drop anything... don't talk. Clear?"

Ghost and Commander Nicolaou made their way to the top of the ridge just as the sun was beginning to cast a faint glow on the eastern horizon. Just shy of the crest the two men dropped to their bellies and slowly crawled the remaining distance, exercising care to remain very low and to move slowly and with fluid grace, avoiding fast or jerky motions that could possibly be seen even from a great distance.

Since the dawn sky was approaching, and with it a ribbon of purple-red glow low on the horizon, Jim and Ghost each set up a standard optical spotting scope. Its light gathering capabilities and superb optical magnification allowed them to see detail even in the dim morning light. First, they could make out the two towers, triangular in shape. Each tower stood taller than any other buildings in the complex. Jim estimated the roof of each tower was maybe 40 feet above the ground.

The top of the towers were completely enclosed, with recessed shutters over what might normally have been windows. Any ladder or staircase for ascending the towers were not visible, and Jim assumed they were enclosed within the core of the structures.

The main buildings—four of them—appeared to be conventional one-story buildings with flat roofs. Each structure was a simple rectangle about four times longer than its width, all about the same size, and all lined up parallel with the others. They appeared to be constructed of concrete or maybe cement block; Jim could not be certain from their viewing distance. One of the main buildings had two vertical columns projecting upward, not quite as tall as the towers but close. Although Jim wasn't sure what they were, he thought they resembled smoke stacks or chimneys.

Jim and Ghost noticed that there were no visible lights anywhere at the compound. But they did take note of three generators and two large fuel tanks. Each machine was about the size of a one megawatt generator. Only one of the machines was operating. The size and number of generators caused Jim to wonder what was inside the compound that required so much electrical power.

For all practical purposes the collection of buildings appeared to be deserted. No trucks or cars were parked outside the buildings and not a single person was visible.

As the sun rose daylight spilled across the land, a wire fence surrounding the compound was revealed by the glint of sunlight reflecting off the coiled razor wire stretched along the top of the high fence. It delineated a boundary that was set about 1,000 yards out from the compound's four buildings. Much closer in, a second fence surrounded an area about the size of a football field adjoining two of the four buildings. Jim surmised this fence was electrified since there was a red light projecting from a pole above the fence.

A single dirt road approached the front of the buildings, and a simple guard shack and gate marked the entry into the facility.

Outside the razor wire fencing a lone vehicle, looking something like a dune buggy, slowly patrolled the perimeter. Jim counted three two-man foot patrols operating a seemingly random pattern. This was the first evidence they'd seen that the complex was inhabited.

Jim and Ghost continued their surveillance in complete silence, each man mentally cataloging the images and details below. Later, in camp, they would share notes and record their observations while the next team continued the surveillance.

Suddenly there was a faint rustle of earth behind Jim. He turned and was face to face with Bull. He nodded as if to say "good morning."

As his call sign implied, Bull was a beast of a man, so named in recognition of his bulk and strength. Like Coyote, Jim had recruited Bull from the Marine Corps, force recon, which was remarkable because nearly all of the SGIT team had been recruited from the Navy SEALs. A California State Champion wrestler in high school, Bull had turned down a full ride to Notre Dame, preferring to follow his family tradition and earn the moniker of Devil Dog, like his father and uncle before him. In the Corps, he regularly lifted weights in addition to the usual regimen of physical exercise. In training, no one had wanted to spar with Bull because they were always soundly beaten.

The largest and strongest man in the SGIT team, Bull was also considered the most gentle. He was their trusted corpsman, braving bullets and RPGs to render immediate medical aid to his wounded comrades—he had patched up most of the team at least once.

As the hand off was being made, Bull noticed a faint odor. It was peculiar and seemed out of place in the arid landscape. He touched his nose with his right index finger while looking directly at Boss Man. Jim nodded and turned back toward the compound. A faint wisp of grey smoke was drifting up from the left chimney.

Bull and Magnum took up their viewing positions and settled in as Jim and Ghost slowly crawled back from the ridge and down the eastern slope. Once they were certain their bodies were blocked from view, they stood and silently walked the final 20 yards to the camp.

Ghost spoke first. "Did you smell that, sir?"

Jim nodded. "Yes, just as we were leaving. Bull caught it, too."

"Kind of reminds me of a barbeque, but not a very good one. You know, like the chicken was burned."

"It was burned alright. But that's no barbeque."

CHAPTER 24

DARFUR
JUNE 13

THROUGHOUT THE MORNING and into the afternoon Jim's team determined that the compound closely resembled a prison camp, despite the fact that no prisoners were observed in the fenced yard. In fact, they had seen no one at all except the two-man patrol teams until two military-green trucks arrived. The trucks stopped outside the main gate for a minute, probably for verbal clearance, and then the gate opened by a remotely controlled electric motor.

The trucks entered the fenced compound and stopped outside one of the four main complex buildings. As uniformed guards removed the covers over the beds of the trucks, a dozen men from each truck jumped out and lined up. More uniformed and armed guards appeared from inside the nearest building, suggesting that these men were prisoners, not volunteers. Their clothing suggested they were native tribal men, and none appeared either older than 40 nor younger than about 17 or 18.

The guards marched the men at gunpoint into the building.

As the door closed, the two drivers climbed back into the trucks and departed.

"So, that's what we know," Jim concluded. He was reviewing the events with his team while also briefing Peter, Todd, Gary, Ethan, and Hamaad. It was late afternoon, and the sun would be setting in an hour or so.

"You said the compound resembles a prison camp. But why aren't there any prisoners out in the yard? You should have seen some people, even if only for a short time. What is the point of a secured yard if the prisoners are kept locked inside the building?" Todd inquired.

"Perhaps the fence is a second layer of security... you know, in case someone escapes from their cell inside the building?" Bull offered.

"I don't think so," Peter added. "In fact, the notion that this is something resembling a maximum security prison makes no sense to me at all. Why here? We're a long way from anywhere. That compound is designed to be very low key. Whoever built it and runs it doesn't want the facility to be noticed. There are no marked roads, no signs, nothing."

Jim nodded agreement.

"And another thing," Peter continued. "You said there are two large backup diesel generators in addition to the main power generator, right?

"That's my conclusion since only one generator was running. The other two must be backup," Jim said.

"Agreed, but why would they require such a high degree of redundancy?"

"Simple. In case the main generator goes down they need power for lights and air conditioning," Bull answered.

"One backup is good enough for that."

"Okay. The cells have electric locks and if they lose power they don't want the prisoners to walk out of their cells," Bull was not easily giving up the notion that this was a prison.

Peter was shaking his head. "No, that's not the case at all. A two-dollar lock keeps the cell door closed and secure. Why would anyone use electronic locks on prison cells out in the middle of nowhere... too expensive and, as you pointed out, too unreliable. No, there has to be a better reason for the backup generators. Buying and maintaining that equipment doesn't come cheap. Those machines are here to make certain they always have electric power—and a lot of it—for some other critical load."

"If you ask me, they're running some electrical or electronic equipment—maybe computers or something—that they can't afford to have go down. Maybe they have a super computer down there; I hear those need a lot of power." Todd offered.

"Makes a certain amount of sense," Jim said. "So, the question is: what is the purpose of that complex? I'd bet my paycheck that we smelled burnt flesh this morning as smoke began coming out one of the chimneys. They could have been destroying laboratory animals used in experiments. If this is a bio-lab, then they would want a backup generator to keep sensitive equipment running."

"Maybe it's a re-creation of a Nazi concentration camp?" Gary suggested in all seriousness.

Both Jim and Peter turned to look at Gary, a spark of insight flickering in each man's eyes.

"My God..." Peter's voice trailed off. He was shocked and horrified by the concept. "Maybe the lab specimens they're destroying are more than little white rats?"

"There's only one way to be sure," Jim replied. "Tonight we're going to infiltrate that facility, and I will report back to Colonel Pierson what we find." Jim looked around the men gathered in front of him before continuing. "We're going in lean—less chance of getting caught. Ghost, you're in."

"Yes, sir!"

"And since I don't have T-Bone and Sulu, that makes you our resident expert on this sort of technology," Jim said addressing Peter. "I want you along as well."

"All right".

"Coyote, Homer—you will be our lookouts from the ridge. I want you in position an hour after sunset."

"Roger."

"Everyone grab some chow and rest. It's going to be another long night," Jim said as his way of dismissing the troops.

"What about me?" Gary inquired.

Jim turned and stared blankly at Gary.

"You need a computer expert. No offense, but that's not Peter."

"None taken," Peter admitted.

"What makes you think we need a computer expert?"

"You said it yourself. You think there's critical scientific equipment in that facility—stuff they would use in biological experimentation. Just where do you think all that data is stored? The hand-written laboratory notebook is a thing of the past. If they're running experiments, they will have terabytes of data stored electronically. It's going to be password protected and likely even encrypted."

"And you can help us access it?" Jim probed, not able to hide his skepticism.

"Look, I've been a programmer for the last two-plus decades, and my wife and I run a computer security consulting firm. Yes, I can bust through just about any firewall. I can get that data. You need me."

Jim studied Gary, contemplating what he had said and, more importantly, considering what it might mean to the mission.

After a long pause, Jim sighed. "Okay, you're in." Then he

mumbled, "I just hope I don't later regret this decision."

Jim turned away from Gary. "Bull!"

Bull jumped to his feet and was standing in front of Commander Nicolaou. "Sir."

Nodding toward Gary, he said, "Make sure his bandage is tight and the stitches haven't pulled loose. I don't want him leaving drops of blood for anybody to find, especially within that facility."

"Yes, sir!"

CHAPTER 25

DARFUR
JUNE 14   0130 HOURS

"THE FENCE ISN'T ELECTRIFIED, and I don't see any motion detectors on either side of it," Ghost said. He and the rest of the team were outfitted with night vision goggles.

Jim simply nodded. He too had been carefully and deliberately scanning the outer-most perimeter fence for any indication that it was more than merely a wire fence. For whatever reason, the perimeter security was lax, comprised of only the nine-foot steel mesh fence topped with razor wire. The motorized patrol they had seen during the day was absent, as was one of the two-man patrols. Able to oversee the entire compound from the ridge, Coyote and Homer tracked the two roving foot patrols and guided Boss Man and his small team toward the perimeter wire.

Ghost cut a two-foot square door in the wire with heavy-duty wire cutters pulled from his fanny pack. He wrenched back the section of fence while Jim, Peter, and Gary crawled through, then eased himself through the opening before putting the section of fence back into place.

Without taking his eye away from his night-vision scope, Coyote spoke into his throat mic. "You are still clear, Boss Man. Both patrols are on the far side of the buildings from your position. Estimate you have three minutes—maybe four— before one of the patrols clears the buildings."

"Roger." Before Jim moved, he scanned the guard towers for any sign of activity. None was visible. He motioned for the team to move forward. In a low crouch, the four men scurried to the near wall of the target building—the one that appeared to be associated with the generators. There was no telling if the electrical power provided from the generator was distributed to all of the buildings or only some, but Jim figured they had to start their search somewhere.

With backs pressed tight against the wall, Jim looked to his right. That was the direction to the door they had seen from atop the ridge. Jim moved deliberately to the corner of the building, taking great care with every footstep to ensure sound footing and avoid noise.

He reached the corner and slowly peered around it... no guards. In fact, other than the two roving patrols, the covert team hadn't observed anyone at all once night had fallen. Jim didn't understand the lack of people, but he was grateful nonetheless. Ghost, Peter, and Gary all pulled up tight behind him.

Jim slipped around the corner and up to the door. It was a standard industrial steel door, hinged on the outside. The door was designed to deter burglars with a protective steel strike plate over the door jam and hinge pins that were welded in place. Although the SGIT team had plenty of options for defeating the door, they would all result in enough noise to awaken the building's occupants.

An electronic card lock was mounted on the wall to the

right of the door, designed to accept a credit-card sized key. Pointing at the electronic lock, Jim made a series of hand gestures and Ghost retrieved a credit-card shaped item from his fanny pack. A ribbon of wires extended out of one end of the card; the other end of the wire ribbon was attached to a small PDA-like device.

Ghost inserted the card into the slot at the base of the electronic lock and then typed some commands on the small keyboard on his device. Two lights flickered red momentarily, and then turned green. At the same time there was a soft click of the lock opening. Jim pulled gently on the handle and opened the door.

Extending before him was a long hallway that appeared to run the length of the building. Above the door was a dim light, probably an exit sign but with no wording, just the light. Down both sides of the hallway, as far as they could see, were doors, each with a small window centered on the door at eye level. All of the doors were closed. The hallway was stark—no signage, no posters, just plain white walls.

At first, Jim only stuck his head in the opened doorway. He was checking for security cameras and motion detectors. Surprisingly, there were none. He entered first and the rest of the team quickly followed.

"This is odd…" Jim commented in a low whisper, speaking more to himself than to the rest of the team.

Seeing the confused look on Peter's face, Ghost translated. "We'd expect to find surveillance cameras, maybe motion detectors. It seems they're not too worried about someone breaking into this place."

Before Jim moved another step, he raised his H&K 416 rifle, tucking the butt stock up tight under his right arm. Ghost followed his commander's lead and did the same with his AA12 automatic shotgun.

They moved forward 20 feet to the first door; it was on the left side of the hallway. While the team stood to the side tight against the wall, Jim slowly peered in the small center window in the door. With his NVG set he could clearly see in the room even though no lights were on. No one was present.

Reaching down, he tested the door—it was locked. To the right was another card lock. Jim motioned for Ghost to use the electronic lock pick system. Since the computer automatically tried the last successful combination, this time it took even less time to open the lock. "Probably the same code," Ghost whispered.

The room was large, maybe 50 feet deep by 70 feet long and devoid of windows as well as other doors. This didn't surprise Jim or Ghost since none of the buildings had windows visible from the ridge. A tiny amount of light was emanating from banks of computers and other electronic equipment that ran the length of the room in four rows. A faint electronic whir punctuated by an occasional click penetrated the silence.

"What do you make of this Peter?" Jim asked.

Peter was still trying to take it all in. He recognized some powerful computers, not simple PCs, but small mainframes. Peter walked to a nearby console. There were two monitors, both off, and a keyboard with Kanji characters, not English. Peter continued his examination of the room as Ghost and Jim followed him with their gaze.

Silently, Gary slipped away and settled in at a computer console with a standard QWERTY keyboard as well as what he assumed was a Chinese keyboard. He turned on the monitor and was immediately greeted by a prompt. Gary guessed it was for a password to access the system although he couldn't read the foreign characters.

He removed a thumb drive from his ever-present PDA and leaned over, inserting the drive into one of three USB ports on the front of the CPU. A few seconds later another prompt appeared on the screen, this time in English. Gary entered a password and a simple command and then leaned back in the chair. Two minutes later the monitor flashed briefly and began rapidly scrolling through data, although it was all moving too quickly across the screen for Gary to understand what it was. He reached over and turned off the monitor.

Satisfied, Gary rose from his chair, removed his thumb drive from the USB port, and rejoined Ghost and Jim who were still gazing at Peter as he was systematically examining the electronic and computing equipment one row over.

"Here are dozens of lab books… all written in Chinese, Japanese, Korean… I can't tell." Peter sounded mildly frustrated.

He opened one of the notebooks and saw the date handwritten at the top of the page. "These are old entries. The optical scanner here is probably for archiving the data recorded by hand years ago. However, that's a very simple function and doesn't explain even a tiny amount of the computing power we have in this room."

"What would explain it?" asked Jim.

"I don't know," replied Peter. "Maybe modeling of complex chemical structures and reactivity, chemical and biological properties… that's very intensive and requires a lot of computing power."

"Okay, let's move on and try the next door, shall we?" Jim was impatient; he wanted answers, not vague speculation, and time was limited.

They exited the computer room and crossed the hallway. As Ghost was electronically picking the lock, the team heard a low moan echoing down the hall. It was faint but definite. This was followed by a grunting sound, louder but still not in the immediate vicinity.

"What the hell is that?" Jim whispered. He looked around,

and seeing no threat he entered the room as Ghost opened the door.

This room was almost as large as the computer lab, but it didn't contain banks of computers. What they all saw made them shudder.

"What the…" Gary mumbled.

The area resembled a medical operating room. Spaced out before them were three large stainless-steel tables. Surgical tools—large and small scalpels, bone saws, clamps, an odd assortment of probes—were neatly arrayed on a tray next to each table. Hanging next to each table was a scale connected to a large pan. The pungent odor of alcohol and formaldehyde tainted the air.

Covering one entire wall was a bank of large stainless steel drawers. "I'm guessing those are cold storage lockers," Peter suggested.

They walked to the bank of drawers and Peter opened the closest one. Empty. He opened the next; also empty. Jim had moved down the row and was checking drawers at the far end of the bank. All empty.

"So we have cold storage for bodies, and three operating tables." Jim was checking off the list of clues.

"This isn't an operating room; it's a dissection lab," Peter concluded. "I don't see any life support equipment. No oxygen stubs, no EKG or ventilators. Plus, there's that bank of cold storage drawers to keep the specimens fresh. Those hanging scales are for weighing organs."

Jim was turning slowly as he listened, visually taking in every detail.

"Medical experimentation… in the middle of nowhere. What are you up to Ming?" Jim asked rhetorically, his voice barely audible.

He focused, drawing his mind back to the present and

pushing away unsupported conjecture. He knew he needed to concentrate on facts. The more hard intel he could gather the better the odds that his team back at The Office in Sacramento would be able to piece together a complete picture.

"We need to know what records are kept here and why they need more computers than MIT has."

Gary had a smug expression as he moved three steps closer to Jim and Peter so he could be heard easily. "The files are being transferred even as we speak to my server back home."

Jim and Peter stared at Gary.

Gary nodded his head. "Really! The transfer shouldn't take long; they have a high-speed satellite link."

Jim glanced at Peter, then cleared his throat. "You're sure…"

"Oh yes. I loaded a little virus I carry on this thumb drive," and Gary removed the small memory device from his pocket, offering it as evidence. "It's a fairly standard hacker tool, but I've modified it—improved it over the years. Basically, the virus overrides the password protection and firewalls before executing a simple program that causes all files to be copied to my server.

"The transfer signal is bounced off at least six international ISPs, so tracing the destination is all but impossible. That's assuming they even discover that the files have been copied… highly unlikely. The virus deletes itself upon completion of the file transfer and resets system log time stamps to what they were prior to the payload hitting the system. Since it is also spoofing a network address, the additional network traffic won't show up on any logs."

"But there must be an enormous amount of data there," Peter challenged.

"Most of it is text, so it doesn't take up much space. Besides, I have terabytes of space available on my server. Even if I can't collect all the files, there will be enough to keep an army of analysts working for months."

"You did that when we were in the computer room?" Jim queried, still finding Gary's story hard to believe.

"Yeah. The three of you were off looking at the rows of computers and other electronic equipment. It was easy."

"I don't believe it," Jim said. "There wasn't enough time; we were only in that room for a few minutes."

Peter had been studying Gary, watching his expressions. "Oh, he did it all right," interjected Peter. Turning to Jim, Peter continued. "You shouldn't have doubted him back there on the ridge when you announced your plan to infiltrate this compound. Gary took it as a challenge. At least the way I'm keeping score, he's one point up on you." Peter and Gary were both smiling broadly now.

Jim scowled. "Whatever. So, if the files from that computing center have been copied over to your server, how can my team at The Office get a hold of them so they can start earning their pay?"

"Oh… that's easy," and Gary removed a business card from his wallet. On the front of the card was printed Gary's name, business and email address, and phone number. He flipped the card over and wrote a short string of letters and numbers on the reverse side, and then he handed the card to Jim.

"Have your analyst go to my web site; the address is on the front of the card. In the search query box at the top right of the home page tell them to type in this password. It's case sensitive. They will be granted access to everything on my server and can download it all."

Jim read the password: PytHoN.357mag.

"You're joking, right? Python dot 357 magnum is your password?"

"Why? Is it too obvious?"

Jim shook his head, "Oh, brother…"

CHAPTER 26

DARFUR
JUNE 14   0245 HOURS

IN THE COMMUNICATION CENTER, a Peoples Liberation army private was sitting in front of a console covered with an array of multicolor LEDs—red, green, yellow, white. At the moment he was reviewing the communications log for the previous day; one of his duties was to initial and date the paper log next to each communication entry.

Because the private was preoccupied with this task, it was several minutes before he noticed a blinking yellow light in the lower center portion of the console display. Actually, a dozen or more lights were seemingly randomly turning on and off, but this one light was important since it indicated an active satellite communication channel was open.

The private put down the logbook and focused on this open communication link. Immediately he thought it odd since no messages were scheduled to be sent until 7:00 a.m. Given the very early hour of the morning, it was extremely unlikely that anyone would be sending a routine status report or request for supplies; the majority of external communications were related to these two topics. Colonel Ming always handled the sensitive communications directly, or so he was told.

After staring at the blinking light for several more minutes, the young private finally decided he should call the officer of the watch. He picked up a telephone handset recessed into the console. There was no keypad because the phone only connected to the watch officer. It rang seven times before a very groggy voice answered.

"Yes?"

"Lieutenant Xu. This is Private Tao in communications. One of the satellite communications lines seems to be active."

"So? You woke me in the middle of the night just to tell me someone is sending out a message? I'll have you washing floors for the next month!"

Private Tao's voice raised an octave and he tried to control his mounting anxiety. "Sir! There are no communications scheduled until 0700 when the daily status report will be sent to Beijing."

"Private Tao. Did it ever occur to you that someone merely forgot to update your schedule log?"

"Yes, sir. But this is a very unusual activity. I rarely see satellite communications at 0250, sir. Procedure requires that I report that anomaly, sir!"

"Very well private. I will be there in ten minutes." Lieutenant Xu slammed down the phone. The loud bang carried through the connection just for a moment before the line went dead, leaving Private Tao with second thoughts about calling his watch officer in the middle of the night.

When Lieutenant Xu entered the communication center, Private Tao was already on his feet standing at attention. He raised his right hand in a salute, his forehead glistening from perspiration.

Xu ignored the military protocol and stopped inches from Private Tao. The two men were of equal height and Xu glared into Tao's eyes.

"Well, private?" said Xu in a voice that made it abundantly clear he was not at all amused.

Tao remained rigidly at attention, eyes locked forward. "Sir, the indicator light on the console... the channel has continued to be active since I reported to you." It was all Tao could do to complete his report without his voice cracking.

Lieutenant Xu turned his head and looked at the communication status board. There were many lights coming on and off, but the three yellow LEDs, each indicating a separate satellite communication channel, were off.

Xu slowly returned his glare to Private Tao. "And exactly which indicator light are you referring to, Private?"

"The active channel indicator..." Tao's voice fell off as he turned his head to the panel. All three indicator lights were dark.

"Sir! I swear! The left LED, channel one, was active! The light was illuminated when I reported the incident to you, sir!" Drops of sweat stung Private Tao's eyes as they ran down his face.

"I'll have you mopping floors and cleaning toilets for the remainder of your tour here, Private. Do you hear me!" Xu's anger was building. Among the enlisted men he had a reputation for a volatile temper.

Tao was desperate. He knew what he had seen, and he knew that reporting it was the correct procedure. But if he couldn't demonstrate these facts quickly, he would be punished for sure. His mind was turning in circles. No, wait... yes, maybe he could prove to Lieutenant Xu that the channel had, indeed, been open.

"Sir! The electronic log... if you check the log, it will prove that I am telling you the truth!"

Xu paused momentarily to consider the Private's suggestion. Yes, he would check the log—and when he saw that there had been no irregularities, he would have Private Tao brought up on charges of insubordination.

Without saying a word, Xu moved to an adjacent computer terminal and entered his password, gaining access to the communication event log. This log automatically recorded all incoming and outgoing communication activity, the channel, and the date and time of day. The log also recorded the source of all outgoing messages, whether from the communication center or from other computer terminals within the four main buildings of the compound.

Xu scrolled back in time 30 minutes; then started to advance the log record one minute at a time. Exactly as he thought—no activity on any of the three satellite channels. A mean sneer began to grow on Xu's face, and then he saw it. Exactly nineteen minutes ago, channel one became active—just as Private Tao had reported. Xu followed the log record forward in time, and exactly two minutes ago, the channel was closed. That would be right about the time he had arrived at the communication center.

So, Private Tao had been telling the truth. But why would someone send an unscheduled satellite communication at this early hour when nearly all the staff were asleep? What message could possibly take seventeen minutes to send? The satellite communications were state-of-the-art and could easily dispatch even the most lengthy status reports in a few seconds.

Xu looked again at the monitor. The message had originated from the science wing, in the computer lab—terminal five, to be exact. It took a moment to sink in, and then Lieutenant Xu realized something was very wrong.

"Get Lieutenant Li on the phone. Tell him to report here immediately!"

CHAPTER 27

DARFUR
JUNE 14   0300 HOURS

GHOST QUICKLY FASTENED several wire ties to bind the cut section of fence, masking the team's entry point. Without wasting a moment, the four men silently retreated from the perimeter fence, wanting to place as much distance between themselves and the compound as possible.

Peter and Gary were both visibly relieved to be outside again, but Jim looked as calm as usual. Peter guessed that he had probably done this a hundred times before.

With Ghost in the lead and Jim bringing up the rear, the team retraced the route they had taken from the ridge overlooking the compound less than two hours ago. The air was cool and refreshing, and the sky was brilliantly clear. The moon, although low on the horizon, cast enough light on the desert to see, but Jim and Ghost still donned their NVGs to make the navigation easier and the travel faster. Peter and Gary simply had to follow Ghost.

With at least some of the data files downloaded to Gary's

server, and a cursory examination of the computer and medical dissection labs conducted, Commander Nicolaou felt they had gathered sufficient intelligence to make a useful report.

Despite this success, deep inside he had an unshakable feeling of dread and primal fear while inside the compound. Whether it was the sights and smells of the medical lab, the unnatural groans they heard in the hallway, or something else, he wasn't sure. His instincts had told him it was time to cut and run—and he seldom failed to trust his instincts.

During the infiltration and exfiltration, no one had seen a single occupant of the compound. As odd as it seemed, the facility appeared to be well maintained by a staff of... what? Robots? Ghosts? No, he knew that people—ordinary people—staffed these buildings and did whatever it was that served the purpose of its existence.

Jim looked again at the business card Gary had given him—he needed to get his team working on this. It was important enough to risk using the com gear. "Bull. Get Lacey on the sat phone. Tell her we have a data dump. She needs to get the analysts working on it." Jim concluded the message with the web address and password Gary had written on his card.

With Ellen Lacey and her team of analysts working over the data files, answers would be forthcoming. But for now at least the mystery remained.

Colonel Ming was not pleased. The clock on the wall signaled the time was 3:30 a.m. Lieutenant Xu, Lieutenant Li, Sergeant Wong, and Private Tao were all gathered in the communication center.

"Lieutenant Li, assuming that somehow this facility has been breached and an unauthorized message was sent from the computer center, what is your tactical assessment?"

"Sir!" Li replied, standing stiffly at attention. "It would have to be a small team, perhaps only one or two skilled operators."

"And?" Ming prodded.

"Sir, if it was me, I would minimize my time within the facility. Given the current time, I would make certain to be well away from here before sunrise."

"Lieutenant, if you were leading this hypothetical band of marauders, where would you be based?"

Li was growing increasingly nervous. He did not like being the focus of Colonel Ming's attention. Even though the room was a cool 68 degrees, he felt himself becoming uncomfortably warm.

Li hesitated momentarily before answering. "The ridge, sir. It overlooks the compound providing an excellent vantage point to observe the activities here. The far side of the ridge is hidden from our view and provides protection from the afternoon sun.

"Sergeant Wong and I have scouted that area and there are several shallow caves on the far side of the ridge, near the crest, that would make excellent shelter. That is where I would base my operation."

Colonel Ming considered Li's words carefully. He was not a man to make rash decisions.

"Lieutenant Li. You will take a squad of twelve Homothals and find the tracks of the intruders, assuming there were intruders..." Ming cast a threatening glance at Private Tao. It would be on him if this proved to be a fruitless chase.

"Sergeant Wong; you will also lead a squad of twelve Homothals but I want you to work around the ridge, flank it. Make certain the Homothals are all given the standard dosage of phencyclidine." This was a common practice to enhance the natural aggression of the creatures as well as reduce their response to pain.

Both Li and Wong bowed, signifying their obedience.

"If there is a hostile military team there I want the two of you to bring back their commander for questioning. He will know something of this transmission, no doubt. The rest are to be killed. Am I clear?"

"Yes, sir!"

"And Lieutenant Xu, I want you to trace the communication signal. I want to know who received that message and, more importantly, what information was sent!" Having given his orders, Colonel Ming stormed out of the communication center.

CHAPTER 28

UNBEKNOWNST TO COMMANDER NICOLAOU and his small recon team, they were not alone on the desert sands. Lieutenant Li and his platoon of Homothals were trailing not far behind. In addition to being much stronger than the average human male, the Homothals possessed certain animal skills including ultra-keen senses—hearing, sight, smell—as well as an animal's instincts.

Many times Li had observed the Homothals during training maneuvers in the desolate Western Sudan desert. It was very common for a Homothal to freeze when he was being observed by an adversary. More often than not, Li never even knew they were under surveillance. It was just a sense that the Homothals had that alerted them to the fact they had, for that moment, become prey—not unlike any wild animal that Li had encountered.

Now, with only moonlight for illumination and barely a whisper of a breeze, Li trusted the Homothals—clad in standard desert camouflage and armed with state-of-the-art QBZ-95 assault rifles—to track the men who had infiltrated the computer center.

On the ridge, observing through spotting scopes, Homer and Coyote could see their small team returning from the compound. The two-man observation team was ensuring that their teammates were not being followed. So far, it looked encouraging; nobody had been seen leaving the compound in pursuit of Boss Man, Ghost, Peter, and Gary.

Then Homer caught just the briefest glimpse of movement maybe a hundred yards behind Jim. Anyone else would have dismissed it as imagination, but not Homer. He spoke softly into his throat mic. The communication was automatically scrambled making it nearly impossible that any eavesdropper could understand the message.

"Boss Man, you have company, maybe a hundred yards on your tail. Can't determine how many, just got a brief glimpse of movement."

"Roger. We're almost to the base of the ridge. Watch our back."

"Roger," Homer replied. He and Coyote were armed with the Barrett rifles; they could easily reach out and "touch" any adversary within a threatening range of the four-man reconnaissance team. But unbeknownst to Homer and Coyote, a second threat was approaching; one that would have fatal consequences.

The second platoon of Homothals, under the command of Sergeant Wong, followed a path further to the south of the position Homer and Coyote occupied. Using the terrain for cover, they moved quickly and without detection. Shortly,

Wong would have his Homothal strike force on the ridge far to the left of the two SGIT observers. With Li striking from the front and drawing the enemy's attention, Wong could approach very close on his enemy's flank without being seen. It would be a textbook maneuver, made possible because of the firsthand knowledge Li and Wong had of the landscape.

With Jim still in the rear and Ghost taking the lead, the recon team crested the ridge single file right in front of Homer and Coyote.

"Any further sight of our followers?" Jim asked, his voice barely audible.

"No sir, nothing. It's as if they vanished," replied Homer.

"I wouldn't bet on it. They had to know they were on our trail." Jim was keeping his voice low, and his men were gathered close around him. The group was huddled just over the crest of the ridge so they wouldn't be seen from any observers below—which meant that they could not see the approaching Homothals until they were only a few yards away.

Due to their superior hearing, the lead Homothal and three others zeroed in on Jim's location and silently converged on their target.

As soon as the SGIT team came into view in the dim light, the closest Homothal charged; a millisecond later, the other three did as well. The four creatures crossed the six yards separating them from their prey in only four short, powerful strides.

Instinctively both Homer and Coyote, who had been facing toward the charging Homothals, leveled their Barrett rifles and fired. The .50 caliber bullets each struck midsection in two of the Homothals, but it was as much the muzzle blast from the rifles as the bullets that threw the two creatures backwards into a lifeless heap.

Peter and Gary dove for the ground.

Jim and Ghost pivoted to face the attack. Ghost had the best angle on the two remaining Homothals and fired without hesitation. The two figures were within five feet as Ghost pulled the trigger of the AA12, the weapon set to full auto. It was a simple matter to nudge the muzzle left and right while discharging five rounds of 00 buck shot every second. Blood and bone fragments sprayed the air as the Homothals were cut down by the automatic shotgun.

The two Homothals crumpled at Ghost's feet. As he looked at them, seeing their features through his NVGs, he could see that they were odd in appearance, maybe deformed, but certainly not like any man he had ever seen. "What the hell?"

"Bull, Magnum! Get everyone! We need you up here on the ridge! Now!" yelled Nicolaou into his communication microphone. There was no point in being quiet any longer.

The high ground was always the best choice, and their camp, 30 yards or so below the ridge, would be a death trap.

The remaining SGIT soldiers quickly scrambled up to join Commander Nicolaou on the ridge crest. Ethan, Todd, and Hamaad were in close pursuit.

Still confident his team could win this skirmish, Jim shouted to Peter and Gary, who were hugging the ground, armed only with the pistols they took on the reconnaissance mission. "Fall back to the other civilians and guard the rear!" Without the training of the SGIT soldiers, Peter and his friends were unlikely to survive the close combat.

Then, using hand signals, Jim indicated for his team to spread out and take cover as best they could. Small rocks the size of a soccer ball became appealing protection. There simply was not much rock or terrain to offer shelter from bullets. But they could use the gross geography, the ridge itself. Whoever their assailants were, they were obviously attacking up the slope of the ridge. Certainly these were the pursuers that Homer had glimpsed.

Regardless of their number, they would have to expose themselves as they came up the ridge and approached the crest. The SGIT team had to get a bead on them first, as they were just coming into view.

Two minutes passed… and then five minutes, without any sign of further assailants. Nicolaou was beginning to think that the assault was over; that the attacking force had only been four men. He moved ever so slightly so he could see Ghost or Bull, whoever was closest.

That's when the bullet struck the rock that Jim's head was resting against. Instantly his entire team opened up in the direction the shot had been fired from. The muzzle flashes exposed his team's positions, and the fire was returned. As near as Jim could tell, there were at least four, maybe five or more, enemy soldiers engaging his team. They had spread out along the edge of the ridgeline, just below the crest. More could be below and Jim would not know until they joined the battle.

Homer and Coyote were using their Barrett rifles at close range, since that was all they had. This placed them at a disadvantage since the weapons only held ten rounds and they were not especially maneuverable in close quarters. The large .50 caliber rifle bullet, on the other hand, was fantastic at splitting even large boulders that the enemy was using for cover.

Jim was sure he had seen two enemy soldiers go down for good—solid hits—but the fire was not letting up. There must be reinforcements below that were filling up the line.

Peter and Gary had crawled to the rear of the fighting and joined up with Todd and Ethan; each had brought their recently issued rifles with them. Hamaad was there as well, AK-47 clutched in both hands and a machete strapped to his hip. In the rear, and slightly lower on the ridge, they could not see any targets to engage.

The SGIT soldiers were all using NVGs. Normally this would have given them an advantage in the dim moonlight, but their adversaries seemed to be able to see just fine. Jim didn't see goggles on any of the enemy, and yet they certainly showed no hesitation in maneuvering and they could quickly pick out their targets.

Two Homothals emerged from a boulder at the edge of the ridge and charged Jim's position. He easily took them down with a short burst from his assault rifle. At this close range it was hard to miss.

No sooner had Jim fired when another Homothal charged, this time toward the middle of the SGIT position. Ghost hit it with a load of 00 buck, and he saw the body shoved backward from the impact of the shot into its left shoulder. But then it regained its balance and continued charging. Ghost fired again, and the buckshot struck the creature in the belly—it continued charging.

Now only ten feet away from Ghost, the Homothal leveled its rifle and Ghost let loose five loads of shot that tore a hole through the Homothal's abdomen. The creature fell, but it still was not dead! It rolled to its side and began to raise its rifle at Ghost who had never seen anything like this before. Any of those hits would have killed a man. This thing... whatever it was... just wouldn't die!

Ghost aimed the AA12 and fired his last shot, hitting the creature in the head. It rolled over, motionless. Ghost ejected the spent drum and loaded a fresh one just in time to face a charge by three more Homothals. Homer and Coyote were doing as best they could with the heavy sniper rifles, but they simply weren't an effective weapon in this close-quarters gunfight.

Still, as long as he didn't run out of ammo, and as long as Boss Man, Bull, Homer, Coyote, and Magnum remained in the fight, Ghost figured they would come out on top. That was before the attack on their flank.

Given the distraction that the frontal assault had provided, it was easy for Sergeant Wong to split his team and maneuver to cover both the flank and rear of the besieged SGIT team. He watched as seven of Li's Homothals were killed. A loss, yes, but these creatures were serving their purpose. Wong felt no remorse over their destruction—he no longer saw them as men.

As the third wave of three Homothals charged the front of the line, Wong unleashed his attack on the left flank and rear.

CHAPTER 29

DARFUR

JUNE 14   0405 HOURS

THE MOON WAS LOW IN THE DARK early-morning sky, casting long shadows across the uneven terrain. The deep shadows made it easy for the Homothals to approach the flank and rear of the defenders position without being seen. The gunfire amply covered any incidental noise of their approach.

Fighters on both sides had become engrossed in the rapidly unfolding events. The group of six Homothals approaching from the rear were so focused on coordinating their attack on the enemy position that they failed to see Peter and his friends huddled beside two large boulders.

As the Homothals broke cover and sprinted toward the crest of the ridge, Hamaad opened up, firing his rifle on full auto until the magazine was empty. In the darkness it was impossible to determine if he hit any of his targets. The attackers continued charging up the slope—only now they knew where the defenders were.

Todd leveled the Barrett at the shadowy figures running

toward him. At the same time, Peter drew his Colt .45 pistol and began firing into the dark mass.

The muzzle flash from the discharge of weapons was like a strobe light briefly illuminating the darkness and rendering the subjects momentarily frozen in time and space.

Gary drew his Python and began firing, the smooth action of the revolver functioning as quickly as a semiautomatic pistol. Gary emptied the cylinder in two seconds and was sure he had dropped at least one, possibly two, assailants.

Ethan joined the fight with his Barrett rifle. He fired all ten rounds in the magazine in four seconds in a near panic. Then the rifle was empty. Neither Ethan nor Todd had brought extra ammunition when they hastily ran up the slope to join their friends. Now, without any ammunition, Ethan had a very heavy and expensive bludgeon.

Todd continued to fire deliberately as Gary and Peter reloaded. Hamaad had no spare ammunition, but he did have his machete.

The Homothals progressed relentlessly, returning fire with their rifles. The boulders were providing good shelter for Peter and his team, leaving the Homothals at a disadvantage. Since they were constantly climbing, they had no ready cover.

"I'm hitting them, but they aren't staying down!" Peter exclaimed.

"Maybe they're amped up on drugs?" Todd suggested, still believing these were ordinary soldiers. Then he poked his head and rifle around the edge of the boulder and fired, striking a Homothal in the chest. He watched for a brief moment as the figure fell backwards and struggled to its feet, slowly regaining momentum.

"Their bodies must be full of adrenaline!"

As Todd pulled back, Peter ventured to look through the gap between the boulders and saw two Homothals, one limping, trying to work around the boulders. They were only fifteen feet away, and Peter had a full magazine of seven rounds. He aimed and fired—the bullet clearly struck home, yet the Homothal barely registered being hit. Peter fired again at the same figure, and still the Homothal hardly showed any physical response from the impact of the bullet.

The two figures remained on track to flank the boulder and their position. Peter raised his sights and fired a third time, this time striking the Homothal in the head. It fell, dead. Quickly, Peter fired at the head of the second Homothal—the bullet struck low, in the neck. It howled in pain, sounding more like a wild animal than a man.

Peter shivered involuntarily. The howl caught Gary's attention, and he aimed for the wounded figure and placed a round through its forehead.

"That's four down," he said.

But there were still two Homothals charging up the hill, and they were quickly upon Peter's position. They rounded the boulder and faced Gary. At this angle, Todd was now at the rear of their position with Peter, Ethan, and Hamaad in between. Todd couldn't get a clear shot with his friends in the line of fire.

When the first Homothal emerged from behind the boulder, it was immediately upon Gary. Staring directly into the yellow-orange eyes of the creature, Gary reflexively pushed the muzzle of his pistol into the creature's belly and pulled the trigger.

The .357 magnum revolver roared and kicked back, raising Gary's hand. Yet the Homothal remained standing. Gary pulled the trigger again and there was nothing but a soft metallic click—the sound of the hammer falling on an empty cylinder.

The Homothal raised its rifle and struck Gary across the face with the butt, knocking him to the ground. His body lay motionless as blood flowed from his nose and mouth.

Rushing to Gary's defense, Hamaad pulled the machete from its sheath and lunged toward the Homothal that had struck his American friend. But the second Homothal, anticipating an attack, had moved to the side and fired a short burst. The rounds hit Hamaad in the chest; he was dead before his body hit the ground.

"No!" screamed Peter, a wave of rage washing over him as he watched Hamaad's chest shredded by the rifle fire. He raised his Colt pistol and fired rapidly, not really needing to aim at this close distance. There were only three rounds left in the magazine and all three hit the Homothal that had shot Hamaad. The creature stumbled backwards but stayed on its feet.

Peter drew his arm back in frustration and anger and threw the heavy pistol at the Homothal. The gun bounced off its chest.

Now it was the Homothal's turn. Sneering, it moved the barrel of the assault rifle toward Peter.

BOOM! The explosion was deafening, and Peter felt the muzzle blast from the Barrett rifle Todd had just fired from behind. The massive rifle bullet, traveling at almost 3,000 feet per second, shattered the Homothal's chest and propelled it backwards with its lifeless arms splayed out.

The Homothal that Gary had shot leapt forward despite its wounds, knocking Peter to the ground. Todd, who was eight feet behind Peter, tried to maneuver the long and heavy sniper rifle to get a shot into the attacking creature. But he couldn't move the muzzle of the rifle quickly enough. He fired, but he immediately knew the round had missed. Adjusting, Todd pulled the trigger again, only now the magazine was empty.

The Homothal barreled into Todd, knocking the rifle from his grip. Todd remained on his feet and swung his right arm, planting a solid blow into the Homothal's face. It merely shook its head lightly. The Homothal, still gripping its own rifle, swung the butt up to catch Todd in the chin. The blow lifted him off his feet and sent him sprawling to the ground. The Homothal raised its rifle, intending to bash in Todd's skull.

Ethan hadn't attracted any attention since he wasn't shooting—his rifle was empty. He was behind the Homothal as it stood over Todd's prone body. Using the only weapon he had, Ethan gripped his rifle by the barrel and swung it like a bat with all his might, striking the Homothal across the shoulder, causing it to drop the Chinese-made assault rifle. The scope on the Barrett shattered from the impact, but the Homothal remained upright. Slowly the creature turned to face Ethan— the yellow-orange eyes boring into him.

Ethan recognized those eyes. He had glimpsed them back at the aid camp when they were under attack. Driven by an instinctive fear more powerful than the urge to fight, Ethan slowly moved one foot back, wanting to distance himself from this demonic creature.

The Homothal took one step toward Ethan and swatted away the rifle-club. Ethan backed up slowly, fear replaced by panic. He stumbled and fell. The Homothal reached down placing a large hairy hand around Ethan's throat. The fingers squeezed, digging into his neck and threatening to rupture his trachea.

The Homothal lifted Ethan by the throat using only one hand—squeezing the life from his young body. Ethan couldn't breathe. He was desperately trying to break the grip and free himself. Tugging and clawing at the iron hand wrapped around his neck, feet dangling off the ground, he couldn't loosen the vise-like grip. His vision began to fade, growing dim around the edge—he knew he was passing out and would soon die. The Homothal pulled Ethan closer—they were almost touching, face to face. Ethan thought his last sensation in life would be the creature's foul, dank breath.

Only yards away, Peter shook the cobwebs from his head

and saw the Homothal strangling his son. Grabbing his hunting knife from the sheath at his hip, he pushed himself to his feet and lunged for the Homothal. The blade plunged deep into the Homothal's lower back. This time it screamed in pain and dropped Ethan.

Peter retracted the knife and drew his arm back to thrust the blade into the creature again. It twisted and swung back with its elbow, catching Peter in the jaw.

The blow knocked Peter to the ground, but the knife was still firmly in his grip. He got up and charged the Homothal only to have the blow deflected. Peter recovered his balance and stood facing the beast. He noticed the eyes and dense hair on the exposed arms and face. He also noticed the relatively large head with shallow sloping forehead. The limbs were extremely muscular, giving it an overall appearance of being rather short and heavy, even though Peter estimated it must have been six feet tall—as tall as himself.

Peter lunged forward again and attempted to stab the Homothal. But he wasn't trained in hand-to-hand combat and his adversary was. The Homothal parried the thrust and grabbed Peter's arm, twisting and bending the limb until Peter was forced to drop the knife. Then the creature wrapped a huge arm around Peter's throat, squeezing and threatening to crush his windpipe. He found it impossible to breath.

Ethan had regained his awareness in time to see his father in a strangle hold. He picked up a grapefruit-sized rock and slammed it into the Homothal's head from behind. The creature dropped Peter and turned to face the new threat. It slammed a fist into Ethan's face, spraying blood and saliva. In rapid succession, the Homothal swung again and again, each blow landing hard on Ethan's face. The tissue around his eyes was cut and bruised from the hammering. Rather than kill cleanly, the Homothal was playing with this victim—trying to slowly crush the skull using only its own brute strength.

Ethan staggered. He could hardly see—his eyes were so badly swollen—and his head felt like someone was hammering a steel wedge into it; every blow another strike to the wedge as excruciating, sharp pain blasted his skull.

Peter was trying to regain his breath. He was on the verge of blacking out, but he was sure he could see Ethan being pummeled by the Homothal. Gary and Todd were lying motionless, either dead or unconscious—he had no way of knowing.

Seeing his son suffering at the hands of the Homothal, fired a final dose of adrenaline through Peter. He slowly struggled to his feet, barely able to hold his balance. He took two steps toward the Homothal and as much fell into the beast as tackled it. The attack was weak and without effect. The creature brushed Peter off like an insect and viciously kicked him in the head and chest until Peter no longer moved.

"Dad!" cried Ethan as he struck the Homothal in the back, trying to make it stop.

It worked, and the Homothal turned its attention back to Ethan.

The Homothal considered its prey and took a moment to savor the pleasure of killing. Yes, one more blow and the skull would crack like an egg. The creature drew back its right arm and rammed it forward, landing firmly on Ethan's cheek bone. The Homothal smiled at the sound of breaking bone. The boy's limp body fell to the ground.

CHAPTER 30

"FALL BACK!" ordered Commander Nicolaou.

One by one, Coyote, Homer, Magnum, Bull and Ghost all made a hasty retreat. Using cover wherever possible and firing to provide protection for their comrades, the SGIT team found itself moving off the ridge crest and back down toward their temporary campsite.

The Homothals made a final rush on the SGIT position, overtaking them in seconds. As the combatants merged, it was impossible to reload weapons—the fighting devolved to vicious hand-to-hand combat. In the frenzied brawl, pistols were drawn and fired at point blank range. Rifles became clubs to be replaced by knives.

The superior strength of the Homothals was proving a decisive advantage. Jim's team was steadily pushed down off the ridge toward the position near the two boulders that Peter and his friends had occupied.

Jim had his Beretta 9mm pistol in hand, rifle slung across

his back, favoring the pistol's maneuverability in the tangled and confusing battle. He fired at any Homothal offering a clear target. The bullets still had little effect, and at first Jim thought that maybe the soldiers were wearing body armor. But as the fighting became more personal, he could see blood oozing from the bullet wounds. The enemy fighters were not registering shock or pain, and they were very difficult to kill.

Bull and Ghost both held tightly to their AA12 automatic shotguns, alternately using them as a bludgeon or firearm. It was taking half a dozen rounds of 00 buckshot to kill each Homothal; they were chewing up their ammunition fast—too fast.

Magnum and Coyote were providing cover fire as Jim retreated closer to the two boulders, expecting to find Peter there. He clearly saw the boulders and wondered why the civilians were not providing cover fire as well. Then he saw the Homothal.

It was punching Ethan violently. How Ethan could still be standing was beyond Jim's comprehension. He saw Peter stagger to his feet and try to tackle the Homothal, only to be knocked down and kicked viciously.

Jim was 40 yards away as the Homothal raised its rifle, preparing to smash Ethan's head where he now lay motionless on the ground. He knew he couldn't reach the monster in time to stop its murderous rampage, so Jim raised his Beretta and fired. The bullet dug deep into the creature's shoulder—it hesitated for a moment, turning to look at the man who had shot it.

Again Jim fired... and again and again. Each time the bullet struck home, but still the beast stood over Ethan, rifle raised. Again and again the Beretta erupted, the bullets hitting the Homothal in the back and shoulder. Jim was shooting and running to close the distance to Ethan.

The Homothal, only five yards away now, looked at Jim defiantly. Staring into the blood-thirsty yellow eyes, Jim saw nothing but death in this thing. He raised his pistol and fired his last round into the creature's forehead, finally killing it, as the slide of his pistol clanged open.

Without pausing, Jim dropped the empty magazine and slammed home a full one. Rushing up to Ethan, Jim saw a badly swollen and bruised face; blood oozed from both ears as well as his nose. Mercifully, Ethan was unconscious. "Bull!" he yelled.

Bull was trying to extract himself from the close-quarters combat as were his fellow SGIT soldiers. His AA12 empty, Bull was swinging it like a truncheon to fend off the attackers. He slammed the butt stock into the skull of a charging Homothal— the blow would have killed a man. The creature barely paused before swinging its rifle, connecting with Bull's stomach. He rolled backward, absorbing the blow.

Two more Homothals broke away from the hand-to-hand fighting and headed towards the twin boulders where Jim was alone with his injured friends. Bull rolled and started to rise to his feet; he needed to help his commander. Suddenly the Homothal he had clubbed—ineffectively—was upon him again, smashing a rock-hard fist into his back. Bull went down onto one knee.

Again Bull started to rise, but the Homothal struck him once more, driving him down. Bull gasped from the sharp pain radiating the length of his spine; he knew his body couldn't absorb this beating for long. The beast kicked Bull in the ribs, rolling him over onto his back. Then the Homothal raised its booted foot, preparing to slam it down on Bull's chest.

As Bull rolled to avoid the blow, he pulled his combat knife. The behemoth closed the distance and swung a downward punch connecting with Bull's cheek. Somehow he absorbed the blow, and while the Homothal was off balance, Bull thrust the knife forward and upward into the Homothal's abdomen.

The face of the Homothal was so coarse and grotesque in appearance that it was hard to see any emotion in it at all. But with his hand still firmly gripping the handle of the combat knife, Bull swore he saw surprise register in the creature's eyes.

The creature recovered and raised its fist, preparing to strike down on Bull. But Bull was not about to let go. He twisted the knife and then thrust down, violently slashing from the belly to the pelvic bone, eviscerating the beast. Intestines and blood spilled from the massive wound. The Homothal bellowed in agony as Bull slashed the knife to the side, enlarging the wound even further. The monster teetered on its feet for a moment before its legs buckled and it collapsed to the ground.

Bull stood with his knife still in hand. He had to get to Boss Man. He picked up his empty AA12 and looked back to the fighting in time to see Magnum level his rifle and take out a Homothal with a short burst of automatic fire. As he swung his head back toward the twin boulders, Bull caught a glimpse of two uniformed men—not Homothals—standing to the side of the battle. *What are they doing?* Not taking time to think about it further, he rose and began running to Boss Man—the two beasts were almost to the boulders.

Jim was ready. As the two savage creatures converged on his position, he holstered the Beretta and unslung the H&K rifle from his back. Verifying a clear line of fire, he dropped to one knee and fired the H&K in controlled three round bursts.

The behemoths returned fire, stopping each time to shoot. They had closed to within 50 yards of Jim, and with so little separation Jim could hardly miss. Yet each Homothal absorbed two bursts of rifle fire—Jim was certain that all the bullets had impacted their torsos—when they both finally dropped dead.

The odd appearance of these things combined with their extreme insensitivity to bodily trauma was something that he would need to report back to Ellen Lacey and the team at The Office. *Maybe we can collect some blood and tissue samples.* His mind continued to function analytically while still not comprehending how bad the fight was going—not anticipating how much worse it was about to get.

"Bull!" Jim shouted again, trying to be heard above the roar of battle.

Two seconds later Bull ran up, short of breath. He had taken a tremendous beating; at least a couple ribs were probably broken. Each breath was labored, punctuated by sharp, stabbing pain.

Bull immediately took in the situation. Ethan was nearest and obviously in serious condition. Bull pressed two fingers against Ethan's carotid artery to make sure he had a pulse. It was barely discernible.

He produced a small penlight and gently lifted Ethan's eyelids when the examination was cut short.

"No time, we've got to get off this ridge and establish a defensive position."

"I've got to get this kid stabilized. He's likely got a concussion and possibly a fractured skull."

"You've got three more patients, too. I don't know what condition Peter, Todd, and Gary are in—but at least they're alive. Hamaad is dead."

Bull looked at Jim, "What the hell happened?"

"There are two dead…" Jim struggled for a word to describe their enemy. They certainly were not men. "…whatever the hell they are, there are two lying over there," he pointed toward the boulders. "I think our friends here saved our bacon by engaging a second squad angling to attack our rear. If they hadn't done so, we'd probably all be dead right now."

Bull persisted. Even with just a quick assessment he knew the injuries were serious "These men are suffering multiple traumas; lacerations, bruising, possible internal bleeding, possible concussion, and possible broken bones. We've got to get them off this ridge and into decent medical care or we're gonna lose some—maybe all—of them."

Jim maintained his vigil while listening to Bull's status report. He glanced briefly at Bull and saw the worry etched in the medic's face.

"We have a bigger problem. Those freakish Sasquatch things are about to overrun our position. We're spread too thin already."

Bull knew his commander was right. They couldn't spare the manpower to get Peter, Todd, Gary and Ethan to a safe location.

"All right," Jim said. "Here's what we're gonna do. I'll join Coyote and we'll split to the right, drawing off some of the fire. Ghost, Magnum, and Homer will pull back—if those hairy bastards pursue we'll flank 'em."

Bull nodded. "You and Coyote will draw fire to allow our guys to retreat and form up on my position here."

"That's the plan. Then you get these men off the ridge and down to the camp ASAP."

"You and Coyote can't hold them off for long; they're gonna break through," Bull protested.

"We're going to buy time. After you get to camp, your job is to stabilize and treat the wounded. That will leave Ghost, Homer, and Magnum to prep the Dillon for action. I want it in position with a second box of ammo. Put Magnum on the Dillon, got it? I want it ready to rock and roll in five minutes."

Each box of ammunition for the Dillon Gatling gun contained 4,400 rounds of ammunition. That would buy them a couple minutes at most with the Dillon capable of chewing through ammunition at the rate of 3,000 shots per minute.

"Give your shotgun to Homer and tell him and Ghost to

load up with frags, got it? Between the minigun and explosive rounds for the shotguns, we'll turn the tide to our side."

"I like the sound of that."

"We'll hold them off long enough for you to get set. When we come running down the ridge to the camp, I want you guys to smoke all of 'em. Got it? Cut them down with everything you got and don't stop shooting until every last one of the mutant mothers is either down and dead or you're out of ammo!"

Bull was still nodding as Jim rose to his feet and sprinted back into the battle.

CHAPTER 31

FOR THE FIRST TIME since the battle started, Jim knew his team was at risk of being wiped out. There was no backup to call in, no air support, and they were losing ground to the enemy. Seeing Hamaad dead and the other civilians seriously wounded shocked Jim into a new reality—they had to retreat and regroup.

Jim was issuing orders over the squad net as he was running toward the fight. He stopped every dozen steps to fire well-aimed shots at the enemy

"Coyote. I'm coming up… 30 yards to your right. Pull back to my position and find some cover. Ghost, Homer, Magnum… give Coyote covering fire."

"Roger that."

The Homothals didn't give ground easily, and Jim was constantly cutting left and right, occasionally diving for the ground to avoid being hit by return fire.

"What's the plan, Boss Man?" Homer asked, his voice

coming in loud and clear through the miniature speaker in Jim's ear.

"We'll draw most of their fire and the three of you are to retreat to the big boulders where Bull is. We've got four wounded, one KIA. Pull back to the camp. Bull knows the plan." The entire SGIT team heard the order, and they struggled to extract themselves from the fighting.

Jim took the last fifteen strides to a rock out-cropping as fast as he could. The rock projected two feet above the surrounding dirt and formed a shallow vee. Each leg of the vee was six to eight feet long, and Jim reasoned this would be the best defensive position for he and Coyote to make a stand. Moments later Coyote slid behind the rock next to his commander.

"What's the situation?" Coyote asked.

"I caught movement over there." Jim motioned discretely with his hand. "I think there are at least four; they're using the terrain and shadows to mask their movement."

All of Jim's team had slipped off their NVGs once the enemy merged on their position and the hand-to-hand combat commenced. Even now, Jim opted not to put the goggles back on since an attack could materialize from almost any direction.

Coyote strained to see any enemy combatants. "That's where me and Homer saw two men in uniform. Maybe the platoon leader?"

"I'd like to get my hands on one of them," Jim said.

"With all due respect, sir, they aren't showing any signs of giving up. And we're getting pretty low on ammo."

"Understood. We only need to hold them off for five minutes. Then we're going to high tail it back down off this ridge and lead our friends here to a surprise back at camp."

Coyote's grin was cut short by a bullet strike against the rock near his head. "Something tells me that five minutes is going to seem like hours."

Jim quickly fired off three shots just to keep the aggressors at bay. "Just stay down. As long as we keep them pinned down the rest of the team can fall back; we have nothing to worry about."

Commander Nicolaou could not have been more mistaken. Lieutenant Li and Sergeant Wong rallied the remaining five Homothals and were preparing to charge the rock behind which lay Coyote and Boss Man.

"They are running out of ammunition," Lieutenant Li surmised. "That is why only two men have remained behind."

"We can rush their position," Sergeant Wong suggested.

Li nodded in agreement. "Colonel Ming ordered that we bring back prisoners. We will split our force. Send two Homothals to flank the left and two to flank the right. That will both draw and split their fire. Then you and I and the remaining Homothal will charge up the front.

"Make certain the Homothals understand; we want to take these men alive."

"Yes, sir," replied Sergeant Wong.

To avoid being seen, the two Homothal teams pulled back from their commanders and split so they could flank their enemy's position. They stayed well behind the protective ridge lip and circled 50 yards before cautiously crawling to the crest of the ridge. There, both teams observed the remaining enemy occasionally firing single shots at the location they had left only moments before.

The four Homothals rushed towards Boss Man and Coyote, brandishing their automatic rifles, firing at the enemy but deliberately missing. This was a calculated maneuver to draw fire away from Lieutenant Li, Sergeant Wong and the remaining Homothal—and it worked.

"Shit!" exclaimed Coyote as he turned to his right to face the two Homothals bearing down on his position. He fired two quick shots from the Barrett, but both missed their mark. Adjusting his position, he aimed again and fired. The bolt remained open as the last spent casing was ejected from the rifle. This time, the massive bullet struck home, smashing into the left upper arm of the furthest Homothal. The impact was marked by a spray of blood and tissue, and the arm dangled limp, held in place by only two strips of tendon and skin. Unabated, the creature continued charging forward, holding its rifle in the right hand and firing continuously.

Jim turned his attention to the left flank; two Homothals suddenly appeared less than a hundred yards away. They moved at blinding speed across the uneven rocky terrain. He admired their strength and endurance, even as he hated their machine-like drive.

Firing single shots to conserve his limited ammo, Boss Man was finding it very hard to connect with the Homothals as they randomly darted left and right, steadily closing the gap. Yet as they drew closer, they also became easier to hit.

Coyote abandoned his empty rifle and was drawing his Beretta when the closest Homothal, only seven yards away launched itself into the air and pounced on Coyote. Landing heavily, the Homothal knocked the gun out of Coyote's hand and brought the butt of its rifle crashing down onto Coyote's nose and cheek.

Jim heard the sickly crunch of cartilage and bone breaking.

Turning, he fired a short burst at point blank range into the Homothal's chest. It stumbled backwards and tried to raise its weapon. Jim pulled the trigger again; the magazine was empty. In a rage, he swung the rifle at the beast, the full force landing squarely across mouth and nose. The pain was intense, and the Homothal dropped its weapon, raising both hands to its face before it fell backwards and died, never uttering a sound.

Jim was immediately overwhelmed by the two Homothals charging the left flank. He swung wildly to free himself from the grip of one of the monsters. Then he kicked viciously at the second creature's groin, his boot making solid contact. This gave him the two seconds needed to pull his side arm from the holster on his thigh. He fired repeatedly at the Homothal he had just kicked. It took four rounds before the savage brute finally went down.

As Jim turned, the other Homothal was on him again, angling to get its thick muscular arm around Jim's neck. Struggling to free himself, yet not willing to lose his grip on his pistol, Jim slammed backwards with his elbow. He felt a solid hit to the rib cage, but to no effect. In desperation, he aimed the pistol down behind his own leg, hoping he could hit the foot or leg of his attacker. He fired… no reaction. Again he fired, this time with effect. The bullet must have hit something and the Homothal loosened its iron grip around Jim's neck, allowing him to break the chokehold.

Jim rounded on the Homothal with a sweeping kick, knocking it to the ground. He raised the pistol to finish the job, but before he could pull the trigger a massive weight slammed into his shoulders, propelling him into the ground. Jim tried to get to his feet, but was halted by a punishing blow between his shoulder blades. He realized the pistol was no longer in his grasp.

Another blow landed on his back, knocking the air from his lungs. If this beating continued much longer, his spine would fracture.

As suddenly as it began, the pounding ceased. Jim forced air into his lungs and became conscious of a voice… not English… maybe Chinese or Korean. He wasn't sure. He felt a strong grip under his arms lift him from the ground and pull his face from the sandy dirt.

Standing now, he faced a uniformed man.

"I am Lieutenant Li and this is Sergeant Wong," the man said in reasonable English.

"You are our prisoner. You will come with me. If you resist, my soldiers will kill you. Is that understood?"

Jim looked at the two men's faces and then at the three Homothals surrounding him—one with an arm nearly shot off, blood dripping off its limp fingers. Slowly he nodded agreement.

Pointing toward Coyote's motionless body, Jim said, "This man needs medical attention."

Li looked toward the nearest Homothal, standing next to Coyote's prone body. Using only the most subtle expression of his eyes, Li communicated his order. The Homothal lowered the muzzle of its rifle and fired a single bullet into Coyote's head.

Jim spun with lightning speed and threw his body into the Homothal that had fired the shot. The two fell to the ground, Jim on top and pounding the monster's face to a bloody pulp.

Quickly the other two Homothals restrained Jim's arms and hauled him to his feet.

"You son of a bitch! You murdered him! He was out of action and you knew that!"

"We are engaged in combat... surely *you* knew that."

"He was no threat!"

"Silence!" screamed Li.

Jim felt the anger boiling inside. Yet he also knew he must restrain his fury. For now he would wait, and he drew strength from the certain knowledge that when the opportunity presented itself, he would avenge Coyote's murder.

"Now... we will return to my base where we will question you. If you resist in any way, we will kill you. Do I make myself clear?"

"Abundantly." The sarcasm in Jim's voice was unmistakable, despite the language barriers.

CHAPTER 32

JIM RECOGNIZED THE MEDICAL DISSECTION LAB. He was standing with his arms held in place behind his back by the two uninjured Homothals who had captured him less than an hour ago.

The wounded Homothal had bled to death on the march back down from the ridge. The creature collapsed beside the trail, and no one even paused to consider recovering its body—leaving it instead for desert scavengers to consume.

Minutes after Jim was escorted into the dissection lab, a senior officer entered. His uniform was Chinese army, sharply pressed, and his rank signified colonel. Lieutenant Li engaged in a conversation with the ranking officer, and it was clear to Jim that the Colonel was not happy with the Lieutenant.

Abruptly the conversation stopped, and the Colonel moved close to square his body directly in front of Jim.

"Who are you?" he asked, his English heavily accented but understandable.

"I am Commander James Nicolaou of the Strategic Global Intervention Team." Ming had already noticed the SGIT insignia patch on the left shoulder of Jim's uniform and the American flag on the right shoulder.

The Colonel nodded. "I am not familiar with your organization; perhaps we will have time to discuss that later. But first, you will tell me what business you have here."

Jim glared intently at the Colonel but didn't answer.

"I asked you a question, Commander. What is the nature of your business here?"

"I heard you," Jim responded. He continued staring at the Colonel. Then it came to him, he had seen this face before, only it was the face of a much younger man.

"You're Colonel Ming, aren't you?"

Colonel Ming was surprised to be recognized.

"Yes, I thought so," Jim continued. "It took me a minute… the photo I saw must have been taken fifteen, maybe eighteen years ago. But it is you."

Ming considered Jim, weighing his thoughts and formulating his reply. "Yes, I am Ming. I command this research facility."

"What heinous experiments are you up to this time, Ming?" Jim demanded.

Sergeant Wong immediately punched Jim in the stomach, causing him to double over in pain. "You will speak respectfully to Colonel Ming!"

"Sure, whatever you say Charlie." Jim was gasping for breath. He slowly righted himself.

"I am asking the questions here, Commander. You would be wise to remember that. Please explain what you were doing inside my facility."

"Had I known you were in charge of this chamber of horrors, I wouldn't have bothered investigating. I would have simply radioed in an air strike and enjoyed a good night's sleep."

"I grow weary with your arrogance, Commander Nicolaou." Ming nodded to one of the Homothals. A knife appeared from nowhere and the creature pressed it against Jim's throat, drawing a narrow crimson line of blood.

Jim pursed his lips.

"Commander, I know you infiltrated my facility. You also sent a message—a rather lengthy message—to someone. Who? Associates of yours? The Pentagon?"

Jim remained silent. The knife pressed harder against his throat and the trickle of blood increased.

"I can trace the message Commander. My technicians have already begun the process. It takes time, though… time that I'd rather not invest. So, you will tell me. Who did you communicate with?"

"Why should I help you?"

Ming's mouth drew wide in a smile that was not reflected in his eyes; they remained cold and hard. "Because I will kill you if you don't answer my questions truthfully."

"You'll kill me whether I answer your questions or not."

Ming glanced at Lieutenant Li as the smile slowly faded from his face. He turned back to face Jim. "Yes, I suppose you are right." He folded his arms across his chest. "But how you die should be of interest, don't you think?"

Jim swallowed despite the knife pressing into the flesh of his throat. He had been in tight spots before, but this was new. He had been stripped of his weapons and was being held by super-human creatures.

"What if I do answer your questions?" Jim asked, buying time.

"Your demise will be swift and relatively painless." Colonel Ming glanced at the Homothal and the knife dug, ever so slightly, deeper into Jim's throat, causing Jim to wince.

"Dead is dead. I don't see any real benefit to helping you."

"Ah. But that is where you are mistaken. See, I can just as easily turn you over to my soldiers whom you have already met on the battlefield. You have seen their animal behavior. Trust me; they are not handicapped by a conscience, as are most men."

It was working; Ming was beginning to open up.

"Whatever these things are," said Jim, "they're not men."

"Yes! Do you realize how correct your statement is? These creations are the result of decades of brilliant work!" Ming's eyes widened with excitement.

"You're delusional," Jim taunted.

"Delusional? You have no idea. My soldiers—we call them Homothals—are my creation, and mine alone! No one can achieve what I have accomplished."

"Really? These things are nothing more than a grotesque deformity. A circus sideshow—freaks—that's all."

Ming leaned forward and shouted at Jim, spraying spittle in his face. "I have created a new species! A new life form!"

Colonel Ming turned in a circle, collecting his thoughts. When he turned to face Jim again, the fire that lit his eyes only moments earlier had dissipated.

"I have gathered ancient DNA from a mummified Neanderthal body found near Gibraltar. Just tiny amounts that were later multiplied ten-million times in *my* lab. Once I had sufficient quantities of Neanderthal DNA, I transferred that genetic material into the cellular structure of common viruses, seeking just the right host."

A flicker of curiosity attenuated with concern flashed across Jim's face, and Ming noticed.

"We tried a great many viruses with years of trial and error before finally finding the right one."

Jim swallowed. He fought a growing fear of what Ming was

about to reveal next.

"We injected it into human test subjects and transformed them." Then he laughed, hard and long.

"You see, Commander... my soldiers... are not men. They are a previously unknown species! A genetic hybrid between Homo sapiens and Homo neanderthalensis. What Nature could not achieve, I have done!"

Disgusted and horrified, Jim was reminded of Mary Shelley's novel. "You're as mad as Dr. Frankenstein."

"I am a genius, the likes of which the world has never known."

Jim narrowed his eyes, already thinking ahead and trying to understand Ming's motive, and goals.

"Why... why do this? Last I heard the Chinese army wasn't suffering a lack of recruits."

"You stupid little man. This has nothing to do with the PLA. I used them to fund my research. But I had other plans."

"It doesn't matter if your Homothals are tough; they still die when shot. And Americans never run out of bullets. That's something even you should know."

"You think small. This is not about simply engineering a superior warrior, although that I have accomplished." He flashed another disingenuous smile.

Jim thought for a moment, but it still didn't make sense. He had to keep Ming talking. He'd try a different angle.

"You don't know who I work for, do you?"

Ming lifted an eyebrow at Jim, and flicked his fingers. The Homothal slackened the pressure on the knife at Jim's throat.

Jim pushed further, trying to trigger doubt and paranoia in Ming's mind. "China and the U.S. are no longer the rivals we once were. I could be assisting the PLA."

"Are you?" Ming asked, directly to the point.

Jim ignored the question.

"So what's your angle Ming? Are you planning to advertise in *Soldier of Fortune* magazine that you're selling super mercenaries to the highest bidder? I have to admit it... you do have a polished sales pitch, and I wouldn't be surprised if there are a half dozen or so dictators scattered across the world who would pay very well for these Homothals. Is that why you are here in Sudan? Working out a deal with the madmen in Khartoum? Are you merely a capitalist at heart?"

"You Americans... you can't grasp the real opportunity."

"I have to give you credit, Ming. It sounds like a good plan to me. What do you figure to net... a hundred million, maybe a hundred fifty million dollars before your freaks are exterminated?"

"Who did you send that message to, Commander Nicolaou?"

Jim didn't answer.

"If you do not tell me what I want to know you will suffer a most horrible death, I can assure you."

"I'm dead either way."

Ming stared into Jim's eyes for a long minute and found the answer he was looking for. The Commander was not going to reveal where he sent the transmission.

Colonel Ming sighed, and his shoulders drooped ever so slightly. "You are a determined man, Commander—a determined, foolish man. The Homothals are more like a wild pack of wolves than they are men. I have seen them tear a weaker comrade limb to limb and then devour the flesh while the muscles were still twitching. They show a preference for fresh meat, even though we have tried to grow them accustomed to prepared food.

"Still, sometimes we allow them the pleasure of hunting a few... primates, shall we say? They seem to enjoy... *playing* with their food. I think you know what I mean... yes? It helps to keep them excited about going into battle against the rebel factions in this wasteland."

"Is that what you call half-starved refugees—primates? You're a sick bastard, Ming." This time Wong slammed the butt of his assault rifle into Jim's stomach. As he doubled over, the Homothal pulled back the knife to avoid cutting through his carotid artery.

Ming chuckled. "They are worthless, a blight on human kind. No one really cares about them. The U.N. and Western countries don't even try to stop us. What has your country done, hmm? Americans spout strong words, but there is no conviction behind those words. I can kill as many refugees as I wish, yet no one even tries to stop me. No one cares what happens in Africa."

"You think the genocide in Darfur has gone unnoticed?" Jim rasped out after catching his breath again.

"And exactly what has the U.S. or Europe done?"

Jim locked eyes with Ming. "I *am* going to kill you, Ming." His voice was solid, confident, authoritative. The way the words were spoken, the message cut through Ming's ego, bringing him to a pause. Should he fear this man before him?

"I shall learn who you sent the communication to when we complete the satellite signal trace. Goodbye, Commander," Ming said, dismissing Jim.

He then turned to Lieutenant Li, who was silently awaiting his orders. "Lieutenant Li. How hungry would you say our Homothals are?"

CHAPTER 33

HOMER MANNED THE DILLON MINIGUN. With a full ammunition box fed into the weapon system, he was ready for the expected charge. Ghost, Bull, and Magnum spread out and took up supporting defensive positions with overlapping fields of fire.

Bull had stabilized Ethan—he suffered a serious concussion accompanied by bruises and lacerations to his face. Both eyes were nearly swollen shut. He was still unconscious and Bull kept him heavily medicated to ease the pain. Without an X-ray, Bull could not be sure if Ethan had one or more broken facial bones.

The rest of the new recruits fared better. Todd and Gary had been knocked out, and Todd was short two teeth from the upward blow to his chin. Peter had taken a serious beating but managed to get away with only bruises to his ribs, throat, and face. Still, Bull had to use smelling salts to bring him completely around.

"Something don't seem right." Bull mumbled to no one in particular. The shooting up on the ridge had ended abruptly almost fifteen minutes ago—plenty of time for Boss Man and Coyote to rejoin the team.

Bull moved close to Homer. "We're going up to see what the hell is keeping Boss Man and Coyote. They should have been here by now."

Speaking into his throat mic, Bull explained the ad hoc plan to Ghost and Magnum. "Keep a sharp eye out and be ready for another flanking maneuver."

The two soldiers cautiously climbed to the twin boulders where they had recovered the wounded men. Using those boulders for protection, Bull slowly peered around at Boss Man's and Coyote's last known position. There were several bodies scattered across the ridge top. He studied the terrain for a long minute before finally seeing the inert body with the American uniform.

"Shit!"

"What is it?" Homer asked.

"We have a man down. From here I can't tell if it's Coyote or Boss Man."

Bull looked again, and not seeing any sign of enemy movement, he slid swiftly around the boulder and dashed toward the prone body. Homer kept close behind, still scanning for the enemy.

As he closed the distance, Bull realized the body was Coyote. Boss Man was nowhere to be seen. Kneeling next to Coyote, it was clearly evident that he had been shot in the head at close range—a pool of blood and gore covered the ground where his head lay. There was no need to check vital signs.

"Damn it!"

There was nothing for Homer to say out loud as he lowered his head and offered a silent prayer. Although Coyote was the newest member of the team, he was well liked.

"Where's Boss Man?" Homer wondered.

Quickly looking around, Bull answered, "I don't know. His body isn't here. He may still be alive."

The two men began examining the physical evidence left in the sandy dirt. There were a lot of boot prints indicating a scuffle, and a great many shell casings, mostly from the weapons Boss Man and Coyote had used.

Bull ventured an interpretation of what had occurred. "Looks like they captured Boss Man and killed Coyote in the process. They fought hard; Boss Man wouldn't give up unless he had no choice."

Homer looked around again and noted the dead Homothals. "They killed a bunch of bad guys. Probably not enough of a force left to carry the attack forward to our camp."

Bull kneeled down and raised Coyote's lifeless body to his shoulder. He was a fellow Devil Dog, and Bull felt a personal obligation to retrieve his body. With a grunt, he rose and turned beginning the trek back down to camp. Never leave a fallen comrade, that's what he was taught in basic training and that was the promise of each SGIT soldier to their teammates.

"We're coming back," he radioed to the remaining team back at camp so as to avoid an accidental shooting.

Ghost replied, "Are Boss Man and Coyote alright?"

There was a pause before Bull could answer. When he did, his answer was short and to the point. "No."

Ghost knew well enough not to press the issue. Whatever had happened on the ridge, it wasn't good.

As Bull and Homer neared the camp Ghost could make out a large object on Bull's right shoulder, but it wasn't until they had entered camp that Ghost and Magnum realized Coyote was dead.

Bull gently and respectfully laid Coyote's body down as

Homer stoically retrieved a body bag from their gear on the mule. The team gathered around the body and afforded as much dignity as possible given the circumstances. Together, the two men zipped the bag closed.

"He was a good man," Homer said.

"What about Boss Man?" Magnum asked.

Bull shook his head. "He's not there."

Homer continued the explanation. "They put up a hell of a fight from the looks of it. I'd say they ran out of ammunition and were overrun. Coyote was killed. Boss Man must have been captured. We recovered his weapon."

"There's only one place he can be—at that compound he infiltrated earlier."

"The tracks lead in that direction, back down off the ridge," Homer agreed.

"Well, what are we waiting for?" Ghost asked. "Let's go get him."

"Slow down," Bull cautioned. "We don't know what we could be walking into. We need a plan."

"The plan is simple," Magnum barked, his voice raised. "We walk into that compound, shoot anyone who tries to stop us, find Boss Man, and leave."

"No, it's not that simple," Bull countered. "We have orders to follow, or have you forgotten?"

"We have a responsibility to retrieve Boss Man, or have you forgotten that?"

"I don't need you or anybody else reminding me of our duty to each other."

Ghost joined in. "I agree with Magnum. I say we take the Dillon down there and turn that compound into Swiss cheese."

"Well, I don't really care what you say. This isn't a Democracy. Boss Man put me in charge in his absence. And until I give you an order to the contrary, we stay put!"

From the fringe, Peter listened closely to the unexpected friction. He didn't care to involve himself in office politics if he could avoid it. Yet it appeared that the SGIT professionalism only went so far when faced with the uncertain status of their missing commander.

"Look, save your fight for down there," Peter interrupted, referring to the occupants of the secret facility below the ridge.

Collectively the SGIT team turned their eyes toward Peter. "Who asked you? You're not part of this team," Ghost said.

"Back off," Bull ordered. "He's fought with us and he's bled with us."

Ghost shifted his focus back to Bull, who offered an olive branch. "We *are* going to rescue Boss Man," Bull said. "But first we are going to put together a plan to ensure our success. The minigun will never make it to the compound, the batteries on the mule are nearly drained after the climb up this ridge.

"Our biggest problem is we can't say for sure where he's being held, assuming he's even alive."

"He's alive," Peter interrupted with a determination that had no rational backing. "Jimmy the Greek is too tough and too stubborn to die." The soldiers looked toward Peter, surprised to hear the emotion in his voice.

"My friends and I can get you in. Once inside, the rest is up to you and your team."

Bull wasn't impressed. "Since when did you three become super soldiers?"

"You need our help. You're down two men. We can do this."

Bull thought for a minute, and then an idea began to gel. He knew his team was, in all probability, severely out numbered. Surely the enemy also knew that. At least he hoped they did—he was counting on it.

CHAPTER 34

"SERGEANT WONG. Take Commander Nicolaou to the cellblock. Release him into the common area where the Homothals can have some sport with him before breakfast," Colonel Ming ordered.

"Yes sir!" Wong replied.

Jim had to stall. He needed more time to come up with a plan. By now his SGIT team would have discovered he was missing, and they would rightly conclude he was being held prisoner in Colonel Ming's research facility. But it would take his team time to formulate a plan of attack.

His best bet was to stall before arriving at the cellblock. Jim knew he stood no chance at all of defeating several Homothals in hand-to-hand combat. He had witnessed their superior strength and phenomenal ability to continue fighting even when mortally wounded. He had heard about wild animals behaving this way—reports from hunters who had shot out the heart of a fleeing elk and then witnessed the animal run for

241

another hundred yards before falling.

He was also familiar with stories of hunters who had been severely mauled, some killed, by an enraged bear or lion that had been shot in the heart-lung vital zone, mortally wounded, yet the beast kept attacking for several minutes.

Jim had no interest in slugging it out with a pack of Homothals. He would have to stage a diversion and try to escape. He knew the odds were slim that he would actually make it out of the compound to freedom, but to surrender to the unfolding events would surely mean death.

An idea flashed; it was risky, but it was the only chance he could think of. As Colonel Ming turned to leave with Lieutenant Li, Jim taunted him once more.

"I have to hand it to you Ming, for all your faults you really are brilliant."

Ming took the bait. He stopped, and looked over his should at Nicolaou, still held in the grip of the two Homothals.

"Yes, but it is too late for flattery to save you, Commander."

"Oh, I'm not flattering you Colonel. Your knick-name is well deserved, I'd say. The MOSSAD calls you the Asian Angel of Death after Josef Mengele, the Nazi doctor who also conducted heinous experiments on captured subjects, Jews mostly.

"History will forever remember Mengele as an evil, sick bastard. I think the Israelis got it right. The analogy to you and your so-called work is perfect. You, too, will be remembered— not as a brilliant scientist—but rather as a psychopath who tortured and killed innocent people, peaceful villagers."

Just as Jim had hoped, Sergeant Wong slammed his rifle butt into Jim's stomach; attempting to defend the honor of his superior officer. Jim doubled over in pain. Then Wong slammed the butt down on Jim's upper back, causing him to fall to his knees. He raised the rifle to strike again. Jim hoped he would survive this beating; he knew it would be vicious—maybe he had gambled too much?

Just as Wong was about to strike again, Colonel Ming shouted, "Stop!"

Wong halted in mid stroke, the butt inches from Jim's head.

"Do not kill him here, Sergeant. It would deprive our loyal Homothals of their enjoyment."

Colonel Ming turned and exited the room with Lieutenant Li close behind.

"I would rather kill you myself," Wong spat.

Jim was trying to catch his breath, hampered by the sharp pain running down his spine from his neck to between his shoulder blades. He remained on his knees, trying to recover some strength and gain more time.

Wong ordered Nicolaou to stand. Jim did not comply, still stalling.

"I said stand up!" and Jim was hoisted to his feet by the Homothals. Wong slapped him across the face. Jim responded with a groan and slowly opened his eyes part way.

Wong was disgusted that Jim could be so easily incapacitated. He motioned to the Homothals to let him drop, and Jim fell to the floor. Sergeant Wong walked to the door where a first aid kit was mounted on the wall. He opened the plastic box and found smelling salts.

Wong returned to Jim and tore open the small packet to release the strong odor of ammonia. The sergeant waved the packet under Jim's nose, and he snorted and shook his head as he had seen others do. He slowly opened his eyes and gently shook his head, the pain still intense and sharp.

"Get him on his feet," Wong ordered the two Homothals.

So far, Jim had just bought an extra seven minutes.

With Wong in the lead, they walked out of the dissection lab and into the main corridor. Turning to the right, the group walked toward the far end. Each Homothal had one hand under each of Jim's arms, gripping the upper arm tightly.

Acting the role, Jim stumbled as he was led down the hallway, allowing the Homothals to carry much of his weight.

Jim reasoned that the cellblock was in another building. He recalled studying the compound from high on the ridge and seeing two long rectangular buildings adjacent to the open, fenced area. He presumed this open area was the common area that Ming had referred to, and that each of the adjacent rectangular buildings housed the Homothals. These would be the cellblocks.

But which one was he being taken to, and how far was it? He had no plan for what to do next.

As they walked down the corridor, Jim observed as much as possible. The doors to other rooms were closed, but many had windows, and he was able to glimpse inside as he walked by. The Homothals, for all their strength and endurance, did not seem to realize that Nicolaou was gathering further intelligence about their facility. *Do they possess the capability of independent thought?* Jim wondered, half shuffling and half dragging his feet.

Some rooms seemed to have a scientific orientation. There appeared to be another dissection lab and one large room held multiple examination tables with a scattering of high-tech instruments and microscopes. Another room looked like a hospital emergency care room. It had several patient beds with surrounding drapes hung from a U-shaped track in the ceiling. Jim glimpsed oxygen lines along the wall and monitors for displaying a patient's vital signs.

With Wong still in the lead, the group left the building into the early-morning air. It was cool, and the fresh air exhilarated Jim. He breathed in deeply, filling his lungs before exhaling.

Wong stopped in front of the door to the next building. This must be the cellblock, Jim thought. As Wong was using his key card to unlock the door, Jim decided it was time to take action. He waited until Wong opened the door and passed through. It was a single door, so his captors would have to pass Jim through, and then follow.

One Homothal grabbed the door before it closed after Wong, holding it open, and motioning for Jim to walk through. Wong had already taken three steps down the corridor.

As soon as Jim passed through the door, he turned swiftly and kicked the door hard, slamming it into the Homothal. Although the door closed, it did not latch. Before the Homothal could regain its balance Jim slammed into the door a second time with all his weight. *BAMM!* The door locked shut with the two Homothals on the outside.

Wong turned at the noise of the door slamming just as Jim barreled into him, bashing his shoulder into Wong's stomach, his momentum slamming him into the wall. Wong dropped his rifle.

Jim punched him hard in the face, causing his head to recoil back into the wall. He slumped to the floor, unconscious.

Picking up the rifle, Jim quickly decided not to kill the sergeant fearing the rifle shot would alert more security guards. He grabbed the key card from the sergeant's breast pocket, and hurried down the corridor.

Jim passed at least a dozen doors, each with a small window protected by steel bars, but he didn't stop to see what lurked inside. He was nearing the end of the passageway. The door directly in front most likely led to the common area. Since that was where Ming wanted Jim to be released, presumably to be mauled to death by hoards of Homothals, that was the last place Jim intended to go voluntarily.

On the left side of the corridor, Jim spotted a doorway lacking the barred window of the cell doors. Jim tried the door—to his surprise, it was not locked. He entered and saw four tables. Each was large enough to hold a man, and the leather straps on the table suggested that was indeed their purpose. And there, on the last table, was a human body.

Jim walked over and saw that the man strapped to the table was dark-skinned, most likely a refugee. He checked the man's pulse... still alive. His breathing was strong.

As Jim was loosening the straps the man startled awake, speaking in a language Jim didn't understand. He continued removing the restraints on the man's arms and legs.

"I am Commander Nicolaou. Do you speak English?"

The man blinked his eyes, trying to regain focus and concentration. His green eyes seemed to communicate understanding. Jim tried again.

"Do you understand English?"

After a moment the man replied, "Yes, I speak English." His words were heavily accented and seemed rough. But they could communicate.

"What is your name?"

After a moment, the man answered. "My American friends call me Daniel."

Jim nodded. "You have been to America?"

"Yes, to Columbia University."

"Okay Daniel, call me Jim."

Daniel nodded.

"Where are we Daniel?"

"This is one of the labs. This is where they perform the treatment."

"We need to find a way out of here and not through the lion's den either."

"There is a way out."

The man raised a shaky arm and pointed toward the back of the lab. Jim ran over to take a closer look at the suggested exit. There he found a supply room. He opened the door and entered. The walls were lined with shelves holding all kinds of lab and medical supplies. The labeling was mostly in Chinese, and he couldn't read it. Some of the cases were labeled in English, identifying the contents as syringes, gauze packs, and other medical supplies. These probably had been confiscated from the Aid Camps.

As Jim reached the back wall he saw that there was another door. He opened it and found himself standing in a second lab, but this one didn't have any patient tables.

Instead, there were shelves lining the walls. On those shelves were large glass jars containing various organs—some looked to be human. Various jars contained limbs and heads, presumably preserved in some sort of embalming fluid, maybe formaldehyde. Judging by the sizes, not all were taken from adult natives.

In the center of the room were three tables with cabinets beneath. "Dissection tables," Jim mumbled to himself.

The air smelled strongly of alcohol. Laid out on white linen towels on a tray at each table were an array of stainless steel medical tools for cutting flesh and bone—scalpels, bone saws, and the like. Jim had no way of knowing that for each new viral infection procedure a dedicated dissection room was established to avoid potential sample contamination.

As Jim was taking all this in, he saw a dark shadow move past the small window in the door opening into the hallway he had just traversed. Like the other rooms he had seen, there was no exit other than to the central corridor. He turned and hurried back to Daniel.

"That just goes back to the corridor. I saw troops coming this way."

Daniel looked concerned. "There is no other way."

The outer door burst opened and two Chinese soldiers rushed into the lab. Jim didn't hesitate. He leveled his weapon and fired two shots, one into each guard. Their rifles clattered to the floor as they fell dead.

Jim picked up the nearest rifle and turned back toward Daniel. "Time for us to leave. Do you know how to handle one of these?" referring to the rifle.

Daniel nodded, and Jim gave him the second rifle. They entered the central corridor. Jim looked both ways before choosing to go back the way he had come. If they could make it out of the building, maybe they could work their way to the perimeter fence, cross through it, and head toward his team on the ridge.

Jim ran down the corridor with Daniel close behind. He expected to see Sergeant Wong's unconscious body, but it was gone.

They were almost at the door when it opened suddenly. A Chinese soldier, a key card dangling from a lanyard attached to his shirt pocket, stood there in surprise at seeing Jim and Daniel rushing towards him. Behind him stood two Homothals.

The soldier and Jim fired at the same instant. Reflexively, Jim dove to the side of the hallway after pulling the trigger to avoid the shots. It was instinctive; training had drilled the response into him. But Daniel had no such training. Caught off guard, he had stayed in place and died on the spot.

The Chinese soldier went down as well, while the two Homothals cleared the doorway seeking cover outside the hallway. The door slammed shut, locking the creatures outside. Jim hoped that neither of them had a key card.

He turned around and ran in the opposite direction, backtracking, trying to get to the door at the far end of the hallway before the Homothals reached it. Maybe he could still get out of the building and evade capture.

The corridor was long, easily a hundred yards. Jim ran, not slowing to look behind him. If a bullet slammed into his back he would be dead. He just kept running—fearing all the while that the door would be locked or have guards posted to prevent his escape.

Fifteen seconds seemed like minutes. Only ten yards to go. He was going to make it. He was at the door. Breathing heavily, Jim pushed the door open just a bit, enough to see a sliver of open ground. *No gunfire, that's a good sign.* He slammed open the door and burst into the early morning dawn.

He quickly looked around... *good, no one's here.* But he had exited into the common area. Looking to his right he saw the gate separating the common area from the general grounds. Jim ran toward the gate.

It was locked securely with a padlock and chain. He pressed the rifle muzzle against the lock, turned his head to avoid eye injury from metal shards, and pulled the trigger. The lock blew apart and the chain clanged loosely against the gate.

Jim deftly removed the remnants of the lock and chain, opened the gate, and continued his rush toward the perimeter fence.

He was close, only three strides away, when he heard the shots and saw the dirt kicked up at his feet. Then the order came.

"Stop! Drop your weapon!"

It was useless. His back was toward the enemy and they could obviously kill him with the next shot. He stopped running and raised his hands.

"Drop the rifle, or the next shot will be through your heart!"

Jim did as he was told and slowly turned to face Sergeant Wong and a collection of Homothals and Chinese soldiers. Admitting defeat, Jim placed his hands on his head.

"I should kill you now," Wong hissed. "But Colonel Ming has other plans for you."

CHAPTER 35

"COLONEL PIERSON, this is Sergeant Beaumont. We have a situation, sir." Bull had used his given name rather than his call sign, not certain Colonel Pierson would be familiar with the latter.

"Get to the point Bull." Bull immediately recognized his error in assuming the Colonel had a faulty memory. In fact, Colonel Pierson had to manage a continual barrage of facts and figures daily, so to him knowing the call signs of his field operatives was a given.

"We engaged an unknown enemy outside the target compound this morning. We took casualties, sir." Bull hesitated before continuing.

"Coyote is dead and Boss Man is missing. We presume he was captured and is now being held in the compound." Bull deliberately avoided mentioning the injured civilians—it would take too long to cover the background story so that Colonel Pierson could understand why four civilians and an SLM rebel had been attached to his SGIT team.

Colonel Pierson remained silent. Inside, he was seething. He had created SGIT, and he was responsible for every team member recruited into the elite organization—a responsibility he took personally. He had selected James Nicolaou from a strong list of highly-qualified and experienced candidates, making Jim the first commander of SGIT. Over the years the bond between Pierson and Jim was as close as that between brothers, despite their two-decade age gap.

"I've been in communication with Lacey. She has extracted substantial information from those computer files you managed to send out. There is still a lot of data to be deciphered, but what we have learned seems to confirm our suspicions. Portions of the research appears to be brilliant... who would have thought Neanderthals and humans were so closely related."

"I'm not following, sir."

"What I'm saying, Sergeant, is that the target compound does indeed appear to be a secret laboratory. Lacey's team has only just begun to examine the data in those records, but what they've seen so far suggests the research involves genetic engineering and human test subjects. That's all we know right now. However, this supports our suspicion that Colonel Ming is involved."

Bull brought the conversation back to the topic of his interest—rescuing his commander.

"Sir, I am requesting permission to infiltrate the compound and rescue Boss Man," Bull paused for effect. "We have reason to believe he is being held and is still alive." These points were fabricated, but Bull was worried that if he didn't press the issue Colonel Pierson would not approve the mission.

"Bullshit, Sergeant. You wouldn't have radioed me if those statements were fact."

Bull clenched his teeth and squeezed the radio handset so

hard his knuckles popped.

"Look," Colonel Pierson continued. "You do whatever is necessary to retrieve Jim—and by God I pray he is alive. But if not, bring home his body along with Coyote's for a proper funeral. They each deserve that much."

"We'll do that, sir." Bull felt a flood of relief wash over his emotions, and then he added, "...come hell or high water."

"I suspect you and your team have a lot of hell still before you. In addition to retrieving Boss Man, your new orders are to destroy that compound. I want all records of their research to vanish—for good. Have I made myself clear, Sergeant?"

"Yes sir!"

"Good. You will have to improvise. I can't authorize an air strike on foreign territory. The Chinese and Sudanese governments would be all over the State Department within the hour."

"What about cruise missiles, sir?" asked Bull.

"Too risky. They would have to fly very low to avoid radar, and if one malfunctions and crashes we'll have an even bigger public relations fiasco. No, you will have to figure it out. Earn your salary. It's a laboratory, Sergeant! There have got to be a dozen different ways to blow it up!"

"Yes sir! The compound is history. All records will be destroyed, sir!"

"Very good. Bull, good luck."

The next thing Bull heard was a click and the line went dead.

CHAPTER 36

BULL GATHERED HIS TEAM and relayed the key elements of his just-completed conversation with Colonel Pierson. He faced Peter. "You say you can get us into that compound?"

Peter had been staring past Bull. His mind kept replaying the terrible beating he had seen Ethan suffer. The worst part was the irrational guilt that would creep into those thoughts. Peter knew he had done everything possible to protect his son, but it wasn't enough. The rational part of his mind was slowly losing the argument to the emotional side of his brain.

"Peter?" Bull's query pulled Peter back to the conversation, his eyes focusing on Bull.

Bull understood what Peter was going through. "Look, you need to focus on the job. Ethan will be okay. Right now he just needs rest so his body can heal."

Peter nodded. "I'm sorry. You were saying?"

"You have a plan to get us into the compound?"

Peter nodded again. "You put Gary, Todd, and me on a

good vantage point with those sniper rifles and lots of ammo. Any target gets in your way, and he'll meet up with a very big bullet."

Bull contemplated Peter's plan. Although Bull knew Peter was not educated as a military tactician, he still recognized talent in the man.

"All right, listen up," Bull announced. "Here's the plan."

All traces of earlier tension between the men vanished; they had a mission to complete.

"We're going to post snipers on the finger coming off this ridge that reaches closest to the compound. You can see it to the left from atop the ridge. We have four Barrett rifles and enough ammo. I want Homer, Gary, Todd, and Peter on the rifles. We'll keep Ethan close by, but still and quiet, and as comfortable as possible."

The four men nodded agreement.

Bull continued. "Ghost and Magnum are going with me into the compound. The rifles are going to clear the path in front of us. Wipe away any threat. We can't afford to be slowed down engaging any bad guys in a firefight—we have to maintain momentum and speed."

Todd was skeptical. "That's going to be a bit tricky, don't you think? I'll admit I'm not completely familiar with this landscape, but it must be a thousand yards or more from the ridge finger to the compound."

Rather than waiting for Bull, Magnum answered. "Probably closer to 1,200 yards if you measure all the way to the nearest building. But those rifles are good out to 2,500 hundred yards. And you boys seem to know how to shoot; I don't imagine this will be much of a challenge."

"Magnum's right," Bull added. "Besides, the first part of your job will be done when we reach the compound. Once there we will enter the nearest building and begin a rapid and systematic search for Boss Man. Then we will toast the entire complex. I want the four of you to engage any target within range of Ghost, Magnum, and me. Whether you kill them or not, your job is to keep them pinned down."

Todd didn't look convinced, but he knew enough to stay quiet.

Homer added, "The electronic sights on those Barrett rifles are fantastic. You can pick out a moving target, get your scope and take the shot a lot faster than you could with the older scopes. You'll love it... trust me." Homer's grin at the end didn't do much to alleviate Todd's concerns.

Peter—his mind now focused on the task at hand—understood the mission's success depended largely on their ability to hit man-sized targets at a distance much farther than he had ever shot before. Although his brief introduction to the Barrett rifle and electronic scope gave him reason to be confident in the equipment, he could not fully shake his doubt.

The four-man sniper squad would have to remove every threat that came within striking distance of the party—without fail. This was considerably different from an afternoon at the shooting range.

Peter chewed on another worry that he left unspoken. He saw how robust these strange enemy soldiers were. He had personally felt their incredible strength, witnessed their inhumane brutality, and seen the pure adrenaline-charged ferocity that kept them fighting even after being mortally wounded. *At least we'll be shooting big bullets*, he thought.

"How do you want us to gear up?" Ghost asked.

"Pack as much weaponry and ammo as you can," Bull answered. "I suspect we'll need every bit of it. When the briefing is over, gather up the weapons that were dropped by the two boulders. I figure the fighting will be close, since I have confidence in our four guardian-angels-of-death." The slight smirk on Bull's face made Peter wonder if he was trying to convince himself the plan would work, or just trying to improve Todd's confidence.

"How do we plan to level that compound after we liberate Boss Man?" Magnum asked.

"Colonel Pierson will not authorize an air strike."

"Then cruise missiles, right?"

Bull shook his head. "Negative. The risk of international backlash against Uncle Sam is too great. The Colonel says we are on our own. Bring along what explosives we have."

"We only have about ten pounds of C4," Magnum replied. "This was a recon mission so we didn't pack for heavy demolition work. It would take at least a hundred pounds of C4 if we really want to obliterate the entire compound."

"The Colonel was very clear on his orders. We are to destroy all records in those buildings. He does not want anything left that someone can later find and use to restart the research they've been doing."

Peter and Gary perked up. "What research?" Peter asked.

"Colonel Pierson didn't go into details, but he said Lieutenant Lacey and her team of analysts had learned enough from the electronic data files to suggest that they have been doing genetic engineering and experimentation on humans."

"What else did he say? What type of genetic engineering?" Peter pressed.

"Look, I'm not a science nerd… Sorry, I didn't mean to insult you."

"Not at all," Gary answered with a smile. Peter was deep in thought. He had an unshakable feeling that he was grasping the end of a ball of string and if he pulled just a bit the whole ball would unravel to reveal the mystery inside.

"There has to be something more, something else that he said. Anything. It could be an important clue."

Bull replayed the conversation in his mind. "Nothing that makes sense to me. He just said that it looked like Ming was conducting genetic engineering, experiments on human subjects. He said that they were still reviewing the data and it would take a long time to go through all of it."

"That's it—nothing else?"

Bull thought for a moment. "Well, he mentioned Neanderthals, but I don't know what that has to do with anything."

Peter's eyes widened in astonishment.

"Think. What exactly did he say about Neanderthals?"

Bull made a face, like a pout. "Just that he never would have believed Neanderthals and humans were so close."

Peter turned to Gary, "My God…"

"Does that mean something to you?" Bull inquired.

Neither Peter nor Gary answered at first, although it was clear they both comprehended Colonel Pierson's cryptic message.

Peter felt the pressure of five pairs of eyes burning into his thoughts. "Yes, this means something."

He paused, struggling to find the right words.

"What your colleague, Lieutenant Lacey, is about to learn is that the genetic engineering documented by those electronic files involves crossing human and Neanderthal DNA."

"How can you be so certain?" Bull challenged.

"Because… those creatures that we've been fighting are the product of that work."

"What?" Homer exclaimed. "You mean we've been fighting the Geico Caveman?"

"Strictly speaking, Neanderthals were not cavemen. They were actually a fairly advanced society that even produced jewelry and held beliefs akin to what we would call religion," Gary lectured.

Homer sneered at Gary like he was the science teacher from high school who no one liked.

Peter went on. "Scientists have recently discovered a substantial amount of Neanderthal DNA in modern humans of non-African descent. Somehow Colonel Ming has found a way to introduce intact Neanderthal DNA into human hosts. That's clear from the reference to experimenting on human subjects. He must have found a way to allow the foreign DNA to fuse with the host DNA."

"How can that be done?" Bull asked.

Peter shook his head. "I don't know. A virus I guess. That's how viruses infect their host—they enter the cell and inject their genetic material into the host, taking over the enzymes that control cell reproduction."

"Except we're not talking about a cold or the flu," Bull said.

"No. What Ming has done has never been achieved before. The result is what we've seen. A hybrid—neither human nor Neanderthal—with characteristics of each."

"That explains their strength," Gary added. Then almost as an afterthought, "And why they're so hard to kill."

"What do you mean?" Ghost demanded.

Peter answered. "The Neanderthal is widely believed to have gone extinct 25,000 to 30,000 years ago. It lived in a much different world and fought for food and survival with primitive weapons. Yet, as a species, it was undeniably successful—expanding its range during a harsh climatic period that we call the Ice Age. Neanderthals had to have been very tough, probably more animal-like in physiology than human."

"Okay, so they're tough. We already knew that, Professor." Bull was growing annoyed. They were losing valuable time.

"So now you know what you're up against. A being that is stronger than you, can out run you, and has better senses—sight, hearing, smell. You are fighting a humanoid creature that has more animal traits than it has human traits."

"And it can shoot," Gary added.

Bull frowned. He didn't like what he was hearing, but that changed nothing.

"Thanks for the science lesson, Doc," Ghost commented.

"I'd feel better if we had the Dillon as backup," Magnum added.

"The battery is nearly exhausted," Bull explained. "No way it can make the trip on the mule, and it's too heavy for us to carry—it would slow us down too much."

Peter looked over at the mule with the multibarrel minigun mounted to the flat deck. "Maybe we can help with that."

CHAPTER 37

Darfur
June 14   0646 hours

FLANKED BY FOUR HOMOTHALS and with Sergeant Wong in the lead, Commander Jim Nicolaou was led to one of the medical labs. He had been in this lab earlier, when he discovered Daniel. He recognized the tables with the wide, thick leather straps for restraining the subject. Prodded by the muzzles of two rifles, Jim was urged forward, toward the closest table.

"Lie down, Commander," ordered Wong.

"And if I refuse?"

Wong cracked a wicked grin. "Then it will be my pleasure to shoot off your left knee cap." To emphasize the point Wong removed his sidearm from its holster and pointed the gun in the direction of Jim's legs.

Reluctantly, Jim stepped forward and slowly climbed onto the table. He lay on his back and allowed his legs and arms to be strapped down tightly. The Homothals and Chinese soldiers stepped back. Jim stared at the ceiling, waiting for the next move.

He didn't have to wait long before Colonel Ming entered.

"It seems that I have underestimated the resourcefulness of your team, Commander. So it would appear I still have a need for you after all."

"Admit it, Ming. You just missed my charming company."

Ming ignored the childish taunting.

"My technicians are having some difficulty tracking your satellite communication. They tell me that your men routed the signal through at least a dozen intermediate stations. Is that true?"

Jim didn't answer. In fact, he really didn't know. The entire data download and transmission back to Gary's server had been done not only without Jim's permission, but also without his knowledge of the technical details.

"It matters not," Ming said. "You will tell me what I want to know."

"Didn't we already play this game?" Jim challenged. He knew that Ming intended to torture him, and he wanted to stall as long as possible to give his team more time. He still clung to the hope that his team would come after him.

"No… we haven't," Ming replied. "You see, before I did not really need your cooperation. Now that I do, the game is about to begin."

"What makes you think I'm going to answer your questions now?"

"Because I will make your existence very painful if you do not."

Jim didn't answer. He found a small stain on the ceiling where he began to focus all his attention.

"Commander. I will ask you a few questions… simple questions, really. They should not be hard to answer for a man of your accomplishments. Now, where did you send the satellite communication?"

Jim remained silent.

Colonel Ming leaned over Jim and stared malevolently. "I will ask once more. Where did you send the communication and what was the content of that communication?"

Jim stared back defiantly, turning his head to make sure he locked eyes with Ming. "Go to hell, Ming."

"I see... we have lost our manners." Ming walked away from the table and turned his back to Nicolaou.

"Do you know what this room was designed for, Commander?"

"To torture innocent civilians, no doubt."

Ming chuckled. "You do have a simple mind, Commander, don't you. Of course, you are right... in a way. What we do in this room is torture, but that is not the intention." Ming walked in a small circle, pausing for effect.

"No, what this room was designed for is nothing less than miraculous. On these tables we create a new life form, the Homothal. This is our Garden of Eden!"

Needles of panic pricked the back of Jim's neck. Ming was completely mad.

The colonel stepped closer to Jim. "Yes, on these tables we transform Homo sapiens into a hybrid creature that is more Neanderthal than human. This is the result of my brilliance!"

"You're sick, Ming," Jim muttered in disgust.

"The process is actually rather elegant. My scientists have learned how to incorporate the Neanderthal DNA into a very basic virus—the cold virus, actually. We tried many—we're still developing the Ebola virus as a carrier—but in the end the cold virus worked very well. The trick, you see, was to find the right viral host that could insert foreign DNA into living human cells such that those cells replicated with the foreign DNA."

Ming was smiling as he spoke, unashamedly proud of his work.

"You're nothing more than a monster."

"I see! And thus your earlier reference to 'Dr. Frankenstein.'" Ming said this with a dramatic flair that surprised Jim.

"And Josef Mengele, let's not forget." Jim added. "Although it would appear that you have outdone his work, if that's even possible."

"I'll take that as a compliment, thank you. Mengele was brilliant, but crude. Of course, with today's tools who knows where his work would have led."

"Mengele was sick, like you. He conducted surgery on children without anesthesia. He maimed and tortured thousands and murdered many more. And for what? What was the benefit?"

As Jim finished, Ming's expression turned cold. "I never said that I am working for the betterment of mankind."

"No, I suppose not, you evil bastard."

Colonel Ming turned away and took the rifle from the nearest guard. The room was silent. Jim watched and waited. Ming slowly turned back toward Jim. Then suddenly and with lightning speed, Ming swung the gun down across Jim's stomach.

The rifle struck hard. Strapped to the table, Jim was defenseless. He reflexively cried out and grimaced in pain.

"You will speak to me with respect, Commander." Ming returned the rifle to the guard.

"Now, you will tell me what I want to know."

Jim struggled to catch his breath enough to speak. His abdominal muscles were trying to double him over, fighting against the straps and causing even more pain.

Jim shook his head from side to side, and through gritted teeth he answered, "Never."

Ming considered Jim for a moment. He really needed to know the transmission's destination. He desperately wanted to know who was coming after him. It could be the Americans, the Chinese, the Israelis, the Koreans, or the Japanese—or any other one of Ming's countless enemies.

"Commander, can you imagine what happens to a man undergoing my gene treatment?"

"No, I don't normally associate with vermin of your caliber."

Ming ignored the insult. "It really is amazing. The cellular transformations that occur are painful, excruciatingly painful. In fact, that proved to be one of the biggest hurdles when we were developing the technique.

"Getting the DNA to fuse with human cellular material was child's play. Getting the patient to survive the transformation… now that was a very difficult problem to solve. The stresses on the human organs, especially the brain and heart, proved too much for 73 percent of the patients. Women and children were especially frail and nearly all died from the cellular disruption."

Jim jerked at his restraints. He desperately wanted to get his hands around Ming's neck, to squeeze the life from him.

"In the end, we had to use a combination of sedatives, steroids, and PCP. Even with this cocktail, we learned to subject only the strongest patients to the treatment."

"So that's why the young men have been taken from villages throughout Darfur. You needed healthy and strong subjects for your experiments."

"Precisely. And as I told you earlier, we needed subjects that would not be missed."

"But they are missed. They left families behind who are telling the world about their abducted husbands and fathers and—"

"Yes, yes," interrupted Ming. "My orders were to destroy the villages and everyone else in them, but a few escaped. Anyway the world doesn't care. We have already discussed this matter."

"I care."

"Your concern is insignificant. You will, however, make an intriguing test subject."

Jim's eyes widened just a bit.

"Don't be too afraid, Commander. I am sure you will be able to endure the pain a very long time. Of course, you could answer my questions and then we can be done with the drama. Sergeant Wong would be more than happy to put an end to your life."

"If nobody cares about what you're doing, why does it matter where the message was sent?" Jim pressed.

Ming remained silent.

"You don't know who your enemies are, do you?" Jim guessed. "You really aren't sure who I work for. What if it *is* the Chinese?" Jim played into Ming's paranoia.

"I have no use for any government. Soon, they will all bow in fear before *me!*"

"Hell is filled with tyrants who thought just like you. You will fare no better."

"Time is up, Commander. If you choose not to answer me now, maybe you will talk once the genetic transformation begins to turn you into one of my loyal soldiers. You will still be able to speak during the initial stages of the infection. Though sadly, as the pain intensifies and the cellular reorganization reaches completion, all speech will be lost along with your humanity. There is no turning back."

Jim stared defiantly at the Colonel Ming.

"Very well." Ming turned to Dr. Hsu who had been silently waiting for orders. "You may begin."

CHAPTER 38

PETER AND TODD HAD WIRED the electric motor on the mule directly to the bank of batteries, bypassing the throttle control. As the mule rolled down hill, this modification allowed the rotating wheels to turn the motor and generate electricity, which charged the batteries. There was no way the men could be sure exactly how much charge the batteries had picked up, but with luck it would be enough to propel the mule within range of the compound.

At the bottom of the ridge, it was a simple matter for Ghost to reconnect the batteries through the throttle to the motor. For now, they left the mule in place, lightly camouflaged. The plan was to leave the mule with its highly lethal weaponry in hiding, only driving it into the open to cover the team as they escaped with Commander Nicolaou.

Homer was designated to operate Bessy using the remote controller from his vantage point on the finger ridge about 50 yards above the camouflaged mule.

Still unconscious, Ethan had ridden the mule down to the finger ridge, strapped to the deck of the machine. There, the team laid him next to a large boulder on a relatively flat, sandy section of ground and made him as comfortable as possible. From this point the sandstone cliff opened into a fissure that extended further up the slope. Peter had placed a folded shirt under his son's head, offering meager padding.

Alone with Ethan, Peter kneeled and spoke in a soft whisper. "You rest here. You're safe, and I won't be far away." He paused, feeling his voice catch.

"We didn't come all this way for nothing." Peter forced a smile as he cupped Ethan's bruised and swollen face. Unconscious and motionless, he appeared to be peacefully asleep. Except that Peter understood all too well the injuries he had suffered and the risk that he may not recover fully, if at all.

He gently wrapped Ethan's hand in his own and closed his eyes. As he did, a solitary tear ran down his cheek. He swallowed trying to vanquish the foreboding from his mind.

Peter could not shake the feeling that he had been here before, when Maggie was in the hospital on life support. As the memory resurfaced he could no longer hold back the tears, and he wept.

No, not again. I can't let this happen again. God, how I miss you Maggie. Why did I have to lose you? It never should have happened. If only I had been driving that night, instead of you.

Peter opened his eyes and looked down at his son. "I'm going to get you out of here Ethan. Just hang on... please hold on... for me."

He folded Ethan's hands across his abdomen and brushed away the tears streaking his face, leaving behind brown smudges. Struggling to regain his composure, Peter began to feel his self-control returning and with it the clarity that always seemed to follow his moments of deep despair. "No," he said a bit louder than before. "You are not going to die here. We are going *home.*"

Still looking down at his son, Peter rose. "I have work to do. And when I'm finished, I *am* taking you home. I promise."

He rubbed the back of his sleeve across his face again, trying to erase all evidence of his frailty, and then placed his right hand on the Colt pistol once again in its holster on his hip. Without ammunition it was pretty much useless. Still, he drew a measure of confidence from its presence. More useful was Hamaad's machete, which Peter had in a sheath slung across his back.

Turning, he marched the few dozen yards to the tip of the finger ridge and joined the other snipers, ready to bring hell to the enemy below.

"Glad you decided to join us," Homer quipped. And then, in a lower voice meant only for Peter to hear, he added, "He'll be fine."

Peter turned his head toward Homer who was occupied with the image through the BORS scope. "Let's get this done."

"Just another day on the job." Homer responded.

The extraction team of Ghost, Magnum, and Bull were moving double time for the compound. The sun was barely below the horizon. The men hoped it would not be hard for the sniper team to pick out their targets.

The extraction team had only covered about 300 yards when the first report from a Barrett rifled echoed off the ridgeline. The men kept moving, not slowing or hesitating. They had to keep moving toward the danger, trusting that any threats would be eliminated for them.

"Remember to lead the target if it's running," Homer urged his fellow snipers. Firing at will, the four men made nearly every shot count, only occasionally missing.

The SGIT extraction team had gained another 70 yards

leaving 800 yards to cover. They were measuring their pace, jogging at a comfortable and sustainable speed. It would take them at least three more minutes to cover the remaining distance... and a lot could happen in three minutes.

From their position on the finger ridge, the sniper team could see everything on the battlefield below them. Another group of four Homothals disgorged from the nearest building and ran toward Ghost, Magnum, and Bull. Right behind the Homothals were three Chinese soldiers. One of the men was lugging a machine gun, and he was closely followed by two others carrying boxes of ammunition in each hand. Bull's squad had no idea they were running directly into a machine gun.

"Todd, Gary... take out the lead group of four; the ones that are running toward our guys. Peter... we'll focus on that machine gun crew setting up down there. You see them?"

"Yes... the three men at the rear," Peter answered as he pointed in the general direction.

"Yeah, that's right. Try to make your shots count, but don't sweat it if you miss. The point is to keep them distracted. We can't let our guys run into that machine gun. Got it?"

Peter responded by firing the first shot. The bullet missed, but struck the ground very close to one of the ammunition bearers. The soldier looked up to the ridge in the direction of the snipers and tapped the machine gunner on the shoulder, and pointed. The gunner pivoted to his right and, pointing the machine gun upwards, began to fire in Peter's general direction.

The shots all fell short, but as long as the machine gun was aimed at the snipers it was no threat to the SGIT trio charging across open ground.

Homer aimed and fired, taking out one of the soldiers carrying ammunition cans. Peter fired again, killing the other ammunition bearer. Amidst the roar of gunfire, the machine gunner had no idea his support team, standing slightly behind him, had just been eliminated. The gunner continued to focus on firing his weapon at the unseen enemy on the ridge above.

Homer took the next shot. He was well practiced with the Barrett. Under these conditions, no wind, stationary target, distance of just over 1,000 yards, the shot was easy for him. He gently squeezed the trigger and watched as a little over a second later the soldier's head exploded in a splash of red.

The three-man SGIT squad was close enough now that they could see the Homothals closing on them. But just as one would raise its rifle to shoot, a silent bullet would strike the enemy down. Like a badly dubbed movie, the sound of the rifle shot came about three seconds after the impact. Bull kept moving forward, trusting that no harm would come to him or his fellow soldiers.

When the last Homothal was shot down, Bull's team arrived within 500 yards of the compound. The fenced parade ground was off to their left.

As they continued their forward momentum, the team was suddenly showered by bullets striking the earth around them, followed immediately by the report of rifle fire. The SGIT soldiers quickly began to dodge left and right, while never slowing their forward pace.

Todd was first to locate the new source of fire. "At the side of the closest building. See them?"

Two Homothals were shooting at the extraction team. Gary swiveled slightly to take aim and fired. Todd fired at the same time and both Homothals crumpled over. The remaining Chinese officer looked up in the sniper team's direction and impotently held up his fist. Peter could imagine the officer cursing him and the other snipers. Homer fired and the officer slammed back against the wall, his chest a massive red stain.

Bull, Ghost, and Magnum continued forward—relentlessly. By now they were all breathing heavily. Each man was carrying about 85 pounds of weapons, ammunition, and explosives. Despite the cool early morning temperature, they were all perspiring heavily.

"Stay sharp," Homer ordered the sniper team. "They're close, but it's not over yet."

No sooner had he uttered the warning when the shutters on the two closest towers opened and machine-gun fire rained down on the SGIT team.

"Shit!" Homer exclaimed. "Gary, Todd—take out the gunners in the closest tower. Peter—we have the far tower."

They fired rapidly, knowing that to fail could be disastrous for Ghost, Magnum, and Bull. The towers fell silent, but not before Ghost took a grazing round to his thigh. It burned like a hot poker, but other than missing a step, it didn't slow him down. At over 300 yards distance, the enemy soldiers were still not able to place accurate fire on the running targets.

Homer feared that replacement soldiers could put the machine guns in the towers back into service. He needed to disable the weapons. Slamming a magazine of explosive rounds into his rifle, he carefully aimed, firing five shots at the gun emplacement in each of the two towers. Only time would tell if he was successful.

Finally, the enemy was driven from the field and the Barrett rifles fell silent. The thousand-plus yard gauntlet now behind them, Bull, Ghost, and Magnum finally reached the nearest building. They quickly ducked inside and disappeared from view.

CHAPTER 39

BULL AND MAGNUM MOVED along the right wall, Ghost along the left wall. Just inside the doorway they stepped over the body of a Homothal lying next to a Chinese soldier.

The objective was simple: quickly and efficiently sweep the building to find their commander. If he was not in this building they would split up and search the remaining four buildings, staying in touch through their scrambled squad-net communication sets.

All three men moved forward deliberately; legs in a slight crouch, senses on full alert, weapons held tight to their shoulders, sweeping back and forth. Magnum was frequently looking back to be sure no one came up from behind them.

A sound from down the hallway caught the extraction team's attention. Two Chinese soldiers, reinforcements for the defenders outside, entered the hallway from the far end. Surprised at the sight of the SGIT team, they stopped and a half second later started to raise their rifles.

Bull and Ghost reacted much faster. Knowing that there were no 'friendlies' other than Jim in these buildings, the extraction team automatically assumed everyone they encountered was a threat to be eliminated.

Bull and Ghost fired short bursts from their automatic shotguns, killing the soldiers before they had even taken aim. The extraction team traveled half way down the hallway and did not encounter any additional resistance, worrying Bull. *Where were the majority of the defensive forces? Would they encounter heavy fighting in one of the other remaining three buildings?*

The SGIT team pressed forward. Each time they came to a door, the nearest man would peek through the small window in the door. If the room appeared empty, he would check the door latch. If unlocked, the men would rush in, sweeping the room with their weapons. Fortunately, they had not encountered any locked doors—so far.

They proceeded nearly to the end of the hallway. Only two more doors remained to be checked, one on each side of the hallway. These last two doors were much further apart from the other doors, suggesting the rooms they opened into were large. Bull motioned to Ghost. They would check both doors at the same time.

Carefully, each man peered into the small window. Ghost abruptly dropped to a crouch and pushed his back against the wall. Bull and Magnum knew this meant trouble and they, too, dropped to the floor and scooted across the hallway to join Ghost.

"Boss Man's in there," Ghost whispered, "and he's surrounded by Chinese."

From his pack, Ghost removed a miniature fiber-optic camera probe connected by a flexible wire to a small hand-held LCD screen. He powered up the device and carefully positioned the probe at the corner of the window, slowly moving it from side to side until he had Boss Man in view.

He could easily see his commander with an IV in his arm strapped to the examination table. A Chinese officer appeared to be questioning him. Another man wearing a white smock stood off to the side and was filling a syringe with something from a small glass vial. Surrounding them were three soldiers and three Homothals.

Ghost was trying to make sense of it. "This room must be soundproof, otherwise the guards would be posted at this door. The bottom of the door seals against the floor; maybe there's an air filtration system—looks like it might be a lab or something like that."

The man in the white lab coat, syringe in hand, stepped toward Commander Nicolaou.

"We have to move now!" Ghost whispered. "It looks like they're preparing to inject something into Boss Man."

Bull nodded. "What do we have?"

"Six armed bad guys, one officer who appears to be interrogating Boss Man, and a mean looking doctor."

"Tight group?"

"Yeah. The bad guys are maybe three feet away from the examination table to the right. The officer and doc are to the left."

"Are the officer or doctor armed?"

"The doc is unarmed near as I can tell... can't see if the officer has a pistol belt on... he's standing on the far side of the table."

Bull nodded again. "You know the drill. Standard hostage rescue. Check the latch, is it open?"

Ghost reached up and very quietly applied pressure to the door handle. There was no resistance; the door was not locked.

CHAPTER 40

"I AM A REASONABLE MAN, Commander. All you need to do is answer my question and we can avoid this messy business." Colonel Ming's fake smile looked more like a grimace.

Jim Nicolaou remained firmly strapped to the examination table and the doctor had inserted an IV into his arm; the shirtsleeve neatly folded up to his bicep. Dr. Hsu was preparing the viral agent that he would inject into the IV drip to infect Nicolaou's body. Jim struggled against the bonds holding his arms and legs to the table, but to no avail.

"You can go to hell, Ming."

"Perhaps… but not before you." Ming looked over at the doctor making his preparations.

"Are you ready with the viral dose?" The doctor was withdrawing a measured sample from a small ampoule into a glass syringe.

"In just a moment, sir," the doctor replied, not breaking his concentration. "It is very important that the dose be correct. The margin between an effective dose and a fatal dose is slim. Too little, and the patient's immune system is likely to overwhelm the virus before it can fully infect his body. Too much, and he will go into cardiac arrest."

"Hmm. That would be a shame," Ming admitted. "The serum you will be injected with is 33vK; it is based on the common cold virus. This is our standard treatment. Dr. Hsu would have preferred to use an experimental serum based on a new strain of the Filoviridae virus—what you know as Ebola—but I told him no because the risk of death is too great."

"Your concern for my health is touching."

"Oh, don't flatter yourself. I am only interested in seeing how you perform as a Homothal. Until now, all my test subjects have been culled from the native population. They had no prior training as soldiers.

"But you… perhaps you will be the first of a master race of genetically superior warriors. I should have recognized these possibilities sooner. This should make you proud Commander, you are at the leading edge of science!"

"Tell me something, Ming. When did you become so perverted—or were you just born that way?"

Enraged, Colonel Ming struck Jim across the face with the back of his hand, drawing a small trickle of blood from his nose.

"Where did you send the transmission?"

Jim remained silent.

"Very well. Doctor, proceed."

Suddenly, the door burst open and the three SGIT soldiers rushed into the lab, weapons raised and firing. The Chinese soldiers and Homothals were focused on their prisoner and were unprepared for the sudden attack.

A barrage of lead cut through the guards; so closely grouped around the table, they had little chance of returning fire. One Homothal, though struck by buckshot and bullets, managed to raise its rifle and fire a poorly aimed burst, but none of the SGIT team were hit.

The SGIT soldiers fired their weapons in full automatic mode. The firefight lasted only three seconds.

When the gunfire ceased, the soldiers and Homothals were all dead on the floor, Dr. Hsu was still standing over Commander Nicolaou, but Colonel Ming had disappeared.

"Get Ming!" shouted Jim.

Magnum rushed forward toward the closing door just beyond the table. Reaching the doorway and placing his back to the wall, Magnum reached down and pulled the door open just a crack.

Bullets peppered the door and frame. "They got us pinned down in here, sir," Magnum reported.

Meanwhile, the doctor moved to inject the virus into the IV drip line. Ghost and Bull were pointing their guns at him. "Let me go—or I will inject him."

"Drop the syringe now," Bull commanded, "or my next shot will take your hand off at the wrist."

The doctor hesitated for a second before dropping the syringe; it shattered on the floor.

Ghost covered the doctor while Magnum and Bull undid the restraints holding Jim to the table.

"To say I'm glad to see you guys would be an understatement. You can brief me later on how you got in, but now we need to get out of here."

"Sir, I spoke with the Colonel," Bull interrupted. "Our orders are to toast the entire compound once we have secured your release. Colonel Pierson was very clear, no research data, records, reports, or related documents are to remain."

"A half dozen 2,000-pound bombs would do the job nicely," Jim suggested.

"Yes, sir. I explained the situation to Colonel Pierson. He

told us to improvise; said he cannot order an air strike or cruise missile attack."

Jim looked around the lab as he hopped off the table. "I was in this room earlier. There's a storage room over there, through the door Ming went out," he nodded his head to the left, "and it's full of chemical reagents and solvents."

"That's fine for taking care of this building, but there are three others, too," Magnum reminded everyone.

Jim thought for a moment, and then turned to the doctor standing silently under Ghost's watchful eyes.

"I think the good doctor will help us."

"I will do no such thing," the doctor answered defiantly.

"Doctor, what are the other buildings used for?" Jim asked casually, as if they were acquaintances exchanging small talk.

"I will not help you."

"Oh, I think you will." Jim walked to the bench where minutes earlier the doctor had been busily preparing the viral agent for injection. The bench, one of several like it in the lab, had cabinets below and open shelving at the back. On the shelving sat an endless selection of chemicals in glass and plastic bottles, all neatly arranged in alphabetic order.

He picked up a bottle, examined the label, and then put it down before moving to the next bottle. He repeated this process several times, not finding whatever he was looking for.

"Doctor, I think I'll take a lesson from Colonel Ming's notebook. He has some rather extreme ideas on obtaining information from prisoners, but perhaps they'll work for me. What do you think?"

The doctor recoiled in terror. He had no idea what Jim was preparing to do to him, and his imagination only amplified his fear. Ghost grabbed the doctor by his shoulders.

"Don't worry Doc," Ghost said, mocking the man's obvious fear. "This won't hurt much, will it Commander?"

"I don't know—depends on what we use as a pain scale."

Jim picked up another bottle, totally at random, but the doctor had no way of knowing.

"I wonder what this one tastes like. Ghost, I think we should let the doctor taste it, don't you?"

Ghost smiled thinly. His hold on the doctor's shoulders tightened.

Jim held the bottle in front of the doctor so he could read the label... potassium hydroxide. Jim vaguely recognized the chemical name and was sure the doctor was well versed in its uses. From the rising terror in his eyes, it was evident he guessed right.

"No, you can't make me eat that. It will kill me!"

"Really? Well, we won't give you very much then... at least, not all at once. We can start with... say... a couple hundred milligrams?"

"No! You can't; you are in violation of the Geneva Convention!"

"So is experimentation on people. Not to mention murder, rape, and genocide."

The doctor's eyes were wide and his face had grown pale. Bull thought he might faint at any moment.

"You can't do this to me. Your country outlawed torture. You have to take me prisoner."

Jim turned to Bull. "Is that right? We aren't allowed to torture any longer?"

Bull merely shrugged.

"I suppose you're right, Doc." Jim sighed. "In the U.S. we wouldn't be allowed to torture you."

The doctor nearly melted in Ghost's grip. He would not have to answer these men, nor be forced to cooperate. How weak, he thought. When the roles had been reversed, as they were not long ago, Colonel Ming would have never conceded.

Jim examined the bottle again. "Potassium hydroxide... you know Doc, I was never very good at chemistry. But this..." he pointed to the label. "This sounds familiar, kind of like sodium hydroxide. It's commonly used in resomation," Jim explained. He turned to his team and added, "that's a form of chemical cremation where strong alkali hastens the decomposition of bodily tissues and leaves only the bones and cartilage behind."

The doctor was non-responsive.

"You know what, Doc. I just remembered something. We aren't in the United States. In fact, I don't even know exactly where we are."

Jim turned to Bull again. "Doesn't the rule book clearly state that we can't torture any prisoner if we're in the U.S.?"

Bull nodded, playing along. "Yes, sir."

"So, I guess it's a good thing we're not at home."

The doctor began to tremble. He was shaking his head. "No!"

"Ghost, you and Bull hold him tight. Magnum, take your knife and pry open his mouth. I'm going to pour in just a little bit of this white powder and then we'll see how long before it starts to liquefy his tongue and mouth. Since he's not going to talk, he doesn't really need his tongue, does he?"

As Jim opened the bottle, Magnum produced his knife. He pushed open the doctor's lips and wedged the knife tip against the doctor's clenched jaws. Applying pressure, the tip pried the doctor's teeth apart. Magnum pushed a little harder and the mouth popped open. He shoved the knife laterally across the teeth to keep them apart. A small trickle of blood appeared at the corner of the doctor's mouth where the blade had cut his lip.

"Now we're making progress." Jim forced a stiff smile. "Magnum, keep his mouth open and I'll pour a little of this powder in. Let's go on three. Ready? One... two... three."

The doctor struggled, but all he got for his effort were more lacerations on his lips and the corners of his mouth. Jim held the bottle over the doctor's mouth and was making ready to tap out some of the white substance.

With eyes wide, suddenly the doctor grunted loudly and nodded his head slightly in the affirmative.

"Bull, I think Doc has something to tell us."

Magnum removed his knife, but Ghost and Bull held their grip.

"All right! I'll tell you!" the doctor cried.

"What are the different buildings in this compound used for?" Jim repeated.

The doctor took a deep breath as he tried to calm down.

"This building is our medical complex. This is where we perform the procedure. Sometimes we might autopsy deceased specimens in this lab."

"You don't even recognize them as people, do you?" Bull interrupted. The doctor ignored him.

"The nearest building to the right is the computer lab and communications center. That is also where the officer's quarters are located. The remaining buildings are quarters for the soldiers, the mess hall and recreation center, and the holding cells for the Homothals."

"You keep them in cells? As in prison cells?" Bull asked.

"They are… unpredictable; sometimes they are very violent and uncontrollable. It is for their own safety."

"Yeah. You mean it's for your safety," Magnum retorted.

"Are you certain there are no records or communications equipment in those buildings?" Jim pressed. He had to be sure. If these other buildings really were as the doctor described, then they could avoid taking the time to demolish them and focus only on the medical and computer buildings.

"I am certain. Colonel Ming does not trust the Homothals or his enlisted soldiers. He insisted the records and communications equipment be centralized under his direct control."

Jim considered the doctor for a moment. He had truly been terrified that he would be tortured. Under ideal circumstances, Jim would not trust information obtained by such means. But these were not ideal circumstances, and he simply did not have time, materials, or other options.

"Ghost, bind his hands behind his back and search him. Take his key card and anything else that might have value."

CHAPTER 41

"BULL, THIS IS HOMER... do you copy?" The squad net communicated the voice message across all headsets. Commander Nicolaou answered.

"Copy. This is Boss Man. Sit rep." Jim requested. He needed to quickly get up to speed on their tactical situation.

"Glad to have you back, sir. I'm with the civilians overlooking the compound. We can provide cover fire to the south and east of the compound. But we have a problem... a new development."

"What problem?"

"A new player is entering the field. Stealth insertion—looks like modified hang-gliders—they're coming in from the south-east."

From the southeast, thought Jim. That meant whoever was crashing the party would have the rising sun behind them. Heat seeking missiles are useless if aimed in the sun's direction; they would most likely lock on to the big yellow orb rather than the intended target. In addition, it would be difficult to discern a small target against the bright sun.

"Roger. Stealth insertion—assume they are not invited. Observe and report. Do not... I repeat... *do not* reveal your position or presence. Is that understood?"

"Roger. Do not reveal presence or position. Will observe and report back when we have some news. Homer out."

"Doesn't sound good," Bull admitted.

"If the job was easy someone else would be doing it," Jim replied. He returned his attention to the task at hand.

The doctor had his hands cuffed behind his back and was sitting on the floor in clear sight. An SGIT soldier always had him in view, and they watched him closely. The last thing they needed was to have the good doctor escape; his knowledge of the compound could still prove useful.

"Magnum, follow me. Let's see what we can find in the storage room that can be used to destroy this lab," Jim said.

The shelves were packed with dozens of bottles of various solvents and reagents, mostly large four liter bottles.

"What are we looking for?" Magnum asked.

Jim was quickly scanning the labels, but without much class time in chemistry, he decided to get advice. "Homer, I need to talk to Peter."

A few seconds later, Peter's voice sounded in Jim's ear. "I'm here. What can I do?" he said.

"We're in a lab. The storeroom has a supply of solvents in four liter glass bottles and a variety of other chemicals. I need something, some method, to destroy this lab. It has computers, and probably notebooks too, but we've not located them yet. The problem is, I don't know what I'm looking at."

"I can help you. You're in the storeroom now?"

"Yes."

"Read the labels to me."

"Dichloromethane. Toluene. Methanol. Cyclohexane. Nitromethane—"

"Stop. Are you sure—nitromethane?"

"Yes, I'm sure. Is that important?"

"Jackpot," Peter said, his voice upbeat. "Everything you named is a fairly standard solvent for sample preparations and liquid chromatography. Most of them are flammable. But nitromethane is a high explosive under the right conditions."

"Isn't it a racing fuel, for dragsters?" Magnum said.

"Yes, that's right. When mixed with methanol it's an excellent fuel; a lot of energy. How much do you have?"

The squad net was silent while Jim counted bottles. "Five bottles, each four liters."

"That's good. Now here's the problem. Nitromethane is very difficult to detonate. Do you have any explosives?

"Magnum has some C4, but not a lot, and we may need it later."

"Got it. If we can find a sensitizing agent, and add that to the nitromethane, it'll be a whole lot easier to detonate. You said there are other chemicals in the lab?"

"Yeah, what are we looking for?" Jim said.

Peter thought for a moment, trying to organize the list in his mind, beginning with the most potent sensitizing agents. "Ammonium nitrate, ethylenediamine, or aluminum powder. These are all solid powders and are probably stored in small plastic or glass jars. They might be somewhere away from the solvent storage area."

"Just a minute." Jim and Magnum left the storeroom and returned to the benches where Jim had found the potassium hydroxide.

"Okay, we're looking now," Jim said.

"The labels will most likely be printed in English—it's too expensive for chemical companies to customize labeling to different languages so English has become universal," Peter explained.

"No ammonium nitrate or aluminum powder. Magnum, you're in the E section?"

"Looking," Magnum replied without taking his eyes away from the bottles. He was systematically checking each bottle, moving his lips as he said each chemical name.

"Bingo! Ethylenediamine. The label says 500 grams and it looks full."

"Good," Peter replied. "You'll need to open each jug of nitromethane and add about two tablespoons of ethylenediamine. The exact amount is not important, so don't worry. Pour in about two tablespoons, put the cap back on the jug, and shake it for 30 seconds. It's okay if all the ethylenediamine doesn't dissolve. When you're ready, cluster all the jugs together. A standard blasting cap should initiate detonation, but to be safe, if you can spare a quarter pound of C4, that will do it for sure."

"Roger that."

"One more thing," Peter said. "Those five jugs of nitromethane—that's a lot of energy. Most likely it'll level that room. Make sure you're far away when it goes off."

Magnum prepared the jugs of nitromethane according to Peter's instructions. Once all five jugs were ready, he packed them in a cluster in the center of the lab where Ghost was piling up computers he had yanked off tables from around the lab. There were no servers or mainframes in the lab, so they concluded that the bulk of the computational hardware was in the next building. Jim hauled a dozen jugs of cyclohexane and toluene from the storage room and placed these around the nitromethane, knowing the flammable solvent would add to the destructive power of the detonation.

Magnum set to work placing a charge of C4 between three

jugs of nitromethane. On Boss Man's order, Magnum would insert a time-delay detonator in the C4.

"Doc, where are the lab notebooks kept?" Jim asked.

At first the doctor refused to answer. He just stared at Commander Nicolaou, eyes blank of emotion.

Jim sighed. "Need I remind you of our deal? You cooperate, and we don't torture you. It's that simple. Where are the laboratory notebooks kept?"

The doctor was entering a mild state of shock. Still, he comprehended the message, and he didn't want to test these men again.

"Over there," he nodded toward a desk and file cabinet across the lab.

Nicolaou walked over to the cabinet and tried to open the top drawer. Locked. He tried the next drawer down… also locked. Having run out of patience long ago, he called Bull over.

"Shoot the lock out."

Bull placed the muzzle of his shotgun within an inch of the key lock and pulled the trigger. A ragged hole replaced the lock.

Jim opened the top drawer—it was full of bound notebooks. He took one out and opened it, verifying the contents.

It was written mostly in Chinese, but there was enough technical jargon and scientific notations, spaced between pages of tabulated numerical data, to convince him that these were lab notebooks. He opened the next drawer down and found more of the same style of books. He again examined a couple to make sure he was not being led astray. He did the same for the last two drawers—four large drawers in all, containing an estimated 150 laboratory notebooks. Each notebook had 300 numbered pages.

"Magnum, Ghost. Help me gather up these notebooks and throw them onto the pile as well. We have to destroy all of it."

After carrying two armloads each, the SGIT team had

emptied the file cabinet of its contents.

"Quickly check all the desk drawers and cabinets. Make sure we aren't missing anything obvious, like CDs, DVDs, or thumb drives," Jim ordered.

Within two minutes the three men had completely ransacked the lab. A small stack of papers in one of the desks and four thumb drives were all they found to add to the pile.

"Throw it all in." The pile was easily six feet tall, spilling over the table and making a large mound on the floor, and at the base of it was the nitromethane bomb and the jugs of flammable solvents.

"Ghost, grab the good doctor. We may still need his services."

Following one final quick look around the lab, Jim ordered Magnum to set the detonator. "Give us two minutes to get clear. If the blast is as big a Peter suggests, we need to put some distance between us and this lab."

Magnum set the time delay and inserted the detonator into the chunk of C4, making one final quick inspection, then he pulled back to Commander Nicolaou and gave him a sharp nod.

"Let's go, gentlemen. Move like you had a purpose!"

The team rushed out the door. No one wanted to be near the lab when the improvised bomb exploded.

Ghost pushed the doctor before him and the team turned to their left, toward the closest exit, when the squad net crackled to life again.

"Boss Man. The new kids are being engaged by approximately half a dozen enemy. Resistance is heavy. So far, it is confined to the open space to the northeast of our position."

"Copy. Be advised, enemy combatants include a genetic hybrid between man and Neanderthal. They call it a Homothal."

"Roger that." Homer had dozens of questions swirling in his

mind, but they would have to wait until later. At the moment he had more pressing issues at hand.

"Are the new kids being engaged by Homothals or Chinese soldiers?" Jim asked, still moving his team to the exit at the end of the hallway.

"Both, sir," Homer replied. "Looks like Chinese officers or non-coms are directing the defenders." There was a brief pause before Homer continued. "More Homothals and Chinese soldiers are now joining the battle."

"Where did the reinforcements come from?" Jim asked.

"From the two buildings connected to the fenced yard."

Jim wanted to be sure, so he asked for clarification. "Did any enemy combatants come from the building to our immediate right?"

"Negative, sir. The bad guys are pouring out of the far two buildings… must be barracks I'd guess."

"Roger that. Our intel says you're right."

"Whoever the new guys are, looks like they're going to get their butts kicked. There must be 50 or more Homothals and Chinese soldiers forming a broad line… and now they're bringing out light machine guns. Those guys are going to be mowed down."

"How many new kids in the party?" Jim needed to weigh the facts and make a decision.

Homer shifted his spotting scope to the right and assessed the situation. "Not enough. Maybe fifteen. And they don't have any heavy weapons, just what they could carry in during their drop."

Jim thought for a moment. Maybe Lady Luck finally took a turn and decided to smile favorably on his team.

"Homer, what's the Dillon's status?"

"It's operational sir. Peter rigged it up to put a partial charge on the battery, so the mule is mobile and we have a full ammo can fed into her. She's hot to trot and positioned at the base of the ridge ready to cover your retreat."

"We still have a job to do, but our friends just provided a much needed diversion."

Homer didn't understand. "Our friends?" he questioned.

"Haven't you heard the Arabic proverb? An enemy of my enemy is my friend."

CHAPTER 42

"USE THOSE BARRETTS TO ENGAGE the Chinese and Homothals! Focus on the machine guns… buy as much time as you can for the new kids and try to pull fire away from them. Got it?" Jim was very short but direct.

"Yes sir, but I can't say I understand. These new players could also be gunning for us."

"Yes, that's a possibility. But we don't know that yet, and since our immediate enemy considers them an enemy… well, that makes them our best ally… our only ally for the time being."

Homer admitted his Commander's logic made a certain amount of sense. "Roger, sir. Will engage and draw fire away from the new kids."

"Get back to me in two minutes. I want to know how the battle is evolving. Boss Man out."

Homer relayed the order to Peter, Todd, and Gary. "We are to engage the Homothals and Chinese soldiers—prioritize the

DAVE EDLUND

machine gunners. View the new kids as friendlies."

Peter had been studying the unfolding events through the highest magnification on his riflescope. He couldn't make out the facial features on the men almost half a mile away. They were wearing uniforms that looked like camouflaged jumpsuits, but the coloring was a mix of blue, green, and two different shades of gray.

"I'm not an expert," he offered, "but I've never seen uniforms like those before."

Homer shifted his viewing angle just slightly so he could take in the closest men. They were beginning to receive machine gunfire. "Could be Chinese Airborne... paratroopers. But that's not our concern right now. Take out those machine guns before they can do any real damage."

Peter wasn't going to debate the issue. He placed the cross hairs on the closest machine gun position. The electronic scope read out the distance using its built-in laser range finder—1,345 yards. The scope compensated for the bullet drop over that distance and a tiny green light illuminated in the upper right corner of his objective lens, signaling that the sight picture had been correctly adjusted and he could take the shot.

Holding steady, Peter took in a breath; rather than holding it he slowly exhaled as he gently increased pressure on the rifle trigger. *BOOM!*

He saw the soldier manning the machine gun take the hit; his right side awash in bright red. The ammunition bearer stepped up to man the gun, and Peter took aim again, almost at exactly the same spot. The rifle roared and kicked, and again the bullet struck its target. With both soldiers dead, this machine gun was at least temporarily out of service.

Homer and Todd were simultaneously dispatching the other two machine gun crews, and the new kids steadily advanced. With the devastating fire from the machine guns halted, this new force on the battlefield began to gain ground.

They were zig-zagging across the open land, running a short distance and then dropping to fire three or four well-aimed shots. They timed their advance so that there was always about half of their force firing and providing cover for the other half that was advancing.

Although the snipers were thinning the defender's ranks, they couldn't do it fast enough. Homer was concerned that the new kids, still heavily outnumbered and now close enough to receive deadly fire, would not make it to the buildings in sufficient numbers to do their job. That thought was followed logically by his next. He started a brief conversation in his mind. *Just what is their job? Not my problem. That's Boss Man's call.*

Homer glanced at his watched—twenty more seconds until he was scheduled to contact Boss Man with a sit rep. As the losses were mounting, he decided not to wait any longer.

"Homer here. We're thinning them down, but there are still way more Chinese and Homothals and the new kids are likely to be overrun soon. We just can't get enough volume of fire down there fast enough."

"Understood," Jim replied. "You have the remote controller for the mule, right?"

"Yes sir."

"Good. Drive the mule out on the most direct line. Engage the Dillon at maximum effective range. Get it moving, now!"

"Yes sir, out." Homer immediately had the mule's electric drive on and the machine pulled out of its hiding spot. Steering with a remote controller that included two joysticks, an LED screen, and one prominent toggle switch, he steered Bessy directly at the defensive line established by the Homothals and Chinese soldiers.

The mule had only traversed a hundred yards or so when

Homer aimed the multi-barrel Dillon minigun at the enemy and pressed the fire toggle switch. To conserve his limited supply of ammo and achieve maximum effect, he fired only short bursts—all the while the mule was inexorably plodding closer to the targets. Homer focused the majority of the fire on the lead elements of the defending force. At first, the defenders did not acknowledge the Dillon. By the time they realized the magnitude of the threat, more than a dozen had been mowed down.

The Chinese soldiers began to fall back. Within three minutes the large ammo can for the Dillon minigun was spent. The battlefield was littered with more than 75 corpses, mostly killed by Homer's squad. Without ammunition, the minigun would be useless for supporting Boss Man's exfiltration. Homer didn't linger on the thought, instead trading the remote for his rifle.

The invading force had been reduced in number to seven men. Homer counted carefully to be certain of the number.

Once they retreated to the building, the defenders had all but disappeared. Only three Homothals remained at the entrance, firing their rifles to keep the invaders from rushing head long to the open doorway. Peter aimed and fired. Two more rifle shots immediately followed and all three Homothals lay dead.

With the doorway temporarily cleared of defenders, the new kids closed the distance and entered the building. As the last man entered, he paused briefly and looked up toward the ridge where Homer and the sniper team were positioned. The man came sharply to attention, raised his right arm, and saluted smartly. Homer watched all this through his scope, as did Peter, Todd, and Gary.

"Well I'll be…" was all Todd could say.

Homer voiced what was on everyone's mind. "I just pray to

God that we helped the right team."

"I suspect we'll know before long," Peter observed.

"I'll let Boss Man know the score. Not much else we can do until the fighting comes back out in the open."

Taking advantage of the break, Peter laid down his rifle and shuffled back to the sheltered spot nestled in a wide fissure in the rock outcropping where Ethan lay. Here he was shielded from stray shots by a group of boulders to the front and the twenty-foot-high sandstone walls that defined the fissure. It appeared to travel further up the ridge... how far Peter couldn't be sure because it took a bend to the right and continued out of sight.

Ethan was beginning to stir. Peter squatted next to his son.

"How are you feeling?"

Ethan groaned and opened his eyes just a bit. "My head is killing me."

Peter smiled, it was a good response. "I'm not surprised. That Homothal was using you as a punching bag."

Ethan squinted his eyes. "The what?"

"Homothal, that's what they're called. A genetically engineered cross between a Homo sapiens and a Neanderthal."

"I don't understand." Ethan paused and a grimace flowed over his face. "My whole body hurts."

Peter rummaged through his field first-aid kit and pulled out a small bottle of ibuprofen. "Here, take four of these," he offered the tablets and his canteen of water.

Ethan took the pills and a big swallow of warm, tepid water. He lay his head gently back down on the rolled-up jacket.

"Dad?" he asked after swallowing the medicine.

"I'm right here son."

"Are we going home soon?"

Peter wanted to tell him yes, that they were leaving right now. But they couldn't leave just yet.

"Soon. We'll be going home soon."

Ethan's eyelids were heavy. "I want to go to Todd Lake and swim in the cool water." Ethan swallowed and even that simple act seemed to drain away his energy. "It's so hot."

"Yes, we're in the desert. Do you know where you are?" Peter's voice was gentle.

"The desert… yeah, I know. It's so hot and my head hurts. I want to go to the lake. Can we go there?"

Peter nodded, fearful that if he tried to speak his voice would break, and he had to be strong for Ethan.

Peter took a moment to compose himself. "Yes, we'll pack a lunch; I'm sure your sister will come along, too. I can imagine the meadow at the far end of the lake. There are still a few wild flowers blooming. Do you see them?"

Ethan allowed his eyes to close and relaxed his head. "Yes, it's so beautiful."

"We'll go soon, I promise. And you can go swimming in the lake. It's too cold for me." Peter attempted humor, hoping to raise Ethan's spirits, if only a little.

A slight curl appeared to Ethan's mouth, but it didn't remain long. His eyes were still closed. "Dad, are you there?"

"Yes, I'm here, right beside you." Peter clasped his son's hand. "You're safe here. Just rest. I won't be far away. Just rest, okay?" Peter's voice was thick with emotion again; he found it hard to speak without choking up. He gently squeezed Ethan's hand and mumbled a prayer, too soft for Ethan to hear.

"God, please get us out of here. Please."

CHAPTER 43

DARFUR

JUNE 14   0845 HOURS

THE SGIT TEAM REACHED the exit doors, knowing they we still too close to the lab. Jim had been through here before and knew that out the doors and to the right they would find the building housing the computer center, the communications room, and—if their prisoner was telling the truth—the officers' quarters. They needed to move without delay, but Jim sensed this could be a trap.

Jim checked his watch, counting down to the detonation. One minute, 17 seconds...

"Doctor, I think you should go first," Jim ordered.

The doctor shook his head. "No!"

Jim, holding an assault rifle he had picked up from a dead guard back in the lab, jabbed the barrel into the doctor's back. "Get up and go out the door!"

"No! They might shoot me!"

"If you don't move, I'll shoot you right here!"

The doctor stood, hands till bound behind his back, and

reluctantly nudged the door with his shoulder. The steel door had no window, so he pushed it open a few inches and yelled out something in Mandarin. Jim assumed he was announcing his presence and telling any Homothals or Chinese soldiers that might be watching the door not to shoot.

The doctor pushed the door open a little further and finally the doctor slowly emerged from behind it, stepping into the morning light. *BOOM! BOOM!* Two shots and the doctor fell dead, his body falling within the door way so that the door couldn't close.

One minute...

"Ghost, snake the fiber optic lens around the edge of the door. We need to know where the shooters are," Jim ordered.

Laying down to conceal his position, Ghost slid the probe along the Doctor's body to the edge of the door. He held the LCD screen close while maneuvering the lens left and right.

"I see two shooters at the corner of the barracks on the far side of the yard... left corner. One is high, the other low."

Forty three seconds...

"Bull, what's the load in that magazine?" Jim asked, referring to a spare AA12 magazine stuffed in a pouch strapped to Bull's waist.

"Frags, sir."

"Good. Load 'em up. When Ghost pushes the door open we all fire where those shooters are. We need to get to the next building. That should be the computer lab. We have to move fast—that bomb is going to detonate."

Jim nodded to Ghost and he pushed the door open. Bullets pierced the door, but none of the SGIT soldiers were hit. Bull raised his shotgun and fired at the corner of the barracks. He was joined by his teammates, all firing as they dashed out the door and turned toward the adjacent building.

Ten seconds...

With weapons aimed across the open space toward the barracks, the SGIT soldiers fired from the hip as they ran for cover.

The explosion was deafening, twice as large as any had imagined. The shock wave shoved the men to the ground and they slid to a stop in front of the door, the card lock above Magnum's head. He stood and inserted the key card, holding his breath for a heartbeat, and then he heard the faint click of the lock opening. He pushed the door open

Magnum entered through the door into the deserted hallway, followed by the rest of the team.

"That door on the left, that's the lab where we found the computers. We'll start there and then search the remaining rooms," Jim said.

As before, the door into the computer lab was not locked. The team quickly dashed inside, and Bull remained on guard while the others surveyed the room.

There were two rows of computer workstations located in the room's center, running the width of the room from left to right. Jim stepped forward and quickly estimated the room's size—100 feet wide by at least 50 feet, maybe 70 feet, from front to back. In this space were a large number of PCs, servers, and other peripherals.

"How much explosives do we have?" Jim asked.

"Not enough," answered Magnum. "We've only got ten pounds of C4."

Jim looked around the room again. They needed another plan.

"We need more explosives or incendiaries… both would be great," Jim thought out loud.

He looked around the computer lab while Ghost and Magnum stared at their commander.

Still muttering to himself, Jim questioned, "Where is a

directory when you need it?"

Ghost and Magnum looked at each other with a question in their eyes.

"You okay?" Ghost asked.

"Never better," Jim replied and then added, "Where would you find explosives in this kind of complex?"

Ghost shrugged, and then said, "Uh, the armory?"

"That's exactly what I think. Now where do you suppose the armory is?"

"Well, in the barracks, close to the troops."

Jim shook his head. "No, not there. Remember what the doctor told us? Colonel Ming doesn't trust his troops. That's why the communications center is located here, in the same building as the officer's quarters."

Magnum understood. "And Ming would want to control all access to the weapons. He lives in fear of a mutiny."

Jim nodded. "Exactly. That means the armory is—"

"In this building," Ghost interrupted.

Jim looked at Ghost. "Now, all we have to do is find it and avoid being killed in the process. Search room by room," he commanded.

The SGIT team left the computer lab and turned down the hallway, continuing their journey further into the building. It was a twin to the other building the team had been in with the long hallway and rooms on each side.

As they searched, Jim hoped they would also discover Ming's office. It was likely critical information would be kept there, which they would need to destroy along with all the other records.

At each door, Magnum tested the handle and so far none were locked. Entering the rooms, they conducted a quick search, taking a mental inventory of the contents so they could come back later and demolish it if needed.

Magnum was testing the latch on the fifth room on the left side of the hallway. This door was locked. Jim motioned for Bull to shoot the latch. Bull switched out the rotary magazine in the AA12 for one loaded with buckshot, but before he could fire, four Chinese soldiers emerged from a door further down the corridor. One appeared to be an officer; Jim recognized another as Sergeant Wong. The Chinese soldiers were startled by the sight of the four Americans.

Immediately recognizing Jim, Sergeant Wong quickly raised his rifle and fired. The shot was wild and burrowed into the wall inches from Jim's head. Jim spun and dropped to his knees. Although the rifle he was carrying was equipped with a 75-round drum magazine, Jim had no idea how full it was. Still, with adrenaline coursing through his blood, he pulled hard on the trigger and fired a continuous stream of bullets into the close pack of Chinese soldiers.

Before Wong got off a second shot, four bullets slammed into his torso. Along with his fellow soldiers, Sergeant Wong died on the spot.

"Get that lock cleared!" Jim ordered, keeping an eye on the hallway for further dangers.

Bull blasted the lock and kicked open the door. They rushed in and closed the door behind them.

From the furniture and decorations in the room it was obvious they were standing in Colonel Ming's outer office.

In front of them was a receptionist's desk with a black phone and an intercom, but otherwise the desk was devoid of paper and other objects. On the wall behind the desk was a framed photograph of Colonel Ming in full dress uniform.

"This certainly confirms the size of Ming's ego," Jim quipped. To the left of the photograph was another door. Jim guessed that this one led into the Colonels' office.

He strode to the door and gently grasped the handle.

Looking back at his team Jim nodded. His team responded by shouldering their weapons and aiming at imagined adversaries on the other side of the door.

Jim turned the door handle and pushed the door forward.

He motioned for his team to move up. They quickly moved through the door and then parted to either side, guns at the ready. Jim immediately followed them through the door. The room was empty.

CHAPTER 44

COLONEL MING'S OFFICE was the size of a two-car garage. In its center lay a large oriental rug in deep shades of burgundy and emerald green. The plush carpet covered a marble floor in light shades of beige. Aged oak panels covered the walls giving the room a mellow honey tone. Nestled close to the back wall stood a large carved ebony desk. Jim could not help but marvel at the beauty of the furnishings.

"Ming may be a monster, but he certainly knows how to select an interior designer. I wonder if his comrades in Beijing know how much of their money he spent to decorate and furnish his office."

"Not quite in the spirit of communism, is it?" Magnum observed, also marveling at the masculine beauty of the room.

"I could get used to this," Ghost quipped. He wandered to the floor-to-ceiling bookcases covering both walls flanking the desk, eyes scanning over the collection like a freshman college student trying to find a particular class-assigned textbook.

There was a copy of *Grey's Anatomy* and two editions of the *Merck Manual*. On another shelf was *Concepts of Genetics* and next to it was a copy of *Human Molecular Genetics*.

Ghost moved to another section of the bookcase. "Hey, check this out. Looks like Ming has a collection of books on Neanderthals. This title is *Neanderthals Revisited*... and here's one called *The Neanderthal Legacy*."

"Think he actually read all these books?" Magnum asked.

"Yeah. It's his reference library," Jim answered.

Bull didn't quite know what to say; he just whistled.

The top of the desk was completely clean and free of clutter. Jim began to rifle through the drawers, looking for anything that might be of value—records, diary, notepads, memory sticks or compact discs, voice recorder—anything.

But he didn't find anything. Only the usual office paraphernalia—pens and pencils, writing tablets, paper clips.

"Looks like Colonel Ming is a neat freak," Bull observed.

Jim kept searching. He turned next to the four-drawer file cabinet. It wasn't locked, and when he opened the top drawer he knew why... empty.

"He's cleaned everything out. There's nothing here. No records, no notes... nothing."

Both Magnum and Ghost were looking through the rows of neatly organized books and artifacts on the oak shelving while Bull was guarding the door through which they entered, shotgun leveled and finger on the trigger.

"What's this?" asked Magnum, picking up a carved wooden figure. It was clearly representative of a man, but with an exceptionally large phallus.

Looking over, Bull replied, "That's an African fertility God."

Magnum just about dropped it trying to get it out of his grip. He didn't want to take a chance that any fertility would rub off onto him. He had a steady legion of girlfriends, but he wasn't ready for a serious commitment and *certainly* wasn't interested in fathering children.

Finished with his search, Jim again scanned the room. "There must be something here, something we've missed…"

Then Jim's eye saw it.

"What is it Boss Man?" Ghost asked.

"The floor," he answered, pointing at a particular section of the marble in front of the shelves. "What is that?"

Ghost and Magnum looked down at the floor near their feet. There were some black streaks, rub marks, on the pale marble. Magnum leaned down and rubbed his thumb against one of the marks. "Feels like a scuff mark."

"Like from a boot?" Jim said.

Magnum nodded.

"Did either of you make those marks?"

The two men looked at each other, and then back at Jim. "No, sir!"

Jim approached and bent down to feel the marks. *Yes, scuff marks from a boot, or boots. Why here at the base of the bookcase?* And then it dawned on him.

"It's a passageway."

"What?" Magnum questioned.

"Behind the bookcase, there's a passageway. These scuff marks were made by Ming and his guards scrambling out of here. They probably were escaping just as Bull shot the lock off the outer door."

"Then there must be a secret lever or something to open it," Magnum said.

"All we have to do is find it."

"But what are we looking for?" Ghost inquired.

"I don't know. I've never seen a real secret passage, only in the movies. Try pulling out the books, and then picking up the figurines and other pieces on the shelves. Something must unlatch the hidden door… maybe a lever under the shelves."

They each took a different section of the floor-to-ceiling bookcase. The moved every book, picked up every art piece, ran hands along the underside of all the shelves. Nothing worked, and Jim was growing discouraged. He sighed and stepped back, collecting his thoughts.

Then he spotted the light fixtures… two of them. Each shaped like a torch held by a bronze hand. They were mounted on either side of the center panel of shelving. He pulled on the left torch, then the right torch. Nothing. Both were firmly attached to the wood paneling

He considered the problem for a moment, and then he tried twisting them. First the left torch… twist to the right. Nothing. Twist to the left. Nothing. It was solidly mounted and not going to move. He approached the right torch and twisted it to the left.

The center panel of shelves swung silently back into a passageway behind the wall. A single bulb cast a dim light that illuminated a landing and a flight of stairs leading down.

Jim looked at Ghost, Magnum, and Bull. "Let's go get him."

CHAPTER 45

WITH JIM IN THE LEAD, the SGIT team rushed down the stairway into the darkness below, weapons raised and ready. As they moved deeper, lights flickered on before them, activated by motion sensors. They descended perhaps 30 feet when they came to the base of the stairway and found themselves entering a wide corridor leading off in both directions. The gray concrete floor, walls, and ceiling were dimly illuminated by bulbs spaced along the wall about twenty feet apart. Tucked up tight against the ceiling were many parallel runs of electrical conduit and a single, wide rectangular ventilation duct.

Pausing for a moment, with Ghost and Magnum training their weapons in one direction down the seemingly endless corridor, and Bull covering the opposite direction, Jim gathered his thoughts. He had absolutely no way of knowing which direction Colonel Ming had gone.

Then he heard it. The noise was faint, but it sounded like a door closing. It had come from the left.

Jim swiveled. "Let's go. We might still be able to catch him. But we have to move fast!"

The men rushed to the end of the corridor where it bent to the right. They had yet to see a door along the vast tunnel, only occasional service panels. After covering about 200 yards from the stairs, they spotted a set of double steel doors.

With the team pointing their weapons forward, Jim slowly opened the door just a crack. The lack of gunshots encouraged him to open the door fully. The room was empty but brightly lit.

It looked like a meeting or conference room. In the room's center stood an oval table with ten plush leather chairs surrounding it. On the wall to their left hung a large projection screen. To their right sat a small table with a neat stack of porcelain cups. On the opposite side of the room was a set of double doors.

"We must have just missed them," Jim concluded. He jogged around the conference table to the double doors followed closely by his team. Jim opened one of the doors just a crack and peered into a junction of two concrete corridors. One broad passageway extended away from their position in a straight line, a second hallway stretched to the left and right.

Still peering around the door, Jim saw a group of Chinese soldiers about 25 yards down the wide passageway. Jim flung open the door. Raising his rifle he shouted, "Stop… or I'll shoot!"

Immediately, Jim's team took up defensive positions using the doorway as cover and trained their guns on the group of six soldiers. Jim stood firmly, legs slightly spread, and sighting down the barrel of the assault rifle.

The Chinese soldiers stopped, standing motionless with their backs toward the SGIT team, totally exposed in the middle of the corridor. Slowly, Colonel Ming turned around and locked eyes with Jim. The other Chinese soldiers did likewise.

"So, Commander. It appears I should have killed you earlier."

"I hear that a lot." Even as he spoke, Jim kept Ming in his sights; finger on the trigger and looking for a reason to fire.

Ming and his soldiers formed a tight group with half his men behind their comrades now facing Commander Nicolaou.

The SGIT soldiers remained firm in their stance. The Chinese soldiers kept their weapons down.

"You cannot win Commander. You are hopelessly outnumbered."

Jim shrugged slightly, but never moved his eyes, or rifle, from his target. "We've done pretty well so far."

Ming nodded, "So you have." At the same time he made an almost imperceptible motion with his fingers. It was so slight that the SGIT team missed it—but Ming's escorts did not. Two men began to slowly move away from Ming, attempting to open up the tight group. They needed to separate a bit if they were all to have freedom of movement necessary to raise and maneuver their weapons.

"I can make you a very wealthy man, Commander," Ming offered, trying to buy time and distract Commander Nicolaou.

"I'm not interested in your blood money."

Colonel Ming shrugged. "Maybe you aren't, but what about your men? I can pay them each more than they could earn in two lifetimes."

The SGIT team remained silent as they continued to sight down their weapons at the Chinese soldiers surrounding Colonel Ming.

"Intriguing possibility, isn't it?" Ming continued. "All you have to do is put down your weapons. That's all."

"No deal." Ghost said. Magnum and Bull held their position and rock-steady aim at the enemy soldiers.

Ming's guards continued to edge away from the group and

gain valuable maneuvering room. Jim realized what they were doing, and understood the tactical implications. "Tell your men to freeze!"

Ming stared defiantly back at Jim.

The Chinese guards increased their spacing and were approaching the point at which Jim thought they could attempt a counter attack. Ming continued to lock eyes with Jim, and a slight smirk appeared on his face. Ming believed that the West was weak because its society felt too strongly about protecting life, preserving rights, and forgiving one's wrong doings.

Ming continued to fatally underestimate his adversary.

CRACK! The sound of the shot was deafening in the confined spaced and echoed off the hard surfaces.

Jim's aim was true, and one guard who had looked most eager to prove himself to Colonel Ming lay dead on the cold, hard concrete floor.

The sound of the ejected shell casing was still rattling on the floor when Jim ordered again, "I said *freeze!* No one moves!"

The remaining Chinese guards were not stupid. Ming snarled, and his eyes filled with hatred.

"Drop your weapons!"

The order came from Jim's right and took Jim and his team completely by surprise.

Reluctant to let Ming go, Jim spun and pointed his weapon at four armed men in camouflage jumpsuits. Bull also pivoted toward the new threat a split second behind his commander.

This left Ghost and Magnum in the stand-off with Colonel Ming's soldiers.

"Put down your weapons! My men will shoot." This order came from one of the camouflage-clad soldiers.

From Ming's position he could not see the new threat to the SGIT team. But he instantly recognized the opportunity created by this diversion and ordered his men to fire.

Jim just caught the movement in his peripheral vision as the Chinese soldiers raised their weapons and opened up.

"Down!" Jim shouted. He and the rest of the SGIT team dove back through the doorway into the conference room. A fusillade of bullets screamed over their heads, tearing up several of the leather chairs and blasting fragments of concrete from the far wall.

As rapidly as it started, the shooting stopped. It was just the break that Ming needed. Surrounded by his soldiers, he bolted down the side corridor and out of sight.

CHAPTER 46

PETER MISSED THE COOL pre-dawn air as the morning heat radiated from the dirt and rocks. It was already beginning to feel like he was sitting in an oven.

With the previous threats outside the compound buildings neutralized, Peter was discussing a plan of action with Homer while Todd and Gary remained vigilant in case a new surprise appeared.

Vultures were already beginning to circle high overhead, drawn by the sight of the battlefield littered with bodies. For the next several days the desert scavengers would eat well.

"We remain in our position, maintain radio silence, and wait for Boss Man to check in with new orders," Homer stated.

"And if those orders don't come in? Then what?"

Homer didn't answer immediately.

"Look, we are completely exposed to the elements here," Peter argued. "There's little shade and by mid-day we'll all be baking. Between the sun's rays and the heat reflected off the rocks, the temperature will exceed 120 degrees. If dehydration doesn't kill us, heat stroke will!"

"I have my orders. We stick with the plan."

Peter couldn't believe what he was hearing. To make matters worse, both Gary and Ethan had suffered injuries serious enough to make them more vulnerable to physiological stress.

"You can't be serious!" he pressed the issue further.

Homer stepped forward to face Peter, and spoke in a low and firm voice. "I am very serious. I have my orders. Besides, I know my commander and my team; I trust them. Perhaps you should have more faith in them, too."

Homer turned away from Peter, returning to his position overlooking the compound. Out of the corner of his vision, up the slope rising a couple hundred feet above them, he saw a brief flash. Pausing, he focused his vision and studied the spot. There was nothing, and he began to question whether he had seen anything at all. He stood motionless and stared at the spot for another 30 seconds. Still nothing. Perhaps it was just a trick of the desert heat.

"What is it?" Peter asked, observing Homer's redirected attention.

"Maybe nothing, but I thought I saw a flash of light... maybe a reflection or something."

Peter also began studying the hillside, even though he didn't really know where to look.

Homer leaned over and retrieved his rifle. Hefting the heavy weapon to his shoulder and arching his back slightly, he pointed it up the slope and used the scope's magnification to search the area where he believed he had seen the spec of light.

All of a sudden, a dark shape exploded from the scattered boulders and started running down the slope! It was a Homothal, and it was firing its assault rifle from the hip as it carried out a suicidal charge.

Peter stared in disbelief when the crack of Homer's rifle sounded. The stocky body collapsed and rolled down the slope another 30 yards before coming to rest.

"What the…" Peter mumbled.

The echo was still reverberating off the surrounding ridges when a barrage of gunfire erupted from higher up the slope.

"Back to the boulders!" Homer shouted.

Peter and Homer ran back to Todd and Gary and began shifting their positions so they could shoot up the ridge from the opposite side of the boulders that had protected them so far.

Led by the Janjaweed barbarian named Korlos, the squad of Chinese soldiers and Homothals had circled around out of sight of Homer's position, climbing the ridge so that they could descend from above the snipers. The plan would have worked had the Homothal not spooked when Homer was using his riflescope. Little did the Homothal know that it had not been seen until it jumped up and charged down the slope.

Automatic rifle fire was raining down onto their position, bullets cratering in the dirt and ricocheting off rocks. Homer was the first to return fire, the Barrett still proving to be a superior long-range weapon. Except that now the enemy was within rifle range, and the snipers had to quickly aim, shoot, and get back behind cover. Without the luxury of time to sight the Barretts with care, the civilians were only connecting on each second or third shot.

The Chinese and Homothals progressed down the slope, using the sparse cover for protection. Todd was taking careful aim at the nearest Chinese soldier as a succession of three bullets slammed in the boulder only inches from his head.

The Chinese soldier was carrying an RPG and was almost within range. The soldier rose to one knee and steadied himself next to a cluster of rocks to aim. At the same time, two Homothals began firing a deadly barrage of automatic fire into the sniper's position. Todd didn't flinch. He concentrated, aimed, and squeezed the trigger.

BOOM! The bullet struck the RPG launcher, shattering the handgrip and the Chinese soldier's forearm at the same instant. The launcher was knocked from his grip; before the soldier could recover, another bullet—this one fired by Peter—struck the man in the chest.

Korlos was yelling orders to his squad. Although Homer couldn't make out his words, it was clear that he was in charge. Homer trained his sights on Korlos and fired. But Korlos was moving too quickly between boulders and rock outcroppings and the bullet kicked up a large cloud of dust only inches from his left foot. He ducked behind a large rock for cover.

Lying on his belly, the Janjaweed leader spotted a shallow draw that led to his right and down the slope, following a wide fissure in the sandstone cliff. He ordered most of his force to keep up the murderous torrent of fire on the snipers while a smaller number—three Chinese soldiers and two Homothals— were ordered to enter the crevice in the sandstone and follow the path down the slope. Following this route, Korlos reasoned, they could flank the snipers and overrun their position.

Peter saw the small group of Chinese and Homothals break off and move to his left where they disappeared into the sandstone outcropping. He recognized what they were planning. Even worse, he feared they would discover Ethan.

Peter rose from his concealed position and ran forward. "What are you doing? Get down!" Homer commanded.

"I have to get to Ethan!"

Then Todd followed suit, with Gary close behind.

"What are you doing?" Homer couldn't believe what was happening. As the three men ran for cover on their way to the rock shelter where Ethan lay, all Homer could do was provide defensive fire. Unable to both return fire rapidly and retreat behind the rocks, Homer remained exposed, sighting from one target to the next.

Bullets were striking all around him, but he continued to mechanically aim and shoot. A Chinese soldier was using hand signals to direct three Homothals to spread out and fire in unison. Marshalling all his training and skill, Homer placed the cross hairs on the soldier's head and squeezed the trigger. He was so absorbed that he was no longer hearing the gunfire. A fraction of a second later he saw the round strike home as an ugly crimson flower appeared where the man's head should have been.

Homer was in the groove. He was sensing the battle unfolding more than consciously taking it in. He had discovered this sixth sense in an early firefight near the Kachin pass along the Afghanistan-Pakistan border.

He felt the sonic *woosh* as a bullet passed within an inch of his body. Twisting his torso slightly to the left, he immediately acquired the new target even as the Chinese soldier squeezed off successive rounds. Homer remained steady in his position— he calmly sighted on the target's center of mass, and fired. He didn't miss.

Moving the rifle barrel only a few inches at a time, Homer swept back and forth across the slope, successfully pinning down the enemy.

"Damn civilians," he muttered. His only option was to lock down the enemy on the slope above him and hope that Peter and his friends could take care of themselves.

Peter ran fast and he made it to Ethan only seconds before the first Chinese soldier came down the fissure and rounded a corner about 20 yards from where Peter stood. He fired the Barrett rifle from his hip with no time to aim. He just pointed and pulled the trigger. The bullet missed and gouged an enormous hole in the sandstone wall next to the soldier, showering him in rock chips and dust.

The Chinese soldier had not expected to encounter the enemy here, believing the snipers were still below the mouth of the fissure. The soldier raised his assault rifle to return fire.

In that instant Peter made a minute correction to his aim and fired again. This time he got it right. The projectile slammed into the man's hip, causing him to cartwheel over, rifle flying in the opposite direction.

Ethan was sitting with his back against the rock wall. In his dazed state, he thought he was secure here, so he didn't easily comprehend the dual that had just taken place.

Peter rushed over to his son and rested the large rifle against the rock face. He helped Ethan up onto his feet. "We have to go. It's not safe here any longer."

Peter's back was to the Chinese soldier he had just shot, thinking he was dead.

"Dad, watch out!" Ethan yelled. Over his father's shoulder he saw the man raising a pistol in a shaky hand, and pointing it at the two of them.

BOOM! BOOM! Todd and Gary had just caught up with Peter; both men fired at the wounded Chinese solder, the bullets striking home. The pistol fell to the ground as the parched earth soaked up the dead man's blood.

"We have to get out of here. There're more coming, and this place will become a death trap," Peter shouted, his ears still ringing from the gunshots. He grabbed his rifle with his free hand to underscore his command.

With Ethan leaning on his father for support, they turned to retreat to the sniper position where Homer was still fighting off the frontal assault. Peter had selected this wide opening in the rock fissure because it offered shade and protection from rifle fire from below. But he had not anticipated that an attack would come downhill from behind their protected vantage point.

Now, the very features that had made this location attractive for protecting Ethan made it indefensible. They had to get out… and fast. It would not take the remaining enemy soldiers long to figure out the surest way to kill them was to begin lobbing grenades down the canyon-like opening in the sandstone.

With Peter in the lead, and Gary and Todd right behind, they emerged from the narrow confines of the crevice just as the first grenade bounced off the rock wall and rolled along the dirt, stopping inches from the rolled-up shirt that Ethan had rested his head upon only a short while earlier. This grenade was soon followed by another, then another.

"Grenades!" Gary roared. Everyone scattered out the open end of the fissure, diving into the hot dirt. Todd and Gary to one side, Peter and Ethan to the other.

The explosions were almost simultaneous… booming louder than the preceding gunfire. Debris erupted from the fissure's open end and dust billowed up the sheer sandstone walls, finally spilling out the top of the crevice 20 feet above the floor.

Coughing from the dust that covered them, Todd and Gary rose first. Then, slowly, Peter stood and helped Ethan up. Dust had filled the fissure, making it impossible to see into it. But they had made it out… if only barely.

They needed to follow the finger ridgeline to their left and join up with Homer. They could still hear Homer firing, and so Peter knew he had not been overrun.

"Let's go."

Todd and Gary went first, rifles held ready. Peter, still helping Ethan, had not yet taken a step when two Homothals burst from the dust. Almost immediately a third man—a Chinese soldier—and a fourth man—wearing a PLA uniform with sergeant insignia—appeared behind the Homothals.

Todd and Gary had already covered about ten yards from the fissure opening and had their backs to the Homothals.

"Look out!" Peter yelled.

The four enemy soldiers, also surprised at running into their quarry so soon after exiting the dust-choked crevice, quickly recovered and turned toward Peter and Ethan, guns raised.

At the sound of Peter's warning Todd and Gary had turned and opened fire, but missed. More shots exploded and Peter saw one Homothal slammed backwards into the Chinese soldier immediately behind him, two bullets having passed through the Homothal's body and instantly killing the soldier. Another round struck the same Homothal, knocking it off its feet.

Peter fell to the ground with Ethan, covering his son with his body. The rough jarring crash sent new jolts of pain slicing through Ethan, the muffled moan emanating from beneath Peter.

Then Peter glanced toward his friends and saw Todd fumble and drop a full ammo magazine in the dirt. Gary was aiming down the barrel of his rifle. He fired his last shot and clipped the Chinese sergeant in the shoulder, causing his body to spin under the impact. He fell, his rifle out of reach.

The wound was hideous; the bullet smashed squarely into his right shoulder and, as it exited, took all the bone and most of the flesh as well, leaving the soldier's right arm dangling. Bright red arterial blood began pooling in the dust and dirt, quickly soaking into the dry ground. His face was already ashen, and his eyes were glazed as shock set in. In less than two minutes the PLA sergeant would bleed to death.

Abruptly the gunfire ceased and Peter again rose to his feet, not sparing the second it would take to pick up his dust-coated rifle. Ethan placed an arm around Peter's shoulder for support.

The remaining Homothal pointed its rifle at Peter and Ethan and pulled the trigger. But nothing happened; the magazine was empty. The beast dropped the useless weapon and charged its intended victims.

Todd was struggling with the rifle bolt and couldn't shoot while Gary was fumbling for another magazine that he didn't have. Helpless, he saw the Homothal crash into the two men, bowling them over and knocking Ethan to the ground. Still suffering from the earlier pounding, Ethan was in no shape to take the blow. He emitted a low groan, and lay still.

Peter was able to roll with the blow and twirled away. As he reached over his shoulder and retrieved Hamaad's machete from its sheath, Peter stepped to the side to place himself between his son and the beast. The heft of the stout blade did little to bolster his confidence.

The Homothal quickly checked its forward momentum and turned. Peter faced the monster trying to figure out its next move, wishing he held a gun rather than the machete. *If only my .45 was loaded*, Peter thought.

The beast struck first with lightning speed, swinging a massive right fist to connect with Peter's jaw. His head jerked back with an audible snap, but he didn't fall. As the Homothal struck again, Peter reflexively swung the machete to block the swing. Somehow he managed to get the blade in the path of the muscular limb, slicing into the Homothal's arm, but momentum carried the hard fist onward, barely checked. Peter's head absorbed most of the blow, but he willed himself to remain standing.

Peter felt like the world was twirling around him, and at any moment he thought he was likely to fall over. The Homothal swung its rock-like fist again landing another solid blow to Peter's face. He staggered, and fell to one knee. With his head drooped, blood dripping from a lacerated cheek and eye brow,

Peter felt his strength ebbing away.

The Homothal raised its right arm, preparing to slam down on Peter's exposed neck.

"Ahhhhhh!" The creature suddenly bellowed.

Peter shoved the machete into the Homothal's knee, just behind the kneecap. It slumped to the ground, propping up its 300-pound body with its arms and trying to take the weight off its knee.

Peter and the Homothal were now face-to-face. Peter on one knee, the Homothal on hands and knees. With its left arm, the Homothal backhanded Peter, smacking him to the ground. The Homothal, seemed to draw a primitive fury from the pain. With Peter knocked down and out of immediate reach, it fixed its eyes on Ethan who was only four feet away.

"I'm out of ammo; you have to shoot!" Gary yelled at Todd.

"The bolt's jammed! I can't even drop the magazine!" Todd exclaimed, frustration rising with his voice.

While Todd continued to struggle with his weapon, trying desperately to clear the jam, Gary drew his Colt Python, aimed and pulled the trigger. Nothing. The pistol was also empty.

Gary charged the beast and slammed the steel gun on its back as he tried to wrap his other arm around the creature's neck. It was a weak attack, and the Homothal easily shook its attacker off. Gary landed hard on his injured shoulder and rolled to the opposite side, trying to get back to his feet.

The Homothal crawled forward, intent on killing all of its enemies. Its reaction was primal—bestial. In its current state of mind, with adrenaline coursing through its body and ripped with pain, the Homothal was easily as vicious and dangerous as any wounded and cornered bear. But the Homothal had a measure of cunning that no other animal could ever possess... that was the major contribution of the human DNA.

Desperate, Todd charged the Homothal, abandoning his

effort to clear the jammed bolt.

Moving his grip to the barrel, Todd swung the rifle down across the monster's muscular back. There was a deep thud as the rifle connected. The Homothal turned to face its nemesis. When Todd swung down a second time, the creature reached out and grabbed the rifle, yanking it from Todd's grip.

The Homothal struggled to its feet, favoring the wounded leg. Swinging the rifle-club one handed, it aimed for Todd's head. But Todd ducked and raised his arm to deflect most of the blow. The beast swung the rifle back and connected a solid blow to Todd's side where his pistol was holstered, knocking him to the ground. He was alive but writhing in pain.

"Peter!" He heard his name and opened his eyes to see the Homothal grabbing Ethan's ankle. Peter rose to his knees—and then to his feet. Rather than moving away, he charged the Homothal.

"Peter! No!" Gary yelled, as he stumbled to Todd's side and retrieved his pistol, hoping it wasn't empty like the others.

Raising the machete with both hands as he staggered forward, Peter swung down with all his strength. The blade slashed deep across the Homothal's back. Again it roared in pain.

The creature released Ethan's leg and arched its back, bringing its left hand around to shield against a further blow. Peter again raised the machete. The creature turned and faced Peter, the crazed, yellow eyes burning fiercely. It snarled and seemed to grunt out something, some message that Peter couldn't comprehend. *Is it trying to talk? Asking for mercy?* In a moment of weakness, Peter hesitated.

The Beretta was there in Todd's hip holster, and Gary quickly drew the gun. Immediately his hopes were dashed when he saw the slide was bent to one side, apparently damaged by the blow. He tried to cycle the action, but it was solidly jammed. So he threw the pistol at the Homothal and charged again, jumping on the back of the beast and wrapping his good arm around its throat.

With ease the monster pulled free of Gary's grip and shrugged him off. Gary collided with Peter and both men went down. Then the beast resumed its attack on Ethan.

The Homothal reached forward and yanked Ethan off the ground. The creature could crush a man's trachea, and it gripped Ethan tightly around the throat.

"No!" Peter yelled.

CHAPTER 47

IT WAS A STANDOFF. Furious over losing Ming, Jim was not about to surrender to the camouflage-clad force. He assumed they were not soldiers under Ming's command since their uniforms were entirely different. *Chinese Airborne uniforms. Maybe these men were part of the attacking force that Homer reported,* Jim thought. If that was true, maybe they were more ally than enemy.

"What are you doing? You're letting Colonel Ming get away!" Jim shouted.

There was no reply from the opposing force. Jim tried again. "I don't know who you are, but I'm here for Ming. We don't have to shoot it out."

Three seconds ticked by, then one of the soldiers stepped forward with his weapon lowered, closing the distance to Jim in swift, purposeful strides. His three companions kept their rifles leveled on the SGIT team.

"I am Captain Wu of the People's Liberation Army... and

you are?"

Jim kept his rifle aimed at Captain Wu while sizing him up. He was of similar height and weight, and obviously very fit. Jim also noticed the green and black sleeve patch. It was a vertical sword with a lightning bolt, indicating that Captain Wu was Special Forces.

"I am Commander James Nicolaou, Strategic Global Intervention Team. We had Colonel Ming in our sights, and you let him get away."

"Yes. I heard you the first time Commander." Wu stared into Jim's eyes, trying to read the man's character. The principle question burning in Wu's mind was whether or not he could trust these men.

"You are Americans. It was your men who gave us covering fire outside?"

Jim nodded.

Captain Wu turned his head slightly and, speaking in Mandarin, ordered his men to lower their weapons. They were all dressed in fatigues similar to Wu's, with black web belt and suspenders for distributing the load of spare ammunition magazines, grenades, and other gear they carried. Each man also had a pistol holstered low on the right thigh.

Two of the soldiers did as Wu ordered, but the third soldier—taller than the rest at an even six feet and with a long scar stretching across his right cheek from just below the eye to his chin—refused to yield. Wu diverted his eyes to the man.

"Lower your weapon!" he commanded.

"The Americans are our enemy!" The soldier responded. He was bordering on insubordination and continued to aim his assault rifle directly at Commander Nicolaou. Jim noted that unlike the other two soldiers, this man appeared consumed with hate.

Jim locked eyes with the man, ignoring Captain Wu for the

moment. "Why would I have ordered my snipers to provide protection for you if I am your enemy? I could have just as easily had them shoot you and your entire team… but I didn't."

Captain Wu turned to squarely face the soldier, and then stepped between him and Commander Nicolaou.

"Corporal Zhao! I said to put down your weapon. That is a direct order, and you will comply!"

Wu was menacing and still completely in control. The other two soldiers stared on, a look of mild disbelief on their faces. No doubt they had never witnessed this type of show-down between an officer and an enlisted man before.

Reluctantly, Zhao lowered his rifle. Wu took in a deep breath and spoke in Mandarin, his voice lowered, "When we return to base you will immediately report this insubordination to the officer in charge, is that clear?"

"Yes, sir!"

Annoyed by the test of his command, especially in front of the American soldiers, Captain Wu turned back to Jim.

"Please accept my apologies, Commander. But I imagine you can understand that armed American soldiers present inside a top secret Chinese military facility presents a rather…" he seemed to be searching for the right word "…unusual circumstance. One in which our extensive training naturally takes over. No doubt your men would react similarly if this was an American base and you had just stumbled onto armed Chinese soldiers?"

Jim nodded but rather than answering Wu he turned his head slightly toward his team and ordered, "At ease." The SGIT soldiers lowered their weapons, but not their guard.

Captain Wu continued. "I have been ordered to retrieve Colonel Ming and to ensure his return to Beijing to face his crimes. Perhaps we can, for the time being, ignore our ideological differences and cooperate since it is clear that we are hunting the same prey."

Jim thought for a moment before answering. He could not let Ming be taken to Beijing—or for that matter anywhere he would be under Chinese military control. He also recognized that some plans are better kept to one's self.

Jim nodded slightly. "Okay. Let's say that we agree to work together and help you get Ming. Then what?"

Wu shrugged as if the question was irrelevant. "I will personally see him locked in chains and placed on a military cargo flight to China. There he will be imprisoned for a long time."

The answer surprised Jim. "Imprisoned? Why?"

"Colonel Ming is a brilliant man; a hero to the Chinese people. He was entrusted to conduct scientific research for the PLA. Unfortunately, he became greedy and his desire for personal wealth overcame the good of the people. It is really quite an embarrassment to the Party."

"Sure, I bet it is. Let me see if I can fill in the blanks. Ming was hired by one or more of your Generals to conduct genetic experimentation, and when he stopped reporting in, someone decided that he was a rogue, no longer to be trusted."

Captain Wu didn't answer Jim, and his face remained devoid of expression. Jim pushed further.

"We have all seen the results of his work—those half-man, half-animal creatures that you fought outside. We know he experimented on human test subjects, subjects that he kidnapped from villages throughout Darfur. He has infected hundreds—perhaps thousands—of civilians with a virus that causes Neanderthal DNA to fuse with human DNA."

Wu's eyes widened. "How do you know this? This is top secret—you can't possibly know!"

"I know because Ming told me so himself. Right before he was going to inject me with the virus." There was a steel-hard edge in Jim's voice and his eyes narrowed, glistening with renewed anger that this monstrous work had been officially sanctioned by any government.

"Fortunately, my men…" Jim nodded over his shoulder to indicate his comrades "…crashed the party just in time."

Captain Wu's mind raced. His orders had not contemplated the current turn of events.

"So why would the PLA be interested in Ming's research?" Jim asked rhetorically. He studied Wu's face for clues. The Captain remained silent.

"Could it be that the PLA wanted Ming to genetically engineer a super soldier?"

The flash in Wu's eyes told Jim all he needed.

"That's it, isn't it? He was to develop a method for crossing human and Neanderthal DNA to make a genetically superior soldier. Only it didn't go as planned. Ming decided he wanted more, so he refused to turn over his research. That's the problem, isn't it Captain?"

At first Wu only stared back in silence. After a long pause he finally spoke. "Yes."

Jim was surprised by Wu's admission.

"As Colonel Ming's research met with success," Wu continued with the story, "he grew ever more egotistical and arrogant. It was suspected that he was not fully disclosing his research results. Finally, he stopped sending any technical reports to Beijing."

"Why not just cut off his funding?" Jim asked.

Wu turned up the corner of his mouth; not a smile, more of a grimace. "You don't understand, do you?"

Now it was Jim's turn to keep silent.

"By the time Beijing threatened to cut off all support, it was too late. Colonel Ming had already perfected the viral infusion process. But, most importantly, he had achieved cell replication. Do you have any idea how powerful that capability is? It represents a new weapon of mass destruction—a *genetic* weapon!"

Jim and his team stood transfixed by the story they were hearing. Jim was trying to fathom the implications of this genetic weapon, as Wu called it.

"There is no antidote?" Jim asked, already knowing the answer.

Wu shook his head. "No. It is perhaps the ultimate weapon of terror."

"Ming said that he is developing a new serum based on the Ebola virus."

Wu thought for a moment before answering. "The Ebola virus is readily spread by contact with infected body fluids. Maybe it could also be engineered to spread by contact with infected water. Regardless, the mortality is very high. Those who unfortunately survived the hemorrhagic fever would be transformed into Homothals. Colonel Ming cannot be allowed to succeed."

"Why strike against Ming now? There must have been plenty of opportunities to stop him once it became clear that he wasn't going to cooperate with your government."

"Ming claimed to have large doses of the virus hidden near all major water sources of eastern China as well as locations in our major metropolitan cities. There are more than 140 cities in China each with a population exceeding one million people!

"He claimed the virus could be spread by air—infecting people who breathe in the virus—or through water by contact and consumption. Our scientists were skeptical, but no one could take the risk.

"Imagine the popular reaction if masses of citizens suddenly began transforming into those Homothal creatures? For sure, many—perhaps most—would die in the process. The women and children, the elderly—most would not survive the transmutation. But those who did survive would be animals, not humans. They would not be able to communicate or function in an orderly society. The result would be complete anarchy."

Wu was shaking his head. "No government could survive that type of attack."

"So, the Generals continued to support Ming's work even though Ming had put a genetic gun to their heads?"

"No. They continued to support Ming *because* he had a gun to their heads."

"Why not just call in an airstrike on this compound and wipe it off the face of the Earth?"

"Ming warned that he had many followers who would carry forth his orders as a final act of revenge."

"If that's true, then why act now?" Jim asked. "Clearly the threat is still there."

"Perhaps. I am just a soldier following orders. But I have heard that despite much effort over the past five years not a single canister has been found."

"So Ming was bluffing?"

Captain Wu shrugged. "No one can be certain. But the PLA has not been sitting still. In the years since Ming first made the threats my government has built massive water sterilization units at all major water treatment plants. They have also installed air sanitizers—tens of thousands of them—in the major cities. Our scientists are confident that a combination of ozone and ultraviolet light combined with nanosilver filtration will be completely effective at killing the virus. The machines were turned on two weeks ago."

Jim understood, but he sensed there was more that Captain Wu was not revealing. If the story was just as Wu claimed, then the PLA's presence was not required at the compound. A half dozen cruise missiles would very effectively destroy the research facility and everything within it. Jim suspected that Wu was sent here to retrieve the knowledge that Ming had acquired over the years and then destroy the complex.

Jim reasoned that since the Chinese government had spent years building internal defenses to destroy the virus and protect at least a major portion of their population, they may not be so fearful of an inevitable release of the virus. On the contrary, if the virus could be carried great distances through human travel, then the government in Beijing may sense an opportunity.

If Jim's suspicions were even partly correct, there was no way SGIT could allow anyone to possess the knowledge secured within Ming's secret compound.

CHAPTER 48

THE DEEP RUMBLING was felt as much as heard. It seemed to be funneled toward them from the corridor where Ming had hastily departed minutes earlier. Jim didn't wait to confer with Captain Wu; he quickly started running toward the source of the rumbling sound with Ghost, Magnum, and Bull following close behind. Captain Wu and his strike team brought up the rear.

Jim reached an intersecting corridor extending to the right and left. He paused only for a second, quickly concluding that the sound was emanating from somewhere to the front, in the direction he was heading.

The SGIT and Chinese soldiers pushed forward, stopping momentarily at the next intersection. Jim was turning his head from side to side, trying to locate the direction from which the rumbling originated. It was getting louder, but the echo off the hard concrete surfaces was making it tough to clearly determine the source's direction. Jim decided it was louder to the right, and he took off running just as the rest of the team arrived at the junction.

There were few markings on the drab gray walls, but at each intersection Jim observed red signs with a brief notation in Mandarin, most likely directional signs.

The hallway stretched out before Jim for another fifty or so yards then turned sharply to the left. He almost slid into the hard wall as he negotiated the turn without slowing down. As he turned, he saw a pair of large steel doors at the end of the short corridor. The ceiling was also sloping upward, so that at the double doors it was perhaps twenty feet high. Jim stopped to allow the others to catch up.

Captain Wu leaned close to Jim and said in a low voice, "This is a flight hangar. I imagine the sound we are hearing is the retractable ceiling being opened."

"You're familiar with the plans for this compound?" Jim asked.

"Yes. I've been briefed on the blueprints. A section of the roof can be closed to obscure the true nature of this structure. It is covered in reinforced concrete one meter thick and disguised on the surface to blend in with the surrounding desert terrain— so your satellites would not see an abnormal heat signature."

"What type of aircraft and weaponry are in the hangar?"

"The roof section is only large enough to allow one helicopter access at a time. The aircraft are lifted to the surface on an elevator platform. As far as weapons are concerned, Colonel Ming has access to attack helicopters, so we can assume that is what he is planning to depart in. The building plans called for a full armory adjoining the hangar."

"Great," Jim said.

Looking to his SGIT team, and then quickly scanning the Chinese commandos, he added, "We don't have any heavy weapons, and the only grenades I see are on your men. If they have access to a full armory, we could be in trouble."

"My soldiers are elite PLA warriors. We will accomplish our objective," Captain Wu asserted confidently. Jim did not share in that confidence.

Jim reached out and tested the door. Not surprising, it was locked.

"I think our first challenge is getting through those doors," Jim declared.

Wu frowned. "We will blow the door open with our grenades," Zhao suggested.

While Captain Wu was considering, Jim addressed Magnum. "Don't suppose you'd have any det cord in your bag of goodies?"

Magnum smiled. "As a former Boy Scout, I'm always prepared." He dropped the pack from his shoulders and reached inside, his hand rummaging around until he found what he was searching for.

Proudly holding a cardboard spool wrapped with layers of yellow cord about a quarter inch in diameter, Magnum offered it up. "Uncle Sam's finest. There's a hundred feet on this spool."

"More than enough to blast through those doors," Jim agreed. Then, addressing Wu, he said, "Save those grenades, we may need them after we blow through the door."

Jim's men quickly began to apply the det cord around the perimeter of both doors, running the cord in a continuous loop down the sides where the hinges were located and across the top and bottom, to cover any slide bolts anchoring the doors when locked. Jim noticed that Wu had stepped to the side with Corporal Zhao and seemed to be engaged in a somewhat heated discussion.

It took a little more than a minute to set the charge. "This is a five second fuse. Everyone, down the corridor!"

Jim popped the fuse and was the last man to move away

from the impending blast. *CRACK! BOOM!* All the men did what they could to prevent permanent hearing damage by covering their ears while holding their mouths open. As the echoes died, they could hear the sound of steel rattling on concrete. The doors were blown cleanly off their hinges and lay alongside pieces of doorframe inside the flight hangar.

The hangar space was cavernous—easily 50 yards on each side and roughly square. In the center of the hangar, on a large platform, rested a Chinese attack helicopter.

The pilot was at the controls going through the preflight check list. In response to the explosion, the pilot switched on the engines. It would take a minute, possibly two, for the powerful turbine engines to warm up. Ming and his bodyguards stood close to the helicopter and were staring at the blown door.

Jim and Captain Wu realized they didn't have much time if they wanted to block Ming's escape.

Wu charged forward followed closely by his men. They all threw grenades towards the helicopter sitting on the lift elevator. The overhead door was open halfway and daylight was streaming into the hangar.

"They don't waste any time, do they?" Jim quipped. There was no cover beyond the door opening, and Jim felt the charge was suicidal. He ordered Magnum, Ghost, and Bull to hug the walls of the corridor as they cautiously approached the door opening, weapons ready.

Each of Wu's soldiers had thrown two grenades at the helicopter. It was an armored gun ship, and grenades would do little more than superficial damage unless one actually detonated within the aircraft—they had no such luck.

Without cover, Wu's men didn't get far. They were pinned down no more than five feet within the entry that had been blasted open. Sprawled flat on the floor, the Chinese commandos tried to will themselves as flat as a pancake. Enemy bullets were ricocheting off the walls and floor. The intensity of fire was fierce, but Wu's men never hesitated and were equally determined in returning fire.

As the fighting erupted Ming's soldiers dispersed throughout the hangar, leaving only two bodyguards and the pilot with Ming. They took up defensive positions behind tool chests, drums of hydraulic oil, and spare parts lockers. This required Wu's commandos to aim at multiple, dispersed targets.

Jim cautiously held his small force outside the open doorway to the hangar. He ordered his men to return fire from the marginal cover of the blasted doorframe. At best, it would only be minutes before the concentrated fire directed at Wu's men resulted in their annihilation. Jim spotted the armory off to the right, adjoining the far wall of the hangar; the over-sized double door connecting the armory to the hangar was open.

"Magnum, how much C4 do you have left in your pack?"

"We placed most of it already as demolition charges. But I still have two blocks."

Each stick weighed one pound, more than sufficient to do tremendous damage… especially in the confined space of the hangar.

"Pull 'em out. Put a ten second fuse in each block."

While Magnum was carrying out the order, Jim turned to Ghost. "Dig into your pack and give me a pair of socks." Given the high value-to-weight ratio of something like dry, clean socks, Jim was pretty sure all team members carried at least one extra pair stuffed somewhere in their packs.

"Say again, sir." Ghost couldn't put the pieces together, so the order sounded like nonsense.

"Your socks! It's called improvising, soldier. Watch and learn."

Ghost did as he was ordered and produced a pair of tan GI socks.

Magnum completed prepping the first block. It had the detonator firmly jammed into the end of the brick of plastic explosive. He handed it to Boss Man and immediately began work to prep the second block of C4.

Ghost's socks were balled together, and Jim separated them while Magnum prepared the second block of explosive with the detonator. Jim inserted one block of C4 into each sock, just far enough that he could activate the detonator and then drop the C4 all the way down into the sock. But he didn't activate the detonators just yet.

"I'm going to move up to the door; you three cover me. I have to get inside the doorway. Then I need about three seconds to activate the detonators and heave these blocks at the armory. If I can get at least one inside, maybe we can cause a little mayhem to even the odds."

Ghost didn't like the plan. "You'll be totally exposed in there," he reminded Jim.

"Do you have a better idea?"

Jim's question was met with silence. "Okay," Jim answered somberly. "I don't either... and those guys won't last long," he said in reference to Wu's commandos. Already two of his men had taken hits; a bullet entering one man's calf and the second man had his left hand shattered by a well-aimed shot.

Jim's team was already positioned at both sides of the former doorway, with Ghost and Magnum on one side and Bull and Jim on the other.

"Hug the walls, but stay low. On my mark you let go with everything you have, draw their fire but keep your heads down. Got it?"

All three men nodded.

"As soon you start shooting, I'll pop up inside the hangar and throw these charges at the armory. The socks will act like a slingshot, and with the high ceiling it should be easy to land them inside the armory. The rest is up to Lady Luck."

Jim sucked in a deep breath. "Ready?"

Nods again.

"Ready… now!" Jim ordered.

The Special Forces commandos were fighting a courageous battle—but one they could not win. Peering around the chipped and fractured concrete wall, Ghost went low with his shotgun while Magnum and Bull went high. They were all firing rapidly, trying to put as much lead down range as possible.

It worked.

The return fire from Ming's forces ebbed momentarily as men sought cover. This was the break that Jim needed. He popped out from behind Bull and, swinging his two tan socks in a large circle, he let them fly.

In the middle of a fierce gunfight, it was perhaps the strangest sight one could image—two GI socks arcing through the air, the tan stretch uppers flapping wildly in flight.

CHAPTER 49

JIM LET GO OF THE SOCKS at the precise point in his
underhand swing to impart a high, looping trajectory. The sock-
bombs separated a bit from each other during the three second
flight, but both landed just inside the door to the armory.

Loaded with one pound of C4 in each sock, they hit the
smooth concrete floor with an inaudible thud and continued to
slide across the polished floor until each came to rest against a
stack of drab-green metal lockers... the kind used to transport
air-to-surface unguided rockets.

Time seemed to advance in extremely slow motion as Jim
watched the socks sail across the open hangar. He was aware
of intense enemy gunfire, some aimed in his direction. In his
peripheral vision he saw bright flashes from the muzzles of
rifles being fired, and he saw Magnum's body convulse as a
bullet plowed through his left shoulder.

Then, as the two U.S.-Government-issue socks came to
rest, there was the expected explosion followed immediately by

a second, much larger blast. A heavy wall of hot air slammed into Jim, knocking him to the floor.

Looking up, he saw that more than half of the enemy troops were down and not moving. It was a massive explosion, much larger than could be accounted for by just the two pounds of plastic explosive.

The C4 had set off a sympathetic explosion of other ordinance in the armory… just as he had hoped. *Better lucky than good*, Jim thought.

Dropping the rifle from his shoulder, Jim rolled into a prone position and joined the firefight. The Chinese commandos, along with the SGIT soldiers, had never let up. Now that the odds were more even, the battle slowly began to turn in the direction of Captain Wu's force aided by the small SGIT team.

Each man was well trained and disciplined, and they remained focused on aiming and shooting rather than reacting to the near misses peppering around them.

One by one, the bad guys were falling—mostly wounded, but many dead. Still, the half dozen survivors fought on tenaciously and showed no sign of giving up.

The armored helicopter easily survived the armory explosion and protected Colonel Ming, who was sitting in the co-pilot's seat. The pilot pushed the engines almost to the point of failure as they were warming up to their required operating temperature.

Realizing that Ming would escape—perhaps for good— if the helicopter got airborne, Captain Wu seized his last opportunity. Eying a control panel on the far wall of the hangar, beyond the nose of the gunship, Wu reasoned it housed the electrical controls that manipulated the overhead retractable roof section.

The section was nearing fully open. The pilot did not wait for the elevator to lift the aircraft to ground level and began to pull up on the collective lever while maintaining maximum power. The helicopter slowly lifted from the concrete floor, a near-gale of wind blasting out from underneath the rotors while it began to ascend toward the opening. In another two or three seconds, Wu estimated, the opening would be sufficiently wide to allow the gunship, with Colonel Ming aboard, to escape.

Aiming with great concentration, Wu fired single shots at the control panel. He did not have ammunition to waste. The first bullet struck the metal box, but nothing happened; the overhead door was still opening. Wu fired again... nothing... again he fired, and this time there was a small cluster of sparks as the bullet pierced the metal electrical box.

The overhead door ground to a halt, just short of being fully opened. But the pilot kept ascending toward the shaft of daylight. For a moment, the men thought they had lost, that Ming would escape. But just as it looked like the helicopter would slip out the opening into clear skies, a rotor blade nicked the retractable door, and in an instant the entire rotor assembly exploded into chunks of metal, hurled throughout the hangar at phenomenal velocity.

Metal bounced off the concrete walls as well as the floor of the hangar, tiny pieces and large chunks alike. One twelve-inch-long piece cut through two of Wu's commandos, killing them instantly. The large shard bounced back off the floor, narrowly missing Corporal Zhao.

Captain Wu was not so lucky; a ragged piece of rotor blade about the size of a baseball ricocheted off the hangar ceiling and slammed into Wu's left leg. The torn metal had razor-sharp edges and it sliced into his flesh, severing the femoral artery in three places. Captain Wu began bleeding profusely. He groaned in agony and clenched his teeth, holding back a cry of pain.

"Bull! Do what you can for Wu—I'll cover you!" Jim screamed, trying to be heard above the mayhem.

Bull handed the AA12 to Boss Man and dropped to his knees next to Wu. Quickly assessing the true danger, Bull removed a tourniquet from his first aid bag. He was in the process of applying the constriction wrap when a burst of rifle fire found its mark.

One bullet sliced through Bull's forearm, breaking the bone; another entered Captain Wu's shoulder. Since he was lying on his back, the bullet traveled deep into his torso inflicting lethal damage through his chest.

"I'm hit!" Bull yelled.

Jim turned and saw what had happened. He also saw fuel leaking out of the downed helicopter and feared that it would burst into flames any second, incinerating the entire hangar and all within it.

"Magnum, Ghost—time to get the hell out of here!"

In an instant Magnum was beside his commander. "Help Bull, he's been hit!"

Ghost continued to lay down a withering barrage of covering fire, pausing only to drop the empty drum magazine and slam in a new one.

Jim shouldered his rifle and the AA12 and then reached down to drag Captain Wu out of the hangar. Corporal Zhao had already retreated to the corridor.

In a weak voice, Captain Wu asked, "Where is Zhao?"

"He's gone. Your corporal is lacking in loyalty." Jim made no attempt to hide his dislike for Zhao.

Wu closed his eyes and shook his head. "No... you must stop him."

Jim didn't understand. "Why?"

Captain Wu's face contorted as a bolt of pain shot through his body. He swallowed before struggling to continue, his voice becoming weaker. "My orders... he's not regular soldier."

"Tell me later. I'm getting you out of here!"

"No—" Wu dug his fingers into Jim's shirt, pulling him closer.

"Zhao will retrieve the data. His orders... he must recover the data..."

"But you said you were sent here to destroy everything."

The Captain nodded slightly, his eyes closed. "Yes. But Zhao has other orders... not under my command... after he transmitted the data, we were to destroy everything."

"We don't have time for this now. The hangar is going to blow."

"Leave me. You must leave the complex."

"We will, but not without you."

Wu resisted. "No, you don't understand. My orders were to leave nothing behind." Wu was fading quickly, his breathing was labored and every word seemed to visibly weaken him.

Jim listened carefully. He suspected what Wu was trying to convey. It was the same order Jim was following earlier when he had set to laying explosive charges and incendiaries to destroy the records of the hideous experiments conducted in the facility.

"How much time do we have?" Jim screamed the question, but Wu didn't answer.

"Captain!" Jim was now in Wu's face, yelling loudly. "How much time do we have?"

Wu slowly opened his eyes, but only part way. Jim could see he was dying, and suspected he only had a few seconds of life remaining before his battered body quit functioning from loss of blood.

Wu moved his lips, but at first there was no sound. Then, a very faint whisper. Jim leaned close to hear.

"Ten... hundred..." the words were soft, feeble. With every shallow breath a trickle of bright red blood dribbled past the corners of Captain Wu's mouth.

He looked at his watch—0951. Nine minutes until the

complex was scheduled to be destroyed.

"Where are the explosives? Can we disarm them?"

Wu shook his head—it was barely perceptible.

"Where are the charges?" Jim demanded, this time shaking Wu.

Again he shook his head. Slowly, in a faint whisper he said only one word. "Missiles..."

Jim's mind was turning over the possibilities. He did not expect an aerial assault, instead assuming demolition charges had been placed at key locations throughout the main buildings.

He looked at Wu. His face was ashen, and his breaths were so shallow and slow that he wasn't even certain the Captain was still alive.

Leaning close, Jim shouted his one burning question. "Warheads! What is the payload?"

No response.

Jim shook Captain Wu and shouted the question again.

Wu's lips quivered, but nothing came out and his eyes remained closed.

Knowing time had about run out, Jim tried again. "What is the warhead?" he yelled.

This time his lips moved more visibly, and a faint rasp emerged. "Tactical..." and then his head fell to the side. Captain Wu had died.

CHAPTER 50

PETER HAD ONLY A FRACTION of a second to react. He pushed himself to his feet and swung the machete down on the creature's neck. The razor-sharp steel, thick and unyielding, severed the Homothal's spinal cord. The monster collapsed motionless on top of Ethan.

Peter dropped the blade and fell to one knee exhausted, emotionally and physically. With Gary's help, they dragged the beast off Ethan. Todd was struggling to stand and Gary helped him up while Peter assisted Ethan to his feet.

"I'll be all right," Todd proclaimed. "Nothing seems broken, but it feels like I was hit by a truck."

Gary wasn't listening, his attention focused elsewhere. "Hear that?" he said.

Peter concentrated, but didn't hear anything other than the faint ringing in his ears. "No... hear what?"

"The shooting has stopped. Homer must have killed the rest of 'em."

Just then Homer rounded the large boulders and burst onto the scene. "We have to get moving! They're right behind me!"

"How many?" Peter's voice was tired.

"A dozen, maybe more. I couldn't hold them off—too many reinforcements."

Just then, Homer received a brief and concise message from Boss Man. "It just went from bad to worse." Homer stole a quick look at his watch. "In eight minutes the Chinese are going to bomb the compound—possibly a tactical nuke. We have to get back over the ridge before it detonates and fries all of us."

With Peter helping Ethan, they began to climb up the ridge, reversing the path they had taken in the predawn hours. Todd picked up the Barrett Peter had been using, discarding his jammed weapon.

Gary jogged up next to Homer, still carrying his rifle but favoring his shoulder. The stiches held, but fresh blood was oozing from the wound. "Do you have any extra mags? I'm out."

Without slowing the brisk pace, Homer pulled a ten-round magazine from a cargo pocket and handed it over. "Raufoss, explosive, armor piercing. Was saving it for a special occasion."

"I think this counts."

The pursuing Homothals and Chinese soldiers were cautiously advancing through the fissure. In groups of two and three they paused every few seconds, weapons aimed forward, searching for a glimpse of the Americans and providing cover while others dashed ahead to the next point of concealment. It was slow progress, but they had already learned that to charge headlong into the sniper fire was suicidal.

The sun was blazing down on the party, making the upward climb even more demanding. Peter had fallen behind, not able to keep up the pace while also helping Ethan who was unsteady on his feet, while Gary and Homer were in the lead.

Gunfire ripped the air and Peter pulled Ethan to the ground

as bullets tore into the dirt behind them. Todd rushed back and helped Peter up. Positioning himself on the other side of Ethan for additional support, Todd urged them forward.

"We have to get moving chief," Todd announced.

Then, as if to punctuate Todd's admonition, the crack of rifle fire erupted again, not far behind and bullets slammed into the earth several feet forward of their position.

Homer pivoted and acquired three targets from his elevated vantage point further up the trail. He fired rapidly and connected with all three bullets.

"Move! Move!" Homer shouted. Then he dropped to one knee and resumed shooting at targets of opportunity as the pursuing Homothals and Chinese exposed themselves.

Gary kept moving up the slope, trying to gain as much ground as possible, not pausing to look back; it didn't take long for Peter and Todd, cradling Ethan, to pass Homer.

The ridge was perhaps another 50 yards above them. Everyone was gulping air. Todd's foot slipped on the loose gravel. He arrested his fall by slamming the rifle butt into the ground. As he regained his balance, he found the rifle made a good walking staff.

Peter's heart was pounding, and he was sucking in huge amounts of air through his open mouth, fixated on the ground before him, one foot followed by the next. It seemed that with every second or third step forward he would slide back one step, making the progress slow and treacherous. His right arm was looped around his son's waist, constantly tugging to keep Ethan moving in the same direction—upward. *Keep going, one more step, just keep moving.*

The sporadic gunfire continued, providing additional—albeit unnecessary—encouragement to climb and cross the ridge. The shots from Homer's Barrett were easily identified as a much louder and deeper boom, so they knew without looking that he was still defending their retreat up the ridge.

And then it stopped.

Peter looked over his shoulder, nearly falling in the process, and saw Homer eject the spent magazine and retrieve a new one, then ram it home into the rifle. He released the slide and was starting to take aim when a bullet finally caught up with him. The round tore into his left calf, and Homer toppled to the side.

With the opposing fire suddenly ended, three Homothals rose from the boulders at the mouth of the fissure and stepped into the open, unleashing a short burst of automatic fire. It was poorly aimed, but the lack of any return fire emboldened the Homothals and they began their charge.

Peter knew they would be on Homer in seconds if they weren't stopped. And even if he wasn't wounded, it was doubtful Homer could fight off three Homothals in hand-to-hand combat.

"Take Ethan and keep climbing! Give me the rifle," Peter grabbed the weapon even as he was still saying the words.

"We can make it together!"

Peter shook his head. "Go! We don't have time to argue! I have to help Homer!"

Before Todd could protest any further, Peter was already running downhill.

CHAPTER 51

GHOST HAD HURRIEDLY APPLIED a dressing to Bull's arm to staunch the bleeding. The three soldiers were waiting for their commander in the corridor outside the hangar bay.

There was no point in trying to recover Captain Wu's body, and Jim had just exited the hangar when the pooling aviation fuel flowed across the floor, reaching the wall where the electrical panel was located... the very same one Wu had shot minutes earlier. The circuits were still sparking from the short, and it only took one spark falling into the flammable liquid to cause it to ignite.

In two seconds that one spark turned the hangar into a hellish inferno. Jim heard a deep *WOOMPF* and felt the intense heat as a fireball engulfed the downed helicopter. The explosion forcefully propelled Jim forward out the opening to the hangar. He landed hard, face down, and slid into the concrete wall, smacking his head on the floor and wall.

"Boss Man!" Ghost bellowed.

Jim slowly rose to his knees, blood matting the raven hair at the edge of his scalp. "Where is Zhao?"

"He ran out of here. Rounded the corner just before the hangar blew," Magnum answered as he pointed down the corridor.

"He's headed for the computer center. We have to stop him before he transmits files back to Beijing."

With Magnum in the lead, the team ran down the sterile concrete hall and rounded the corner that opened onto the main hallway, intending to retrace the route they had followed from Ming's office to the underground flight hangar.

The team spotted Zhao at the far end of the corridor. Gunfire reverberated off the walls as Zhao fired a short burst at some unseen threat down an intersecting corridor to his left. Then he was running again for the exit.

"Looks like we have company," Jim announced.

The men reached the intersecting corridor quickly. Magnum cautiously glanced around the corner. Not more than 50 yards away, an enemy squad was advancing on their position.

"I count a half dozen Chinese soldiers and Homothals. They're hugging the walls on both sides of the passageway," Magnum reported as a dozen rounds ricocheted off the walls and passed harmlessly down the corridor.

Looking across the faces of his team, Jim gave his orders. "You have to take them out quickly and get out of here—same way we came in. The entire compound is targeted for a Chinese missile strike in less than eight minutes, possible nuke. You need to be well clear by then… got it?"

"What about you?" Bull asked.

"I'm going after Zhao. He can't be allowed to transmit even a small portion of the data from Ming's experiments back to the PLA."

"I'll go with you," Ghost suggested.

"No. You three need to eliminate that squad and get the hell out of here. Is that clear?"

All three heads nodded, but it was apparent no one liked the idea of leaving Boss Man on his own.

"Besides, as soon as I cross the hallway I'm going to draw a lot of fire. The three of you need to lay down heavy suppression."

Jim drew in a deep breath and tensed his legs, preparing to launch himself across the ten-foot wide opening.

"Ready?"

As one, Bull, Ghost, and Magnum nodded.

"On my mark. Three... two... one... mark!"

Jim sprang forward and made a running leap across the open corridor, arms flailing as he scrambled to get his legs in front of his body, preparing to absorb the landing impact. Immediately, the SGIT soldiers opened fire down the hallway in the enemy squad's general direction. Weapons on both sides were being fired on full auto, hoping for a hit.

Jim crashed to the concrete floor and rolled another eight feet before coming to a stop. Not wasting any time, he scooped up his rifle and rose to his feet, dashing off in pursuit of his quarry.

Jim ran through the intersection of hallways where Captain Wu had first confronted his team and headed towards the conference room. Its door was still slightly ajar, and Jim paused before opening it.

Using his rifle barrel, Jim nudged the door open. The door moved about six inches when the hinges squeaked. Instantly, a barrage of bullets tore through the door and Jim dropped to the relative safety of the floor. More bullets ripped through the door, the sound of gunfire replaced by the clatter of brass cartridge cases rebounding off the floor.

As Jim was considering his next move he heard the distinctive sound of a bolt being racked back and forth. Either

Zhao was out of ammunition or his rifle was jammed.

Jim slammed the door open and dove into the conference room. Rolling to the side, he came up firing the remainder of the rounds in his assault rifle in the general direction he expected Zhao to be.

But no one was there.

Casting the rifle to the side, Jim leapt over the conference table, pushing aside the leather chairs impeding his progress as he scrambled for the double doors on the opposite side of the conference room.

Bursting through the doors, Jim entered the long hallway at a full run. He saw Zhao ahead and Jim was closing the distance. Zhao caromed off the wall at the end of the hallway where it turned to the left, unable to stop his bulk in time to make the turn. That mistake brought Jim several yards closer.

As he rounded the same corner, Jim saw Zhao make another critical error—he overshot the stairway branching off to the right of the corridor; the stairway leading up to Colonel Ming's office.

As Zhao corrected and retraced his steps, Jim caught up with him, grabbing his shoulder and spinning the man around. Zhao lashed out, swinging his arm, connecting with Jim's face. Jim recoiled, still suffering from the effects of the hangar explosion. Every beat of his heart sent a spasm of pain through his skull.

Zhao dashed up the stairs, taking them two at a time.

Fatigued, winded, and with his head throbbing like nothing he had felt before, Jim had enough.

"Stop!" Jim ordered.

Corporal Zhao stood at the top of the stairs, his hand on the latching mechanism that would open the hidden door to Ming's office. Perhaps it was the authority in Jim's command, but Zhao hesitated.

"I know what you're up to Zhao… I won't let it happen."

Zhao laughed but remained with his back toward Jim. "What do you know?"

"Wu told me, after you left him to die. You are not regular army, not under his orders. You have independent orders to recover the records and data from this facility."

Zhao was surprised at how much Commander Nicolaou knew.

"You're a coward, Zhao. You left your commanding officer to die."

"Captain Wu was not my commanding officer. I take my orders from the Second Department of the PLA General Staff Headquarters—similar to your military intelligence."

"And your orders are to transmit the records from Ming's experiments to the PLA. Why? Even you can see that this is the work of monsters!"

Zhao snickered as he slowly moved his hand across his belly toward the holster on his hip. Zhao gambled that Jim wouldn't notice the subtle movement.

"The Second Department is charged with collecting and evaluating information that may have relevance to weapons and tactics. We analyzed the wreckage from your Black Hawk stealth helicopter that crashed in Pakistan and obtained a sample of its 'stealth skin'. We analyzed all the electronic countermeasures and surveillance equipment onboard your EP-3 spy aircraft after it entered our airspace at Hainan and rammed one of our J-8II fighters. Iran, a valued ally, allowed us to inspect the predator drone in their possession. We have even penetrated your most secret nuclear weapons laboratories at Livermore, Sandia, and Los Alamos." He paused to let Jim absorb this admission.

"Why would we ignore the research at this facility? After all, it was funded by the PLA."

"You're a lunatic, Zhao. This isn't a weapon that can be controlled. It's a weapon of terror."

"History is filled with such weapons! In the sixth century BC the Assyrians poisoned enemy wells with rye ergot. Throughout Europe in the Middle Ages rotten corpses, often infected with plague, were catapulted over city walls—arrows were dipped in infected blood or manure. And let's not forget how your own government distributed thousands of smallpox infected blankets to the Native Americans in your often over-looked genocidal war to conquer their lands."

Zhao's hand was inching closer to his holster, his torso still screening the motion from Jim's view.

"The world no longer lives in that age. Terrorism is no longer accepted as a legitimate means of settling disputes," Jim argued.

"You would have me believe that diplomacy works? That the United Nations has made the world a better and more peaceful place? Nonsense! Look at the atrocities that America committed in Iraq. You killed over one million Iraqi civilians in order to discover those 'weapons of mass destruction' that existed only in the mind of your president. When chemical weapons were deployed in Syria, the UN did nothing more than issue speeches expressing moral outrage."

His fingertips were now brushing the clasp on the holster, his head turned, trying to gain a glimpse of Commander Nicolaou's exact location. Just a little further and he would have a grip on the pistol.

"You can't win, Zhao."

"Who's going to stop me—you?" Zhao laughed deeply this time, the sound masking the metallic click as he unsnapped the strap securing his pistol.

"Wu confessed that cruise missiles are scheduled to strike in six minutes."

"Enough time to send the most recent research data in a burst transmission." His hand was now on the pistol grip. "The historical data offers nothing more than an interesting perspective on Ming's trials and errors before he achieved the current success."

As Zhao finished speaking, he yanked the pistol from its holster and spun, simultaneously raising the weapon to fire.

Jim was no fool. His Super Hawg .45, was already drawn and aimed. Both guns roared.

Zhao fell forward, tumbling down the staircase. He was dead by the time his body came to rest at Jim's feet.

CHAPTER 52

LUCKILY, PETER HAD GEOGRAPHY in his favor. Running downhill, Peter slid to Homer's side, cradled the heavy rifle, and fired at the exposed creatures. All three Homothals fell dead, but Peter was out of ammunition.

"I'm out," he announced to Homer.

With one hand firmly pressed against his calf, Homer shook he head. "I don't have any more. Only the full mag in my rifle."

Peter swapped weapons and scanned the boulders below for more enemies. Not seeing any, he turned back to Homer. "How bad is it?"

"Missed the bone, but went through my calf. I can't walk." He grimaced as a spasm of pain shot through his body.

"Let me see," Peter said. He leaned over and gently pulled back Homer's hand. Then he pulled back the cloth of the pant leg, exposing the bullet wound. As the cloth gently brushed against the wound, Homer stiffened and stifled a yelp.

"Bleeding's not too bad. Let's get behind some cover and

then put a bandage on it." Homer nodded toward a large rock behind Peter.

"That's gonna be our best cover."

It wasn't far to go, and Homer crawled into position behind the rock while Peter used the rifle scope to search again for enemies amongst the boulders—he didn't find any.

"Maybe they're all dead." Peter said.

"No, I saw at least ten, probably fifteen."

Homer retrieved a field dressing while answering Peter, and then deftly wrapped it around his leg, securing the ends of the bandage. Peter pulled the pant leg down over the bandage to provide a further barrier to dirt.

When Peter looked up again, two more Homothals had emerged from the boulders and opened fire at Peter and Homer. The bullets slammed into the rock and Peter ducked. He placed his rifle against the solid support and took aim. Ignoring the bullets whistling overhead, still more striking their sandstone barrier, he aimed carefully—it was close enough he didn't need any ballistic computer helping his aim. He pointed, aligned the crosshairs, and squeezed the trigger.

"You have to get over the ridge," Homer ordered.

Before Peter could reply, fourteen Homothals and soldiers began a charge.

Peter stole a quick look over the sandstone rock and was rewarded with a barrage of bullets. He quickly pulled his head back. "I can't get all of them."

"In about two minutes it won't matter much anyway. Give me the rifle. I'll slow them down so you can make it over the top."

Time slowed almost to a stop in Peter's mind. He closed his eyes and was engulfed in conflicting emotions. *I can still make it over the ridge and be with Ethan. I want so much to go home with him. Maybe I can forget it all. I just want to be home again with my son.*

He opened his eyes and turned his head, facing Homer. "Give me the gun and get outa here. You have to go... now!" But it was more than his words. Homer's eyes were pleading, begging Peter to go and reunite with his son.

Peter's brain continued to swirl wildly, refusing to settle on a course of action. He'd felt this obscene confusion moments before Maggie died, taking part of his soul with her. Peter dropped his head and squeezed his eyes shut, grasping frantically for a logical thread to latch onto.

I can leave now. If I run hard I can make it to Ethan, we can go home together. But if I go, Homer won't come home. He'll never see his family and friends again. How can I abandon him? Ethan and Joanna are young adults; they don't really need me anymore. God, how I will miss them.

A sudden calm descended and Peter knew what he had to do.

"Not gonna happen," he said, fixing Homer's glare with determination and grit. Then he aimed and fired the last of his ammunition, taking down six.

Homer had his service pistol in hand and began shooting as well, the pistol braced against the rock. He managed to drop three Chinese and another Homothal before the slide clanged open.

As bullets were gouging out chunks of sandstone, Peter hunkered down low for safety. He spied a larger outcropping further off to his right. It wasn't far, and if he could drag Homer over they would be shielded from the expected air blast over the compound.

"How much time?" Peter asked.

Homer studied his watch while bullets zinged overhead and smashed into the rock. "About 90 seconds," and then, as an afterthought, he added, "It's been good knowing you."

"We aren't dead yet. There's still enough time. I can drag you over there, behind that rock formation."

"We'll never make it."

Tossing aside the useless rifle, Peter placed a firm grip on Homers load harness. "Come on, we have to try."

The shooting ceased, perhaps the remaining enemy realized that the Americans were out of ammunition.

"We'll be sitting ducks as we cross in the open. You make a run for it. I'll just slow you down!"

"Let's go!" Peter began tugging, his boot heels digging in the soft dirt as he pulled. At the same time he looked down the slope and saw three Homothals and one soldier approaching. They were advancing with determination, and Peter noticed that the soldier had a dark beard, his face looking more Arabic than Chinese. Although they were all armed with assault rifles, none were firing.

That changed as soon as Peter pulled clear of the rock cover. Quickly, he dived back for protection.

Without warning, there was a deep crack from above. It sounded like it came from the ridgeline. The distinctive report was that from a M107 rifle, which could only mean Gary was in position to provide covering fire. Within milliseconds of the rifle report there was a second *BOOM* as the Raufoss round entered the lead Homothal and exploded.

"Now's our chance!" Peter renewed his effort; only this time Homer was helping to pull himself forward. They had to crawl across ten yards of open slope, then they would have the protective cover of the massive stone outcropping.

Although Peter didn't know it, Todd was behind Gary helping to spot targets. They reasoned that the only chance Homer and Peter would have was to hunker down behind a large boulder. As soon as Peter started to pull Homer, Gary knew where they were going, and he opened up with the

Raufoss ammunition.

Gary kept shooting, Todd leaning close and shouting targets in priority of threat. Another Homothal went down, and then the third one, it's chest blown apart.

"Soldier," Todd announced calmly. "Last one."

Gary aimed and realized this was not a Chinese soldier. The man stopped and aimed his rifle at Peter, but before he could pull the trigger Gary fired. The explosive bullet hit low and severed both legs. Korlos bled to death within 30 seconds.

All threats eliminated, Gary and Todd dashed over the ridge and rejoined Ethan, who was sitting in a patch of shade, his back against part of the rocky ridgeline. Gary didn't bother to take the rifle figuring it would only slow him down.

Ethan still appeared disoriented and unsure of recent events. "Where's my Dad?"

Before either man could answer, the first missile detonated.

CHAPTER 53

THE SMOKE WAS STILL WAFTING from the super hawg's muzzle as Bull, Ghost, and Magnum jogged around the corner to meet up with their commander. Jim leaned down and felt Zhao's neck for a pulse and secured his sidearm.

"We have to get out of here," he reminded his men. "We have only a few minutes to evacuate."

The team hustled up the stairs faster than they thought possible. No one wanted to be present anywhere near the compound when the missile struck.

Turning the latching mechanism, they passed through Ming's office and emerged into the outer hallway, leaving the dull interior for the bright morning light. Jim glanced at his watch... 0958.

"I hope that missile isn't early," Jim declared as he pointed in the nearest direction that would lead them away from the group of buildings. The four men took off running.

They had covered almost 200 yards when the first cruise

missile came in low and fast. Traveling at just under the speed of sound, they heard it seconds before detonation.

"Down!" Jim shouted, and the team dove in unison for the ground, covering their heads as best as possible.

The warhead detonated over the aircraft hangar and was quickly followed by a second explosion as the next missile arrived on target. If they had been armed with nuclear warheads the SGIT team would have been vaporized.

Despite their injuries, they all rose to their feet and kept running. Jim's head was pounding, and a wave of nausea washed over him. It was as if someone was hitting his head with a bat with every step he took.

Ghost felt the burning pain from the bullet wound to his thigh. Magnum was trying not to move his upper body as he ran but found that every time he stumbled and twisted his torso to maintain balance, the sharp stabs of pain thrust through his shoulder. The bandage on Bull's arm had a slowly spreading red stain, and his ribs were on fire.

Still, they continued running. To stop now meant certain death.

Seconds later the next missile arrived. This one altered its flight path at the last moment, maneuvering into a steep climb followed by a dive almost straight down. The missile plowed through the earth and exploded 20 feet underground. The shock wave caused all four men to stumble and fall.

Jim was up fast, and Ghost, too. But Magnum had landed on his left shoulder and was writhing in pain from the impact.

"Ghost... give me a hand!"

As Bull slowly rose, Jim and Ghost converged on Magnum and helped him to his feet. Then they were running again for safety; handicapped by their wounds, the pace was slowing.

The next four missiles arrived almost simultaneously. Two plowed into the earth and exploded deep under the complex.

The other two were air bursts aimed to destroy the structures above ground and ignite fires in the rubble. The combined explosive force threw the four men forward. Luckily, there was enough separation between ground zero and the men that the blasts only caused additional minor bruises.

Looking out over the smoldering wreckage, Jim had a strange sensation. He feared that the complex may not be totally destroyed. Yes, only rubble existed where buildings were minutes ago, and there were a few small debris fires. Surely the equipment must all be in ruins. Certainly the explosives his team had rigged would have destroyed all electronic records and notebooks in the laboratory.

But what of the data in the computer center, and virus samples? Jim wondered. Would the heat of the explosions be enough to kill the viruses? Could there have been biological samples and other records stored in secure vaults deep under the complex? He couldn't shake the notion that something important had survived the attack.

If the virus had survived... if data from the heinous experiments had not been totally destroyed, then maybe someone could replicate Colonel Ming's work. Jim shuddered at the thought.

Yet the political leaders in Beijing—and maybe some military leaders as well—had ordered the air strike to destroy everything. They clearly feared what Ming had developed and sent in Captain Wu and his team to ensure complete destruction.

Or had they? At that moment Jim realized his mistaken assumption. With a sudden sense of urgency, Jim shouted to his men. "Get moving... it's not over yet!"

Long ago, Ghost, Magnum, and Bull had learned to never question Boss Man. If he gave an order there was a damned good reason for it and they knew to carry it out... no questions, no discussion.

This learned reaction saved their lives.

Despite their pain and fatigue, they pushed their battered and bruised bodies onto their feet and ran for a low rocky drop off that marked the edge of the dry streambed. The men dove over the ledge and fell four feet to the sandy, gravel-strewn ground. Quickly, they all squirmed back up against the ledge. Now out of sight of the compound remains, they could not see the approaching missile… but they heard it.

The explosion occurred as two successive blasts. The first was not very big, but it was almost instantly followed by a much larger explosion… a massive blast and fireball. The intense light from the explosion and the heat blasted over the edge of the streambed. Nestled tight against the rocky wall, Jim and his team were safe in the shadows. From their protected position, looking away from the blast, they saw smoke rise from tinder-dry tumbleweeds exposed to the intense thermal radiation.

As the fireball rose it created a backdraft, sucking dust and debris up into the conflagration. Four seconds later the fireball consumed itself and vanished.

Jim raised his head. The destroyed compound was fully engulfed in fire… everything would be consumed in the intense blaze ignited by the final missile, one armed with a tactical thermobaric warhead, just as Wu had tried to warn.

Finally, Jim began to relax, if only slightly. He still wondered if the compound was built with a well hardened bunker that could have survived the onslaught, but then he reasoned that the Chinese had access to the original architectural plans and they would have chosen the missiles' warheads accordingly.

The virus and lab data must have been destroyed, and Colonel Ming was dead as well. It was likely that all of Colonel Ming's men and the Homothal army he was creating had also perished. Still, Jim couldn't feel assured without personal verification.

Under different circumstances, he might be able to search the smoking ruins, to be confident the destruction... and their mission objectives... were complete. But with so many wounded men, in hostile country, and low on ammunition and medical supplies, he didn't have the luxury of waiting around. With a sigh, he accepted that he had to let it go.

His eyes still focused on the flames reaching 50 feet into the clear desert air, Jim said, "Our job is done. It's time to get out of here."

EPILOGUE

"THE VIEWS FROM HERE ARE INCREDIBLE. I don't imagine one would ever tire of it." Jim stared out the panorama windows at the Three Sisters, three distinctive volcanic peaks in the Cascade Mountain range, still lightly coated with snow. Standing next to Jim, Peter was also absorbing the beauty.

"I think I've heard you say that before," Peter replied with a smile. "It's always awesome... no matter how many times I look at those mountains, it's never enough."

"Colonel Pierson asked me to pass along his commendation for a job well done. All of the American hostages were reunited with their families eight days ago... they're going to be fine. The Colonel has officially listed you as an approved contractor. My office will send some paper work to you, and they have already started the process of elevating your security clearance."

Peter seemed not to hear what Jim had said, his eyes still focused toward the Three Sisters to the west.

Jim turned and faced his longtime friend, addressing what

he knew was on Peter's mind. "That was close."

Peter diverted his gaze to the floor. *Too close*, he thought.

Following the destruction of Ming's secret compound, the SGIT team had radioed for an air evacuation. Although against the rules of engagement because the team was within a country considered hostile, and was present without official sanction, Colonel Pierson authorized the medevac anyway. There was no way he was going to leave his team wounded and without support.

The entire team was flown to Landstuhl Regional Medical Center in Germany where the wounded were treated and cared for. The SGIT team departed Landstuhl after four days of convalescing. Peter, Ethan, Todd, and Gary remained at the medical facility until they were placed on a military transport five days later and finally flown home.

Even though Gary lived in California, he opted to stay on a few days in Bend—he needed time to allow the soul to recover. His wife, Nancy, had just flown up to join him.

Ethan had suffered the most serious injuries with a severe concussion, fractured cheekbone, and extensive bruising and muscle strain over most of his body. The attending doctor commented that the damage to Ethan was similar to what he had observed on soldiers blown up by improvised explosive devices in Afghanistan and Iraq. Perhaps because of this experience, the medical staff at Landstuhl was well prepared to treat Ethan's wounds. Fortunately, the fractured zygomatic bone did not require surgery or plates to reconnect the bone, and in time, the doctor was confident Ethan would fully recover.

Gary, Todd, and Peter all suffered from exhaustion, bruising, and, in Gary's case, a grazing bullet wound across his shoulder and back. Fifty-three stitches were required to close the gash after the medical team had removed Bull's field dressing and debrided the wound.

The SGIT team was also on the road to recovery. Ghost, Magnum, Bull, and Homer would all enjoy some time off to rest and let their wounds heal. Rambo was sporting a cast while his broken wrist healed, and Sulu was expected to regain normal functioning of his legs and arms following successful surgery to remove the grenade shrapnel.

All still mourned the loss of Coyote and T-Bone. It was rare for the SGIT team to suffer casualties, and on this mission they had paid dearly.

Peter lifted the glass in his hand and swallowed the last of the microbrew. "Can I get another for you?" he asked, noting that Jim's glass was also empty.

Together they walked to the bar and Peter ordered two more Mirror Pond pale ales. He had booked the reception room on the second floor of Deschutes Brewery for this gathering. Peter thought it would help if he and his friends could spend the evening together once more, only this time in peace, and he could not imagine a more peaceful place.

Peter's friends had walked to hell and back to help him rescue Ethan from the Janjaweed militia halfway around the world. In the process, two good men sacrificed everything and would not return to their loved ones. He knew he could never repay them, but he would try.

As Peter and Jim were absorbed in quiet reflection, Ethan walked up, breaking the silence.

"Commander Nicolaou," he began, and then corrected his posture, standing tall and straight at attention. Looking Jim firmly in the eyes, he continued. "Sir. I have not formally thanked you for all you and your team did to save me. Not just me, but also my friends… out there in the desert." Ethan paused for a minute to regain his composure.

"Also…" Ethan's eyes grew moist and his voice cracked. He swallowed hard, and then continued. "Also, I want to thank you, Sir, for ending the terror that was waged for so long on the people of Darfur." He would never forget Bebe or Hamaad.

It was clearly important to Ethan that he express his gratitude with the full degree of respect and protocol that he knew Commander Nicolaou deserved. Once he did, the tears came forward.

In the brief time he spent in the refugee camp... what seemed so long ago... he had met an innocent population that had suffered beyond imagination. People who had no idea why they were being brutalized and terrorized. People who simply wanted to live in peace like anyone else.

Jim put his hand on Ethan's shoulder. "It's okay son. Let it go."

Ethan bowed his head and tried to hide his tears, ashamed of his emotional display.

Jim spoke gently. "Ethan, there is nothing to be ashamed of. You witnessed the worst elements of mankind. You, your father, and your friends stood up to that aggression. You demonstrated to every man on the battlefield your compassion, your humanity, and your bravery. Thanks are also owed to you."

Peter wrapped Ethan in a fatherly hug.

Gary and Todd overheard the conversation. Without prompting, Todd raised his glass and offered a toast.

"Here's to all our service men and women. Wherever they are, they're keeping the wolf at bay."

There was a unanimous "cheers" as each man took a drink. Not to be outdone, Gary raised his glass and added, "And here's to the Oregon Ducks! May they not only get to the Rose Bowl this year, but actually win it again!" Everyone laughed, including Ethan.

As the laughter died down, Peter became serious once more.

"Jim, did your team learn anything from the data files Gary

downloaded?"

"Ellen Lacey is still leading the analysis. It will take time, but she suspects that the data is sufficiently complete to be able to reconstruct Ming's formula."

"Formula? I don't understand," Peter replied.

"The picture is not yet complete, but Lacey tells me that Ming developed a formula for using a common virus to insert Neanderthal DNA into human cells. The trick was finding the right cocktail, or recipe, that resulted in self-replication of the infected cells. Once the complete formula is uncovered, then it can be reproduced."

"Why in God's name would anyone want to recreate that demonic work?"

Jim shook his head. "The experts say it will open entirely new areas of research—new possibilities to clone extinct species and genetically cure a long list of diseases."

"You've got to be joking. This can't be allowed… that data must be destroyed before it's too late!"

"It may already be too late. Once knowledge is gained, it cannot be eliminated. There is no going back." Jim didn't seem upset in the least.

"How can you stay so calm?" Peter demanded. "After all we just went through… you saw those hideous beings. They nearly killed me, my son, and my friends… and they did kill Coyote. Ming's cloning of Neanderthals could never possibly benefit mankind."

Jim glared at Peter. He didn't like having Coyote's death brought up.

"I'm well aware of what happened," Jim countered, staring directly into Peter's eyes, measuring his words before continuing.

"You still haven't learned to trust me, have you?"

Peter thought back to the beginning when he had sought

Jim's help and Jim seemingly refused. Only later to find that Jim was, in fact, working the back channels.

The conversation was interrupted when Jim's cell phone rang. Recognizing the caller identified on the phone's display, he said, "Excuse me. I need to take this." He walked to a deserted corner of the large room where he could speak in relative privacy.

Peter turned around to again look out the windows to the west. He could always trust those mountains to bring peace when he was most troubled. He would go there tomorrow—to Todd Lake—with Ethan, and maybe Joanna, too.

Jim pocketed his phone and returned to the bar. He had a slight grin and the shine had returned to his eyes, displacing the heavy fatigue that had been there since they left Sudan.

"Aren't you going to ask?" Clearly, Jim couldn't keep the news to himself.

Peter didn't understand, but he played along. "All right. What am I supposed to ask about?"

"The phone call, of course."

"What about it?"

"That, my good friend, was Lieutenant Ellen Lacey."

"And..." Peter's voice betrayed a growing irritation.

"She reported a problem... with the main computer. Well, actually not with the main computer CPU, but really with the disc drive storage system... the servers. You know they hold a fantastic amount of data—"

Peter cut him off. "Yes, I know. Just get to the point, would you?"

"The point? Oh, yes." Jim was obviously enjoying himself now. "The point is... you know that data Gary downloaded from Ming's servers?"

Peter stared back and frowned.

"Well, that data was stored on two secure servers at The

Office. It was backed up just yesterday."

"And?" Peter urged Jim to continue.

"Well, it seems both servers—the primary and the backup containing all of Ming's data—failed. Apparently, it was a hard crash... completely unrecoverable. Truly a shame." Jim's grin turned into a full smile.

For the first time since the ordeal began, Peter knew he would sleep through the night.

AUTHOR'S POSTSCRIPT

BEFORE I BEGIN, A BRIEF WARNING—I urge you to read the story first, and then these comments. To do otherwise will deprive you of some of the suspense that I hope you enjoy as the story unfolds.

If you read *Crossing Savage*, you know that a foundational plot theme in that novel is energy independence; an optimistic subject. In this second Peter Savage novel, I have embraced a darker theme—biological terrorism. This is a real fear for me, something that keeps me awake at night, something our society is vulnerable to. The reason is simple; humankind has embraced biological warfare for centuries—and it's a relatively simple weapon of mass destruction and terror.

In contrast, nuclear weapons are very complex, extremely difficult to handle, and, thankfully, the detonation sequence has to be done just right (to the millisecond) or you have a dud. Chemical weapons are difficult to manufacture and deploy.

If sanity prevails, I'll never read about biological weapons other than the occasional misplaced lab samples at the Center for Disease Control.

On a lighter note, I've wanted to write a story involving a cross—or hybrid—between modern humans and another, more animal-like, species for a considerable time. This interest stems from two hobbies: I love to shoot and hunt, and I'm quite fond of werewolf movies.

Now, these may seem unrelated interests, but not to my mind. Many times, walking back to camp through a dark forest, I have pondered what it would be like to challenge an animal—with all its physical and sensory excellence—if that animal also had mankind's cunning and weaponry.

Scary concept—one that inevitably leads to thoughts of werewolves and lycans. But the problem with every werewolf (or lycan) story I'm familiar with is the transformation process; it just isn't remotely believable. And I suppose it doesn't have to be.

So when I sat down to write *Relentless Savage*, I wanted to incorporate a scientifically plausible transformation process; a believable means by which people might be changed into something else, something decidedly not human. The answer, of course, has to reside in DNA. This is where the science is actually well understood, and is fundamental to the story.

Viruses are wonderful and strange organisms. They do not contain the necessary enzymes for cellular growth and replication. Until a virus invades a host cell, it simply exists—stretching the definition of life itself. When a host cell is infected the virus highjacks the DNA and replication enzymes of a host cell, ultimately reproducing more viruses. This process may be relatively rapid (as with a cold or flu infection) or the virus may lay dormant, viral DNA inserted into host cellular DNA for months, even years, before the virus replicates (e.g., herpes and HIV).

Even more bizarre is that a substantial part of human DNA is believed to have derived from viruses. It is estimated that as much as 8% of the human genome was inserted by viruses. Although scientists speculate that much of the virus DNA is so-called junk DNA—serving no purpose at all—schizophrenia and some mood disorders are thought to originate from this virus genetic material. So it is plausible that viruses might insert active foreign DNA into human host cells in a manner that allows the DNA to replicate and change our nature.

As pointed out in the Author's Note, the human genome was deciphered many years ago. Also, the genome for Neanderthals has been mapped (from samples recovered from well-preserved remains), and we know that Neanderthal DNA is present in modern humans, albeit not of African descent. It appears that modern humans (Homo sapiens sapiens) originated in Africa and crossbred with Homo neanderthalensis. In all likelihood the male offspring were infertile, and eventually modern humans won out over Neanderthals.

Scientists are already debating cloning Ice Age mammals in order to bring back these extinct species. We know that Homo neanderthalensis and Homo sapiens sapiens have a remarkable degree of genetic commonality. In the search for medical cures, how long will it be before we start to investigate adding sections of Neanderthal DNA to human DNA? This will be the first step toward engineering a human-Neanderthal hybrid.

ABOUT THE AUTHOR

DAVE EDLUND is the author of the *Peter Savage* series and a graduate of the University of Oregon with a doctoral degree in chemistry. He resides in Bend, Oregon, with his wife, son, and three dogs (Lucy Liu, Murphy, and Tenshi). Raised in the California Central Valley, he completed his undergraduate studies at California State University Sacramento. In addition to authoring several technical articles and books on alternative energy, he is an inventor on 97 U.S. patents. An avid outdoorsman and shooter, Edlund has hunted North America for big game ranging from wild boar to moose to bear. He has traveled extensively throughout China, Japan, Europe, and North America.

THE PETER SAVAGE SERIES
BY DAVE EDLUND

Crossing Savage
Book 1

Relentless Savage
Book 2

Deadly Savage
Book 3
(Coming Soon)

Follow Dave Edlund at www.PeterSavageNovels.com, tweet a message to @DaveEdlund, or leave a comment or fascinating link at the author's official Facebook Page www.facebook.com/PeterSavageNovels.

CPSIA information can be obtained
at www.ICGtesting.com
Printed in the USA
FFOW05n1203110315

9 781611 531299